D0685472

The Foundling's War

Michel Déon is a member of the Académie Française and the author of more than fifty works of fiction and non-fiction. He lives in Ireland with his wife and has many horses.

Julian Evans is a writer and translator from French and German. He has previously translated Michel Déon's *The Foundling Boy*.

WESTHAMPTON FREE LIBRARY
7 LIBRARY AVENUE
WESTHAMPTON BEACH, NY
11978

Praise for *The Foundling Boy*:

'Remarkable ... deserves a place alongside Flaubert's *Sentimental Education* and *Le Grand Meaulnes*' *New Statesman*

'A big-hearted coming-of-age shaggy-dog story ... [Déon's] novel leaves you feeling better about life' *The Spectator*

'It is shamefully parochial of us that this eminent writer has been so ignored by the anglophone world' *Sunday Times*

'Quiet, wryly funny prose ... a delight' *Independent on Sunday*

'Michel Déon is a storyteller par excellence, and if *The Foundling Boy* is your first encounter with him, you couldn't have a better introduction' *Irish Times*

'As witty as its English forebear [*Tom Jones*] but with French savoir-faire, *The Foundling Boy* may win new readers for books translated from French' *New York Times*

'I loved this book for the way, in its particularities and its casual narration, it admitted me to a world I knew nothing about and the many ways it made me care. It is not just a glimpse into the past, but the study of the heart of a man and his times' Paul Theroux

'*The Foundling Boy* is a legitimate, if not yet fully grown, heir to the great line of storytellers running from Fielding to Giono' *Le Figaro*

'This is a book to devour, savouring every last mouthful' Pierre Moustiers

The Foundling's War

WESTHAMPTON FREE LIBRARY
7 LIBRARY AVENUE
WESTHAMPTON BEACH, NY
11978

The Foundling's War
by Michel Déon

translated from the French
by Julian Evans

Gallic Books
London

This book is supported by the Institut français du Royaume-Uni as part of the
Burgess programme.
www.frenchbooknews.com

A Gallic Book

First published in France as *Les Vingt Ans du Jeune Homme Vert*
by Éditions Gallimard, 1977

Copyright © Éditions Gallimard, Paris, 1977

English translation copyright © Julian Evans, 2014
First published in Great Britain in 2014 by Gallic Books, 59 Ebury Street,
London, SW1W 0NZ

This book is copyright under the Berne Convention
No reproduction without permission
All rights reserved

A CIP record for this book is available from the British Library
ISBN 978-1-908313-71-3
Typeset in Fournier MT by Gallic Books
Printed and bound by CPI Group (UK) Ltd, Croydon, CR0 4YY

2 4 6 8 10 9 7 5 3 1

Jean's view of the band as it turned into the avenue leading to Place de Jaude, was obstructed by Palfy's nose. It had always been of noble dimensions, with nicely arched nostrils that quivered particularly sensitively at the smell of grilling meat or a ripe Camembert but never, never before had it aspired to block an entire avenue. From the front, Palfy's nose suited his bony face, and its bump, emphasised above its bulbous tip by a white scar, actually seemed somehow cheerful and promising. But then suddenly, seen from the side, it underwent a curious mutation: protruding, it transformed Palfy's expression utterly, turning him into a sort of predator, a gourmand (or sensualist, if you like) of an extreme and quite possibly sadistic kind. Abruptly his eyelashes seemed too exquisitely brushed, his eyes to retreat into their orbits, exaggerating the pink, living caruncle into a pustule at the corner of the eye, and his arched nostril revealed the cartilage inside, as smooth as the wall of a cavern.

Jean told himself he must never really have seen his friend's face in profile before, which was both a pretty peculiar and pretty improbable state of affairs, given that they had known each other for three years and been through nine months of fighting together, eating from the same mess tins, sleeping on the same straw, throwing themselves down in the same mud. He had had to sit at a café terrace in Clermont-Ferrand on a July morning in 1940 to discover Palfy's nose for the first time. How long would it take to get to know the rest of his face? Jean closed his eyes and tried to imagine Palfy's hands. His attempt to conjure up a precise picture of them was unsuccessful and when he opened his eyes again the band, having filed past Palfy's nose, had arrived at the café. Children dashed along the pavements. Women in sleeveless dresses waved. One of them stopped in front of the café terrace, and through the thin blue lawn of her dress the sunlight outlined soft thighs, delicious hips, and a slim back. For a second or two she stood without moving, offered to their gaze, an unknown, fragile-looking young woman with ash-blond hair falling over her cool neck. She turned to walk away and her face appeared with its childlike nose, pale lips and sun-lightened eyebrows.

'Did you see?' Jean said.

'Yes. We are visited by grace herself.'

'Fleetingly!'

'However fleeting, she must always be acknowledged. And we shall see her again.'

'She might be really stupid.'

'I guarantee she won't be!' Palfy declared, in a tone that brooked no contradiction.

Sergeant Titch was passing them now, chest out, marching stiffly, tossing his beribboned baton high above his head. The band followed, drummers first, ahead of the buglers, whose instruments festooned with blue pennants embroidered with a red design – a devil and his lance – glinted in the sunlight. These gaitered, white-gloved cherubs, cheeks bulging under their greased and gleaming helmets, were being menaced from behind by Pegasone, the strawberry roan mare of Colonel Vavin, a fine figure of an infantryman on horseback. Mounted uneasily in his saddle, the colonel, knowing the mare hated the cacophony of brass and drums, feared she would throw him at any moment. And behind Pegasone lay further danger in the shape of the baby-faced subaltern who, flanked by heavily decorated NCOs, was carrying the regimental standard at far too acute an angle, threatening Pegasone's hindquarters with its metal spike. One false move and she would be off.

'Come on!' Palfy said.

Jean looked for a waiter to pay for their beers.

'What are you doing?' Palfy asked.

'I can't see the waiter.'

'Don't you know that we won the war? Have you ever seen the winning side pay for its drinks? Let's get out of here.'

They dived into the crowd, which grew thicker as they approached Place de Jaude.

'I think you're overstating it,' Jean grumbled. 'We didn't win the war. In fact I don't think we can ever have lost a war as shamefully as we did this one.'

Palfy shrugged.

'We must have won. At the last minute it all worked out for us. The miracle of the Marne. *La furia francese.* Otherwise they'd never dare parade like this.'

The regiment flowed into the square, its companies marking time as they waited to take up their positions in front of an empty stage backed with red curtains that looked like an open mouth. Squeezed into khaki jackets buttoned to the throat, trussed up in cartridge belts stuffed with bread, chocolate and tobacco, and weighed down by new cleated boots that threw sparks as they hit the ground, the soldiers looked as though they were on the verge of apoplexy. Company sergeant-majors, lieutenants and captains scuttled back and forth, issuing orders to their companies that were raggedly obeyed. Rifles were stacked, and at a signal from section NCOs each man pulled a rag out of his cartridge belt to polish his boots. An admiring 'ah!' of astonishment ran through the crowd massed on the pavements, held back with some difficulty by a police cordon. A new era was dawning. Groomed and gleaming, newly issued with MAS-36 rifles (prudently kept back during the fighting to make sure the old rifles from 1914–18 were used first), the regiment with its distinctive red epaulettes and dashing, self-important officers seemed to have survived its recent battles without so much as a scratch or losing a single one of the buttons Gamelin had promised to the government.

When the boots were polished, the rifles were unstacked and companies lined up once more. An official in a black-edged jacket, stiff collar, striped trousers and bowler hat appeared on the platform.

He scrutinised the two rows of chairs, looking for the one with his name on. He looked like a clown or a tiny Jonah, about to be swallowed by the curtains' open mouth. Having found his seat, he settled himself, mopped his brow, and suddenly saw that more than a thousand spectators had him in their sights. Swiftly replacing his bowler, he disappeared as if swallowed by a trapdoor, followed by a wave of laughter.

Moments later, the prefect made his entrance. Instructions rang around the square and battalion commanders ordered their men to shoulder arms.

Jean and Palfy found themselves in the front row, among the ex-servicemen, who wore their berets tugged down over their ears and carried children on their shoulders. Jean could have named nearly every officer and NCO now standing to attention in the square, but the veterans of the regiment – the men who had still been fighting three weeks earlier – had been redistributed among the re-formed companies, which had then been joined by the last contingent to arrive. He and Palfy recognised Hoffberger, fat as ever, and the huge Ascary, little Vibert, still furious-looking, the seminarian Picallon, their friend the boxer Léonard, and Negger, the pacifist primary-school teacher – all of them easily distinguishable from the young recruits drummed up after the armistice by their visibly casual way of standing to attention.

'I can hear Ascary swearing, "God oh God oh God in heaven",' Palfy said.

'And Hoffberger going "hmmph".'

'Good to see they're both still with us.'

'To tell you the truth,' Jean said, 'I'd prefer to see that nice blonde, the one we saw just now with the sun behind her.'

'Is that all you can think about?'

A general was inspecting the regiment. When the inspection was finished, it was time to award the decorations. Colonel Vavin added a bar to his Croix de Guerre, which already reached his belt. Three captains and four lieutenants received the official embrace. Next it was the NCOs' turn. A dozen sergeants fell out.

'You see, we won the war. No question about it,' Palfy said.

Next to them, an ex-serviceman curiously sporting a faithful copy of a Hitler moustache hissed at them, 'Shut up, you bloody layabouts!'

'Forgive me, Monsieur,' Palfy said contritely, 'I was only joking.'

'This is no time for jokes.'

Jean's elbow connected with Palfy's ribs. One of the sergeants, good-looking in a thuggish way, was taking his three paces forward to receive a Croix de Guerre.

'It's Tuberge! They're giving Tuberge the Croix de Guerre! They're out of their minds!'

'Not that bastard who trousered my watch!'

There was movement and a murmuring around them. The ex-serviceman put up his fists.

'Now you're insulting our heroes!'

'I make a hero like that every morning,' Palfy said.

'Shut up!'

'Oh, belt up, you old fart.'

The ex-serviceman attempted to grab Palfy's shirtfront. Shoving him back, Palfy broke free and, cupping his hands around his mouth, yelled, 'Sergeant Tuberge! You're a fairy! Coward! Bastard! Looter! Murderer! Shit! Thug!'

The general, about to pin on Tuberge's medal, stopped dead, although he did not deign to turn towards the heckler. Nor did the colonel, who beckoned to an aide-de-camp. In the reverential silence that reigned across the square, Palfy's shouts had been heard by everyone. Tuberge himself, fists clenched, appeared to be about to dive into the crowd towards his tormentor, who was now brandishing his fist, having just shoved the infuriated ex-serviceman to the ground.

The ex-serviceman was shouting, 'Arrest them! Arrest them! They're agitators.'

The aide-de-camp ran over to a police sergeant. In the ranks of his old battalion Jean could see Ascary doubled up with laughter,

Hoffberger scarlet with amusement, and Negger, who had put his rifle on the ground to underline his pacifism. Despite the many hands trying to restrain him, Palfy was not finished.

'Bloody coward! Bloody bugger! Bloody … navvy!' he went on shouting.

'Let's get out of here,' Jean begged him.

The police were running towards them. Ducking low, they shoved their way back through the crowd, which watched them dumbfounded. Breaking free, they found that they were face to face with a *garde mobile*,[1] who tried to grab their arms. They tripped him and he fell.

'This way!' Palfy said.

They ran down one side of the square. No one tried to stop them, but several policemen in the square were still following them, running parallel to the crowd, which might have thinned out enough to let them through if it had not been distracted by a new development. Overcome by heat, weakened by dysentery, three soldiers who had been standing presenting arms for ten minutes crashed to the ground. They were followed by a fourth. A bugle call and a series of drum rolls covered the yells of the police and the growing noise of the crowd. Reaching the corner, Jean and Palfy found a narrow cobbled street that led up to a church. They had left the *garde mobile* a hundred metres behind them. Palfy swerved right. Jean was following suit when he suddenly saw, directly in front of him, the young woman with ash-blond hair. Their eyes met. The woman's were amused. Jean was lost for words, feeling the same inexpressible emotion he had felt when she had innocently stood in front of the café terrace with the sun shining through the light lawn of her dress.

'What's your name? Tell me!' he blurted out.

She stopped, and smiled.

'Quick!' he said.

'Claude.'

Not hearing his friend behind him, Palfy spun round and shouted, 'Jean!'

'I'm here!'

The *garde mobile* was gaining on them. The young woman was still smiling. Jean, wrenching himself away, caught up with Palfy and together they ran up to the church then turned left into a small square where an area had been roped off for some roadworks. Palfy stepped over them, put his shoulder to the door of a small wooden hut till it gave, and pulled out two pickaxes and a pair of straw hats.

'Take off your shirt!' he said.

Seconds later they were breaking up the earth with their picks as the *garde mobile* and a dozen policemen arrived.

'Oy! You lads! Did you see a couple of men scarpering like rabbits?' the sergeant asked breathlessly.

'That way!' Jean pointed to a side street.

The sergeant mopped his brow and turned to his men.

'They'll be the death of us! Right, let's go!'

The group jogged out of sight. Palfy dropped his pickaxe and pounded his bare pectorals.

'Now,' he said, 'given the combined brain power of a middle-aged police sergeant and a youngish *garde mobile*, I reckon it will take them a good five minutes to work out that no one works on the roads on a Sunday and that actually we are Sergeant Tuberge's tormentors. So no need to hurry. Put your shirt on, my fine friend, and let's get out of here and find a drink.'

'I've met one of the women of my dreams,' Jean said.

'Your little shadow puppet in the blue lawn dress?'

'How did you guess?'

'I have a talent.'

'I spoke to her.'

'Are you going to have many children?'

'We're going to make love endlessly, but we'll only have two children, and not until several years after we marry.'

'I want to be godfather to the eldest.'

'You shall.'

They put their rough wool shirts back on and left the roadworks behind. The streets behind Place de Jaude were deserted, the citizens of Clermont-Ferrand having gathered en masse to watch the parade. The army, decried and scorned for years, had again become a symbol, one of the values the French were trying to cling to. The first parade by Jean and Palfy's regiment since the armistice belied the merciless thrashing Germany had inflicted on it and cast a pious veil over the missing, the million and a half prisoners who at that very moment, crammed into livestock wagons or straggling along distant roads, were being herded to camps in Silesia and Poland.

Palfy seemed to know where he was going. Jean followed him, but so absentmindedly that his friend stopped and said, 'Hello! Where are you?'

'A small part of me's with the lovely Claude, the rest is with our friend Tuberge. The look on his face …'

'Yes, we mustn't forget it. One day, Tuberge, one day I'll have your guts for garters. When I think about that poor priest …'

The night had been calm except for a few volleys of tracer rounds fired over the canal, mostly either to let off steam or soothe nerves, or just for the pleasure of emptying a magazine and watching a salvo describe a clutch of luminous parabolas like a storm of meteorites in the warm June air. Early dawn light spread along the canal's banks. A trickle of water carried with it planks of wood, a hat, a dead cow with a monstrously distended stomach and a pair of corpses, two men tied together at the wrist and obligingly floating on their stomachs to hide their mortified expressions. Then, from out of nowhere, a fat, bare-headed priest appeared on the enemy side of the canal, walking along the towpath and reading his prayer book. His incomprehensible appearance seemed to cause time to stop, forcing a respite at the exact moment when the fighting was due to restart.

'It's a truce from God!' Picallon, the seminarian, said, and for once no one laughed at him.

A damp freshness enveloped the numb men in their hastily constructed dugouts. Mosquitoes had devoured their hands and exposed faces. Lance-Corporal Astor had woken up blind, his eyelids swollen and stuck together with pus. He was led off to the command post, where a hypothetical ambulance was waiting. Jean and Palfy, smeared with lemon juice, had escaped the onslaught and subsequent wholesale itching. The priest followed the towpath, hard by the water's edge, as far as a destroyed footbridge, where he turned round and, with his nose still in his prayer book, retraced his steps. The last shreds of grey night were drifting away in the sky. The cleric's florid face was visible, as was his unkempt white hair and too-short cassock that revealed a pair of skinny calves ending in stout ankle boots very like those worn by the abbé Le Couec.

Behind the group to which Jean and Palfy belonged, Sergeant Tuberge and Lance-Corporal Pomme had dug themselves a comfortable hole which they had reinforced with planks and sandbags. Thirty metres to the rear of his men, Tuberge claimed it was a good command post because he could receive orders from the main CP without endangering a runner. In reality it was clear that his location would, at the first sign of trouble, allow him to take to his heels down a well-protected trench, at the end of which lay one of those elastic positions so beloved by communiqué writers at headquarters. But Tuberge, a loudmouth well skilled in the boasting arts, still managed to impress with his physical presence and underworld vocabulary. A one-time lathe and milling-machine operator at Renault, he had prepared himself for battle by wreaking havoc among the female population of the villages where the regiment had been billeted during the phoney war. Jean and Palfy had not been surprised to find that the first shots fired in anger had revealed the sergeant's possession of a hitherto unsuspected virtue: enormous caution.

The priest once again about-turned, impervious to the threatening silence that accompanied his reading and private prayers. He was like a tightrope walker exorcising his vertigo at the war to right and left and keeping his balance on the high wire with a long pole, in this case, his prayer book, the word of the Church. At that hour, with the day still undecided, a priest's innocence and the word of the Church seemed truly supernatural. They held the guns silent, forbade bloodshed, and returned to its state of French grace the whole tract of peaceful countryside whose colours were beginning to awaken. Everyone felt the moment, except for Tuberge, who grumbled something about fifth columnists and parachutists disguised as priests, then picked up a light machine gun and raked the black cassock with a volley of fire. The priest's hands flew to his flushed face, and his body, after a moment's hesitation, toppled into the canal, joining the dead cow whose horns had become tangled in the weeds. As the echo of the machine gun died away a sudden breeze sprang up, rippling the surface of the canal. The cow moved off again, dragging the priest behind, his wet cassock floating just below the surface.

'Bastard!' Picallon yelled, standing up in his dugout and shaking his fist at Tuberge.

'You shit, it'll be your turn next!' Palfy shouted in the sergeant's direction.

Tuberge prudently kept his head down, but shouted back, 'The next one to complain gets a bullet in the back of the neck from me.'

'Do we shoot him?' Jean asked in a low voice.

'He won't show himself,' Palfy answered. 'He may even be making his way to the rear at this very moment.'

Five hundred metres away on the far bank, from behind a half-ruined wall, a machine gun fired several rounds and jammed. Silence fell again between the lines, as if death were taking a last deep breath before exhaling its fire across the meadow and through the willows. Everything looked frozen: the cumulus clouds in the pale sky, the canal's greenish-black water, the leaves in the trees and the tall grass stained with the red spots of poppies that had been winking there since sunrise. The stillness might have carried on for an eternity if a crow had not suddenly swooped low over the canal, attracted by the corpses that floated there. Someone muttered that it must be the priest's soul, as the crow settled on a willow branch, but the priest's soul must have been as cursed as his body. The first mortar struck the willow, splitting it in two, and the blast scattered black crow feathers in every direction. Shells began falling far beyond the canal, behind Jean and Palfy, shredding trees and blasting funnel-shaped craters out of the meadow. Then a salvo hit the canal, sending up geysers of brackish water. Progressively the range was adjusted until at last it started pounding the bank held by the French in their foxholes. For an hour, shells arced through the sky, emitting soft whistles as they fell. They could be seen climbing merrily, twisting as they rose, then gliding and hesitating, as if choosing their targets, and boring their way down through the air to land in a spray of earth, grass and stones, their dull thud as they burst putting an end to fear.

For no discernible reason, the mortars fell silent. The Germans failed to show themselves. Trees and bushes were ablaze. At eight in the morning the sun was already sweltering. Packed into their foxholes, their necks protected by their packs, Tuberge's group was sweating as much from fear as heat. The corpses of the cow and the priest had disappeared. In their wake drifted dead branches, a boater, and a cutter with a smashed gunwale. Palfy raised his helmet on the tip of a bayonet, but no one shot at it and he crawled gingerly out of the foxhole. On the far side of the canal, in the deserted meadow, the wind was bending the tall grass.

'Tuberge,' he called.

Nothing.

'Maybe he's been blown to bits,' someone said with unconcealed joy.

'I'd hate to miss that,' Picallon said, crawling towards the sergeant's shelter.

There was no one in the shelter but it was piled high with tinned food, wine and ammunition. On a plank Tuberge had pinned a photo of a donkey with an erection sodomising an enormous Hindu woman.

'They've cleared off!' Picallon shouted.

'Try and get hold of the command post.'

The seminarian disappeared down the trench. He returned two minutes later.

'Scarpered! With the 75.'

The 75's disappearance was no news to anyone. Ever since war had been declared the self-propelled field gun, commanded by a reservist officer cadet, seemed to have had as its principal objective staying out of sight of the enemy. With three shells it could have silenced their mortars, but that would have meant risking an artillery piece destined to feature in a museum with a caption that read: '75mm cannon, having succeeded throughout the war of 1939–40 in not aggravating relations – already very bad at that time – between Albert Lebrun's France and Adolf Hitler's Germany'.

'We're buggered!' Noël, a railway worker who was always depressed, said. "We'll have to surrender. Who's got something white we can wave?'

'Not on your life,' said Pastoureau. 'The Krauts don't take prisoners. If I have to die either way, I'm for scarpering too. But who's going to take command?'

'You, Palfy, you're the oldest!' Joël Tambourin, a Breton, declared.

'All right,' Palfy said, having expected the nomination. 'Jean will be my NCO.'

'What's happening?' Picallon called from his hole. 'What are we doing?'

'Palfy's taken over command!' Tambourin yelled back with the joy of a man who had been liberated. 'We've got a chief!'

Palfy smiled and murmured, 'The frogs need their prince.'

Jean crawled across open ground to the next foxhole. For some incomprehensible reason, the Germans were holding their fire. The other group was dug in about twenty metres away. Jean hailed them.

Getting no answer and tired of crawling, he got to his feet, ran and jumped into the hole: into a tangle of pulverised heads and crushed faces, of men whose spilt guts were already attracting flies. Two, possibly three mortars had fallen directly into the shelter and Jean found himself floundering in a pulp of blood, shredded flesh, and pieces of bone. His right boot finished the job of crushing a man's chest. As he pulled it free, he pulled white ribs away with it and squashed the heart, from which thick black blood trickled. A ghastly nausea gripped him, and his whole body seemed to turn over in an excruciating pain that affected his arms and legs, as if his own life was being dragged out of him by giant pincers. He vomited not just the hunk of bread and corned beef he had eaten during the night, but all the food he had ever eaten, all his innards, his blood, his saliva, his snot. Intolerable throbbing drilled into his temples as he shut his eyes and clawed at the parapet to try to get out of the hole and flee the horror. Standing up, casting all caution to the winds, he wanted to run but collapsed, his foot caught in a length of someone's guts. A machine-gun volley rattled over his head and his mouth was filled with earth.

'Crawl, you bloody idiot!' Palfy shouted.

Jean disentangled his foot and, green and trembling, let himself drop into the foxhole, where Palfy broke his fall.

'Well …? Oh, I see. Right.'

Palfy in turn crept to the nearest position in the opposite direction, which was better protected by a parapet, but there the men had decamped, abandoning kit and ammunition. Another machine-gun volley punctuated his return.

'Nothing for it but to do the same.'

'Forget it. I'm not moving,' Boucharon said. 'All things considered, I'm all right here. Demob!'

'I'm going,' Palfy said. 'If I make it to Picallon I'll cover you.'

He climbed out. The enemy machine gun fired, kicking up dry sprays of earth around him, but he reached Picallon and set up the light machine gun.

'Doesn't fill me with joy,' Noël said.

'You'd have to be mad!' Boucharon added.

'Would it fill you with joy if I get across?' Jean asked.

'Maybe.'

Jean got across. A bullet ricocheted and hit his heel, another holed his jacket.

'Three of us! The holy trinity!' Picallon said, laughing uproariously and helping Jean back to an upright position.

'Your turn, Noël,' Palfy called.

The machine gun scythed through Noël's spine when he was halfway across. He did not even flinch, just fell with his face flat on the ground. His fingers untensed and slid away from his rifle. Tambourin, whose turn it was next, hesitated at the shelter's edge, then scrambled forward, crawling level with the immobile body. Palfy's light machine gun discharged a magazine over his head towards the invisible German machine gun, which responded with a volley of bullets that riddled the earthwork of Tuberge's shelter just as Tambourin was sliding into it. Palfy caught a dead man in his arms. He placed him in the bottom of the foxhole and sat him up. His face was already waxen, his lips pulled back to reveal his gums.

'Palfy?' Boucharon called from the shelter.

'Yes.'

'What happened to Tambourin?'

'You want to know?'

'Yes.'

'Dead.'

'In that case, all things considered, I'm staying put. They're not cannibals, the Germans, after all. Demob!'

'Please yourself!'

And so Boucharon, who had been expecting to throw away his uniform that day, kept it for another five years. On the other hand, he travelled and got to know the camps of Poland, Silesia and Württemberg where, working as a farmhand, he impregnated the wife of a farmer who was freezing at Stalingrad. Not the worst life he might have had, as he admitted, free of worries, his board guaranteed, and plenty of available women. He talked about it for the rest of his life after he got back to his family in Creuse, over whom the war had passed without a trace. From time to time, he still roared, 'Demob!' when he had drunk a bit too much at the Café des Amateurs, but no one knew what demobilisation he was talking about, and nor did he. For a few years after he got back he dreamt of his German companion, of her delicious breasts and her strong smell of milk after she had been milking, but the memory gradually faded and he arrived by degrees at a princely state of apathy for everything that did not belong to his little world of food, wine and work on the farm, where he lived alone with his dogs, cows and two pigs. In which case let us speak of him no longer (in any case his role in this story is about as episodic as it could be) and return to Palfy, Jean and Picallon who, having bid Boucharon, huddled in his hole, farewell, reached a long hedge and then a clearing that they crossed on their stomachs, and finally a sheep pen next to a duck pond. This had been the command post. A table set up outside the door was still strewn with tins of corned beef and sardines, red wine and country bread, and cigars.

'I'm hungry,' Picallon said. 'I could eat a horse.'

'Eat, young priest, eat. I shall keep you company. What about you, Jean?'

'No thanks.'

He would never again be able to swallow another mouthful. The smell of blood and human flesh clung to him, and he gagged again, all the more painfully because his stomach was empty. He leant against a tree and stayed there for a long time, staring at a landscape as blurred as the sea bed. Picallon gobbled down three tins of corned beef, a litre of wine, and an entire loaf of bread. The enemy machine gun, still close by, was regularly audible, firing at random in the direction of the canal bank where Boucharon had decided to see how events turned out. Turning away so as not to see the other two gorging themselves, Jean walked into the house. A headquarters map was spread out on the kitchen table, dotted with white and red flags as if for a lesson at the École de Guerre. In their scramble to retreat the staff had left behind the stock of flags, a pair of binoculars, a swagger stick, even a monocle attached to its black string. Jean looked for their canal position on the map and understood why the Germans had not attacked. They had settled for a flanking movement via a bridge ten kilometres downstream. Alerted, the command post had ordered a withdrawal so hasty that only the NCOs had known about it. But the map indicated the local paths as well, and the enemy could not be in possession of all of them. If they moved at night or kept to the woods, they would eventually rejoin the French lines. As propositions went, it was optimistic but not so absurd as to be impossible. Nor would it be the first optimistic proposition formulated by members of the French army since 10 May 1940.

Lacking communications and at the mercy of idiotic wireless broadcasts and a hopeless romanticism, France, its retreating army and its refugees lived in a whirlwind of rumours and lies that, despite the majority being instantly refutable, ricocheted from village to village and unit to unit. The strategic discussions at a thousand Cafés du Commerce had never been blessed by such a unanimous belief in success before, and as the retreat gathered momentum a veritable torrent of misinformation received the same serious consideration: the very night of the German forces' entry into Paris, Hitler had gone to the Opéra to hear *Siegfried* and gliders had dropped a battalion of parachutists disguised as nuns on the outskirts of Tours, where they had taken control of the aerodrome without firing a shot; other parachutists disguised as farm workers were giving false directions to the French armoured division and sending it straight into the lion's den; Roosevelt was about to make available to France and Great Britain five hundred fighters and more than a thousand bombers, with aircrew; a famous singer had been shot: her coded songs broadcast on the wireless had given away troop numbers at the Maginot line; two trains filled with gold ingots were going to buy Mussolini's neutrality; the German armoured division had only a day's fuel left and the bombing of the Ruhr was causing strikes in the armament factories; some units were already running out of ammunition; in any case, the president of the Council had announced with a tremor in his voice that 'Germany's iron supply line has been cut' and it had not a gram of steel left.

Jean went outside again, map in hand. Using a spirit stove Picallon was heating up some coffee he had found in a flask, and Palfy was coming back, smiling broadly at his discovery: a hundred metres away, in the shelter of birch woods, were two working tankettes with trailers stuffed with mines, sub-machine guns and ammunition. The tankettes, with which the French army had been supplied in abundance for want of battle tanks, had been assembled at high speed at arsenals to the south of the Loire and lined up under the proud gaze of sergeant-majors to be counted and re-counted. They had proved utterly useless. They looked like cartoon tanks, the kind of thing rich men's children might play with on the family estate. What terrifying toys they could have been in childish, cruel hands, flattening hens under their tracks, crippling the children of the poor!

With the turret raised, there was room for two inside each one. Picallon could not drive and in any case his height – close to six foot three – made him too big to fit into a tankette. He settled himself on the bonnet of Jean's instead, accepting, as a consolation, a new sub-machine gun still covered with the oil applied by the regimental armourer, who must have relinquished it only under the most extreme duress.

The convoy jerked into motion, heading south on a forest track through the woods. The tankettes advanced slowly, doing ten kilometres an hour at best. Sheltered by summer foliage and twice cutting across roads that helped serve as landmarks, they reached the edge of the forest where they were forced to move without cover through a hot, empty landscape in which the hay roasted by the June sun was starting to wilt. Three Stukas passed overhead, way up, at well over a thousand metres, mission accomplished, dazzling birds in the midday sun. The road led through a deserted hamlet, then a second where, suddenly, a scarcely human form emerged from a doorway, a ball of sound slumped in a wheelchair. The man was working the wheelchair's wheels desperately, trying to get away from a pack of excited dogs. Picallon slid off the bonnet and walked towards the invalid. He had been abandoned there with a plate of rice and bread and water that he was protecting, groaning inarticulately, from the starving dogs. At twenty paces he reeked of excrement and urine. Picallon stepped back.

'What do I do?' he asked.

'Kill the dogs before they make a meal of him!' Palfy ordered.

The sub-machine gun silenced the wheelchair's famished attackers, and Picallon nudged the corpses into a ditch with his boot. The man shrieked with joy and clapped.

'That's enough, young priest, you can't do any more!'

'It's disgusting.'

'No going soft. Come on.'

They set off again, and the man in the wheelchair tried for a moment to follow them, burping and coughing in the cloud of dust and exhaust gases. Re-seated on the tankette's bonnet, Picallon began to heat up as if he was being grilled and started to pray aloud to St Lawrence, offering his apologies for not hitherto having appreciated his martyrdom. Jean, having familiarised himself with the tankette's various directional levers, was following the tracks made by Palfy, who had dived into a series of dusty paths bordered by yellowed, overripe wheat and parched grass. The harvest of 1940 was superb, but there were no men to take it in. From time to time across the fields they saw the distant figures of women in white headscarves, cutting wheat by hand and forking the crop into carts drawn by Percherons whose coats trickled with sweat. But no one turned to watch the two strange vehicles lurching noisily into and out of view in plumes of dust. Jean felt an intoxicating sense of freedom. No more yapping NCOs to order pathetically inadequate defensive fire or a premature withdrawal. He and crazy Palfy were going on holiday, to tour France's agricultural heartland and discover its bistros where the *patronne*, in vowels as round as her hips, served 'her' *pâté de campagne*, 'her' beef stew, 'her' local wine and the pears from 'her' garden. But the farms looked like the *Mary Celeste*, the famous brigantine discovered still under sail in the middle of the ocean, without a crew, with breakfast served on the table, the fire still lit in the galley and not a soul on board. They stopped at some of these farms and called out, and no one came. There might be a dog barking, pigs snuffling in the rubbish, cows with swollen udders mooing in the pastures, but apart from the few women they glimpsed, busy bringing in the wheat, France had been emptied of its population by the wave of a magic wand, with the single exception of a disabled man in a wheelchair whom the pigs would eventually deal with too, for lack of anything better to eat.

His mouth painfully dry from the dust, his stomach empty, his head burning, and still with the taste of his exhausting nausea on his tongue, Jean's mind began to wander. The war was ending just when it could have become amusing and comfortable, riding in this tracked contraption after having marched themselves to a standstill ever since the Ardennes, chasing the ghosts of promised trucks that would miraculously allow the regiment to rest and re-form. But the trucks had archives of documents to save, tons and tons of archives that headquarters were relying on to exact their revenge one day.

The first evening they broke open the door of an abandoned farm. A slab of butter still sat on the pantry shelf. Picallon, brought up in the country, milked the cows and brought a jug of cream to the table. They found ham and *saucisson* in the cellar, and some bottles of light red wine and apples. Unmade beds told of a hasty flight. Palfy went looking for bedsheets and found piles of them in a cupboard; picking up a sheet, he rubbed the linen between his thumb and index finger.

'Obviously it's not satin, and there's no trace of a monogram. But the mistress of the house washes her own linen and hangs it to dry in the meadow. Even in London you won't find whiteness like this any more. We must make do. In any case we have no right to ask for too much, my friends. I must remind you that there's a war on, in case you've forgotten, for youth is terribly forgetful.'

'You're amazing,' Picallon said. 'You've seen everything, you know everything. Without you we'd either be dead or have been taken prisoner.'

'Perhaps I'm actually God!' Palfy suggested, modestly.

'No, definitely not, I know you're not Him. I may be naive, but I'm not that naive.'

Night was falling. They lit candles and stuck them in glasses on the big table in the main room.

'Look at us, back in the good old days at Eaton Square all over again,' Jean said. 'All that's missing is Price and his white gloves.'

Picallon was astonished that his friends had seen so much of the world. He was particularly dazzled by Palfy, who was way beyond the experience of a country boy from the Jura. He watched in amazement as Palfy laid spoons to eat the melons that he had cut in half and scooped out.

'My dear Picallon,' Palfy said, his voice tinged with regret, 'I know that at your seminary no one would ever have dared to serve melon without port. Unfortunately I've run out. My butler drank it one evening when his boyfriend cheated on him. I sacked him of course, but the damage is done and there's not even a drop of white wine left to help you save this melon. Just this red which, incidentally, as you'll note at once, has the same lightness as your Jura wines. I hope you won't be cross with me for inviting you and offering you such simple fare …'

Picallon was not cross with him at all. He found the entire dinner marvellous, down to the candles that cast the room's soot-blackened chimney, post office calendar and portrait photo of a lance-corporal in the engineer corps into gloomy oblivion. The war had been banished and no longer filled their thoughts. Around midnight they stumbled on a bottle of what they thought might be plum brandy.

'When you're a bishop—' Palfy said.

'Me a bishop! Not ruddy likely. I don't like tricky situations. As you're my witness, I shall be a priest and stay a priest ...'

'You lack ambition.'

'Ambition is a sin.'

'Picallon, you're an imbecile.'

'Yes, maybe I am, but you're too clever, you know too many things. Doesn't he, Jean?'

'No. Palfy doesn't know anything. He guesses it all. And because he doesn't know anything, he dreams up fabulous schemes that make him a multimillionaire one day and a conman the next.'

'Conman is harsh,' Palfy said without irritation.

Picallon, his mind opened to life's great adventures by the plum brandy, wondered whether the things he had been taught at the seminary still meant something. The invader was trampling France – the Church's elder daughter – underfoot, and of his only two friends one was disenchanted and the other a conman. His mind a little fogged by alcohol, he tried to work out whether it was all a very good joke, or a dream inspired by the Great Tempter.

'You're mocking me, both of you,' he said. 'You're incapable of being serious ...'

And he went to bed, in a bedroom that smelt of wax and straw dust, which was a reassuring atmosphere for a country lad from the Jura.

We shall not elaborate now (or later for that matter) on the conversation that took place between Jean and Palfy after Picallon had gone to bed. More serious than usual, it went on until around two in the morning, after a last glass of plum brandy. The bottle was empty. To find another they would have had to break down the cellar door and they were neither vandals nor looters, just soldiers abandoned by a republic in flight. A minimum of careful thought was vital. Where had the French army gone? Even in the absence of official news, it was plain to see it had evaporated. The worst part was that there did not seem to be a German army either.

Standing on the doorstep, admiring the warm starry night that enveloped the farm and the countryside, Palfy sighed.

'If we were genuine optimists,' he said, 'we'd be imagining that both armies have put the wind up each other. The Germans have turned round and nipped back across their beloved Rhine to stroke their Gretchens with their blond plaits, and the French have laid down their rifles and put in for their paid holidays, a month's leave on the Côte d'Azur ...'

'I wouldn't mind going down to Saint-Tropez myself ...'

He thought of Toinette and the sweet letter she had written him when he enlisted. But dreaming was forbidden! Palfy reminded him of it every time he weakened, and did not fail to do so this time as well.

'My dear boy, one doesn't sleep with one's aunt. It's no more unhealthy than sleeping with anyone else, but it may bring misfortune on your head. Now is the time to be superstitious again, believe me. I would not have messed up my last two projects in London and Cannes so stupidly if I'd paid attention to certain signs ...'

'You'll never fail to make me laugh,' Jean said. 'Let's go to bed. Tomorrow—'

'*Mañana será otro día.*'

'Don't get clever with me. I know those are the only four words of Spanish you know.'

'Mm, they're all I need. In them lie all the hopes of the world.'

*

Tomorrow was indeed another day. The tankettes had to turn out onto a short stretch of departmental road that might be used by the Germans. As soon as they were under way they glimpsed a motorcyclist in the distance, bent over his handlebars and riding flat out in their direction, like a fat cockchafer. The insect swelled disproportionately and they made out a green jacket, black boots, a sort of large, gleaming kettle crowned with insignia and, beneath it, a face grey with dust. The rider did not slow down, acknowledging them with a friendly wave as he flashed past and immediately disappeared behind a hill. Palfy, driving in front, stuck out his right arm, indicating that they should turn onto a dirt track between two large fields. The track led to a barn and a ruined farm. Picallon jumped down, opened the gate, and the two tankettes concealed themselves behind the barn's stack of hay.

'That was a German!' Picallon yelled, as soon as the two engines cut out.

'Thanks for telling me!' Palfy sighed. 'I came to the same conclusion. I must say, strong emotions make me hungry and thirsty.'

They found some shade and sat down to some *saucisson* and the two bottles of light red wine they had liberated unrepentantly from the farm that morning.

'It should be drunk cooler than this!' Picallon observed, the taste of the light wine reminding him of haymaking time on his father's farm.

'I say, young priest, you do know how to live!'

'Don't make fun of me, Palfy. I went straight from my farm to the seminary and from the seminary to the army. You've seen the world; I haven't. So perhaps you know why that German didn't stop and didn't shoot at us.'

'It's probably perfectly simple: a humble soldier on the winning side finds it impossible to imagine that behind his army's lines are three chaps in French uniforms out sightseeing on a couple of tankettes.'

'Are you saying he took us for Germans?'

'Precisely, my dear young priest. In which case, it also occurred to me that a semblance of thought might run through his fat head and perhaps cause him to turn round and come back. Which is why we are sitting eating *saucisson* in the hay in the shelter of a barn while there's a war on somewhere.'

'All right,' Picallon said, 'I get it. We're in the hands of divine Providence again …'

Providence was no slouch. From the haystack they watched the road for more than an hour. It remained empty. They set off again in the summer heat. Their tracks chewed the soft tarmac. Picallon sat cooking on Jean's bonnet while the tankette advanced at a stately pace and Jean alternately dozed and watched anxiously as the fuel gauge neared zero. They had been on the move for two hours when they glimpsed a village whose church pointed a tentative spire into a sky empty of aircraft. Palfy held up his arm and they halted outside the *mairie*. The tricolour hung despondently from its pole. There was not a soul on the street, not even a stray dog. A grocer's had been looted and the Café des Amis had barricaded itself behind wooden shutters. It was an ordinary French village, pleasant, neither ugly nor handsome, lacking all arrogance as it lacked all pretension. Windows closed, it slumbered quietly in the warm afternoon. On nameplates they read: Jean Lafleur, solicitor; Pierre Robinson, doctor: surgery hours from 2 p.m. to 4 p.m. and by appointment; Auguste Larivière, contractor … Where had they all gone, these peace-loving citizens, exiled one morning in panic from their village, from their memories, their family portraits, the little gardens you could picture behind their houses, tidy and neat, with an apple tree, a few rose bushes and some geraniums? Crammed into wheezing cars, they had fled the war without thinking that the war would travel faster than they could on the congested roads. The single petrol pump was, predictably, padlocked, and hung with an unequivocal sign: 'No more petrol, so don't ask.' The situation seemed perfectly simple: they would have to continue on foot.

Palfy said bad-temperedly, 'God, what fools you French are!'

Picallon's hackles rose. 'You're French as well.'

'I do apologise, young priest, I haven't regaled you with my life story yet. My mother was English, my father Serb. I'm wearing the same uniform as you are merely because I happened to be born at Nice while my father was trying out an infallible system at the Casino on the Jetée-Promenade.'

'An infallible system?'

Palfy raised his arms heavenwards and called Jean as his witness.

'Must I explain everything? Listen to me, Picallon: my heart belongs to France. I could have steered clear of this war, but it amused me and came at the right moment, when I had one or two problems as well—'

Jean interrupted him, pointing his finger at a window on the first floor of a grey house with a shale frontage.

'I saw the curtain twitch and a hand, just a hand …'

A cat sauntered calmly across the square, walked up the stairs to the *mairie*, and sat down to watch them.

'The curtain twitched again!' Picallon said.

Someone was watching them from a window. The village was not entirely dead. A hand and a cat still lived here, and things began to look more lively as a breeze rustled the leaves of the ash trees shading the avenue with its inevitable war memorial, which for once was reasonably discreet, an obelisk decorated with bronze laurels beneath which was inscribed the fateful date '1914–1918', followed by a list of names. At a second gust of wind a door creaked, and the three startled men whipped round: one of the doors of the church had swung open onto a dark space streaked through with reddish flashes of sunlight from the stained-glass windows.

'Blimey!' Picallon said, crossing himself.

The seminarian went in, crossing himself again after dipping his fingers in the font. Jean did the same, and both felt the incense-scented coolness of the holy place buffet their hot, dry faces. Picallon knelt to pray while Jean, moved by the silence and innocent simplicity of the church, which reminded him of the abbé Le Couec's at Grangeville, stayed standing in the nave. A splintering sound distracted him. Palfy was trying to force the poor box underneath the Sulpician statue of St Anthony. Their gazes met. Palfy shrugged and went out.

'Why do you keep doing that?' Jean asked, following him outside to the porch. 'It's like an illness with you. I thought you'd got over it.'

'I'm not harming anyone. I believe I explained it to you years ago, when we first met. What's in the poor box is for the poor. And we're poor: twenty-five centimes a day is nowhere near enough to live on. Particularly as our government no longer knows where we are.'

'You're forgetting the postal orders Madeleine sends you. And that I always share the ones Antoinette sends me.'

'Money from women doesn't count. It's dishonourable. Can only be spent on things you shouldn't spend it on. The only money I respect is the money I earn.'

'By stealing?'

'There are risks.'

'Not in churches.'

'Jean, you're being tiresome.'

Picallon was still praying. They walked back to the square. Again the curtain fell back. Someone was spying on them. Approaching the front door, they read the enamelled nameplate 'Jacques Graindorge, surveyor'. Palfy rang the bell. They heard chimes: three notes repeated three times. The house remained silent.

'Perhaps it was the wind twitching the curtain,' Palfy said. 'Or just a mirage. I don't know how many days it's been since we saw a civilian, apart from that handicapped chap in his wheelchair, whom the pigs must have eaten by now.'

'I saw a hand the first time.'

The cat, licking its paw on the top step of the *mairie*, stretched, arched its back, and padded towards them. An ordinary cat, black spotted with white or white spotted with black, in no hurry, pausing to bat playfully at a piece of paper before proceeding with remarkable casualness across the deserted square. Jean watched it closely: it was clearly well fed, so there was no question of it making do with rummaging in dustbins or hunting mice. No, this was definitely a proper, bourgeois moggy, returning from a short stroll after its lunch. Nothing surprised it, not even the two men in khaki shirtsleeves who had arrived from another planet in their big noisy toys that were resting further down the avenue. It walked between Jean and Palfy, lifted a paw to push a flap that swung back in the bottom of the door, and hopped through it. The flap closed automatically.

'There's someone inside,' Jean said.

Palfy rang the bell repeatedly. The only reply was the sound of meowing. The cat did not like the noise of the chimes.

'I know what to do,' Palfy said, walking back to the tankette and pulling out a machine pistol. Of course, the classic tactic: a quick burst to shoot the lock and you push the door open.

But there was no need: above them the window opened and an anguished voice called out, '*Kamerad! Kamerad!* Don't shoot! Me friend Germans. You speak French?'

'Like your mother and father,' Palfy said calmly. 'My friend too. Open this door or I'll shoot it open.'

'I'm coming! I'm coming! Don't shoot!'

The house suddenly came to life. A door slammed, hurried steps made their way downstairs. A chain was slipped and a key turned in a lock. In the doorway stood a man in his forties, his red hair tousled, his lips pale and quivering in an almost purple face.

'Gentlemen, forgive me, I thought you were French soldiers. I swear' – he put out his right arm – 'I swear I'm a friend of the Germans, a friend of Grossdeutschland and its leader, the Führer Adolf Hitler.'

Palfy put on an interested expression.

'So you're definitely not hiding any Frenchmen?'

'I'm the only Frenchman in the village.'

'You don't listen to the lies on the English wireless?'

'Never. Anyway I don't understand a word of English.'

Palfy turned to Jean and said to him in English as guttural as he could make it, as though it was spoken with a German accent, 'This bugger deserves to be taught a lesson. Go and get Picallon, and tell him not to utter a word of French.'

In French he said to the surveyor, 'That's all very well, but we're an advance force. The regiment is following behind and we're here to start the requisitioning. What do you have for lunch?'

Monsieur Graindorge raised his arms heavenwards.

'Requisitioning! What an awful word, Messieurs. You won't be requisitioning anything here. You are my guests. My maid – a very stupid woman – has gone off pushing a pram filled with everything she holds most dear. But I can do without her. Give me an hour and I'll have the pleasure of offering your German palates – a little basic, I'm sure you won't mind me saying – a lunch worthy of French discernment and quality. I trust you accept?'

'Of course, Monsieur Graindeblé,' Palfy answered with blithe artlessness.

'Graindorge!' the surveyor corrected him. 'Strangers do sometimes muddle up my name.'

Blushing and still trembling, the man was sweating with unctuousness. Jean went to warn Picallon, who was where he had left him, on his knees, communing with himself before the altar, thanking God for having saved his life and entrusted it to such resourceful friends, even if they did not seem very promising at first sight. Jean's hand on his shoulder roused him from his reverie.

'Are you hungry?'

'Very,' the seminarian said.

'Come on then.'

As they crossed the square he explained the situation.

'I'm not setting foot in there!' Picallon said indignantly. 'He's a traitor.'

'I thought you said you were hungry?'

'Yes, but such a man's bread shan't pass my lips!'

'You only have to open your mouth and eat.'

'You're both mad.'

Palfy was in the sitting room, stretched out in an armchair, his feet on a velvet stool, holding a glass in his hand.

'What are you drinking?' Picallon asked, thirst getting the better of him.

'Monsieur Graindemoncul's pastis. Help yourself. The bottle's over there and the water's cold.'

'Where is he?'

'In the kitchen, knocking us up a chicken fricassee.'

Picallon helped himself to a glass of pastis and stared around the sitting room, finally exclaiming, 'It's really nice in here!'

'Personally, I think it's revolting,' Palfy said. 'I wouldn't live in a room like this if you paid me. The worst of French bad taste …'

Picallon was quiet, suddenly anxious. The black furniture polished to a dusky red, the dresser and its shelves of travel trinkets, the reproduction Corot that was so dull it made you want to throw up, the bone china on the mantelpiece had astounded him, but Palfy's confident and violent antipathy cast doubt on all of it. He turned to Jean, who saw his discomfiture.

'Listen, I grew up in a kitchen. My father's a gardener, my mother was a washerwoman and a nanny. A house like this would have been the height of luxury to them. My father would say the same as you. He's an honest, good man and I'll never be ashamed of him. You stick to what you think, Picallon.'

'But what about you, what do you say?'

'I say the same as Palfy, but I've been lucky, I've learnt how to live.'

They heard footsteps. Palfy put a finger to his lips.

'You got the message, Picallon? Keep mum. You don't speak a word of French.'

Their host entered, smiling and happy. He grasped Picallon's hand and shook it vigorously.

'I hear you don't speak French. Your comrades will translate. You are welcome in my house. I am a friend of Germany.'

'Don't waste your breath, Monsieur Graindorge,' Jean said, 'our comrade is an excellent soldier but a complete dimwit. The only thing he's interested in is eating.'

'In that case just give me half an hour, and forgive me for receiving you like this, with whatever's in the larder ...'

The surveyor was wearing a blue pleated apron much too big for his narrow waist and he had turned up his cuffs, revealing pale, skinny wrists.

'What do you think of my pastis?'

'Drinkable!' Palfy said without enthusiasm.

'For German throats it must be a novelty.'

'Don't you believe it, Monsieur Graindavoine. Before entering France like a knife through butter, we had an intensive course in French language and customs. We were taught to appreciate garlic, red wine, accordions and women who wear little silk knickers ... Don't laugh, Monsieur, I'm not making it up. Our Führer is very far-sighted. Helmut here is quite different from my friend Hans and me. He may be a giant and rather crude-looking, and he may not have followed the course we did, which was somewhat beyond his intellectual capacity, but instead he was taught how to kill and he now belongs to a commando unit that specialises in terminating suspects with extreme prejudice. I've never seen anyone kill as cleanly as Helmut does. You can trust him, he eliminates without fuss, and if you like, if you have an enemy, I don't know, anyone, just let me know, don't be shy, all I have to do is lift my little finger and Helmut will get rid of him for you ...'

Picallon, furious, was about to explode with indignation. Jean gripped his arm and urged him to drink. The so-called Helmut's sullen expression fully convinced Monsieur Graindorge, who quivered with excitement and fear at having such a redoubtable fighting machine as a guest in his house.

'As you see, the village is deserted,' he said. 'So I have no enemies here any more. In peacetime it was a different matter ... The mayor was a leftist and a warmonger. No one would mind seeing the back of him … but as I say he's not here … We'll talk some more. I need to see to my saucepans.'

Jean thought of his father. Albert Arnaud would definitely not have left Grangeville. At the beginning of the phoney war his pacifism had made him several enemies. Now his leftist ideas would make him a sitting duck for the Graindorges of the world.

'I'll have you for this,' Picallon said to Palfy. 'If you take the piss out of me once more—'

'Drink your pastis, young priest, and belt up. You are about to eat like a prince and we're about to empty this ass's cellar.'

'Then what?'

'Then we'll see.'

'It will end badly.'

'Everything always ends badly. So if it's a bit sooner or a bit later than expected, who cares?'

Monsieur Graindorge was a competent chef, though it was hard to judge on the basis of a hastily prepared chicken fricassee in which he had had to use tinned mushrooms. His sauce lacked body.

'Forgive me—'

Palfy interrupted him.

'Monsieur Graindemaïs, let me say that we are listening to you with the closest attention. The truth is that you are our first real contact with the French population. But on Adolf Hitler's instructions – very strict instructions – we were ordered categorically never to say "Forgive me" but "I beg you to forgive me". I can't believe our Führer would have made a mistake on such a point …'

The surveyor blushed deeply. He was not an ugly man, having an average nose, mouth and eyes, but the rush of blood to his cheeks and forehead and around his neck, in large splotches, coloured his face so violently and artificially that it looked like a mask tortured by fear and anxiety. Have I mentioned that this was a man who had only just turned forty and was therefore in what is commonly referred to as his prime, and what is more a bachelor, which in general keeps you young; that he enjoyed a level of material comfort as a result of his technical abilities, which were sought after in the region; that he was a gourmet, a trumpeter in the village band, always jockeying for position on official occasions, but unhappily secretly undermined in his pleasure by a deficiency that, at another time and place, would have earned him highly trusted status in a harem? I'll admit that that is a lot to reveal about the character of a man whom the author will feel obliged to leave behind fairly swiftly. Jacques Graindorge, then, was ignorant of the subtleties of the French language that Palfy was disclosing to him with a calculated ingenuousness. Querulous, he started to stammer, then, feeling his self-importance rapidly slipping away, made a superhuman effort to get a grip on himself and hide his petulance.

'Your Führer is right … I have made a mistake in French and what you have been taught is absolutely right … but look, you must excuse me. So as not to seem like a pedant in this village, inhabited by honest but unrefined citizens, I tend to adjust my speech to stay in tune with them. Stupidly, in your company, I forgot myself …'

'I'm not annoyed,' Palfy said, 'because our Führer is right on this point. I'm not aware that he has made a single mistake in his life.'

Picallon was shovelling down his lunch, apparently devoting himself to the pleasures of his plate. He served himself a second helping without a word or gesture to his host. Monsieur Graindorge ventured a timid smile.

'Your killer has a healthy appetite, anyway. It's a real pleasure to see him eat. What a face! A real animal. I expect he was born in some remote province in Germany …'

Under the table Palfy applied sudden sharp pressure to Picallon's foot, sensing he was about to explode, and to calm him served him a third full plate of fricassee. Monsieur Graindorge noticed nothing. Crouched at his sideboard, he was looking for a box of cigars that was so well hidden that for a moment he suspected his housekeeper of having made off with it in her pram. He eventually discovered it under a pile of napkins. Palfy sniffed one with suspicion.

'Hm,' he said. 'Rather dry … Well, there's a war on.'

The surveyor offered him the flame of a petrol lighter. Palfy drew back in surprise.

'Well, well … that is remarkable … We were taught that the French were as painstaking about their cigars as they were about their wine, and they only lit them with wooden matches … Might our Führer have been mistaken?'

Picallon grabbed a cigar from the box uninvited and chewed a piece of it before spitting it on the floor. Graindorge rushed to pick up the flakes of tobacco scattered over his flower-patterned carpet. Picallon took advantage of him bending over to make an expressive gesture, placing his hands around an imaginary neck and wringing it.

'Once again,' the surveyor answered, 'your Führer did not deceive you but, well … I haven't any matches left. The *tabac* is closed, and a fortnight before you arrived my fellow citizens panicked and started hoarding matches.'

'This is extremely serious!' Palfy said. 'You are aware of course that looting and hoarding are both punishable by death. Our comrade here – who I would agree is a little coarse – is responsible for executing all summary verdicts by courts martial. It seems to me he would have his hands full in this area. What sort of brandy do you have?'

'I haven't a very big selection.'

Palfy cast a suspicious eye over the bottles and glimpsed an unlabelled one behind the run-of-the-mill brandies.

'Thank you, no, this gut-rot isn't for me; I look after my health. But tell me what's in your bottle there.'

'A raspberry liqueur,' Graindorge said, looking devastated.

'What brand?'

'There's no brand.'

'Interesting! Interesting! Then I suppose it must be the gift of a private distiller?'

'How did you know?'

Palfy waved his hand disdainfully: he was hardly going to go to the trouble of explaining. Graindorge served them with a sinking heart and made to put the bottle back in the sideboard. Picallon took it from him threateningly. The surveyor, who was partial to his raspberry liqueur, tried to reason with Jean.

'You shouldn't let your comrade get drunk. Men like him, real forces of nature, they don't know their limits. When a brute like him gets alcohol inside him, he'll be unstoppable and very dangerous.'

'We have him well under control, Monsieur. He only kills to order.'

A ray of sunshine cutting across the dining room splashed onto the tablecloth. In the golden light the curls of cigar smoke stretched out languidly, forming silvered snakes and mobile geometric shapes. Picallon was indeed drunk, but the naive and good-hearted seminarian was more ready to burst into tears than fly into a rage at the role he was being forced to play, of a poor country lad among the ways of gentlemen. Their host, he saw, was a proper bastard, and there is always something sad about the first bastard you ever come across, about discovering the multiple ruses by which Satan attaches himself to a human being. One day when the war was over and the seminary reopened, he would unburden himself of all these thoughts to his spiritual director, the abbé Fumerolle …

The reader is already aware of the author's warm feelings for Picallon, who reminds him of the parish priest at Grangeville, Monsieur Le Couec. Between the country boy from the Jura and the elderly Breton there exists a certain bloodline: a now vanished race of French priests whose only reasoning was their brazen faith and who lived among their parishioners in poverty, charity and hope. They taught children their catechism in simple, idealised pictures that seemed fascinatingly magical. And yes, in their sermons Jesus was always a great magician, whose feats would never cease to dazzle the world. At the time this story begins, the integrity possessed by young men such as Picallon is already under threat, but so far our seminarian has been immune to the new order. His model is the village priest who awoke his own vocation, just as for Jean, already half disillusioned in faith, the model priest will always be the abbé Le Couec, that rough Breton 'exiled' to Normandy. Picallon of course is fated one day to confront the influences of his community, but we shall not see him in those circumstances. Meanwhile he is here, in this bourgeois dining room in a French village with a full stomach and a dry mouth, and it is too late to stop the game his comrades are intent on playing. The afternoon wears on, the bottle of raspberry liqueur is emptying, and now and then Picallon rocks back on his chair and lifts the white tulle curtain to keep an eye on the still-deserted square and the two tankettes parked on the avenue with the surveyor's cat asleep on the bonnet of one of them. Palfy is on his third cigar, Jean has excused himself twice, and the dreadful noise of a toilet chain that refuses to flush properly has been heard. Picallon would like to go too, but is unsure of his ability to remain upright, and in a foggy dreamlike state he recalls the wedding feasts in his village at which the laziest would slip an empty bottle under the table and use that. He has hiccups, pins and needles in one leg and above all he is sick of listening to the nasal tones of Jacques Graindorge, surveyor, toady and coward, watching his every move with a terrified expression. When Picallon finally gets to his feet, the dining room sways and without Jean's steadying hand he would have fallen over. Moving gingerly, he reaches the front door and there, in the middle of the square, opens his flies and sprinkles the cobbles as he gazes gloomily at the flag drooping from its flagpole.

'What do you think of it?' he asks Jean, who is still holding his arm.

'Of what? What you're doing?'

'No. The flag.'

'It looks a bit limp.'

'And what about liberty, equality and fraternity?'

'I'm afraid the moment for them is past.'

'Why are you holding my arm?'

'So you don't fall down.'

'Am I drunk?'

'Not half.'

'It's the first time in my life and it'll be the last, but I want it to be a drunkenness I'll never forget, one befitting the Apocalypse. We'll empty that stinker's cellar, and anything we can't drink we'll smash up.'

'All right, old chap ...'

'We'll smash it up, we'll smash it up!'

Picallon, his bladder much lighter but suddenly distracted by his obsession with smashing up what could not be drunk, forgot to put his organ away and, supported by Jean, remained standing unsteadily there, limply facing the erect flagpole on the *mairie*'s pediment.

It was in this posture that he was first observed by Unterscharführer Walter Schoengel as he arrived at the village square in an armoured car, his body emerging from the green turret, ramrod straight in his black SS uniform, his face darkened by the sun beneath his peaked cap. Jean, for a second, imagined that in this victorious warrior he was seeing his friend Ernst, his companion from his famous cycling tour of Italy which had taken them to Rome in 1936, but – as we already know – Ernst and Jean will never meet again, and no chance meeting in the long war now under way will revive the friendship born four years earlier between a young Frenchman indifferent to politics and a handsome member of the Hitler Youth with straw-coloured hair.

Unfortunately this particular warrior was not Ernst, but a run-of-the-mill SS NCO with no sense of humour whatsoever, who was greatly offended by the sight of these two men in khaki shirts and trousers, staggering and with flies undone. Leaping athletically from his armoured car, revolver in hand, he walked up to them, barking a sharp order. Jean understood and put his hands up. Picallon remained bewildered. The Unterscharführer barked again. Jean translated.

'Put your hands up, you idiot, otherwise he'll shoot us.'

Picallon did as he was told, forgetting his open flies and limp penis, which was enjoying its exposure to the fresh air with an utter lack of curiosity for the events unfolding around it. The puddle on the cobbles bore witness to what had occurred only moments before. Walter Schoengel circled it with disgust and patted both men down. Reassured as to their inoffensive character and that they were a couple of strays, he sniggered and delivered a good kick to both their backsides. The driver of the armoured car had raised his goggles and was observing the scene with ill-concealed ribaldry as the square suddenly began to fill with motorcycles and sidecars, a further two light armoured cars and an open-topped car on whose rear seat sat Obersturmführer Karl Schmidt, his face hidden in the shadow cast by a gleaming helmet adorned with the SS lightning flashes. Schmidt was a lieutenant with a plump face and small, piercing grey eyes, and to begin with he paid no attention to what was happening. With a gesture he motioned to a young Obergrenadier to lower the French flag, then ordered a house-to-house search. Jacques Graindorge's door was still open. Two grenadiers jogged into the hall and returned with the surveyor and Palfy, who were propelled forward by the rifle butts in their back and then lined up with Jean and Picallon. The Obersturmführer knew a few words of French.

'You ambush behind Wehrmacht! Shoot you!'

Jacques Graindorge realised that there had been a mistake and smiled apologetically.

'Mein Herr, I believe you are mistaken. These three men are some of your comrades. They are German soldiers. I invited them to lunch. I'm a friend of Germany.'

The SS lieutenant reddened with fury.

'Shut up, pig. Shoot you as well. Harbouring irregulars.'

The grenadiers quickly broke down the doors of several houses. They were empty. They reported to their section chief, who nodded and set sentries to hold the square against fire from all four corners.

Palfy yawned in a way too forced to be real and said to Jean, almost without moving his lips, 'Now's the time to produce your famous letter from the prince.'

'It's in my tunic pocket.'

'And your tunic?'

'In the tankette.'

Soldiers were searching the tankettes and had already removed several pots of jam, chocolate biscuits, and three sub-machine guns. Jacques Graindorge was shaking so much that he was on his knees. A soldier forced him to his feet with a rifle barrel to the ribs. The Obersturmführer studied the square in search of a wall against which he could line up his four captives. The firing squad could not do its job with the sun in their eyes. But behind him his grenadiers were doubled up with laughter and, wanting to understand what had caused his men's hilarity, he scrutinised his prisoners until he noticed Picallon's ill-adjusted uniform. A roar of laughter blew across the square and the Obersturmführer summoned Walter Schoengel who walked over to Picallon and, with the barrel of his revolver, flipped the flaccid member back into his trousers.

'Pig!' the officer repeated, putting into the one insult of which he was confident all the scorn that seethed inside him.

Picallon was sobering up slowly. He was regaining his lucidity and faith at the same time, already glimpsing his final moments, for which he was better prepared than his two friends. He began, under his breath, an act of contrition: 'My God ...' Palfy told him to shut up and then Jean told Palfy to shut up. Karl Schmidt was enjoying the unprecedented moment. In Poland, where his section had advanced into a zone already cleared by the Wehrmacht, he had never been favoured with a moment as dramatic as this. The French campaign was at last offering him an opportunity worthy of him. He dispatched a grenadier to fetch his camera. When it arrived he took several pictures of his prisoners. The surveyor, his throat constricted, attempted to explain the appalling error that had been made, but not one articulate sound emerged from his mouth, which was distorted by a rictus that the Obersturmführer interpreted as insolence. Handing his camera back to the grenadier, Karl Schmidt walked up to Graindorge and slapped him twice, hard. Blood flowed from the corner of the surveyor's mouth and he fell to his knees again.

'Pig too!' the officer said. 'Get up!'

Palfy helped the foolish man to his feet.

'I thought——' Graindorge said.

'We fooled you, you stupid twerp,' Palfy said. 'All three of us are French. Now you're paying for your stupidity.'

'Quiet!' the Obersturmführer said.

'No!' Jean retorted. 'We're not irregulars. And you don't shoot prisoners. Now, if you like——'

'May God forgive you!' Picallon finished his sentence, then lowered his arms and put his hands together in prayer.

The SS lieutenant pointed to the façade of the Café des Amis, and the grenadiers shoved the four men towards the wooden shutters. The sun was going down. A pink light bathed the square and fell gently on the church porch. Graindorge's cat jumped from the bonnet of the tankette and followed its master, its back arched, its tail bristling. Walter Schoengel selected the twelve men of the firing squad.

'It'll all be over very quickly,' Palfy said gloomily.

'Yes,' Jean answered.

'The raspberry liqueur was really good.'

'It's a consolation. There's none left for them.'

'They'll be pardoned!' Picallon said.

'Not by me!' Palfy said.

Karl Schmidt made a sign to a grenadier to bring him the cat, which let itself be picked up and settled in the Obersturmführer's arms.

'*Schön!*' the officer said tenderly. 'How he called cat?'

Graindorge started with indignation.

'It's not a male, it's a female. She's called Sarah.'

'Sarah! A Jew name!'

The Obersturmführer threw the cat down, tried to kick her but missed, unholstered a revolver and emptied its magazine at Sarah, missing her again as she dashed to hide under an armoured car. A ricochet hit the Obergrenadier who had taken down the French flag, injuring him in the calf. The lieutenant paled, pressed his lips together and swore at the man, who stood to attention with blood flowing down his boot. Jean, Palfy, Picallon and Graindorge lined up in front of the wooden shutters of the Café des Amis. Karl Schmidt issued a brief order and a grenadier ran to his car, from which he returned carrying a violin case. The firing squad took up position under the orders of the Unterscharführer, who then inspected them. Karl Schmidt took out his violin and bow with an ecstatic smile, pressed the instrument against his cheek and tuned it before walking over to the Frenchmen.

'Do you like Brahms?' he asked, a delicate smile lightening his porcine features.

'No!' Jacques Graindorge shouted, seized by convulsive trembling and convinced this was another trap. He would never like anybody again.

'Don't listen to him, Lieutenant,' Palfy said. 'He's a fool who knows nothing about music. I can assure you, and I speak for my comrades too, that we all like Brahms very much, and that if you were to do us the honour of playing his Sonata No. 1, Opus 78, we could die happy.'

'You know?' Karl Schmidt said, astonished not to be dealing with brutes.

'Obviously the piano will be lacking, but I feel sure that playing solo will allow your musical temperament to be given full expression. We are your humble audience.'

The grenadiers stood to attention. The officer advanced between them and the prisoners, legs apart, eyes lowered to concentrate before his first bow stroke. Karl Schmidt was a fine violinist. Before joining the Waffen SS he had been second violin in the Stuttgart city orchestra. His father was a virtuoso and his two sons played the flute and viola respectively in a Hitler Youth orchestra. Since being commissioned he had missed playing in public. Not any old public. One that was thoughtful, contemplative, ready to feel the music's emotion. Who could be a more attentive audience than four condemned men? Four was not many, but the future promised bigger audiences, much bigger, and one day Karl Schmidt would have the great public his talent deserved. Music transfigured him. Under podgy skin that shone with heat and effort the fine features of a blond child could be discerned, a little German boy who could have been generous, trusting, enthusiastic. The little German disappeared with the last bars of the sonata.

'Clap!' Palfy whispered to the others.

They lowered their arms and clapped with a fervour that surprised Karl Schmidt so much he straightened and bowed his head as if he were on stage in a concert hall. The sight of Graindorge's pasty face brought him back to earth. The surveyor was not applauding. He was dribbling. He no longer existed, he was already dead, his back slumped against the shutters of the Café des Amis, a village amenity he had always scorned.

'You, not happy?' Schmidt yelled.

Graindorge heard nothing. His brain was no longer functioning. Palfy came to his aid.

'I think he is a little overcome by the situation we find ourselves in.'

'Overcome? What is overcome?'

'The idea of dying.'

Karl Schmidt roared with laughter and turned to the firing squad to explain in German that the Frenchman on the left was afraid of dying, then turned back to Palfy, whom he had identified as the leader of these outlaws.

'My soldiers, they not fear to die! Heil Hitler!'

The squad responded with a unanimous 'Heil Hitler'.

'Would you play us another piece?' Palfy asked politely.

'Shut up!' Jean muttered.

'Another? *Nein!*' the Obersturmführer said contemptuously. Where did these bandits think they were?

'Play for time,' Palfy hissed at Jean.

Picallon seemed lost in thought. He was praying. Jean envied him his ability to escape so far from the world, to see nothing of the scene that was unfolding: these soldiers in black uniforms that bore the silver lightning flashes of the SS, the lengthening shadow of the church, the swallows darting over their heads. It looked like a film set into which actors destined for other roles had strayed. Where had the real actors gone? The mayor with his tricolour scarf, the priest in his round hat, the teacher in his black jacket, the drummer in his blue shirt, the children in the choir, and the few scattered old men and women to occupy the benches that lined the avenue in the shade of the ash trees. Instead, an absurd misunderstanding, had placed, like a screen across the deserted square, still warm from the setting sun, a row of black statues masked by shadows, their lips tight and jaws tensed, stretching their chinstraps. The shadows of these men had in turn lengthened beyond the lead actor, violin in hand, almost to touch the condemned men. The real actors meanwhile wandered the roads, lost, crushed by fatigue more than sorrow, their feet bleeding, their mouths dry, their stomachs empty, driven by a fear whose incommensurable futility they were just beginning to understand.

'Our comrade would like to take our confessions!' Palfy said.

'Confession?' Karl Schmidt repeated, unfamiliar with the word.

'Yes, before he gives us absolution. He's a priest.'

'A priest?'

The SS officer looked Picallon up and down, staring incredulously at this emaciated beanpole who a few moments before had stood in front of him with his flies undone, offering a sight of his sleepy organ to all and sundry.

'The pig is priest?' he repeated.

Picallon made a gesture as if to deny the description: he was neither a pig nor a priest, just a seminarian. Jean's expression beseeched him to shut up as he knelt down first.

'Listen to me, young priest,' he said in a low voice, 'first make the confession last as long as you can, then you're to ask God to forgive me for two things: I caused pain to my father by joining up instead of deserting, and I caused pain to my dear guardian, the abbé Le Couec, by showing myself to be a very poor Christian.'

'You're already forgiven,' Picallon said.

'No, that's too quick—'

'*Schnell!*' Karl Schmidt yelled.

Palfy knelt down in turn and murmured, 'You're going too fast, you numbskull. We have to play for time …'

'The ways of God are impenetrable.'

'Shut up, for God's sake, get down on your knees and let's all pretend to pray together. That means you too, Graindorge …'

'I'm … a … freemason!' the surveyor stuttered.

'That's all we need!'

The Obersturmführer was growing impatient. He summoned a grenadier, handed him his violin, and marched up and down in front of the firing squad, repeating, '*Schandlichbande! Schandlichbande!*' Picallon got to his feet and smiled at him. He was ready.

'It really upsets all my plans, having to die!' Palfy said.

'I'm starting to panic!' Jean admitted.

They lined up again in front of the Café des Amis. A gust of wind swept the square, raising a dry cloud of dust which got into Karl Schmidt's eye. He called an orderly, who cleaned his eye with gauze. Rubbing it, the officer barked a rapid order at the Unterscharführer and walked back to his car with a disgusted expression. The grenadiers stood to attention …

The French are very patriotic deep down. A few bars of a military march and their dormant fighting instinct is aroused. Clermont-Ferrand was throwing itself into the parade. Men unfit for military service wandered in the neighbouring streets, brooding on their shame, and were joined by a few stone-deaf pensioners. Palfy was walking briskly, Jean struggling to keep up behind him, his thoughts still on Place de Jaude where the woman in the lawn dress had vanished into the crowd. He was cross with his delicious apparition for letting herself be taken in by such a dubious spectacle. Did she have a taste for heroes? If she did, Palfy's noisy interruption must have surprised her. Her amused smile when she had glimpsed Jean with the *gardes mobiles* in hot pursuit planted a hope that she had a critical turn of mind. If I'd had to, Jean mused, I'd have accepted a Croix de Guerre from her; her cool kiss on his cheeks was infinitely more tempting than the rough embrace of some colonel or general. But what chance did he stand of chatting her up on a big day like this, dressed in a ghastly pair of old corduroys two sizes too big and a rough wool shirt? Something about her reminded him of Chantal de Malemort: the outline of her figure, a neatness about her, her smile when she answered an unexpected question. But Chantal, gone to earth in Grangeville, was bringing in the harvest and Jean would never forgive her for having betrayed him.

Palfy stopped. They had taken the wrong street. They retraced their steps, looking for a crossroads in the old town that led to where they had decided to go. A short, elderly man in an alpaca suit and a boater with a black ribbon, walking with the aid of two sticks, offered to show them the way.

'Follow me – it's a long time since I've been there, but I know the way. When I had my legs, I used to go there on Saturday nights. Around 1925 there was a Negress there, Victoire Sanpeur was her name; everyone in Clermont remembers her—'

'Victoire Sanpeur?' Jean asked.

'Now, now!' the old man chuckled. 'Just listen to the youngster! My dear young fellow, in 1925 you were still suckling at your mama's breast. Yes, Victoire Sanpeur, that's who I said; everyone in Clermont remembers her. An unforgettable head of hair! She was here a year, before she was kidnapped by a député ... I can't walk very fast. It's because of my arthritis ...'

Palfy winked at Jean and asked in a deliberately innocent voice, 'Not because of an old dose of the clap, perhaps?'

The old dodderer raised his stick.

'You blooming rascal, you deserve a good hiding!'

His anger was short-lived. The allusion to his past exploits helped him forget what a wreck he had become.

'No, Monsieur, throughout my life I have only ever frequented establishments that maintained the highest standards of cleanliness.'

'Never an honest woman?' Palfy enquired politely.

'Never! Honest women, as you call them, that's where the trouble lies. No sense of cleanliness.'

He stopped, gathered his sticks in one hand, mopped his brow, and blew his nose noisily before breathing again. Jean gave up being astonished. How did Palfy know Clermont-Ferrand? He was a vagrant who was at home everywhere: in London, Cannes, Deauville, Paris, and now in the Auvergne. In fashionable society or the demi-monde he fell on his feet with staggering ease: penniless one day and dressed up as a priest to rob the poor boxes in church; elegance itself the next, driving his Rolls-Royce around London, served by a butler who was straight out of an English novel; one day a swindler, the next a successful wheeler-dealer. Beside him Jean measured his own clumsiness and naivety, discovering that life is made up of such differences: one child is born into a glittering, false milieu that gives him a passport for the rest of his existence; another, born in a caretaker's lodge at Grangeville in Normandy, will always feel the weight on his shoulders of his humble origins as the child of a washerwoman and a gardener, and have to discover everything by himself. The fact that Jean had known his real mother's name since Antoinette's revelation at Yssingeaux – Geneviève du Courseau – changed nothing. Only Albert and Jeanne counted. The couple had brought him up with strict principles, boring virtues and flat homilies that had proved useless in the present circumstances. As for Geneviève, she had offered him only the most ambiguous feelings. He was once again hanging on to Palfy's coat-tails, as he kept the man with two sticks company.

'My sister keeps house for me,' the arthritic old man said, each step producing a grimace of pain. 'She leaves me a few francs for my tobacco. I've been rolling my own since 1914, shag, nothing but shag. And enough to order an Amer Picon before lunch. What do you drink?'

'Champagne or vodka,' Palfy answered.

'I've drunk vodka … in the past. No taste. Champagne is for marriages, christenings and the sick … Here we are … This is it.'

He jabbed his stick at a massive, freshly painted door. A mermaid's tail in gilded bronze served as a knocker beneath the iron grille. The shutters were closed.

'There won't be anybody home,' the old man said. 'They'll all be at the parade. You'd be better off coming back – and making yourselves more presentable. They won't let you in like that. It's a place with a good reputation. It belongs to the diocese.'

In the distance the band struck up the first bars of 'Le Téméraire'. The companies were marching past the general.

'It's over,' Jean said. 'They're returning to barracks.'

Palfy lifted the knocker. The little old man stamped his foot and banged the pavement with his stick.

'They're not there! And they won't let you in anyway.'

Having led them there, he was regretting his kindness. Good

heavens! Two workers did not seriously think they were going to slake their appetites in a house that had seen Clermont's political and municipal elite pass through its doors, not to mention distinguished men of the cloth and numerous respectable husbands and fathers.

'They won't let you in, I tell you!'

A creaking warned them that someone was sliding the grille aside to observe them. The door opened a fraction. A birdlike head, thin and with a long curved nose and jutting chin, crowned by a meagre but severe bun, appeared.

'Now look, Monsieur Petitlouis, you know perfectly well that your sister does not want to see you coming here any more. Be reasonable. You're past it now!'

Monsieur Petitlouis, choked with fury, banged his walking stick again.

'My sister? Bugger my sister. And you too, you blooming madam.'

Palfy inserted a foot between the door and frame. The woman saw it and tried to force it back.

'The establishment is closed.'

'Not to me,' he said.

'The staff are watching the parade.'

'We'll both wait for them together then.'

'You'll wait outside …'

And more energetically than expected, she let fly a kick that connected with Palfy's shin and dislodged him. The door shut again.

'Didn't I tell you you wouldn't get in?' chuckled the ghastly old man.

Through the grille the woman called out that she would call the police if they continued to make a scene in a street of respectable citizens. But Palfy was not to be deterred. He knocked again with the mermaid's tail. The grille slid half-open.

'What are you wanting now?' the haughty, shrill voice demanded.

'The correct form is, "What do you want?" but it's a small detail and we shan't let ourselves get hung up on grammar. I want to see Monsieur Michette. I have a message for him.'

'Monsieur Michette is doing his duty. He's gone to war.'

'Allow me to point out to you that the war is over.'

'Madame Michette will be here shortly.'

The grille slammed shut. It was clear this time that the door would stay closed. The assistant madam had her orders. Monsieur Petitlouis almost burst with pleasure. He spat into a checked handkerchief. Have I mentioned that on this particular day in July 1940 the temperature had risen to 31 degrees in the shade, overwhelming a town far more used to a temperate climate? Jean and Palfy had been running. Their throats were parched. Monsieur Petitlouis offered to take them to a bistro where they served home-distilled pastis, on condition naturally that they bought him a glass.

'My sister will never know!'

He laughed so hard he almost choked again. Jean looked anxiously at Palfy. The night before had left them with no more than a few francs in their pockets, hardly enough to buy half a baguette and some mortadella. As the reader will have realised, Palfy was not a man to let such a detail bother him. One on each side of the arthritic old devil, they reached a café at the bottom of the street. Back from the parade, the *patron*, in a black jacket and homburg hat, was raising the shutter. He served them at the counter, philosophising about the morning's spectacle.

'Well, Monsieur Petitlouis, you really missed something at that parade! You have to hand it to our army and how it's put itself back together, two weeks after the armistice. The Germans won't want to brush with them a second time, I tell you. You can see it in our chaps' faces: they're raring to go. It's the government that's not. A fine bunch of traitors in the pay of Adolf, I tell you ... That armistice business was all for show, with a fat lot of cash changing hands to stop us pulling off another Marne like we did in '14, on the Loire ...'

Monsieur Petitlouis agreed. Traitors were everywhere. Customers were arriving, red in the face and breathless. They listened to the *patron*, nodding or choosing their words carefully to express mild doubts. The pastis was served in cups, in case a policeman came past and decided to apply the new law on the consumption of spirits. Jean kept an eye on the street. In the distance he caught sight of about a dozen women, led by a matron in a blue skirt, white blouse and red hat, walking up the middle of the street. They fanned themselves with little paper tricolours, and as they passed the café he saw, sashaying in the middle of the group, a black woman with straightened hair, her back hollow and her buttocks stretching the pink satin of her skirt. She reminded Jean of the girls from the Antilles who had brought up Antoinette and Michel du Courseau and simultaneously been their father's bit on the side. And what an odd coincidence: one of them, Victoire Sanpeur, had come to live at Clermont after her departure from La Sauveté. He decided to tell that part of the story to Monsieur Petitlouis, who was sipping his pastis like a greedy child.

'You really knew Victoire!' the old hog exclaimed. 'You were lucky. They say she's still living with her député. She comes back sometimes to see her old girlfriends. She's been known not to turn down the odd customer, even now. For fun – know what I mean? Ah yes, that's a real establishment, a proper family if you're with the Michettes. Not one of those nasty whorehouses where they chuck the girls in the street when they're a bit past it. No. They teach them a trade, how to spell and use a knife and fork; then they find them a job somewhere ...'

The women walked past, looking straight ahead and ignoring the customers' ribald comments. Madame Michette glared at those responsible for the coarsest comments. Two girls giggled. Palfy ordered another round of pastis and made a sign to Jean.

'We'll be back in a couple of minutes,' he said to the *patron*. 'Look after Monsieur Petitlouis, he's a friend of ours.'

*

This time Madame Michette herself opened the door and asked them, disdainfully, what they wanted. The house was closed. The ladies were having lunch.

'We won't disturb them. We merely wanted to have a word with Monsieur Michette and deliver a letter to him from a mutual friend.'

'And who might that be?' she asked, with the suspicion of someone accustomed to the kind of subterfuge her business inspired.

'It's a matter between Monsieur Michette and ourselves.'

'Monsieur Michette is still serving in the army.'

'In that case we shall come back later.'

It was a risky move. It depended entirely on the curiosity and high regard in which Madame Michette held herself, after having taken over the reins of the establishment. The two workmen rightly inspired very little confidence, although the older one talked very correctly and the younger one had a handsome, open face. These were tumultuous times. Clothes no longer made the man.

'Come in!' she said, in a more accommodating tone.

We shall not linger over a description of a brothel interior at Clermont-Ferrand in 1940. It would be tedious. There is a whole literature full of such images of the good old days, when lonely men could take themselves to a so-called 'house of ill repute' and find a family to welcome them, to provide tenderness and a sympathetic ear to their preoccupations large and small. Let us merely say that at the Michettes' (another fateful name, but the author cannot help that)[2] a very strict code of discipline and morals was applied. Monsieur Petitlouis was not exaggerating. Madame Michette was convent-educated and Monsieur Michette had had an exceptionally distinguished war in 1914–18, coming out of it as an infantry sergeant-major. The sum of physical and spiritual human misery that found respite and forgiveness in their establishment was incalculable. One might, without irony, describe the Michettes as belonging to that category of society's benefactors that provincial life shunned, stifling it in the straitjacket of moralistic disapproval. Lastly – a supreme luxury in a town whose relative enlightenment as the capital of the Auvergne did not stop gossip being rife – the Michettes had made discretion the watchword of their profession. No large number over the door, and obviously no red light. A stranger could walk past the house a dozen times without suspecting anything, unless his gaze should rest for a second upon the little mermaid whose fish's tail curled to form the knocker and gave its name to the establishment.

The diocese valued this self-effacement and the punctuality with which its rent was paid. Seminarians were offered concessionary prices and popular opinion had it that senior clerics paid by handing out absolutions. Numerous were the Clermontois who remembered with feeling having lost their virginity there before their marriage. In the arms of Nénette, Verushka or Victoire they had learnt many imaginative alternatives to the missionary position, alternatives that they would later teach their wives. Those violated, humiliated, ashamed and overwhelmed brides, at first taken horribly by surprise at what marriage involved, would later be secretly grateful to the girls of Michette's. Not for them the harrowing labours of Mesdames de Rênal and Bovary, pursuing experience with clumsy youths. I am being perfectly serious. France's brothels – the serious ones, in any case – contributed to both the moral welfare and mental stability of her people. They were her universities of sex. Anatomy was taught there and love acted out with far greater talent than was to be found in a marriage arranged by a notary. They were, in fact, where men passed their exams in licentiousness before setting out on the business of life. Suppressed after the war by a prudish republic, they were so sorely missed by the French that a generation later the state was forced to take measures to introduce the theory and practice of sexual matters into schools. We then witnessed the spectacle of a generation of benighted adolescents receiving the cobbled-together guidance of schoolteachers and demonstrating just how far the civilisation of love had regressed.

There is no need to remind ourselves that our two heroes had different conceptions of love. Palfy, as a gentleman, kept his preferences to himself, and Jean, thanks to his physique, had not had to go to the same school as everyone else. As a result, coming across such a place for the first time, he found Madame Michette's establishment gloomy, especially its large sitting room with its walls decorated in a design of pale-skinned mermaids with crimson lips and golden tresses, where Madame received them standing up, not inviting them to sit as she would have done for the humblest customer before the girls processed past him. A scent of cheap face powder hung in the air, along, perhaps, with other odours less pleasing to fastidious nostrils. Tall, solidly large, with the physique of a grenadier, with workman's hands, and hairs sprouting from her animated chin, Madame Michette banished from their minds any further thought of playing practical jokes.

'Do you have the letter you mentioned?' she asked Palfy.

'I have it with me, but its sender, Monsieur Salah, was very insistent that we deliver it personally. It's a shame Monsieur Michette isn't yet back from the war.'

Jean patted his back pocket. The famous letter he had been given by the prince, in case he ever found himself in difficulty, was not there. His friend's latest deceit infuriated him. He would happily have strangled Palfy, who intercepted his glare and gave a forced half-smile, half-grimace. Madame Michette, whose eyes had opened wide at Salah's name, took the smile as a shared understanding. She was dying to know the letter's contents.

'I have the same authority as my husband to receive Monsieur Salah's orders. His friends are our friends.'

'It's a delicate matter,' Palfy murmured in a reticent undertone.

Jean decided that if Palfy showed the letter to Madame Michette, he would grab it and make a run for the nearest exit, but a diversion saved him from such an extreme step. A face framed by red curls appeared in the half-open doorway.

'Madame, the lamb's done. Shall I pour the sauce over the flageolets?'

'Wait for me, Zizi, I'm coming. Serve the asparagus first and leave the lamb in the oven.'

Zizi's head disappeared.

'We shall leave you,' Palfy said.

Madame hesitated. Despite her position and her responsibilities, she was still a woman. Suspicious but curious. She would have that letter.

'Come and join us for lunch. We had a gift of a shoulder of lamb, and it's sitting waiting for us.'

Jean felt his resistance weaken. Palfy was already accepting, begging Madame Michette to forgive his and his friend's state of dress.

'We trust you, Madame, but I must ask you not to enquire as to the reasons for what we're wearing. We are on our way back from an ultra-secret mission and haven't yet been able to change …'

The reader will find his excuse less than subtle, but I ask him or her to remember the period. Over the next four years numerous people would live in disguise and under borrowed identities. The world would lose count of the colonels and generals who popped up like jack-in-the-boxes, only to disappear again immediately; of the bogus priests and phoney nuns concealing sub-machine guns or explosives underneath their skirts, and the inflated numbers of commercial travellers, an easy profession to assume for those who carried false papers. A great intrigue was on the wing, undertaken by amateurs who would dazzle the readers of adventure and espionage fiction. Madame Michette, ordinarily exceptionally sceptical and trained by years of experience at sniffing out men's lies, felt so flattered by Palfy's half-confidence that she instantly adopted an expression of complicity.

'I promise you *we* shall say nothing.'

So they went through to the dining room, where the residents had already sat down. They stood up again as Madame entered, and for a moment Jean wondered if she was going to say grace. He and Palfy were introduced as 'friends' to Nénette, Claudette and one or two others. Indicating the young black woman, Madame added, '– and our black pearl, Victoire from Guadeloupe. Her real name is Jeannine, but the customers have such fond memories of the first black resident we had here that they demanded we call her successors Victoire as well. Since our motto has always been "put the customer first" …'

At the Sirène, behind closed shutters, life carried on in the glare of electric light. Jean noticed the poor girls' anaemia, their skin coarsened by make-up, the rings round their eyes and their bodies' lack of firmness beneath their thin dressing gowns. Their eyes were the only part of their faces that still showed signs of a life of joy and pleasure. They nudged each other and giggled, and there was general hilarity when Madame scolded Zizi for eating her asparagus in a manner that might have given pause to those with dirty minds.

Palfy liked to put his friends on the spot. Jean's silence made him feel disapproved of, so he swung the spotlight back on him.

'To be perfectly honest' – he leant towards Madame's ear – 'I know Monsieur Salah very slightly. It's more my young colleague who knows him well. Before this absurd war they saw each other often, in Rome, in London and even, I believe, at Grangeville in Normandy.'

'And how old are you, young man?' she asked Jean.

'I'm just twenty.'

'Twenty years old, and you've already seen the world!'

'Not the world: only Italy and England.'

'Well, I had to wait forty years before I went on a pilgrimage to Rome. That was the year I brought Maria back.'

Across the table from Jean a girl with brown hair and bright eyes smiled. Less pale than the others, she revealed behind her plumply rolled lips the compact teeth of a Roman she-wolf.

'And do you speak Italian?' Madame enquired, making at the same time a gesture to Nénette that she should extend her little finger when drinking her glass of wine.

'Only a few words, but I speak English.'

'Education always comes in handy. I say it again and again to my young ladies.'

The young ladies, who usually chattered non-stop at the arrival of a customer, whoever he might be, had understood that a certain decorum was called for at this lunch in the company of two strangers. Madame fortunately was well versed in the art of what she called 'lathering' her customers, and secretly hoped that the two messengers would take flattering reports back to Salah about the way her establishment was run.

'Who knows where that man is now?' she said with an anxiety that was only half feigned.

'In Lebanon,' Jean said.

Questioning looks were exchanged around the table, but no one dared ask where Lebanon was. Madame Michette's anxiety was not allayed.

'There's no war there, I hope?'

'Not yet!' Palfy said with a knowing air.

Zizi, the establishment's cook, had prepared a surprise: a chocolate gateau topped with whipped cream. Everyone clapped. Madame Michette injected a melancholy note.

'Cream is getting hard to come by. Apparently the Germans are commandeering whole trainloads of it. If we let them, they'll take it all. However, Monsieur Cassagnate, who is a little in love with our Zizi, has promised to keep some by for us. From his farm! Real cream.'

'He's such a sweetie!' Zizi said.

'A sweetie filled with cream,' Nénette added.

Madame tapped on the table with her spoon.

'Nénette always talks too much,' she said. 'When she was little her parents took her to pray to St Lupus, who cures the timid. He cured her too well.'

Palfy played up to her, listening attentively, and when the Bénédictine was served (what else, in such a right-minded establishment?) Madame Michette and her young ladies launched into stories of their favourite saints with healing properties: Saints Cosmas and Damian who would cure you of anything at Brageac in Cantal, St Priest at Volvic who restored the infirm (although, as Victoire observed, he had had a failure with Monsieur Petitlouis), Notre-Dame de la Râche at Domerat who was good for getting rid of impetigo, and at Clermont itself a pair of saints who were not short of work: St Zachary who restored the power of speech and St George who eliminated the harmful effects of embarrassing diseases ...

Madame protested. They had no need of him at the Sirène. It was a decent establishment, very *hygienic*. The girls cleared the table and carried the dishes to the kitchen. In half an hour the first customers would be arriving. They had just enough time to make themselves up and slip on the négligées they wore for work. The assistant madam, who had received Jean and Palfy so disagreeably, appeared looking pinched and officious and summoned the young ladies. The bedrooms needed to be clean and tidy.

'It's Sunday,' Madame explained to her guests. 'And after that parade we'll be seeing a fair few soldiers. Oh, if only Monsieur Michette were here ...'

'He won't be long now.'

'One often needs a man on such occasions. Military men are such children.'

'My colleague,' Palfy said, 'has exactly the physique you require to preserve respect for the conventions. If he can be of any use to you ... I can't personally: I've a very hollow chest, and at thirty my reflexes aren't as quick as they were.'

Before accepting his offer, Madame Michette again expressed her keenness to know more about the letter. Might she not just see the envelope? Palfy put his hand in his pocket and turned pale.

'I had it a moment ago.'

Jean let him search for it. Madame Michette, her face flushed a little from red wine and Bénédictine, started to look suspicious. Palfy ran to the sitting room and Jean took advantage of his absence to get out the letter he had surreptitiously removed from his friend's pocket. The outer envelope had already been slit. It contained a typed list of town names, and next to each town someone's name. Against Clermont-Ferrand was the name 'Michette, René', underlined by Palfy. This addressee was to be given a second sealed envelope, which he would open and reveal the important person whose intervention would save Jean, if it ever became necessary.

'I can't show you any more,' Jean said regretfully to Madame, reclaiming his property as Palfy returned, looking yellow and sheepish.

'You had it?'

'You gave it to me this morning, remember. For safekeeping,' Jean lied, to save face for his friend.

Madame Michette had seen the list for long enough to scan the names.

'I know some of these people,' she said meaningfully. 'They're acquaintances.'

'Yes,' Palfy said, 'but we must ask you to be very discreet. Since you're clearly a trustworthy person, we can tell you that great plans are being made. The Germans have not won the war, as some benighted souls imagine. They have lost it. It is for that defeat that my friend and I are working. We are, I'll be completely frank and open with you, secret agents.'

'My lips are sealed!' Madame Michette breathed, closing her eyes and pressing her hand to her stomach, which was making a joyful gurgling sound.

Jean tried very hard not to laugh. Madame Michette led them to a small ground-floor office from where, through a spyhole, they could monitor her customers arriving and leaving. As soon as they were settled, they fell fast asleep in their armchairs, full of lunch and exhausted from their recent forced march, and were undisturbed by the noise of the knocker and the comings and goings in the hall. Her uniformed customers, that day at least, refrained from behaving like conquering heroes. They came, mostly in groups of three or four and pushing a blushing virgin ahead of them, and the authority of Madame and her assistant madam impressed them deeply. There were no brawls, nor Bacchic outbursts.

Let us make the most of the moment while our two heroes slumber to satisfy the reader's curiosity about a point of history that the author has, in his Machiavellian way, so far left blank. What happened when the twelve rifles of the SS Grenadiers took aim in the little village square where Constantin Palfy, Jean Arnaud, Francis Picallon and the surveyor Jacques Graindorge had been lined up to be shot? Of course, apart from themselves and Obersturmführer Karl Schmidt, no one *really* thought they would be shot. We would not have undertaken the narrative of Jean Arnaud's long sentimental education if we had had to call a halt at the age of twenty because a uniformed idiot who played the violin had ordered a platoon of his men to execute four Frenchmen after a good lunch. No. Jean Arnaud and the strange Constantin Palfy will have a hard life, but it is Karl Schmidt who will be the first to die, which no one, except for his wife and children, will greatly mind. But let us abandon Karl Schmidt, whose only virtue was to add a grotesque element to a macabre spectacle. The thing we need to know is that the SS Grenadiers did take aim at our friends. It was a ghastly, melancholy minute and few who have survived such a thing can bring themselves to talk about it. Twelve black holes and an NCO, his boots squarely planted where he stands, revolver in hand for the coup de grâce, are an image you don't forget. If you escape, by a miracle, that image awakens a deeper respect for life, and the three-line notices announcing the death of a hostage jump out of the news with a significance so harrowing that it can become unbearable. What does one think about at such a moment? It is as difficult for the survivor to remember as it is for anyone else to imagine. If we were to ask Jean Arnaud, he would answer, 'I don't know. Nothing, maybe. Two or three fleeting memories: Maman in the kitchen of her house, holding the iron up to her cheek, Papa limping across the garden, Antoinette showing me her bottom at the foot of the cliffs, Chantal in our bedroom in Rue Lepic, or Geneviève, my real mother, embarking at Cannes to escape from the war. But all of it very fast, very superficial. Nothing, in fact. And not even a thought for my soul's salvation. No, really, nothing dignified or interesting, not the sort of thing you read in classical tragedies, romantic plays, or heroic novels.' Come to the point, I hear you say. But the author cannot help but go on hesitating to say what saved Jean and Palfy that day, so utterly improbable does it seem here. It would be so much easier to explain that it was all a poor and violent joke on the Obersturmführer's part to test the four Frenchmen's equanimity, or, more prosaically, to divert himself after a campaign so rapid that the SS units intended for the fiercest fighting had not had to fire a shot in anger. Valiant warriors who had advanced with the thought of heroic battles to come had experienced considerable frustration. They had been drilled for war, not sightseeing. The firing squad was thus not merely a macabre joke. A few seconds longer, and Jean and Palfy would have been shot. So we are left with no alternative but to invoke Providence, that benevolent entity that sometimes stoops to take a hand in human destinies and delay deaths without giving reasons, just to amuse itself, or so it seems, to toy with existences that are no more or less dear to it than others and that it only identifies by caprice or a taste for sarcasm.

On this occasion, then, Providence appeared in the guise of an open-topped car belonging to the German army, an elegant high-bodied vehicle driven by a helmeted chauffeur whose chinstrap was immaculately placed. On the rear seat sat three individuals: two French soldiers in forage caps, flanking a Wehrmacht colonel. They had come from the south and been on their way for more than an hour, which showed how far behind the lines the tankettes were. But was there still a line on 20 June 1940? One wonders. The car was crossing the square when the colonel caught sight of the drama in which the Obersturmführer was already losing interest. He tapped the driver's shoulder. The car braked in a cloud of dust. The Unterscharführer ordered his platoon to about-turn and present arms. Karl Schmidt attempted to inject an offhand note into his salute, but the colonel ordered him to approach.

'What do you think you're doing? Are you shooting civilians?'

'They're irregulars, Herr Oberst.'

'They are not, because there aren't any. And if there were, they would first of all be answerable to a court martial, not to an SS lieutenant.'

'Herr Oberst, I assure you that they are dangerous bandits.'

The colonel sighed and stepped from his car to approach the men lined up in front of the Café des Amis.

'Will you excuse me,' he said in French to the two prisoners who flanked him, pale and with clenched teeth, on the rear seat.

The colonel approached Jacques Graindorge, who was seized again by a mad hope.

'Were you sheltering these soldiers?' he asked scornfully. 'If one may call them soldiers …'

'I thought they were Germans, General! I'm a friend of Germany, General, of Greater Germany, General.'

'A friend of Germany ought to be able to tell the difference between a colonel and a general and a pair of khaki trousers and a pair of field-grey trousers. Or alternatively he's an idiot, but even if he is we aren't going to shoot every idiot on earth – we'd be here for years.'

One of the prisoners got out of the car and walked up to the colonel. Had it not been for his uniform, he could have been taken for a German: a tall Celt with curly blond hair, eyes of a clear blue, hollow cheeks.

'Colonel, will you allow me to ask these men a question?'

'Of course, my dear fellow.'

The man stared at the prisoners in turn, with great concentration.

'Are there any Bretons among you?'

'I am Anglo-Serb,' Palfy said.

'I'm Norman,' Jean said.

'From the Jura!' Picallon sang out.

'And you, Monsieur?' The prisoner turned to Graindorge.

'From the Auvergne!'

The man turned back to the colonel and shrugged.

'They are of no interest to me at all. Having said that, Colonel, spare them if you're able and if you believe, as I do, that we should begin our project in a spirit of reconciliation rather than hatred.'

'Consider it done!' the colonel said.

He called Karl Schmidt and ordered him to release the prisoners. The Obersturmführer protested. The officer reminded him of his rank. There was much heel clicking and more presenting of arms and the SS section drove away in its armoured cars.

'Do we have you to thank?' Palfy asked the Frenchman.

'No. Thank the colonel.'

'There are always blunders when two great peoples such as Germany and France are reconciled,' the German said, 'but it is well known in Berlin that your country has been plunged into a fratricidal war by unscrupulous politicians … Now, leave your two tankettes and try to rejoin your army …'

Laughing, he added, '… if you have strong legs.'

Jean studied the French prisoner who had spoken to the colonel with such assurance, and to whom the colonel spoke in a tone close to deference. In the colonel's car, the other prisoner was looking both furious and bored. It was the combination of the two faces that reminded Jean where he had seen them before, one open and friendly, the other sarcastic and closed.

'I'm wondering whether I might possibly know you,' Jean said to the prisoner whose incomprehensible contribution to the situation had saved their lives. 'You wouldn't be a friend of the abbé Le Couec?'

'Yes.'

'Then you know me too, and your friend sitting in the car owes his freedom to me. My name is Jean Arnaud and I led him by bicycle from Tôtes to Grangeville eight years ago. I was a little boy then.'

'Jean! Jean from Grangeville!'

He kissed him. The colonel smiled. Things had been going very well ever since the morning. When he had asked a group of prisoners of war for any Bretons among them to make themselves known to him, he had had the surprise of coming across two senior members of the Breton National Party. The reader who still has a vague memory of Jean's childhood will already have guessed that these two are Yann and Monsieur Carnac, names that in the underground denote the two separatists who, having taken part in the attack at Rennes on 6 August 1932, on the eve of a visit by Édouard Herriot, had fled and met up again at the abbé Le Couec's rectory at Grangeville. A terrific coincidence, I will agree, having promised that these kinds of magic meetings would be putting in no further appearances, yet it must be admitted that in the general chaos of that time anything was possible. Monsieur Carnac stepped from the car and shook Jean's hand.

'I wouldn't have recognised you. You're a man now.'

The colonel (I have not given his name as we shall not be seeing him again in Jean Arnaud's life; he is no petty Prussian squire with a monocle screwed into his eye – there really would have needed to be a fantastic reservoir of petty squires to supply the entire German army with officers – but a professor of Celtic studies at the University of Mainz whose detailed report on Breton separatism, published at the outbreak of war, had attracted the attention of the German high command), the colonel seemed over the moon. His grand political design was taking shape: the two prisoners he was taking to Dortmund, where separatists of every stripe, Breton, Basque, Corsican and Alsatian, were being assembled, had sympathisers in the rest of the country. They were not disliked, far from it. France was behind them!

We shall cut short the scene that followed. The colonel was in a hurry to return to Germany. He signed three safe-conduct passes for

Palfy, Jean and Picallon and assured Graindorge of his protection.

'If I may give you a word of advice,' he said to the three soldiers, 'it would be to throw away those uniforms and lose yourselves on one of the farms around here. Marshal Pétain requested an armistice last night. The war is over ...'

The village square returned to a state of calm, and if the two tankettes had not still been parked in the shade it would have been easy to imagine that it was any summer's day at siesta time. Graindorge, his fear evaporated, and overcome by shame and rage, hastened to his house and locked himself in. The three friends walked across to a clothes shop which they opened with a boot through the window. Inside, they found that all that was left were trousers and jackets that were either too large or too small. They spent the next two weeks on a farm bringing in the hay, heard that the armistice had been signed and the ceasefire had come into effect. Picallon, ever dutiful, left on his own to rejoin the regiment, said to be stationed at Clermont-Ferrand. Palfy and Jean took longer to get themselves organised. They had become fond of the farm, where they were looked after lavishly in the evenings when they came in from the fields. But once the hay was in, there was no longer any need for their services, and they set out. It was on the morning of their arrival at Clermont that we first caught sight of them on a café terrace, enjoying their regiment marching past and moved by a glimpse of a pretty young woman with ash-blond hair, wearing a dress of translucent lawn.

Their siesta, deepened by Madame Michette's red wine and Bénédictine, was succeeded by a conversation which we can summarise briefly. Palfy felt quite at home at the Sirène – he would happily have spent several days there – and urged Jean to hand over the secret letter to the *patronne*, a woman of intelligence, well organised and enterprising. She was capable of getting them out of trouble at a time when contacts, ideas and courage would not bear fruit so easily. What could Clermont-Ferrand offer them by way of resources in these difficult days? With the frontiers closed, there was no leaving France now, and even more inconveniently, to get across the demarcation line from the northern zone to the southern was impossible without a special pass. Despair would obviously have been absurd. The cage in which they found themselves was still a large one, and the freedom of movement it offered was not so very different from before the war. The newsstands were still covered with names of newspapers that reminded them of Paris: *Le Figaro*, *Le Journal*, *Paris-Soir*, *Le Temps*, *Action Française*, now proudly launching into the subject of the 'national revolution'. In short, one had to be there in order to see what would happen. Jean, however, wanted to keep the prince and Salah's letter, which was intended to be used only in extreme necessity. What, in any case, could it contain? Probably a recommendation to some powerful person who controlled the destinies of thirty such welcoming establishments scattered here and there around France. As such, that person was likely to have close relations with police and politicians, and Jean, more by instinct than serious consideration, recoiled from using such a recommendation, to the point where he was willing to leave Clermont if he could not find work there ...

'We've got nothing to eat this evening!' Palfy objected.

'I'm not hungry.'

'Very well ... let's wait till tomorrow.'

This was stating the obvious. The truth was that Palfy was becoming bourgeois. He was less fond of the risks that for so long had been a prime feature of his character. Jean, on the other hand, felt that the situation was tailor-made for them: a few francs in their pockets and nowhere to stay.

'I know,' Jean said, 'let's play a little game while we're at it. To unearth, in this town where we know neither streets nor habits, a pearl beyond price lost in the crowd ...'

'Yes, she's very pretty. But you're not going to make me wear out my shoe leather. In all sincerity I prefer Zizi. Firstly because she's a good cook—'

'Palfy, you think of nothing but eating these days.'

'Yes, and it's my impression that that is going to become more and more difficult. We're not even allowed to go to Switzerland, where they've hollowed out mountains to fill them with chocolate and butter. So we might as well get a head start here. The establishment is very welcoming—'

'Nothing says that old woman Michette is going to be happy keeping you for a single night.'

'You're out of your mind! She's quivering with anticipation at the idea of harbouring secret agents.'

Palfy was right. Madame Michette offered them a room without any prompting.

'After midnight we're closed. Nénette and Zizi will sleep together. You can use Zizi's room. We'll give you clean sheets. Tomorrow perhaps we'll have some news of Monsieur Michette. An officer told me that his regiment has reached Perpignan at last, after defending heroically. He'll be here soon; he knows his duty now that the war is over.'

Palfy explained that they had another problem: to find their contact, a pretty young woman who answered to the name of Claude, green eyes, ash-blond hair, a blue lawn dress (but well dressed enough not to wear it two days running), whom they had just missed this morning because of the crowds gathering for the parade.

'Naturally,' he pointed out, lowering his voice, 'we are still talking about a secret mission, and as I'm sure you're aware, when a meeting between agents fails, they stand a strong chance of not making contact a second time. Safeguarding security is of the utmost importance in our work.'

Madame Michette threw herself into her two guests' predicament with an eagerness that astonished them. The truth was that she had recently become a devoted fan of a serial in L'Avenir, the Clermont-Ferrand newspaper, about the adventures of a secret agent whose name, Soleil, had particularly captivated her. Ever since her breathless daily dose of Soleil's adventures, which had had her hurrying to the newsstand before she drank her morning coffee, she had dreamt of offering her services to her country. She had begun raiding the bookshops for spy novels. Accepting that her appearance was unlikely to allow her to seduce an enemy agent and extract his secret from him, she had been waiting for an opportunity that would reveal her deeper qualities of courage, intuition and decisiveness. In this bourgeois woman brought up to respect the virtues on which an honest and hard-working society was based, there seethed ambitions that her position as madam of a brothel did not allow her to satisfy. She suffered from not being 'accepted' in society. The great and the good of Clermont were as friendly to her as good taste allowed, but in public either barely greeted her or failed to acknowledge her entirely if they were with their wives. Their disregard made her miserable and she had complained bitterly about it to Monsieur Michette, who himself had no such sensibilities and contented himself with scrupulously keeping the establishment's accounts for the benefit of its powerful patrons. Palfy and Jean could not have guessed upon what marvellously fertile soil they had fallen, or what an ally they were making for themselves by asking this honest woman for her help. In a flash Madame Michette had glimpsed an incredible opportunity in the challenge they had set her. If she came out of it well she would be eligible for other missions, and one day, like her husband, be entitled to wear the Croix de Guerre, and earn the respect of all.

She nevertheless made it clear to Jean and Palfy that what they were asking was tantamount to finding a needle in a haystack. Thousands of refugees were flooding into Clermont-Ferrand. The hotels were full. There was not a bed to be had in any private house. And the inhabitants of Clermont, secretive at the best of times, recoiled from showy behaviour. Families lived discreetly, rarely showing themselves. Perhaps there were, all the same, two or three streets and Place de Jaude where one might position oneself in the hope of meeting the desired person. But their description of Claude was vague. Madame Michette promised to give the matter some thought.

The next morning the street's residents were highly surprised to see the young women from the Sirène emerge as a group from their lodgings. This was not part of their routine. Speculation ran riot: the girls were on their way to the railway station to greet Monsieur Michette, who was returning with another palm to add to his Croix de Guerre; they were going to present a petition at the prefecture calling for their status as workers in a reserved occupation to be recognised, which would entitle them to extra food rations: 350 grams of bread instead of 250, a bar of chocolate a month and an extra 100 grams of butter; they wanted to complain en masse to the regional military commander about his rumoured decision to send the glorious 152nd infantry regiment to Montluçon – the 15–2 – first regiment of France, recently re-formed at the Desaix barracks. The spectators watched them go, their bottoms swaying briskly down the street, led by Madame Michette dressed soberly in grey, the appropriate colour for a secret agent. The girls were not laughing and walked with their eyes lowered, their faces unmade-up, swinging their patent handbags. In short, only Monsieur Michette was missing for them to start walking in step with each other.

As soon as they arrived in the town centre they dispersed according to a prearranged plan. Madame Michette installed herself at the Café Riche, next to the telephone booth. Palfy and Jean sat at a table some distance away, pretending to ignore their new friend, who ordered a beer and immersed herself in a spy novel. With a passion unexpected in a person as down to earth as she was, she had, in the space of a night, taken the bait put down by Palfy and decided, by every possible means including the consumption of pulp novels on the subject, to begin her training as a secret agent.

The wait lasted all morning. Palfy rejoiced in his machinations. Jean was the only one not to believe it would work, even though the preparations had crystallised in his mind's eye an idealised image of the young woman he had glimpsed during the parade. In the shabby, heavily perfumed surroundings of the Sirène, that image was like a window open onto a scrap of sky, a hope that a world more sympathetic to his tastes and his aspirations still existed despite the debacle of the past month.

'I feel we're on our way to great things,' Palfy murmured. 'The era is eminently favourable to those who venture all. We shall have fun.'

'I'll admit it hasn't got off to a bad start. I adore Madame Michette.'

'France is full of Madame Michettes. We shall fill their heads with dreams.'

'You'll fill their heads. Not me.'

Palfy waved his hand irritably.

'Are you starting again? Listen, dear boy, I don't know how many times you've tried to back out, but it's time to stop. I know your excellent soul, your rectitude, your honesty, your courage and loyalty. All well and good, I'm in the picture. You can't shock me any more. But from now on, life is about living, so put all that on one side for the next few years. We own nothing, hardly even the shirts on our backs. We're starting again from nothing. I have a few ideas and you've got a sweet mug – women like you. On my own I can't do anything, and if you go it alone you'll end up doing ghastly little jobs: delivering parcels, or bouncer at a nightclub. Think about it ...'

'Then explain to me,' Jean said, 'why your cheating makes me feel so uncomfortable. I should be getting used to it and recognising that it's justified most of the time, because all you're really doing is taking advantage of human stupidity. But I can't help it: every time something inside me says no.'

'My dear chap, I'm afraid these scruples of yours are metaphysical in origin. They're an artificial distinction, produced by centuries of tradition, between good and evil. Trust me on this: get out of the habit, or you'll be doomed to play the game of a society that doesn't give a shit about your soul and will happily exploit you like a slave ...'

A slave? Wasn't one a slave to everything? To one's social status, one's passions, one's stupidity or clear-sightedness for that matter? Jean would have liked to muse on the question at greater length, without immediately answering yes or no to Palfy, for whom, ever since they had enlisted, he had felt real friendship, even something close to admiration. Palfy shone a light on life, painted it in bold colours, set traps for him. Unfortunately, every time events seemed to point to perfect happiness, they had a tendency to come to grief and everything went back to square one. Staring out of the café window, Jean felt sceptical about the possibilities Palfy saw in the situation: he saw only a quiet street, women carrying shopping bags, a queue outside a butcher's twenty people long, several closed steel shutters. After the emotions sparked by the parade, life was returning to normal, as dull as before, with the same hardships making themselves felt and starting to monopolise people's thoughts, as night followed day. How could one hope to succeed in a defeated country that, since the unprovoked massacre of its sailors at Mers el-Kébir, no longer knew whether yesterday's allies were not today's enemies and whether the enemy currently occupying half the country in such a disciplined way would not become tomorrow's friend? To be able to see clearly these days demanded a particular lucidity, one that no single person possessed. Reason dictated simply surviving until one could see things more distinctly. No one knew what was happening in Paris or the rest of France. Jean thought about his father. How was he feeling now, the old leftist pacifist who had remained so loyal to his ideas that he was willing to insult French officers in the street while a war was going on? Jean had disappointed him deeply by enlisting on the eve of the conflict.

'I need to see my father,' Jean said.

Palfy shrugged.

'Forget it. You've got to leave all that alone now too.'

One of the girls from the Sirène came into the café. She brought an address. Madame Michette made a note. By the end of the morning she had half a dozen other addresses. Posted at different crossroads, the girls had observed six possible Claudes and trailed them to where they lived. Six was too many. Jean did not hide his scorn. He found Palfy's new ploy risible, an ugly caricature of the carefree pleasure to be had from a sudden encounter with a desirable face and a tantalising outline in the morning sunshine. After lunch he refused to accompany Palfy when he set off, list in hand, to find the real Claude. He was thrown into an even greater panic when his friend returned triumphant. Claude existed! And she was waiting for him, in a café on Place de Jaude. First they had to put on an elaborate act for Madame Michette, whose chest had swelled to bursting and who expected a medal at the very least.

'Get going!' Palfy ordered. 'I have a hunch that you've got an incredible opportunity waiting for you this time, one you can't pass up. She's much more beautiful than we thought when we first caught sight of her. A refugee from the north. Lives in Paris. Get a move on, I tell you! The future is yours.'

'I won't know what to say to her, I don't know her.'

'You'll think of something.'

He went, pursued by Palfy, who, suspecting he might try to run away, did not want to give him the opportunity.

'What did you say to her?' Jean asked as they reached the café.

'Nothing. I didn't need to. She guessed.'

'I haven't even got enough to buy her a drink.'

'I thought of that. Here.'

He held out a 500-franc note.

'Where did you get that?'

'What do you care?'

'Was it Zizi?'

'Yes, clever dick. She's mad about us.'

'It makes me feel sick.'

'We'll pay her back a hundred times over.'

The time for hesitating was over. Palfy turned and walked away. Inside the café the young woman was sitting at a table on her own. She smiled when she saw him walk in.

'So it is you,' she said.

Jean had never read *On Love*.[3] Had he ever opened it, he would probably have shut it again immediately. Theories left him cold, and the philosophy of love had not yet revealed itself to him. Jostled and pre-empted by reality, as spoilt as a little prince and punished as only the innocent are, he had never thought love could be expressed in cut-and-dried formulas. The cold-eyed clarity of Stendahl's Julien Sorel, punctuated by outbursts of frenzy, left him annoyed and disbelieving. In truth, being incapable of calculation, he found it natural that fortune should smile on him more than other young men of his age. Life had granted him, very young, two capital experiences and he felt they would never be repeated, at least not in the same way. A shred of reason restrained him – reason that was swept away by the words 'So it is you' and by the amused look the speaker directed at him. He felt suddenly awkward and ridiculous, and so inferior to the lovely woman staring at him that it was all he could do not to take to his heels. Sitting facing her, he was unaware that the crystallisation around her fleeting outline had turned into a real love that was almost comfortable in its reciprocity, however undeclared it was, and that he was preparing for this young woman with her nose dotted with pale freckles, her unmade-up mouth that scorned lipstick, and short hair that exposed her lovely, gazelle-like neck, to be the love of his life – even long after everything was finished between them – and that his only distress, as it is with every happy love, would be not to know how to love her enough. In short, as she sat in front of him with her chin resting on the palm of a hand ornamented at the wrist by a green malachite bracelet, she was the natural intermediary a boy of twenty needed in order to embark upon manhood.

It would be so much kinder not to smile. Jean's feeling for Claude and hers for him have coalesced within a drama containing plenty of burlesque elements. We ought to overlook the participation of Madame Michette and the girls at the Sirène. Let us just lament, by way of excuse, that the ways of love are impenetrable. Fortunately that's all too true. The situation and timing are ill-chosen: the country is split down the middle by a defeat that has left it stunned. People are nursing their bruises and wounds, counting their dead, their missing, their prisoners. Without the saving grace of a cowardly relief that the adventure had been no worse, there would be little place left for the love that is blossoming, masked by a discreet ruefulness, between a young man of twenty and a young woman of twenty-five.

There is no mistaking some raising of eyebrows at the mention of their ages. Is Jean destined for ever to love women who are older than him? Let us remember that in those distant times women did not start making love as soon as they reached puberty. It was thus inevitable that a fine figure of a boy, as the novelists have it, should experience his first amorous awakenings with women who are a little more, or even much more, experienced than he is. With of course one exception: Chantal de Malemort, who by her conduct at Jean's age had wrecked the idea of a pure love blossoming in a sylvan paradise, dawning in a provincial mansion and rudely sundered from its ideals in a cramped bohemian bedroom in Paris, in Rue Lepic. So here they are, these two, Jean and Claude, each subtly attracted to the other, and I am very tempted to talk of magic. In fact magic it certainly is if we enumerate the combination of circumstances necessary to bring this encounter about. If a single detail were out of place, the whole thing would be impossible. If, for instance – as Jean imagined, thinking about his Italian journey of 1936 – a thief had not stolen his bicycle, if the consular official had not shown him the door instead of offering him his help, if he had not met the truck driver, Stefano, the lover of Mireille Cece, if Mireille had not squeezed him dry with her insatiable appetite, if, as he fled from her, he had not met Palfy disguised as a priest in his elderly Mathis, and so on ... he would never have found himself, one July afternoon, at a café table on Place de Jaude facing a young woman who, in any other circumstances, he would have had no reason to be meeting. We might ask ourselves some questions about the impressive intelligence of chance, which has been preparing for a long time for this inevitable event, and preparing for it with such minute attention to detail that no electronic brain could match it. It is an observation that leaves us with few illusions about our freedom of choice, but what does it matter if the result is the one we have been preparing for from birth? Out of the air we plucked the theft of Jean's bicycle at Ostia, but there are a thousand other events whose sequence is equally necessary. And so must we also, in the same context, thank chance for having thrown Chantal into the arms of Gontran Longuet and Sergeant Tuberge for abandoning his men in their foxholes. The backstage scene is one of an immense watchmaker's mechanism of cogs and wheels of such complexity that they pass all human understanding. Only the result counts, and for now Claude and Jean are face to face.

We shall compress the account of the first meeting of these two beings, already in love and still swimming in that atmosphere of happy awkwardness and sweet felicity that precedes the moment of fateful pronouncements. So as not to keep the reader in suspense any longer, we shall provide some details about Claude, at least the ones we know, unconnected with her character, whose slow discovery is Jean's business. She is French on her father's side, Russian on her mother's. We shall refrain from mentioning Slavic charm, out of consideration for those who witnessed the arrival of the first Soviet troops in Poland, Silesia, Pomerania and East Germany, and, later, the triumphal entry of the liberators into Hungary and Czechoslovakia. That so-called quality may well be one of those ghastly clichés you still hear bandied about in nightclubs. Claude's aura expresses itself in a different way, more like a poem whose lines are arranged in the form of drawings, in words that write themselves around her when she speaks and smiles.

I am conscious of having mentioned her smile a great deal already. That is because each time it appears in her natural, unmade-up features it is an extraordinary summons, an instant temptation, an expression one would give one's soul to see appear. So why is she not surrounded by a swarm of admirers battling to get closer to her, elbowing each other aside, loathing their rivals and planning their victorious offensive? For the simple reason that charm and grace are not apparent to everyone and this exquisite young woman lacks one crucial quality that excites and fans men's passions: she is incapable of being a bitch.

So far only one man had disregarded this shortcoming. His name was Georges Chaminadze, and Caucasian blood ran in his veins. He was the father of the small boy with blue-green eyes who we shall encounter a few days after the first meeting with Claude, in a third-class railway carriage steaming slowly up to Paris. In the same compartment are six other people, all with set faces, who clearly dislike the presence of this boisterous child with the strange name of Cyrille. Jean is trying to get him interested in some drawings of monsters that he is sketching in an exercise book, while Claude stares out of the window at the countryside rolling past on the other side of the demarcation line.[4] France is in the fields. Between Paris and the Loire the war has left few serious scars on the land. There is no sign of crops flattened by tanks, and only occasionally an abandoned truck at the side of the road or an aerodrome where planes were burnt where they stood on the morning of 10 May, at the sacrosanct coffee hour. A horse drags a wagon with a cot balanced on its roof. The crossing keeper chases his children, playing on the level crossing. The sun is shining. The summer of 1940 is superb, soft and golden. Three fighter planes – Messerschmitt 109s – fly over the train, showing their camouflaged undersides decorated with the black cross of the Luftwaffe. On a river bank there are even some fishermen sitting with their rods, two wearing straw hats, one in a beret. Paris is approaching: suburban burrstone houses and sad-looking apartment blocks, their shutters closed above shops still locked and dark. The train slows. Cyrille is at the window. Scrambling onto Claude's knees, his feet have made her skirt ride up. Jean sees her knee for the first time. He places his hand on it, and she gives him a glance of reproof. The other passengers pull down their suitcases and parcels. Impatience and clumsiness make their natural rudeness worse. They would trample you underfoot rather than face a second's delay.

Jean has very little with him, just a small bag containing a shirt and a sweater, his razor, a toothbrush, and a book. He is a long way from the ambitious Rastignac's 'It's between you and me now!',[5] yet the future lies here: he must live to deserve the beautiful being at his side, whom the war has left defenceless. Georges Chaminadze is in England. He has managed to get a message through via the Red Cross. Claude is going back to her apartment and an uncertain livelihood. The train draws into the platform at Gare de Lyon with a long screech of brakes. German railway workers mingle with French. There are no longer any porters and no taxis.

The mêlée of passengers jostles and pushes its way to the Métro, which greets them with its smell of burnt electricity and disinfectant. Claude holds Cyrille's hand. Jean carries the two cases. He escorts Claude to her apartment on Quai Saint-Michel. Apart from the occasional German car, the streets are empty. Paris smells good. The chestnuts are in leaf. The booksellers have reopened their stalls and there are soldiers flicking through pornography or buying engravings showing little urchins peeing in the gutter while a girl with an upturned nose watches spellbound. The lift is out of order. Four floors.

Claude pushes open the shutters and there is Notre-Dame, to which France's government of freemasons and secularists filed on 19 May to pray to the Holy Virgin to save the nation. A *Te Deum* that fell on deaf ears. France has vanished but the witnesses to her past have remained: the Conciergerie, the spire of the Sainte-Chapelle, and in the distance the Sacré-Cœur, as ugly as ever, the work of a pretentious pastry chef. Cyrille tugs off his socks and lies down on his bed among his favourite animals. Claude closes his bedroom door and walks back to the hall with Jean. She raises herself on tiptoe and kisses him quickly on the cheek.

'Thank you,' she says. 'Tomorrow?'

'Tomorrow.'

As he goes back downstairs he reflects that so far he has not even held her hand. But his palm has kept the memory of her knee that he stroked for a second on the train. Where to now? He knows no one and has only a few francs in his pocket. He feels a strong urge to turn round and retrace his footsteps. He reaches the Opéra. On the terrace of the Café de la Paix there are green uniforms and women sitting at the small tables. Rue de Clichy is deserted and the Casino de Paris is closed. Paris looks like a city drowsing in the sun, unwilling to wake up because it feels too early and there is no sign of the familiar morning noises – the buses and their grinding gearboxes, the milkmen and newspaper sellers – yet different noises are audible, as if in a bad dream – the two-stroke engines of German cars, the distant rumble and squeak of armoured units driving through the city back to the north, and the whistle of dispatch riders' heavy BMW motorcycles. Drawn by a Percheron, a charabanc passes, transporting cases of beer. And on the giant billboard above the entrance to the Gaumont a poster for a German film.

Jean had thought he would never see Rue Lepic again, but here it is, and as he walks up it he recognises the Italian fruit-seller, the pork butcher from Limousin and the café-*tabac* run by the Auvergnat, though it is no longer Marcel behind the counter but his wife whose breasts are as large as ever. And finally the filthy, poetic building from which Chantal de Malemort escaped one morning, carried off in a Delahaye driven by that dandified thug, Gontran Longuet. Nearly all the shutters are closed, but two are open on the fourth floor. Jean climbs the stairs. Nothing has changed. He rings the bell. A sound of footsteps. The door opens wide. Jesús Infante stands with his mouth open.

'Jean!'

He throws his arms wide, seizes Jean and crushes him, knocking all the air out of his body and thumping him on the back, Spanish-style.

'Jean!' he repeats. 'You are 'live!'

On a bed behind him, draped with black satin, lies a girl with dyed blond hair.

'Com' in!' Jesús shouts in a booming voice. 'Make yourself at 'ome!'

The girl gets to her feet to look for a dressing gown and finds a piece of cloth that she knots above her breasts.

'Coffee, Zorzette! A real one!'

Jesús is the same as ever, shirt unbuttoned on his hairy chest, five o'clock shadow, gold-filled smile. On his easel is a canvas of depressingly anatomical realism. He intercepts Jean's gaze.

'Yes, it's revolting, I know. But i' sells, i' sells. You 'ave no ide'. I make one a day. So – tell me everything!'

Jean tells his story quickly. Jesús's reaction is decisive. Jean has nothing, so he must live with him. He has a camp bed he can put up in the studio. The Germans buy his nudes by the dozen. The gangster from Place du Tertre who sells them visits three times a day and has doubled his price. Anyhow, Jean's not here for that. They'll talk about it later. Jesús jerks his chin in the direction of Georgette, pouring boiling water into the coffee pot. She is not in on the secret. Jean studies her as she bends forward to fill his cup: she has a tired and listless face with smudges around her eyes. She bleaches her hair carelessly and smells of the same cheap scent as the girls from the Sirène. Jesús taps her on the bottom.

'Go an' get dress'. 'E's finish' for today.'

She goes to change behind a screen.

'What time tomorrow?' she asks.

'Today, tomorr', we celebrate Jean. I le' you know. An' fuck the painting!'

She shrugs and holds out her hand. He puts money in her palm and she vanishes. Jesús tells Jean about his 'war', which has been as simple as can be: he has stayed exactly where he is. The only one left in the building, he went to the Étoile to watch the Germans march past, their band leading the way, in front of General von Briesen. Life has slowly returned to something like normal. Jean, remembering his friend's strange eating habits, asks if he can still find peanuts and red wine. No, there are no more peanuts.

'The peanut supply line 'as been cut!' Jesús says, imitating Paul Reynaud, former president of the Council and much given to vainglorious announcements.

'So?'

'I eat wha' I find! War is war. You 'ave to survive.'

His face takes on a sorrowful expression. There is a question on the tip of his tongue, but he is hesitating. Finally he speaks.

'An' 'ow is Santal de Malemort?'

'I don't know,' Jean says.

'You forgive 'er.'

'I haven't thought about it.'

'You 'ave to forgive.'

'That's rich, coming from you!'

Jesús puts his hands together. He would like to swear but there is no God, so Jean will have to believe him. This is the truth: he, Jesús, never slept with Chantal, although it is true that she came to see him when Jean was working nights and offered to pose for him. Jesús would not have dreamt of touching her. He hadn't known how to say it to Jean, and then afterwards he realised the misunderstanding.

'I don't care,' Jean said. 'And you're a chump not to have screwed her.'

'You is telling me that I'm chump?'

'A very big chump.'

'Okay, I'm chump. She was a girl who like' to show 'er tits ...'

Jesús wants to know everything. Why did she go back to Malemort when Gontran Longuet was offering her the high life, sports cars, hotels, travel? Women were incomprehensible; in fact they were completely mad. An Andalusian philosopher, a man from Jaén, Joaquín Petillo, declared in the eighteenth century that female seed came from another planet. An unknown object, smaller than a whale and bigger than a sardine – but in the shape of a fish – had several thousand years ago deposited an unknown seed on the surface of the earth. Until that moment our fathers (and mothers), all hermaphrodites, had lived happily and immortally together.

'So how did they reproduce?' Jean asks.

'By the masturbación, dear Jean, the masturbación, mother of all the virtues.'

Unfortunately the seeds of this strange planet, so remote it took a hundred years at the speed of light to get from there to here, had mingled with those of the men who had been calmly masturbating as the sun passed its zenith, and so the first women had been born, bringing discord into an idyllic world. From these strange and remote beginnings they had retained a quality of mystery that even the greatest seers had never managed to unravel. They were incomprehensible, completely mad, acting with a total lack of masculine logic, and you ended up asking yourself if they were not somehow ruled by an interplanetary logic evolved by their seed during the long voyage through space, a logic purely and exclusively feminine and incommunicable to any human not possessing ovaries.

'Even a transvestite can' understand it!' Jesús declares, raising his finger. 'Tell me abou' your friend Palfy, who interes' me ...'

Jean tells him that Palfy badly wants to come and live in Paris. Unfortunately his papers are not in order. He is waiting for clearance from the Kommandantur, which is investigating his past. Palfy has no alternative but to wait: the Côte d'Azur is closed to him, London likewise. He needs fresh pastures and a clean slate for his great schemes.

'Madeleine will 'elp 'im!' Jesús says.

'Have you seen her? Is she doing business again?'

'You mus' be barmy! She lives with the colonel who is commanding the cloths!'

Jean is baffled. His understanding was that colonels commanded regiments. But no, this is a German colonel who occupies an office on Rue de la Paix. Buying stocks of available French cloth for the Wehrmacht. Of every type; even organdie, jersey and satin. The German army is an exceptionally chic fighting force, which conceals beneath its aggressive flag a passion for frothy and seductive undergarments. The important thing is that Madeleine has not forgotten Palfy and Jean. Only last week she was voicing her anxiety that they had been taken prisoner. If it were true, she would move heaven and earth to have them released.

'She will fin' you work!'

'I don't know if I've the means to work. Unless someone pays me weekly. I haven't got a sou to my name.'

'Sous, I'm making plenty o' them. We share. This nigh' dinner is on me …'

Jesús, then, is assuming importance in Jean's life, having been in the first part of this story no more than a face glimpsed between two doors. The author is well aware of how irritating it is to see reproduced phonetically the words of an individual afflicted with such a strong accent. We get tired not just of the accent, but even more of the crude, overblown caricature a foreigner speaking our language imperfectly feels obliged to give to the least of his ideas, as though the nuances are likely to be completely missed because their refined and distinguished French equivalents (as we like to think) are lacking. Make no mistake though: like Baron Nucingen jabbering his execrable French, dunked in low German like bread in soup,[6] Jesús, sucking his way through a French as beaten and twisted as a Spanish omelette, is no fool. As a young man he fled the mediocrity of a petty bourgeois Andalusian family, shopkeepers in the torrid city of Jaén, to breathe a different air that, even befouled by occupation, he continues to call the air of freedom – not political freedom, about which he does not give a damn, and will continue not to give a damn to the point that, when France is finally liberated, he is still a member of the Communist Party, but freedom to shock, sexual freedom, of which his own Spain at that time has not the slightest idea. In truth, his great dilemma – about which, out of embarrassment and naivety, he dares not speak to anyone – can be expressed in four words: where is painting going? Impossible to discuss it with other painters, especially those who have made it. The only talk he hears from them is about money, girls and food. With Jean it is different. Jesús can unburden himself without fear of ridicule: Jean is not an artist and will not retaliate with sarcastic remarks that conceal all the jealousy, envy and contempt with which his contemporaries are riddled. To Jean and Jean alone he can confide, without being mocked or scoffed at, his unspeakable misfortune in having to prostitute himself in order to survive and keep his hopes alive. Despite the difference in their ages – Jesús is thirty and Jean now twenty-one – they are children from the same stock: friendship is the only asset they possess. It is quite true that Jesús did not sleep with Chantal de Malemort. He could have, but did not want to. Preserved by his disinterested ambitions, Jesús will never grow up, whereas Jean will become an adult in small steps that will each break his heart a little more. Oh, what price must a youth not pay to become a man one day! Jean, back in a Paris it sickens him to return to, possesses neither love nor friendship enough to keep his courage alive. Fortunately Claude is there, and in her presence nothing is inevitable, everything is simple, and there is no shade of ambiguity from the beginning. I would not like to say more at a time when Jean himself still knows nothing. Let us attempt, in some measure, to act as he does, and feel our way towards this woman whose smile will light up two of the four dark years to come.

*

Jean recoiled from meeting Madeleine. In two days and as many journeys across Paris on foot he had taken in the reality of the occupation: the parades at the Étoile, the signposts, the flags of the Third Reich stamped with the swastika flapping in Rue de Rivoli. Small signs, yet they sufficed to stop him forgetting and to allow him to guess that an iron fist existed, gloved in velvet for now but an unspeakable and indeterminate threat in the sky of the future. The free zone could play its games of smoke and mirrors, parade with its bands blaring and its comic-opera army of a hundred thousand men, unfurl all the modest pomp of a new regime, but the undeniable, naked, crushing truth was here, in Paris.

Next morning Jesús introduced Jean to the director-owner of the gallery who sold his grotesque and obscene nudes at Place du Tertre. This person, who before the war had mocked the Spaniard with merciless sarcasm, nicknaming him 'Papiécasso' for his unsaleable collages, had spotted in the defeat a new and much more interesting clientele than the American and English tourists of the inter-war years. Short, fat, blue-eyed, his neck pinched by a celluloid collar, his cheeks red and his short legs swamped by trousers even more voluminous than his backside, Louis-Edmond de La Garenne claimed to be descended from a crusader who would have covered himself in shame had he seen one of his descendants keeping a shop. Jean was deeply put off by his lack of eyebrows and his jet-black hair (with its unnatural reddish glints) which clashed with a face that was smooth, chubby and apparently completely hairless. Jesús had forgotten to warn him that Louis-Edmond wore a wig, ever since a strange illness that had robbed his body of all hair. Louis-Edmond de La Garenne looked Jean up and down.

'I know my way around men,' he boasted. 'I'm never wrong. The first impression is the only one worth having. Afterwards you get bamboozled into all sorts of feelings and nuances. You'll do. Do you speak German?'

'Not a single word. Only English.'

'Perfect. Our clientele at this time is exclusively German. It demands flattery. Either these imbeciles imagine they speak French or they will address you in the language of our hereditary enemy: English. You're the man I need. You'll start straight away. I'll give you five hundred francs a month. With tips you'll do very nicely for yourself.'

'Louis-Edmond,' Jesús said, 'you take us for stupid bastards who is workin' for nozing. You give Jean two thousan' francs an' a commission on what 'e sell 'imself.'

'Jesús, no one is indispensable.'

'No, is true. No' even you. Especial' you. You understan' me?'

'You're ruining me. I accept only to give you pleasure.'

Jesús treated him to a vigorous thump in return.

'You are intelligen', Louis-Edmond. Very intelligen', you old sweendler.'

Jean discovered that the gallery already possessed a salesperson, a middle-aged woman with a dignified but ravaged face named Blanche de Rocroy, the last of her line, beggared and humiliated at every turn by La Garenne, suffering his criticisms in silence as she had suffered since childhood, the only daughter of decrepit and déclassé aristocrats whose one remaining pride was the name they carried. Her fiancé had been killed at the front in 1918. What chance did she have of finding another when she looked like a battered, abject old owl with no bust? La Garenne had slept with her once during her period of greatest misery and still requested, in a tone that brooked no refusal, minor services from her which she provided in his office after the door had been locked behind her. For the first few days Jean could not get a word out of her. He tried to reassure her that he had not been taken on so that La Garenne could get rid of her, but because only a man could deal with customers interested in canvases of nudes. She half believed him and for a long time continued to look as gloomy as the rural landscapes that she sold with barely disguised apathy. Business boomed. Soldiers on leave in field-grey uniforms crowded outside the gallery windows, shoving each other with their elbows, smothering their guffaws, embarrassment and curiosity pressing them together. Their NCOs walked past, ramrod straight, eyes front, outraged in the name of the Reich at the sight of these bottoms, nipples and pussies, the very symbols of the moral and physical corruption that had led France to its destruction. The officers, on the other hand, strode in, leafed through the gallery's catalogue and asked to see what Louis-Edmond proudly called his 'hell', a collection of pornographic prints, licentious drawings and Jesús's most daring canvases. It was understandable that Blanche de Rocroy should feel uncomfortable displaying such horrors to male customers who were in the habit of screwing monocles into their eyes so as not to miss the smallest detail. Jean's days were therefore mostly spent in 'hell', with Louis-Edmond only appearing when a customer started haggling too much. Moving from honeyed charm to outright disdain, and from disdain to perfectly pitched indifference, he would close the sale with his ineffably glib tongue. The examples of extreme erotica sold fast. Jesús began to be unable to satisfy the demand, and La Garenne started to look for new artists. He found a few, but their work did not sell: talentless and sleazy, they failed to meet La Garenne's customers' exacting requirements. From Jean Jesús learnt what was happening and slammed the door on his dealer. Jean laughed. Louis-Edmond, frantic at the idea of running out of merchandise, sent him back as his ambassador, bearing a very large cheque.

'Tell 'im to come 'ere hisself,' Jesús answered. 'I wan' to see this shit climb my stairs on 'is 'ands an' knees.'

The dealer came, and climbed. Jesús let him off the hands and knees, though La Garenne was ready to submit. Puce-faced, perspiring, so breathless he could not speak, he listened without protesting as he was called every name under the sun, his head bent, twisting his plump hands with their filthy nails. When Jesús ran out of insults La Garenne sobbed, 'I am a wretch.'

'A wretch stuff' with cash!'

'I'm not talking about that. I'm talking about my name, which I've allowed to be dragged through the mud. Me! The descendant of a crusader!'

'An' fuck your crusades!'

But La Garenne had got his breath back, and with it his snooping instinct, and was glancing around the studio. Ignoring the daubs he usually bought, he went up to an easel on which stood one of Jesús's new canvases, a black and luminous landscape, a violent confrontation between a lava-covered land and the sea, under a blazing sky.

'This is brilliant!' he said. 'I'll buy it.'

'Eh?' Jesús said, dumbstruck.

La Garenne took out his cheque book.

'How much? You tell me.'

'I don' feed the jam to the pig.'

'Jesús, I'm not asking for compensation for your insults. Where genius is concerned, everything is allowed. How much?'

'No.'

La Garenne signed his cheque, dated it, left the amount blank and handed it to Jesús.

'You put down whatever you like.'

'Go fuck yourself!'

As we may imagine, La Garenne walked away with the picture, leaving behind a cheque for twenty thousand francs and the promise that Jesús would deliver within the next week a series of six etchings for 'hell'.

'Edition of fifty, not one more!' the dealer promised, his arm extended as if for a fascist salute.

Jean had reason to believe that, with the help of subtle manipulation, the fifty would turn into two hundred, plus several dozen artist's proofs. La Garenne fiddled the documentary evidence and had already for a long time been forging the pseudonymous signature Jesús used for his bread-and-butter work. To buy Jesús's landscape as he had, almost with his eyes closed and with an impressively faked passion and a cheque to match, had been a stroke of genius. Jesús wavered. For a time he even stopped heaping insults on Louis-Edmond, making an effort, without great conviction, to acknowledge a flair beneath his crudity, a sort of instinct for painting that only the treacherous circumstances and frightful materialism of the French prevented from showing itself. Jean refrained from pouring cold water on his friend's enthusiasm and opening his eyes to the Machiavellianism of La Garenne who, almost as soon as they were back at the gallery, had handed Jesús's canvas to Blanche, curling his lip contemptuously.

'Put that in the toilet or the cellar. Yes, in the cellar. If I had that in front of me I couldn't deal with two shits at once.'

Perhaps the important thing was that Jesús had found a buyer for a painting that he had begun to think was unsaleable.

What about Claude? I hear you say. We have not forgotten her. She explains everything. Without her Jean would not stay a single day longer in this new Paris, slowly beginning to fill with people again and to face the autumn with a kind of fearful, courageous expectancy. He puts up with the ignominy of working for La Garenne, with Blanche's relentless gloom, with the disheartening experience of spending his days in the gallery's hell, because when he finishes work Claude's smile and the cool welcome of her cheek is waiting for him on the fourth floor of Quai Saint-Michel.

Cyrille would open the door: a pale little boy with curly blond hair and blue eyes sparkling with pleasure.

'Maman, it's Jean!' he would shout.

'Who else did you think it would be?' she would answer from the next room.

She would appear, her face half turned to his, offering her cheek and the beginning of her smile. Cyrille would go back to his toys, and when the weather was fine they would lean on the balcony and look out over the city slowly disappearing in the twilight, the Seine velvet and immobile, its banks empty but for pedestrians hastening home.

The first evening Claude said, 'It's terrible!'

'What's terrible?'

'Everything. Not knowing anything about the people you love, or even the people you don't love. Not being sure of anything. What will happen to us? We're using up the best years of our lives wanting to know, wanting to have an answer.'

'I close my eyes. You should do the same.'

'You don't have anyone else.'

'I'm the same as you. I have you.'

'You don't have me. You have to remember that.'

'Well, I think I have you, whether you like it or not, and deep down it doesn't matter if you do or you don't.'

Yes, let us dispel the ambiguity. Nothing has happened between them since their meeting at Clermont-Ferrand, and it is Claude's wish that nothing should happen. To all appearances that is not how things are: they are together, they see each other every day. When the gallery closes, Jean walks down from Montmartre to Saint-Michel. He likes crossing Paris like this, among crowds of Frenchmen and -women hurrying about their business, paying no attention to the signs in Gothic script that they encounter en route. The occupiers are still tourists. There were others like them before the war, and no one is surprised that this new wave of curious visitors responds to the same siren songs as their predecessors, making straight for the Opéra or the Folies-Bergère. Jean loves Paris for other reasons; for him the city is intimate and full of secret places. Turning a corner, catching sight of a theatre or a cinema, revives memories that no longer cause him pain. Claude is there, and she drives out Chantal de Malemort. As he crosses Pont Saint-Michel he looks up to see Claude's windows and is flooded with happiness. Cyrille has his tea and goes to sleep in his mother's bed. Claude has laid a table for two. They sit and talk. From time to time Claude looks down and the divine smile that Jean adores leaves her face. Then quickly, in a few words, he takes back what he has just said and what has upset her. Since the day he put his hand on her knee in the train that brought them to Paris, she has never had to be wary of him. Little by little she has learnt who he is and where he comes from, and is surprised that he has no desire to go and see what is happening at Grangeville.

'Aren't you worried about your father?'

'He's not my father. I love him, but I don't feel I have anything in common with him any more.'

'What about Antoinette?'

'I'd like to see her again. There's no urgency.'

'And Chantal de Malemort?'

'We have nothing to say to each other.'

He would love Claude to talk, as he does, about the people close to her, about her family whom she sees, he knows, during the day; but she seems to prefer to be without attachments where he is concerned. A single woman with a small boy, the two of them perched on a Paris balcony. Not a word about the husband. There is a photo of him in the bedroom, on the bedside table on Cyrille's side of the bed. Jean hates this bed. He finds it hard to look at it when he goes to kiss the little boy on his damp forehead before he leaves. One night they go on talking for so long that when they stop it is after curfew. Jean sleeps on a couch in the sitting room; he has to curl up like a dog under an eiderdown. The night seems endless to him. Is Claude asleep? He swears that she is. A single police car speeds past along the embankment, then there is no other noise until the dripping, cold dawn reveals a lugubriously grey Paris.

Claude makes coffee and toast. Cyrille is in a bad mood. Jean cheers him up and the boy does not want him to go. After that night there are others, and now Jean sleeps practically every other night at Quai Saint-Michel. Sleeps properly. Lightly, in case Claude were to get up in the adjoining room and come to him. But, as we have guessed, she does not come. Occasionally he wonders what progress he has made since the day he first sat awkwardly opposite her. In all honesty he is obliged to say: none. The curious thing is that it does not make him feel bad, and little by little he has settled for this friendly and affectionate distance that she has assigned to him, like the trinkets – a silver snuff box, an ivory sweet tray, a tortoiseshell dance card, a crystal perfume bottle – laid out on a small side table that she often strokes with her finger as she walks past, familiar mementoes of life in Russia that her mother has saved. Jean is there, just like them, though he is not from Russia.

In fact he would feel perfectly comfortable where she has put him, if he did not, at certain moments, desire her with a painful intensity. During the day she knows how to keep his desire at bay, but at night, asleep behind her bedroom door, she loses her advantage and Jean has a trio of images that help remind him of her reality: the silhouette of her body placed between him and the sun, beneath the transparent material of her dress; her knee on the train (which will stay with him for the rest of his life); and, one morning when she bent over to butter Cyrille's bread, her dressing gown falling open and revealing a bare breast. Not both, just one; although with a modicum of imagination one could picture the other as very similar. She did not notice and Jean averted his gaze to avoid embarrassing her, but at night, as soon as he closes his eyelids, he sees again the curve and delicacy of this breast that looks like a young girl's. It is maddening and unbearable. The funniest part of it is that his days are spent sorting, exhibiting, putting away, and selling Louis-Edmond de La Garenne's 'hell', an unbelievable pornographic *vomitus*, an ocean of the most extreme erotica, of which Jesús is the chief supplier. In all honesty, Jean fails to understand how anyone can feel the slightest emotion at the sight of an obscene engraving, and he would need very little persuasion to consider all the customers who throng the gallery in Place du Tertre as suffering from some form of mental illness. And so, step by step, he is discovering what is particular to his own notion of physical love: almost total indifference when he is not in love, and contrarily, hypersensitivity when he is. He would not need much persuasion either to believe that all lovers of erotica must be impotent. Who among his customers would feel their heartbeat race when they looked at Claude because she had innocently worn a sleeveless dress or because, as she sat down, she had revealed her knee?

Jesús, when Jean attempts to explain these nuances, opens his eyes wide. In Spain only virginity can trigger an erotic frenzy. A married woman, the mother of a child, is totally uninteresting. Several times the discussions that follow last till dawn. The next day Jean is reeling. He accuses himself of naivety and clumsiness. Any man with any experience would already have obtained from Claude what he so passionately desires; and later, as he crosses Paris to see her again, he spends the journey making cynical resolutions he is determined to keep and every time fails to keep. As soon as she is there in front of him, he is disarmed. First there is Cyrille, who every day shows him more and more affection, then there is Claude herself, talking to him as if she has guessed his resolve and is herself determined to head it off.

'Jean, I think you and I are going to make something wonderful, something completely unique in the world that no biologist could even think of. Born to different fathers and mothers, we are going to have the same blood.'

'What do you mean?'

'That you are my younger brother.'

'Haven't you ever heard of incest?'

'Yes. And haven't you ever heard of the curse that strikes down those who engage in incest?'

He tells her she is being overdramatic. She smiles and they talk of other things, of Jesús whom she wants to meet, and of Palfy, about whom there is still no news. Jean wonders if his friend has moved into the Sirène with all its comforts, continuing to dupe Madame Michette mercilessly. It is so unlike him to put up with the same fate as everyone else! No one who knows him can imagine him waiting for a visa along with three hundred thousand hopefuls waiting to cross the demarcation line and get to Paris. He has failed to reply to the inter-zone postcard Jean sent at the beginning of September. It probably sounded baffling to him anyway, with its series of permitted formulas, almost all to do with food or family.

The truth is that no one knows what is happening on the other side of the militarised border. When Parisian newspapers are not lampooning the Vichy government, they are dismissing it as a den of traitors coolly plotting vengeance. In Paris people live in a closed and isolated world. Beyond the palisade people might be mobilising or they might not: if the German communiqués are to be believed, in London, Coventry and elsewhere everyone has gone to ground.

The army of occupation continues to conduct its war without a scratch, a superb fighting mechanism whose resources were criminally concealed from the French. It has fuel, leather, endless supplies of machinery, perfect discipline, and all it can eat. The exotic London Jean once knew is impossible to imagine now, under a storm of steel: the majesty of Eaton Square that he loved, the doll's houses of Chelsea, the elderly ladies in Hyde Park, the boats that steamed up the Thames to moor at Hampton Court among the oarsmen. It seems so distant now! The French are winding themselves into a cocoon, like a small child, while the Heinkel 111 bombers drone through the night towards

Britain. They remain in a state of shock. The most pressing question is that of subsistence, a difficult problem for which the country is unprepared. At least love can make everything else go away. Jean does not stint himself. In the evening when he arrives at Saint-Michel there is always a package under his arm, something to make the dinner go better, whatever he has managed to extort from the grocer in Rue Lepic. Blanche de Rocroy's cousin, who lives in the Seine-et-Marne region, sends her parcels of butter, lard and even game that she shares with Jean, who passes it on to Claude and Cyrille. The lift in their building is sealed off and he has to walk past the lodge of the concierge, a ghastly woman who wears her spitefulness on her face. Whenever she opens her door a crack, a smell of stew and decomposition fills the lobby. Jean is unaware that she has bought herself an exercise book in which she notes down the comings and goings of the tenants and their visitors. For the moment she does it because she enjoys it, with the thought at the back of her mind that one day it might be useful. Who to? The German police, or the French? She doesn't know, but she tells herself she is a patriot and that if there had been more like her France would not be in the state it's in now. Jean hurries up four floors. Claude's cheek is waiting on the other side of the door.

'You're late!' she says.

To excuse himself, he opens his package, which contains a hare. They skin it together on the kitchen table, an operation Jean has seen his father carry out a hundred times with an Opinel painstakingly sharpened beforehand. Alas, their own knife is far from razor-sharp and the skinning is a laborious business. The blood dries on their hands and Claude begins to feel sick. They will be cooking all evening, using up their last onions, a scrap of flour, four potatoes, some herbs and a glass of red wine. Cyrille proclaims that he does not like eating dead hare. He wants a live one. Because they have eaten late, Jean is to sleep on the couch in the small sitting room. Claude is on the other side of the wall. He strains to hear her breathing. Nothing. Not a sound. Neither the other tenants on this floor nor those on the floor above have returned to Paris. The ghastly concierge maintains they are all Jews; she has proof they are, in the form of the miserable New Year tips they used to give her before the war. In fact the only Jew is an upstairs tenant called Léon Samuel-Roth, a professor at the Sorbonne who for ten years has been writing an essay (eight hundred pages of his final draft are complete) on the Marxist aspects of the thought of Jean Racine as developed in his two Jewish plays, *Esther* and *Athalie*. At this moment Professor Samuel-Roth is hidden away in the Auvergne, missing his books terribly. Having succeeded in avoiding the increasingly widespread arrests, within four years he will nevertheless finish his essay (another four hundred pages), bring the manuscript back to Paris in October 1944, a few months after the Liberation, and leave it on a bus, a loss he will get over surprisingly easily, frequently telling his students that it was actually a fairly superficial piece of work, an academic's distraction, and that at the age of fifty he felt the time had come instead to write a novel, whose action would be located in the same Auvergne where he lived for four years without seeing a thing, buried in his writing and with his nose, bristling with grey hairs, constantly to the grindstone. The other absent tenants on Claude's floor are an elderly Alsatian couple, the Schmoegles, the husband a former officer in the Coloniale[7] and since his retirement a technical adviser to a company manufacturing lead soldiers. No one knows what became of them when Paris fell and we shall hear no more of them; perhaps they died in the general exodus, hastily buried without anyone taking note of who they were. The fact that their apartment is empty will soon be passed on by the concierge to the German police, who will requisition it for one of their informers, who in turn will be denounced by the same concierge at the Liberation, be arrested and have his throat cut in a cellar, to be succeeded by an FFI colonel[8] who will finally take his ease among the late Schmoegles' belongings.

In the silence insomnia gnaws at Jean. He knows it will make his frustration worse, but he cannot stop himself from fantasising. He has to clench his teeth, get up and go out on the balcony, where the sudden numbing autumn cold freezes his temples. Quai and Pont Saint-Michel, Quai du Marché Neuf and the forecourt of Notre-Dame are deserted. Jean remembers a film by René Clair, *Paris Asleep*, that Joseph Outen had showed at his film club in Dieppe in the heyday of his cinema period. Alas, it is not the charmingly cocky Albert Préjean, his cap tilted over his ear, who is making the most of the sleeping city, but a German motorcyclist, fatly girdled in black leather and preceded by a brush stroke of yellow light, whose machine rips into the silence as it dashes past. What message can be urgent enough for the rider to wake up thousands of sleeping Parisians along the road to his destination? And talking of films, where has poor Joseph Outen got to? Has he been killed, taken prisoner, wounded? Did he make it back to Normandy, to a new hobbyhorse and another pipe dream? Freezing, Jean closes the window, moves across to the communicating door, and hears the parquet floor creak in Claude and Cyrille's bedroom. The door opens, and in the doorway a figure is vaguely outlined against a black background. Claude closes the door behind her.

'You're not asleep,' she murmurs in a reproachful voice.

'Nor are you.'

He stretches his hand out towards what he guesses to be her bare arm, grasps it, and presses his thumb against the vein beating in the crook of her elbow. Her skin is warm and smooth. Claude, usually sensitive to all physical contact, does not pull her arm away.

'That motorcyclist woke us both,' she says.

'I wasn't asleep, I was on the balcony.'

'In this weather?'

'In this weather.'

He goes on stroking the crook of her elbow and the skin whose taste he so longs to know.

'Why aren't you afraid?'

'Of you? Never.'

'I'm an idiot.'

'Don't say that! I can't bear it. And I wouldn't love an idiot anyway.'

It is the first time she has said it. An icy shiver runs down his spine that he finds it hard to make sense of.

'You said you love me.'

'Of course. Could you have doubted it? Would I be here if I didn't love you?'

'So?'

'So we wait ... Go to sleep. Cyrille will wake up.'

At daybreak he leaves for Rue Lepic, to wash and shave. The elation he feels makes the human beings pressing into the entrances to the Métro look sadder and greyer than usual. He notices how much thinner they are already. The well-fed crowds of 1939 have given way to men and women whose clothes flap around them. Poor diet makes them more sensitive to the cold. Jean usually walks back, varying his route. It's his only way of maintaining his physical fitness, under threat from the sedentary existence he leads. He longs to have his bicycle with him but it is out in the country, in Normandy, assuming no one stole it during the exodus. He decides to write to Antoinette.

Jesús is already up. Winter and summer, he rises at five, lights his stove with wood from a friendly joiner in Rue de l'Abreuvoir, boils the water for his coffee or something with the colour of coffee if not the taste.

'I wouldn' min' meetin' this girl!' he says.

'She isn't a girl!'

'So she's what?'

'A ... woman ... Thanks very much ... So you can suggest she poses naked for you straight away, I suppose.'

They laugh at this. Before going to his easel Jesús does ten minutes of weight training in his underwear. In the mornings he works for himself, but no collages now, no borrowed technique. He had plenty of excuses; anyone coming from Jaén has a good excuse. Everything's fascinating and new when you haven't seen anything yet, but two or three visits to museums quickly reveal Surrealism showing its age, and now Jesús has decided not to listen to or admire anyone but himself. The result is landscapes. And for him these mean a return to Andalusia every time: scorched earth, melancholy vegetation, an oily sea, skies crushed by light. As he remembers the landscapes of his childhood, he feels such thirst for austerity and absolutism that he simplifies his colours to their extreme. From a short way away the spectator could be looking at abstract canvases and must examine them close up to grasp the pictures' tormented life.

'You understand, my friend. I am 'appy, 'appy ... I do wha' I wan'. And I tell you, fuck La Garenne ... Fuck 'im, fuck 'im ...'

In truth, Jesús is a long way from being able to send La Garenne packing, and at ten o'clock when his model arrives he bundles his canvas into a wardrobe and whips out a sketchbook. Jean leaves for the gallery. Blanche has the keys and is already there as he arrives. Through the window the sight of her scrawny figure fills him with pity, even though, despite the endless stream of insults and obscene remarks La Garenne subjects her to, she has somehow always managed to cling to something like dignity. She has a distinguished voice, which verges on affectedness in her pronunciation of certain words, as though she intended to remind whoever might get the wrong impression from her physical appearance that she remains a Rocroy. She has only just turned forty, yet it is impossible to guess how old she is. Bad luck ages people: they go grey, bags appear under their eyes, their shoulders droop, their legs become so thin they look like broomsticks. Handling

Jesús's series of drawings for La Garenne's specialist clientele, she smiles unembarrassedly, observing how 'saucy' they are, which is the very least that might be said of them.

In front of the building in Rue Lepic a German car was parked. Sitting on the bonnet, a blond soldier with soft features and cap at a rakish angle lit a cigarette and smiled at a girl who hurried on her way. Jean went up. Madeleine was sitting in the studio's only armchair. Her elegance jarred with its tattered upholstery and missing foot, replaced by three books. She looked like Lady Bountiful, come to console a poor artist. Behind her back Jesús made a frustrated gesture of apology for Jean's benefit. Since coming to Paris Jean had avoided Madeleine, who had called at Rue Lepic several times to try and find him. He hardly recognised her. She had taken full advantage of Palfy's lessons and now knew how to sit in an armchair and smoke a cigarette with poise. There was no longer any trace of what had once been so garish about her: the handbag that was too big, the over-thick make-up, the jarringly jaded tone. She kissed Jean and he noticed she was wearing good perfume. There was an air about her, an attitude that suggested a deeper transformation. Perhaps it was the result of security, of a feeling that she had a strong, powerful man to rely on, who asked her only to be the woman she wanted to be. In a few sentences of conversation it became clear that, after years of unhappiness in a milieu in which she had felt fear more than any other emotion, she was suddenly blossoming at an age when Blanche de Rocroy was withering. She must have kept up her elocution lessons: her diction was smoother and her level voice had lost its vulgar cadences. Jean had been fond of her for her naturalness and generosity. The naturalness had gone but her generosity remained, and now with evident resources at her disposal she had not forgotten her friends.

'I was beginning to think you were avoiding me,' she said.

He lied, assuring her she was wrong. She wanted news of Palfy. He briefly told her the story of their war, not omitting their encounter in the village square with Obersturmführer Karl Schmidt.

'Ah, the SS!' she said knowingly. 'That doesn't surprise me. Julius hates them …'

'Who is Julius?'

'Oh, you'll meet him. You'll like him instantly. He's a big manufacturer from Dortmund. The Kommandantur has put him in charge of getting the French textile industry going again.'

'We could do with that,' Jean said, having managed with great difficulty to buy himself a suit.

'Don't be silly. If there's anything you need, all you have to do is tell me. In any case tonight you must come for dinner – we're going to Maxim's.'

'Dressed like this? They'll turn me away at the door.'

'With Julius? You must be joking. But if you feel uncomfortable, we can go to a bistro at Les Halles.'

'Listen, Madeleine, I'm going to say no, for a simple reason that Jesús is already aware of. Very simple and stupid: there's a woman in my life—'

'Well then, bring her, you goose!'

'She can't go out. She has a little boy and there's no one to look after him in the evening.'

'You are disappointing. Isn't he, Jesús?'

Jesús raised his arms to the sky.

''E's in love, Mad'leine, 'e's in love!'

'What about you? You could do with getting a move on in that direction.'

'Never! I love the art. Is the only zing!'

This made Madeleine laugh. She wrote her address and telephone number on a piece of paper.

'Whenever you feel like seeing me, ring me. And now give me Palfy's address. I'm going to get him an *Ausweis*.'

'A what?'

'An *Ausweis*, my little bunny … A travel permit. Do try to keep up a bit. Come down off your cloud. You're still a good-looking boy. I'm very fond of you, you know.'

Jean wrote down the Michettes' name, but suddenly could not remember either the name of the street, or the number.

'It's at the Sirène, Clermont-Ferrand.'

'The Sirène? A hotel?'

'No. A bordello.'

'Are you saying that he lives in a bordello?'

'The *patronne* is a fascinating woman.'

Madeleine looked baffled. She found it difficult to imagine 'Baron' Palfy in love with the *patronne* of a bordello. It was undeniable that in the new world born from defeat, old values had been turned upside down. She, for now, was at the top of the ladder. She supposed that since places were limited, it was natural that some were obliged to take a step or two down.

Jean and Jesús stood at the window, watching Madeleine leave. The soldier opened the car door for her and, standing behind her, made an obscene gesture in the direction of her backside before she turned to sit down.

'Respect is dead,' Jean said.

'You can say that again! And there are even some pricks who says no to dinner at Maxim's.'

'With Julius? You must be joking. I know exactly what that would be like.'

'Madeleine ez an angel.'

'Steady on. Let's say she's all right.'

Thoughtfully Jean watched the car turn round and drive down towards Clichy. He thought how far Madeleine had come. Two years earlier she had been living in that same building and hanging out on the stairs in her dressing gown, with tired skin and breath soured by alcohol. She had led a wretched life until she met Palfy, who had offered her a lifeline before the ship went down. What would have become of her if she hadn't met him? A new woman had been born out of those chance events. She still had much to learn, of course, and even if her destiny looked rosy she still ran the risk of committing some serious faux pas that would not escape a trained ear. What more reliable audience could she have chosen for her performance than an industrialist from Dortmund? Madeleine's reappearance and her ascent in society, despite Jean's efforts to ignore her, were a sign. At the age of twenty-one it is no easy matter to leave the past behind.

He wrote to Antoinette. She answered him in a long letter which we shall quote in full.

> *Jean darling, what a relief to have your letter. We have all been thinking of you. I ran up- and downstairs, shouting everywhere, 'Jean's alive, Jean's in Paris!' The only person to greet the news with no emotion was your father – well, I mean Albert, because I don't know how you think of him any more in your heart. The fact that he isn't your father isn't really important in the end, is it? Our parents are the ones who bring us up. To tell you how he is, first of all: still working with the same fortitude and self-sacrifice, despite the arthritis in his hip that hurts him dreadfully. The abbé Le Couec says simply that he's a saint. A cranky saint because we made him plant cabbages, potatoes and carrots in his borders. Yes, it's not very pretty, but we have to make do as we can and we suddenly have a lot of new 'friends' who happen to drop in on Sundays, always around lunchtime, from Dieppe and Rouen. Maman bought some hens and rabbits and Michel came down from Olympus for long enough to build us a henhouse and some hutches out of wood and chicken wire. Oh yes – Michel's back. He came back at the end of June, dressed as a farmhand … You know what he's like: he took one look at our expressions and insisted that he was a gardener, not a farmhand, and quoted St John's Gospel: 'And*

they did not know he was Jesus … thinking he was a gardener.' We're no less complicated than before, as you can see. We had some difficulty getting him proper papers. The gendarmes at Grangeville claimed he needed to get himself demobilised at the Kommandantur. In other words, our poor darling looked very much as if he might end up in a stalag. Finally Maman's brother, Uncle René, who's something important in Paris in some new political movement, got involved. Now Michel has papers and even a permit to go to Paris when he needs to. I wouldn't be surprised if he didn't drop in on you one day soon. He was very interested in your work in the gallery and would like to know if you only sell well-known painters.

Maman is the same as ever. So active she exhausts us all. She cycles down to Dieppe in the afternoon to volunteer as an auxiliary for the Secours National:[9] blankets, powdered milk and medicines for those in need. She's in her element and her only complaint is that there aren't enough who need her services.

The abbé Le Couec suffered terrible depression after the defeat. We were worried he would have a complete breakdown, right up until two mysterious friends of his came to visit him. I met them one day and they told me a quite fantastic story, that you would have been shot by the Germans if they hadn't intervened. You can imagine my panic! The abbé assured me that the Blessed Virgin was protecting you, and perhaps there's some truth in what he said because no one could possibly believe that it was chance that put the abbé's two friends in exactly the same place as you at exactly the moment when the Germans were about to shoot you.

The Marquis de Malemort was taken prisoner and is in an oflag somewhere in Silesia. After two terribly worrying months, his family finally got a letter. They're sending him weekly parcels. He dreams of saucisson, cider and turkey, apparently. It's all he can think about. Do you want to hear about Chantal *or not? If you don't, cut off this part of my letter and throw it away now.*

Chantal has taken over from her father. She found a couple of Percherons from somewhere to replace the tractor and she drives the plough now as if she's been doing it all her life. You'd never have suspected the energy that lurks inside that frail-looking creature. Living the way she does, in the open air, has given her a ... Norman complexion, to put it politely. No more beautifully manicured hands, no more life's little luxuries. She's out in her overalls all day long. Gontran Longuet went to see her in a car he'd had fitted with a wood-gas generator. She set the dogs on him. Oh yes, apropos the Longuets: they came back in July. They've two German officers living with them, 'visiting' the region, taking photos and writing things down. Apparently one of them was asked, 'Are you here to stop the British from landing?' and he burst out laughing rather rudely and said, 'It's more the other way round.'

End of paragraph about Chantal and the Longuets. I've still got lots of news to tell you, but if I write too much you won't read my letter. Let me know if there's any way of getting word to my father. He's never mentioned here. I'm the only one who misses him. Terribly. Don't laugh. Your affectionate aunt,

Antoinette

His affectionate aunt? Yes, it was true, even though they were so close in age, she twenty-four and he twenty-one, a difference of no significance now, but one that had been so great in his childhood that he had repeatedly been tripped up by it. Had it really been his 'affectionate aunt' who had celebrated her nephew's thirteenth birthday by taking him down a gully to the bottom of the cliffs at Grangeville to show him her bottom, two delicious globes that dimpled where they met the small of her back? Had it been his affectionate aunt who had led him into the hay barn for altogether more serious games? To a bare mattress in the new house her mother was having built? And to a night of melancholy goodbyes in a hotel at Dieppe before he left for England? When he had found out he was Geneviève's son, it had opened up a gulf between Antoinette and him. But perhaps it was better that way. It was to her he owed his transition to manhood, still more because of her that he had felt jealousy for the first time and suffered his first and greatest disillusionment, although these negative experiences had in the long run been of little use to him, nature in her generosity having endowed him with the ability to forget and to hope. So that the part of her letter that talked of Chantal de Malemort, though it still made his heart ache, no longer deeply affected him. Claude had wiped out all his bad memories. Thanks to her, the world was now a spectacle he could observe with a detached, almost untroubled gaze, a vantage point that let him take things as they were, without disapproval or indignation.

Which was useful, for he needed a healthy dose of indifference to deal with Louis-Edmond de La Garenne's salacious mischief-making. We have not much discussed this character, except to describe his physical appearance, unflatteringly some will think. It is, admittedly, not kind to point the finger at a man in a wig who imagines he's the cat's whiskers, nor to make fun of excessively wide trousers or pointedly hold your nose when a person with bad breath speaks to you. Nature is cruel enough without us adding caricature to the blemishes with which she already makes so free. And since two wrongs don't make a right, it ill becomes us to invoke Louis-Edmond's lack of scruples and then display the same fault when speaking of him. But how are we supposed to stifle our laughter when we're faced with his schemes, and our brickbats when they fail, and how can we feel pity for a wretch so bent on humiliating Blanche de Rocroy? Jean was dismayed and moved by Blanche. She would for ever be downtrodden and ridiculed, or treated with sadistic delight as a pariah by her employer. If he were to sack her, she would starve; at least that was what he let her think. But Jesús – who also felt sorry for her – reassured Jean. He was convinced she liked to be whipped, and that if Louis-Edmond abandoned her she would simply go looking for another tyrant capable of humiliating her to the point of complete degradation.

However, an unexpected meeting that took place in October 1940 was to alter Louis-Edmond's attitude.

Shivering in a Spanish shawl her grandmother had brought back with her from a pilgrimage to Compostela in 1865, Blanche watched gloomily through the gallery window as the procession of uniformed tourists wended their way around Place du Tertre. These young Teutons did not feel the nip of autumn, with their pink cheeks and blue eyes, their polished boots and black leather belts with buckles stamped *Gott mit uns*. They lingered in front of the open-air exhibitions, buying their miniature Eiffel Towers and Sacré-Cœurs and postcards of Le Lapin Agile, admiringly contemplating the painters seated on their stools, bearded, their berets tilted down over one ear, pulling on their black pipes and begging tobacco from their audience of *nouveaux riches*, those soldiers who should have been taken captive with a pot of French jam or a quarter-kilo of butter but who now represented prosperity, strength, the new order.

It was just after lunchtime. Business was slack. Jean was cataloguing his drawings in hell. Louis-Edmond was shut in his office, supposedly working, but in reality asleep with his feet on his desk, trousers and waistcoat unbuttoned, revealing a triangle of rumpled, dirty shirt and a waistband of grey cotton underpants. Blanche stood up as a German officer came into the gallery. She had learnt to recognise the ranks: this one was a colonel. He nodded to her, put his cap under his arm and glanced around at the canvases hanging from the picture rail, a smile of distaste curling his lips. Blanche was about to summon Jean when the officer asked in almost unaccented French, 'You haven't anything of interest apart from these horrors, have you? I'm looking for a Utrillo.'

The rule laid down by La Garenne was to make it clear that the gallery possessed many valuable reserves, far from the public's vulgar gaze.

'I'm sure we have. I'll have to ask Monsieur de La Garenne. He's an unusual proprietor and a very bad dealer. When he finds a picture he likes, he refuses to sell it. He'd like to keep everything for himself. But he can be persuaded ... if you're a genuine lover of art.'

The German smiled.

'In that case I'll leave you my name. You can call me in the mornings at the Hôtel Continental.'

Removing his black leather glove, he wrote in the visitors' book 'Rudolf von Rocroy'.

'Von Rocroy!' Blanche exclaimed, her heart beating fast. 'My name's Rocroy too, Blanche de Rocroy. I was always hearing my father talking about the German branch of our family ...'

'Yes, we do come from France originally; we emigrated to Germany after the revocation of the Edict of Nantes. My father used to keep in touch with a cousin of his: Adhémar de Rocroy—'

'That was my father.'

'So we're cousins too.'

Blanche clasped her hands together. Fortune was smiling on her at last, in the shape of this cousin with clean-cut features, piercing blue eyes and manners she had straightaway identified as perfect. The last of the French Rocroys, the pitiful straggler of a once great line, had rediscovered her pride in the family name. All was not lost. The younger branch had kept the flame firmly alight, and its representative was both a dashing officer and a victor.

'Do you have children? I do hope so!' she innocently exclaimed.

'Four. Two little Rocroy boys to be on the safe side, and two girls.'

Praise be! The Rocroy line was indeed assured.

'In that case, come and see me tomorrow at the Continental instead. We'll lunch together and you can tell me what interesting things you have in your secret reserves … I've already forgotten your owner's name.'

'Louis-Edmond de La Garenne. He doesn't awfully look like it, but he's descended from a crusader.'

Rudolf von Rocroy raised an eyebrow in silent approval. He kissed his cousin, as cousins do in well-born families, and the following day over lunch he even addressed her as *tu* and Blanche, who had only addressed three people as *tu* in her entire life, was clearly required to respond in kind. She had brought von Rocroy good news: La Garenne owned a number of paintings of the sort that interested him – Utrillos, Derains, Braques and Picassos – although it would take a little time to have them brought to Paris from the country where they had been stored since the outbreak of war.

'We are very interested,' he said, so archly discreet that his interest was glaringly obvious. Even Blanche felt that his royal 'we' was a bit too much, and it took her until lunch was over to realise that her cousin was in fact acting on behalf of a German organisation that wished to add to the collections of contemporary painters in a number of German museums. The new Germany, he told her, needed French art just as the new France needed German order. The two countries were bound in a common hope, the birth of a united Europe, which in future would be the only conceivable way to bring peace to the world.

By now Blanche was no longer listening. She was thinking of La Garenne, who, after what she had told him about Rudolf von Rocroy, had scented a big client and big business. But who would ever have imagined that that diabolical man possessed such unexpected treasures? That he had modern masters hidden away that he had never mentioned before? In her blindness Blanche decided it must be because of his genius for discovery, and she rejoiced to think that he would now have a chance to sell at inevitably astronomical prices canvases he had shrewdly bought for peanuts when their artists were unknown names. She made her way back to the gallery, her cheeks flushed after an over-rich lunch that had finished with champagne. La Garenne was waiting impatiently.

'Well?' he asked. 'Is he serious, your Roc-of-my-arse-roy?'

'Perfectly.'

'Did you pin him down?'

'I did not pin him down. He is a Rocroy and his motto is the same as ours: "My word and my God".'

'What blasted use is your motto to me? "My word!" Only one? Like the poor! And "my God"! When the ancients had thirty-six ...'

'Your ancestor would not be at all pleased to hear you talk like that, Louis-Edmond!'

'Well, that twit ... instead of copping a dose of the clap in Jerusalem he'd have done a lot better for himself, and made a lot more money, if he'd stayed at court. Then I wouldn't be here selling filth to perverts and ruining myself dragging artists out of the gutter and having them repay me with their contempt and ingratitude. When does your Rudolf want his paintings?'

'As soon as you've brought them to Paris.'

Louis-Edmond beat the air with his arms, like a wounded duck.

'Oh I see! I'm at his beck and call, am I? Art on a plate for the Fritzes! They open their mouths, they require, they decide. Monsieur the colonel would like his Utrillo with his breakfast. Thinks we're at his feet, does he! Well, he can forget it! He can wait, like everyone else. Join the queue, Messieurs Boches ...'

'In that case, perhaps he'll go somewhere else!' Blanche said, more mischievously than she would have believed herself capable of.

'Oh, no! No! No, he'll be robbed blind if he does. Explain that to him. It's your job from now on. Go out with him, show him round, talk to him about your family, and make him wait, patiently. He'll get his blasted pictures.'

*

Jean observed this scene without saying a word. He knew where La Garenne would find his Utrillos and Picassos. It would depend on Jesús's skill and whether he was in a good mood, but Blanche was not to know that. With a gesture that he considered dashing, La Garenne swept up his battered broad-brimmed felt hat with its grubby ribbon and clamped it on his head, apparently heedless of his wig, though in reality he knew it was in no danger, thanks to a new gum. In his black cape he resembled an elderly portrait photographer, despite lacking any of the courtesy of such a person and gesticulating madly with his arms as if, like some horrible plucked bird, he was trying to take off over Montmartre and dive down onto the city below to peck out its heart with his beak. From the direction in which he strode off, Jean guessed that he was on his way to Jesús, and was sorry he could not be a fly on the wall.

Blanche, left behind, radiated happiness that afternoon: to have, all in the last twenty-four hours, discovered a noble cousin and possibly secured a fortune for her persecutor supplied her with all the reason she needed for existing.

That evening Jesús recounted the arrival of the grotesque but skilful La Garenne, who had come as a supplicant and left with the promise that in a week's time the Spaniard would deliver a fake Utrillo and two fake Picassos.

'You understand,' he said, ''e's more 'ard to make an Utrillo. I 'ave to forget I knows 'ow to pain'. Picasso, 'e knows but 'e doesn' want, so you make a Picasso the same way you smok' the cigarette or you fuck the girl. But an Utrillo, an Utrillo …'

To help him make up his mind, La Garenne had also left with one of his canvases under his arm.

'We goin' to be rich, my young friend. Rich. And then one day we say fuck to them all, to that crook La Garenne, to the dealers, to the painting. Fuck, you 'ear me, the biggest fuck in the 'istory of the art.'

Jean lamented the disappearance of the canvas La Garenne had taken, a red-brown bull in the Andalusian light, a sublime bull in sublime light, a vision that on the mornings when he woke up in the studio was waiting at the foot of his bed, splendid and overlooked, a door open onto a landscape that gradually, as Jesús talked it into life in his stories, he wanted to get to know. What would La Garenne do with it? The bull was destined for his toilet wall. Jean said nothing. Yet again he had the uncomfortable feeling of being, if not implicated in something crooked, then at least a witness to it in a way that pained him. Was he not making himself an accessory by staying silent? He had to put it out of his mind.

Going to Claude's that evening, to the taste of her cool cheek and to her mysteriously indulgent smile, put an end to his remorse. He continued to long to take her in his arms and bury his face in her neck so that he didn't have to think of anything but the smell of her hair and the tang of her skin that drove him mad with hunger. So why did it have to be on this evening that he noticed two half-smoked Virginia cigarettes, stubbed out carelessly or nervously, in an ashtray? Claude did not smoke. Jean was so preoccupied by what he saw that, since he did not dare say anything, dinner passed very glumly, despite Claude's efforts and Cyrille's questions.

'What do you do to earn money? Why don't you live with us all the time? I'll tell Papa when he comes home that you're my best friend.'

The absent husband was suddenly between them. When Cyrille was in bed Jean finally turned to Claude.

'For the first time since we've been together, I'm not happy.'

'I can tell … Have I said or done something to upset you?'

'You couldn't if you tried.'

'Then it must be because of Cyrille. But I can't stop him talking about his father. The longer the war goes on, the more he'll forget him. It's a horrible situation but it's not my fault.'

'I'm jealous!' he burst out.

117

She smiled, reassured and reassuring.

'Well, that's something new, and on the whole rather nice to hear. I was a bit afraid you might not be. Although I know someone else who has much more reason to be jealous of you. But why talk about it?'

He knew she was thinking of Georges Chaminadze, whereas he was simply suffering from not knowing who had smoked two cigarettes in her apartment that afternoon. Curiously he had to acknowledge that the idea of a husband aroused no animosity in him. There were few signs of Chaminadze's former presence at Quai Saint-Michel, as if time had already erased this man of whom only a snapshot remained, a photograph of a tall, blond man with a rugged face and short hair in tennis whites. The picture could not come to life; it fixed its subject for ever as someone who would never grow old, a tennis player who had not even met Claude when it was taken, who spoke Russian and French, who, born at Makhachkala on the shore of the Caspian Sea in 1910, had fled to France in 1919 in the great Russian emigration. That was all Jean knew; he had no idea how Georges and Claude had first met, where they had got married and Cyrille had been born, what Georges did. They had apparently lived without material hardship, but not in any luxury either, and Claude knew how to do everything for herself. Jean had found her several times with a pattern on the table, a dress she was cutting out and sewing from pieces of cloth she had kept from before the war, a precaution that had appeared full of foresight since rationing had been introduced. She made Cyrille's clothes too. When she cooked she had that discreet, subtle way of making ingredients go a long way that has to be admired for its dignity. Jean remembered his adoptive mother's exhausting attitude to thrift: matches split in two, one lamp for the whole house every evening, the leftovers from Sunday lunch served up cold two or three times on Monday and Tuesday, socks darned to death, bed sheets sewed edge to middle (how that seam in the middle of his bed had rubbed him!), and yet they could have lived better, but Jeanne went without from a feeling that she ought to, saving up her sous at the savings bank the way people did when a lifetime's thrift guaranteed one's old age. She had not understood or even noticed how money had collapsed, and had been distressed by what she had called the 'folly' of her little Jean when he had bought himself a bicycle with the prince's first postal order. Albert, with the soul of a contrarian, though at heart he lived by the same strict principles of 'a sou is a sou', let Jean spend his money, recognising perhaps unconsciously that the younger generation no longer relied on the same values to ensure their future. In the era ushered in by their defeat in June 1940 the French were about to rediscover Jeanne's virtues, the stubs of candles, the meanness of locked cupboards. Claude had adapted without complaint to privations that her grace dispelled. She was a strange person; her character appeared too simple and too decent for one to dare believe that she was real. Yet there were those two cigarettes in the ashtray, which, by the way, she made no attempt to hide as she emptied it after dinner.

With the butts out of sight Jean felt calmer. They belonged to a bad dream, whose scenes Claude had swept away in a single gesture. Her power was very great.

'It's over!' Jean said. 'You're with me again.'

'Was I not with you?'

'No. I'm an idiot, aren't I?'

She was silent for a moment, absorbed in thought that she tried, as she always did, to articulate with a precision and clarity that gave her more serious conversations a faintly bookish tone.

'Do you somehow imagine,' she said at last, 'that this situation is only hard for you?'

It was true that he had never thought about it from her point of view. In fact the truth seemed to him so glaring and his egotism so awful that he felt ashamed and threw himself at her feet, burying his face in her lap. And could she have made a sweeter indirect confession? He looked up at her. Her eyes were wet with tears, and she smiled with the same indulgence she showed when Cyrille had done something silly.

'I don't know,' she said. 'I truly don't know what we should do. Perhaps we shouldn't see each other any more.'

There was so little conviction in her voice that Jean regained his courage and the sense of humour that had saved them from awkward situations before.

'Yes,' he said, 'that's definitely the solution. It's such a clever idea, only you could have come up with it. I suggest we put it off a bit – only because to start this evening would be too easy – and definitely start in ten years' time, when we're completely used to each other and the separation would be really heart-rending ... yes, heart-rending ... and so romantic it would make a gravedigger weep.'

She offered him her cheek, laughing.

'Go and sleep!'

In the stairwell, happy again, he ventured to ask the question.

'Who came to see you this afternoon?'

'My brother!' she said. 'How do you know?'

'He smokes, doesn't he?'

'Ah, that's what it was about, was it? Well, you'll meet him one day.'

He jogged as far as Place Clichy before slowing down. His fitness was returning. Jesús had lent him his weights. They had a punchball and took turns at it, ten minutes each, wearing wool vests. Jesús insisted that it allowed him to do without women. There were, of course – at least for others if not for them – a variety of ways of solving that particular problem. La Garenne, seeing the fame of his gallery spread far and wide as whole coachloads of uniformed tourists began arriving to visit, intended to satisfy every taste, but despite his best efforts had not been able to find a painter who knew his way around homosexual subjects. A hissed word from a diminutive, baby-faced major with a glass eye had put him on the right track. 'Photos!' Why had he not thought of that? He instantly set about adding the new line to his gallery.

'Photography is an art!' he explained to Jean. 'A new art. The only new art invented since Phidias's time. Yes indeed, Monsieur Arnaud, Nicéphore Niepce is as great an artist as Phidias, the divine Leonardo and the genius Picasso. The philistines think you just have to press a button, click!, and there's a photo of Grandpa and Grandma and little Zizi with his hoop. The morons! When I say "morons" I'm being polite. As much composition goes into a photograph, Monsieur Arnaud, as into a still life by Chardin, and light plays as important a role in a photograph as it does in a Rembrandt. There is no phrase more absurd than the term "objective lens" when applied to the eye of a camera. Nothing is less objective than an objective lens. That transparent glass, which one imagines to be inert, is both a third eye and a brain but that eye, that brain must have a spiritual motor, which is the genius of the photographer, his vision of the world, his culture, his sensibility, his responsiveness. Painting is perhaps an expression of the human; photography is an expression of life ...'

Jean assumed that this speech was a prelude to some new mischief-making by La Garenne, who always felt the need to dignify his muckiest transactions with the name of art. Thus his erotic drawings became, as he saw it, a means of psychological liberation for sexual misfits. He was even armed with a fine quote on that very subject by Freud that made of him, the purveyor, a benefactor of humanity, a saviour of inhibited couples and a generous supplier to lonely masturbators. His glibness, which never lacked conviction, was in every respect a match for his greed. The only question that remained was how he would spend the piles of money he had been amassing since the beginning of the occupation. There was no danger of it being wasted on women. Blanche de Rocroy was enough for that very restrained libertine, too

121

stingy even to treat himself to a tart. He was not a betting man and he spent nothing at his tailor's, being always dressed in the same black suit of the tenth-rate painter who has called himself a bohemian for far too long, on top of grubby shirts that he wore until they fell apart with, for a necktie, a greasy black ribbon that might once, in its long-distant youth, have been an ascot. In the mornings he would appear in his shiny, crumpled, dust-flecked suit as if he had slept under a bridge the night before. In his office, on the door of which he had inscribed in large capital letters the only play on words he had ever deserved credit for – 'The bosom of bosoms' – he would remove his trousers and throw them at Blanche, who piously set to ironing them in the stockroom, as if this garment, rigid with unnameable grime, represented some sort of thaumaturgical vessel for the Holy Grail, while her master (what other word can we use?), in his long grey-coloured cotton drawers, scratched his crotch and explained his grand designs to Jean. No one knew where he called home. Did he even have one? It was doubtful.

Photographs, then, began to be added to the stock of drawings in hell. Mostly they depicted young boys with erections. Their creator, an antifascist refugee called Alberto Senzacatso, lived in an artist's studio on the top floor of a respectable building in Rue Caulaincourt. His models were occasionally to be encountered on the stairs, mostly the sons of the other residents, cheeky boys with roving eyes. Truth compels us to add that Alberto was not the sort of man to inspire repugnance, and might have resembled a fruit and vegetable wholesaler more than a maker of pornographic photographs if it had not been for the way his face lit up in a faintly mad way whenever he talked about his models. As a boy he had been force-fed with castor oil by Mussolini's Blackshirts, and from the severe diarrhoea that had followed he had been left with an anal obsession that verged on mania. His models, all volunteers, emerged tight-lipped from their posing sessions and returned to their families on the floors below. Alberto's customers sometimes bumped into them on the landings and recognised the models who were the subjects of the very special photographs they had just purchased.

Their excitement can be imagined. The Italian lived alone in a studio stuffed with books and paintings. Open-minded and curious, he was writing a history of Mannerism which, after years of contemplation, he was hoping to reduce to three volumes of five hundred pages each. He counted a number of writers among his regular customers, whom he referred to only by their Christian names – Monsieur André, Monsieur Roger, Monsieur Julien – recognisable even to the uninitiated from the odd detail slyly slipped in by the garrulous photographer about their propensities. Two or three times he had been within a hair's breadth of getting arrested, and Jean would find out later that he had succeeded in avoiding arrest by passing on details about his buyers. The police turned a blind eye and added to their files. Alberto showed no remorse. That was life, and staying in Paris was worth the occasional piece of information that in most cases was never used, the parties in question being protected by their standing and their periodic contributions to the *Revue Littéraire de la Préfecture de Police*,[10] or in some cases their status as patrons of a non-profit-making organisation known as the Amicale des Gardiens de la Paix.[11]

Alberto was a good judge of character and understood straight away how disgusting Jean found his business. Handing over an envelope containing around twenty photographs in exchange for a sum of money, he would move quickly on to another subject, for preference one of his choosing, which at that time meant Il Bronzino, whom he referred to familiarly as Agnolo and with whose painting he had a relationship that can only be described as love. He even claimed to have unearthed a very late sketch for the portrait of Jean, the son of Eleanor of Toledo, at the flea market. This modest canvas sat on an easel, mostly concealed under a piece of velvet. He uncovered the picture to talk about Bronzino, as though he was inspired by the inquisitive gaze of the child with the round face, and the plump hand laid upon the brocade dress of the beautiful Eleanor. Listening to him,

Jean realised that, underneath his crude, kinky exterior, innocence and passion remained, that it was unfair not to give him some credit for such feelings, and that clearly life demanded, if only out of a sense of justice, as much indulgence as Manichaeism. But what about La Garenne? A full-blown shit, without the slightest outward sign of anything that might be considered a redeeming feature. And yet there was one.

Sometimes in the afternoons, stifled and sickened by the gallery's atmosphere, Jean slammed the door behind him and escaped to stroll the streets of Montmartre village, to breathe fresh air and banish the accumulated fetid vapours of hell. What he found most unendurable was not being able to see how he could get away from a society so fearfully turned in on itself. In Paris he knew only Jesús and Claude. And Madeleine, in her new life of affluence and suspect relations. The situations vacant in the newspapers were starting to offer work in Germany, but the world at war required specialists, die- and toolmakers ... And to take the first job that came along, for the sake of being dramatic, would mean parting from Claude, which he could not bear. What would a single day without her be like? He would die of loneliness and fear of losing her, convinced that her charm and naivety would render her easy and innocent prey, forgetting in his blindness how much that lovely and tempting being had preserved of her own defences. But what she gave to him – however small it was – would she not give it to others? Did she really have a brother? One doubt led to another in a process that would be irreversible if he did not retrace his steps back to the start, to his trust in her candid and natural features. When, too unhappy to bear such thoughts alone, he opened his heart to Jesús, the Spaniard consoled him in his own way.

'It's true that the women are easily turnin' into the 'ores!' he said. 'It's subleemly true, and it's a stupidity to make a man weep. En we, wha' are we, the men? The sons of the 'ores, for sure! *Claro!* The women are in ou' imáge! You, you is a good imáge. The wimmen in you' life, they will be like you ...'

'What about Chantal?'

'That one, se sowed 'erself to be a 'ore without knowin' it. Don' speak to me of 'er ...'

Jean could not quite believe that Chantal had been a whore. The idea wounded his self-esteem, despite everything being over between them. No, she had lost her head, like a little country girl, and now she was making amends the fashionable way, going back to the land, and when all was said and done that was a laudable way to atone for a moment of madness with a gigolo in a red Delahaye convertible. He must not think about her. Not ever, despite all the memories lurking in the lanes of Montmartre that he kept stumbling across, surprised to find they were still so vivid.

When he returned from his brief forays away from the miasmas of the gallery, he would be greeted by La Garenne looking furious, but the gallery owner had kept his fury bottled up ever since he had been reminded that it was upon his salesman's welfare that Jesús's continued goodwill depended. It was Jean, too, who took care to deliver the fake Picassos and Utrillo from Jesús's studio himself. Rudolf von Rocroy admired them and requested a few days to think about the purchase. When he returned to the gallery he was accompanied by a tall, severe-looking and haughty person. Jean learnt that this was Émile Dugard, an art critic who was highly regarded, whose services the German had enlisted. Dugard, showing no enthusiasm, examined minutely the signature and the composition of the sky over Rue Norvins and declared that the painting was a Utrillo from his early period, when he was still living under his mother's influence. Subsequently, as he explained to Rocroy, who was listening attentively, Utrillo had weaned himself off alcohol but in the process had lost part of his genius and begun peopling his canvases with the famous little couple who walked hand in hand through the pale streets of Montmartre. As for the Picassos, there was absolutely no doubt about them either; they belonged to the so-called Synthetic Cubism era, almost monochrome, with different shades of brown playing off against each other. Rocroy left with the paintings. The following day Dugard presented himself at the gallery to collect his commission. Raised voices were heard coming from La Garenne's office, and Dugard pretended to flounce out. If he had not achieved everything he had demanded this time, at least he had succeeded in agreeing the terms of his future services.

Louis-Edmond felt the critic was robbing him blind and bared his soul to Jean with unfeigned indignation, forgetting that his listener knew better than anyone where the paintings had really come from.

'Ponces and crooks, art critics, the lot of them! Sons of Barabbas, selling themselves to both sides, taking from every honest party. That Dugard is the worst, with his high and mighty airs. And tell me, young man, tell me if there's a single man on earth who has the right to criticise Art? Eh? "Art critic" – it's so pretentious you could die laughing. All ponces, I tell you. In my day ... How old are you, actually?'

'Twenty-one.'

'I'm two and a half times your age ... I was around when this buggers' century started ... I tell you, they were full of it. It was going to be the triumph of civilisation, humankind delivered out of servitude by machines. And the sum total: two wars ... Yes, in my day, Monsieur Arnaud, artists and their public had no need of bribed intermediaries – yes, you heard me, bribed – to reach each other. The spark jumped between them *on its own*. There were still patrons, truly inspired art lovers then. Now it's all speculation, percentages – do you hear what I'm saying? Beggars with their hand out! A real racket, as the Americans say.'

He waved his arms like a scarecrow to chase away the predators who wanted to wheel and deal in Art with a capital A. Blanche listened to him starry-eyed. She did love her Louis-Edmond! Especially when he let fly with a good rant, belabouring the middlemen, chasing the moneychangers from the Temple. His honesty would condemn him to poverty for life. But the defence of Art was a long ascent to Calvary, and at its summit one could not even be certain of seeing one's efforts recognised. She would climb the path of that Calvary with him, bent beneath the world's opprobrium, stooping to gather up crumbs of genius and the bitter tears of ingratitude.

Jean shrugged his shoulders. What was the point of reminding La Garenne of the truth? Especially as a customer had just arrived, a tall, thin young man whose deep, dark gaze settled on those present with a gentleness that was too earnest to be genuine. Michel du Courseau was honouring Paris with a visit. Blanche thought he looked distinguished, but Louis-Edmond, scenting an artist in the gallery, prudently vanished into the 'bosom of bosoms'. Michel favoured Jean with a rather formal hug and these words, which seemed to encapsulate an affection of long standing: 'Dear old Jean!'

'Steady on, people are going to expect us to start weeping in each other's arms.'

'I've found you again!'

'And it's not over yet.'

'You're still my little brother, you know.'

'Your nephew, you mean.'

'Ah yes, of course, you know the truth now: Antoinette told you everything.'

'Antoinette has never kept anything from me.'

He almost added, 'not even her bottom', but managed to stop himself, reining in his feelings of aggression in Michel's presence; his uncle was, after all, his mother's brother and Antoinette's.

'I don't know that she should have!' Michel said. 'I hope you don't find it painful being Geneviève's son.'

'Not a bit. I think she's wonderful. Oedipus's dream woman. Every chap would love a mother like her: her beauty, her charm, the pathos of a life threatened by tuberculosis. In short, an awfully modern story, a slightly muddled version of *The Lady of the Camellias* and *The Bread Peddler*. It's a shame that she's so elusive and maternal feelings aren't her strong point, but you can't have everything.'

'One mustn't blame her,' Michel said sententiously. 'She was left to her own devices. Maman was torn between Geneviève and us. In the end she chose us.'

'I can't quite see my mother sitting darning socks by the fire.'

'Listen,' Michel said. 'We'll talk about it another time. Now's not the moment. Shall we have dinner this evening?'

'I can't. I'm busy.'

'Tomorrow then?'

'I'm busy every evening. We can have lunch if you like. The gallery's closed from midday till two. Will you excuse me for just a moment?'

Two German officers who had just walked in were asking to visit hell. They left swiftly, their choices made, concealing their Alberto Senzacatso prints under their arms. Michel had remained with Blanche de Rocroy, who had naively tried to interest him in a series of horrors: fishing boats against a setting sun, Parisian girls on a swing, flowers in a vase – paintings for innocent tourists.

Seeing her look discouraged, Jean said, 'There's no reason you should know, but Michel is a real painter.'

'Oh ... in that case I'll leave you alone.'

She was not cross; she made mistakes all the time. The name meant nothing to her and all painters were real painters. Some just grabbed their chances better than others.

As might have been imagined, Michel du Courseau's visit was not without motive. After abandoning a singing career he had returned to Grangeville to devote himself to painting, though without an audience or friendly voice to encourage or guide him.

'Solitude is very necessary for my work, but I need warmth too, particularly as I've started on a risky path: religious inspiration, you see, is the only kind that moves me. Secular subjects leave me cold. Art has lost its faith. I want to give it back ...'

'Listen,' Jean said, 'this gallery isn't really the kind of place you need. I tremble at the thought that you might discover what we have for sale back there ...'

'You mean that old spinster—'

'She's not so old … only just forty. And it's not her who sells the stuff in what we call hell, it's me. The owner, Louis-Edmond de La Garenne, is a crook. Paris is a cut-throat place. Everyone's on the fiddle. Only idiots don't make anything. In this city honesty is an unforgivable sin.'

Michel looked genuinely shocked. He had never come across anything like the situation Jean was describing.

'I see now the terrible isolation our family has lived in. If I'm honest, all we know is our little Grangeville world, satisfied, happy, hiding its little wounds. If what you tell me is true, and if in coming to Paris I have to fall in with your pessimism, then it's Maman who is guilty for having made me live too long in a state of innocence. What is so special about this hell of yours?'

Jean supplied a full account, with a vulgarity we shall not venture to repeat. He enjoyed seeing Michel's reaction.

'Someone like that Italian,' Michael said, paling, 'should be denounced, and arrested instantly. He's a criminal. He's contaminating a society that he lives from by perverting it.'

'This isn't a time for denunciation.'

What was Jean saying? He was still unaware of what had already started to happen, too rarely among his fellow Frenchmen to grasp the purulent frenzy of denunciation that had erupted in a country still stunned by the blow it had received. It was a shame he had not read Céline, who was hunched over a manuscript that very day, that very moment, writing, all illusions abandoned, with the penetrating acuity of the visionary: 'Censors and informers are at every corner … France is a pitiful donkey, the Kommandantur stuffed with people who have come to denounce each other.' He was heedless even of the gnawing unease corrupting a population tempted by an authority known for its prompt reactions; yet Michel's threatening words chilled him. Denounce? Who to? How?

'There is no right time for denouncing or not denouncing,' Michel went on agitatedly. 'Evil is evil, whether France is occupied or free.'

'Now you're annoying me,' Jean said. 'Go and enjoy your painting and leave me alone.'

Michel flinched, wounded, cross and surprised. He had arrived with good intentions, wanting to bury an awkward past. Why was Jean unwilling to take the olive branch he was offering?

'You sound bitter,' he said.

'Bitter? Well ... now you mention it ... I am. And it's a very mediocre emotion. So forgive me. Did you bring any of your canvases?'

'Five. Not enough for an exhibition, but I've several pictures in progress: a Last Supper that's nearly finished, a "Suffer the little children ..." I've just started. Nothing but sacred subjects. A great Christian revival has taken hold in France. Artists cannot stand idly by.'

Jean suppressed a shrug of his shoulders. Generalised ideas like Michel's bored him to death. He found his pompousness beneath sarcasm.

'I'll ask who you should introduce yourself to,' he said. 'La Garenne knows all that sort of thing. But don't say he was the one who sent you. He's a crook.'

'In that case I don't want to have anything to do with him.'

'Save your fine words for later. At the moment he's the only possibility I can offer you.'

'I'll leave it to you in that case.'

Jean walked a short distance down the street with Michel, and in doing so learnt that Antoinette had been ill with a stubborn bout of influenza that she could not shake off, that Marie-Thérèse du Courseau was astonishing Grangeville with her energy, and that there remained, as expected, no news of Antoine.

'I suppose he's in the southern zone,' Michel said. 'Antoinette knows his address, but she'd let herself be cut into little pieces before she'd tell Maman or me. Anyway, neither of us is insisting. Papa has gone from our life. Now that he can't get hold of petrol to keep his Bugatti on the road, he must be a shadow of his old self. He's one of those men who only have a personality when they're behind the wheel. If you'd known Gontran Longuet better, you'd understand why I put them both in the same boat, or rather car. Did you know Gontran is currently impressing the Norman coast with a wood-gas car …'

'You're unkind and unfair about Antoine. He was my only friend. It makes me happy to know that he got away from you both.'

'Oh, I know you've always had a soft spot for him, and more than ever now you know you're his grandson.'

Jean thought about this.

'Actually you're wrong. It makes me uncomfortable more than anything else. I feel tempted to believe in blood ties now, whereas before it felt like something more noble, an affinity between two men, which is something so rare it doesn't happen more than once in a lifetime.'

Michel suggested they might agree to differ on the subject of Antoine, without coming to blows. Like a coward, Jean accepted the offered platitude, which got them both out of a situation that left them feeling awkward. They stopped on the forecourt of the Sacré-Cœur, turning their backs on the hideous basilica, looking out over an impassive Paris, a sea of roofs glittering in the cold winter sun. Children were playing on Square Willette and soldiers in green uniforms seated on the steps contemplated the El Dorado of a city below them, which in truth looked from this height like almost any other city, as long as they could not put names to the church steeples, domes and palaces. The absurd Eiffel Tower was the only landmark that wholly reassured them, and perhaps the wavering line of the Seine. Jean pointed, lower down, to Rue Steinkerque and a small bistro there.

'Second on the left as you go down. I'll meet you there tomorrow at one. It's Wednesday. There'll be black pudding. I hope you like black pudding?'

'I'll make do.'

'See you tomorrow.'

Jean watched him go down Rue Foyatier and disappear, swallowed up by this Paris that succeeded, in so many different ways, in cloaking the most singular individuals in anonymity. He did not hate Michel, he had never hated him despite his deviously spiteful behaviour that had dogged his, Jean's, childhood, despite all the scorn Michel had poured on him because he had thought, in those days, that he was the gardener's son. The emotion he felt was simpler than hate: he did not understand him and would never understand such gratuitous and spontaneous spite. Michel had arrived in Paris like a provincial youth greedy for conquests. Perhaps it had not even entered his head that the city might not recognise his talent any more than it had the first time at the Salle Pleyel, on the occasion of his recital accompanied by Francis Poulenc. The audience then had not been able to appreciate his quality. Or had he sensed, from a lack of warmth and despite having a fine baritone voice, that he would never, in that sphere anyway, be in the first division? Painting offered him a second chance in a confused era. He was no less talented an artist than he had been as a singer, but would he again have to be satisfied with a *succès d'estime*? With music lovers thinking of him as a gifted amateur, and art critics as a talented dilettante?

Jean returned to the gallery. Blanche, sitting on a stool by the door, was observing the comings and goings of the passers-by through the window. Her chapped, reddened hands lay on the shiny cloth of her skirt, stretched tight by her bony knees. Rudolf von Rocroy had not appeared at the gallery for a week. The elation of their first meeting and the success of the first sale had begun to evaporate. That same morning La Garenne had reproached Blanche for not looking after her cousin.

'The idiot's buggered off! You didn't know how to keep hold of him. He's running around the other galleries now, where they're robbing him and cheating him. And you, Mademoiselle de Rocroy, don't care. Quite cynically, you do not give a tinker's cuss. Telephone him.'

'I have. He's never there.'

'Not there for you, perhaps. Because you're always talking to him about family: Papa Adhémar, Cousin Godefroy, Aunt Aurore and Grandfather Gonzague. He doesn't care a fig about your family, you goose. He came to Paris on his own, to enjoy himself. Take him to the Folies-Bergère, find him a girl, go to the Bois de Boulogne at night. Show the old aristo a thing or two ...'

'Me?'

'Oh for God's sake, don't be such a bloody goody-goody.'

Powerless, Blanche suddenly came face to face with her failure to help Louis-Edmond. Instead of taking a lunch break, she walked all the way to the Hôtel Continental to deliver a letter. Would he answer? Jean's return produced a timid smile.

'Your visitor is absolutely charming!' she said. 'Is he a relation of yours?'

'My uncle.'

'So young and already an uncle! Your mother must be very young, then?'

'Yes, very young.'

'I'd so like to meet her.'

'Not much chance of that, at this precise moment. She's in Lebanon.'

'In Lebanon? How extraordinary! I've got a second cousin there. She must know him. Colonel Pontalet. A colonel in the Foreign Legion. Quite an old scrapper.'

'Perhaps they'll meet!' Jean said kindly, doubtful whether the prince and Geneviève spent any time at all socialising with army officers.

At seven that evening Jean walked into the apartment building on Quai Saint-Michel. The concierge appeared from her stew-ridden lair.

'You're Monsieur Arnaud?' she asked.

'Yes.'

'Madame Chaminadze has gone away. She left a letter for you.'

'Gone away?'

'Yes, gone away. Don't you understand French?'

'Yes.'

He took the letter. The concierge did not move, perhaps in the hope that he would open the envelope in front of her and tell her what was in it. She had tried hard to steam it open and had not succeeded. But Jean put the letter in his pocket and went out without hearing her affronted mutter. 'And not so much as a thank you for it.'

He walked a hundred paces before stopping at an illuminated shop window. His hand was shaking. He felt sick and afraid.

> *Jean, I have to go away for a few days. Shut your eyes. Don't try to find me. As soon as I get back I'll let you know. Loving and kissing you, Claude*

'Already?' Jesús said when he reappeared at the studio. '*Hombre!* You look like you 'as jus' been to a funeral. Is you angry?'

'She's gone.'

'Ah the bitch!'

'Just for a few days.'

He held out the letter to Jesús, who held up his arms to heaven.

'My friend, 'e's a crazy. Your Claude 'e's comin' back. I tell you is true. Is family business.'

'Do you believe in those sorts of excuses?'

'Yes, idiot, I do b'lieve. An' tonight you is dinin' with me at old Coco's. She 'as got leg of lamb for us, real lamb.'

'There's no such thing as mock lamb.'

'Shu' your mouth, you argumentin' boy.'

The door bell rang. A pretty, slightly over-made-up young woman stood in the doorway. Jesús kissed her and said to Jean, 'This is Irma.'

He led the woman onto the landing and Jean saw him press a note into her hand. Irma frowned, sulking, but turned away.

'Why don't you have dinner with her?' Jean asked.

''Cause I am 'avin' dinner with my frien' Jean.'

So Jean learnt that evening that Jesús was his friend.

So many loose ends need to be tied up, the reader will say, if only from time to time. It's not fair to introduce new characters into a story when the old ones are still alive and kicking. The author feels the same, and he begs forgiveness for this unavoidable chain of events that leaves Jean no time to meet again those who knew him, helped him and loved him in the early part of his life. All we can do is try to keep up with him, hero that he is of this incredible adventure that we call the birth of a man. An adventure that begins all over again when a woman arrives and blots out her predecessors, when all of a sudden events overtake you that before seemed so distant, of concern only to others ... those who don't suffer in their own lives suffer from the infinite, vertigo-inducing distraction of being in love. So no, we shan't slide into a pointless universalism but will regret and carry on regretting the fading into the background of so many characters whom Jean, in his discovery of life, is leaving behind, leaving to their emotional (or physical) unhappiness – or even their modest happiness – and will not see again.

So it is with his adoptive father, Albert Arnaud, wounded equally by loneliness, the devastation of his pacifist dreams and of France, by the country's occupation under those he continues to refer to as 'the Uhlans', and by Marie-Thérèse du Courseau's practical initiative to plant cabbages, carrots and potatoes where there should have been rhododendron beds, azaleas and oriental flowering cherries. Perhaps his reaction was absurd and disproportionate, but let us reflect for a moment on the kind of existence Albert Arnaud had had: a childhood and adolescence that was far from well-off, a coming of age at a local brothel and then marriage to a kind and generous woman who nevertheless could hardly be said to have lived her life with a deep sense of romance. Then had come the four years of the Great War and the loss of his leg at the bottom of a muddy shell-hole. The unexpected arrival of the baby Jean had swiftly turned into a mixed blessing, as Albert had watched his adopted son grow up with the children from La Sauveté, Michel and Antoinette du Courseau, and privately felt that nothing good could come of it. He sensed, not without reason, that Jean would be happy neither at home nor with the du Courseaus, tugged in two directions by different worlds that would both reject him as a hybrid, belonging to neither. And Jean would certainly not become a gardener.

Albert's accumulated knowledge – his only capital – that he would have liked to bequeath to the boy, Jean did not want. In any case, he did not have green fingers: whenever he planted something, it almost never turned out well. So let us not mock Albert's disappointment when, instead of his flowers, he sees vegetables growing, and let us compare him to a man who has spent his life reading and suddenly finds himself in a universe purged of books. Without twisting words and their meaning, let us say that flowers are his culture. Without flowers, existence lacks the one gratuitous element that justifies it: the creation of beauty. They are his poetry, the thoughts he can't manage to articulate, the pictures he dreams of and that the earth has given him, perfect and complete, the symbols of a world of exquisite grace.

Jean had not wanted flowers, or political ideas; instead, in 1939 he had enlisted. Albert had felt deeply wounded and the wound had been, in the larger sense of destiny, like a denial of justice. The abbé Le Couec's patient explanations were to no avail. The facts were there. Albert did not reproach Jean. His elevated and democratic notion of individual liberty forbade it. Adoptive father and adopted son will not see one another again. Jean writes phrases of such banality that even he finds them depressing. From Antoinette, their go-between, he gets conventional answers: 'Your father's in good health and hopes you are too.' She faithfully writes down these sentences, adding as a PS, 'He's sad, grumpy, stoical and never smiles.'

When Jean finally has an opportunity to travel to Grangeville, it happens to be on 19 August 1942, the morning a commando unit of Cameron Highlanders from Winnipeg lands at the foot of the cliffs, slips between the German bunkers and reaches the village. At Puys and on the esplanade at Dieppe the remaining commando units are pinned down by the German defences. But at Grangeville and a little further south, at the Pointe d'Ailly lighthouse, Lord Lovat's No 4 Commando at the foot of the cliff – at the spot where Antoinette first showed Jean her bottom – and the Cameron Highlanders have met no resistance. They blow up a coastal artillery battery, the one placed in the former garden of Captain Duclou, Jeanne Arnaud's uncle, and for a time their advance is practically a victory parade as they hand out cigarettes and sweets, pat children's cheeks and then, joining up with the South Saskatchewan Regiment which has surrounded Pourville without succeeding in taking it, return to their landing craft. Albert is at the roadside. He recognises the khaki uniforms and the soldiers in their tin hats.

His memories of 1914 are like a lump in his throat. Forgetting his neutrality, he limps as fast as he can towards them, waving his arms to stop them turning onto a path where a Wehrmacht patrol is lying in wait. German and Canadian bullets riddle his body, easily a hundred or more, for no one counts the bullets when they're waging war. Let us merely record that when it is over, there is nothing left of Albert. The pieces of him are collected with a fork and spade and tipped into a sack.

Jean is turned back at Rouen without explanation. He nevertheless manages to get through to Antoinette by telephone and from her learns that Albert, according to his oft-expressed wish, has been buried without a religious service. The ceremony is attended only by the du Courseaus, Captain Duclou, stunned and muttering and making no sense, Monsieur Cliquet who repeats over and over again, 'That's what happens to pacifists', and the abbé Le Couec, who is wearing an ordinary suit so as not to disturb his friend's soul's rest but who, through the long night that follows, will pray for him at the foot of the altar. It is all over for Albert, and we shall miss him. He will no longer pitch his stubborn ideas against an unreliable and inconstant world in which men and women of his ancient stamp have no place. A little of France as she once was has been extinguished with his passing.

And while we are on the subject of the dead, let us mention too that a year earlier, in the summer of 1941, the prince slipped away at Beirut. That enigmatic figure simply stopped breathing one night. At dawn his secretary/chauffeur/right-hand man, Salah, bent over him to wake him up. He lightly touched the hand that lay on the sheet, and it was cold. The prince was a wax statue, his papery yellow skin stretched over a bony mask. He was buried according to the rites of his religion, and that afternoon friends gathered at Geneviève's. She displayed impressive dignity. Perhaps she was already aware of what the prince's will contained. She had inherited a substantial fortune, but not its management. Salah with his dark complexion was stepping into the light, and there were those who murmured spitefully, in Beirut as in Alexandria, that he was now more than merely Geneviève's legal representative, which was untrue. And she herself was at risk. Lebanon's climate did not suit her. She felt she needed to get to Switzerland, which, despite her possessing influential contacts, looked to be almost impossible, and it took her until December 1941 to make it happen and find her way to a small village in Valais, hidden away in the mountains, called Gstaad, where she rented the first floor of a modest country hotel.

As for the famous letter given to Jean by the prince before the outbreak of war, it remains unopened. To be honest, Jean attaches no importance to it, and the only person to suspect its true value is Palfy.

Which is, one imagines, why his first question when he arrives in Paris on Christmas Eve of 1940 is, 'Have you still got the letter?'

Jean is no longer even very sure where he has put it, and it has to be said that at that moment it is the least of his worries. Claude left him the day before, and he has not yet got over this latest sudden twist of fate. During the night Jesús and he have polished off a bottle of calvados between them, a present in a parcel from Antoinette. Waking up has been exceptionally painful and there is no respite: here is Constantin Palfy, knocking at the door in an elegant grey flannel suit.

'You're my first port of call,' he says. 'You look like death warmed up. I bring you "real" coffee and "real" croissants. Everything is real!'

'Even me, who's a real idiot.'

'Ah, *delectatio morosa* … that is you all over, my dear Jean.'

Jesús was no more awake than Jean but glimpsed, standing behind Palfy on the landing, the girl who had come to pose for him. She was called Josette and had generous breasts, and portraits of her in outrageous style already furnished the rooms of several German officers and their most bountiful dreams.

'Not today, Josette! Is the wrong time …'

She cried and he pressed a note into her hand, a remedy he considered, not without justification, to work very effectively whenever disappointment manifested itself. Once Josette was gone, they boiled water for 'real' coffee, which they drank with 'real' warm croissants. Palfy, finding it hard to sit still, went to the window. Paris was enveloped in a purifying cold, its roofs covered in frost in the clear light of the end of December. A city unlike all others, whose gentle blue and pink breath misted the windows and broke up the sun's rays.

'You're not about to say, "It's between you and me now!" are you?' Jean said.

'Don't worry. Not a bad idea, though.'

'Is it all thanks to Madeleine that you got your permit to cross the demarcation line?'

'Of course! The dear girl. She's complaining that she never sees you. We saw her last night. Marceline's very impressed with her.'

'Marceline?'

'Ah yes, you didn't know ... Marceline Michette.'

'The *patronne* at the Sirène?'

'So what?'

'You're not going to tell me you're shacking up with the *patronne* of a brothel now?'

'No, you ninny! Zizi's the one I'm after ...'

Jean tried to remember the foxy, mocking features of the red-headed Zizi at the Sirène, apparently Palfy's sort of girl.

'What about ... Marceline's husband?'

'Taken prisoner, dear boy! Bravely falling back to Perpignan, his regiment left him behind. There are, sadly, some colonels not worthy of being called the father of their regiment. Now our dear sergeant-major is atoning for France's sins. Let us salute a warrior and a gentleman. Monsieur Michette! A hero! Not to mention his wife, who yearns to serve her country. Her talents cannot be allowed to lie fallow. In Paris there'll be no stopping her.'

Jesús poured himself more coffee.

'The best I 'ave ever drunk!' he said. 'This war 'as got to be made to las'.'

'We're working on it in high places,' Palfy assured him. 'And what about dear Claude? Are you still seeing her?'

'Every day,' Jean said, 'but yesterday she had to go away for a few days ...'

'So everything going all right there then. Good!'

Jean and Jesús looked at each other. Why say more? If Claude returned, her sudden departure – once explained – would be no more than a moment's upset that was swiftly forgotten, and if she failed to return Palfy would not even notice. Jean's affairs of the heart had always seemed to him to be pointless aberrations, weaknesses unworthy of a young man destined for a great future. So Jean said nothing: Jesús knew what had happened, and that was enough. In any

141

case Palfy had already moved on, asking Jesús to recount in detail La Garenne's rackets. The scale of the gallery owner's hoaxes thrilled him. He immediately wanted to meet this master swindler and have lunch with him.

'He doesn't have lunch with anyone,' Jean said. 'He'd be too afraid he'd be left with the bill.'

'I'll take him out!'

'You haven't got any money!'

'I'll borrow some from him.'

They burst out laughing.

'Even supposing you succeed,' Jean said, 'which, just between ourselves, would be a stroke of genius, I ought to warn you that as soon as he opens his mouth to speak he'll start spitting into your food.'

'I'll buy him some new dentures.'

'He'll resell them as a Surrealist sculpture.'

'You won't stop me, you'll see.'

Jean believed him. His friend had spotted an opportunity and was already plotting to join forces with La Garenne. After all, yes, why not? Jesús was delighted by Palfy.

'This La Garenne 'e's a slob. 'E put everyzin' in iz own pocket. What I like 'e's that 'e's connin' the Boches. For that you need a *hombre* with big *cojones*.'

'No hurry. Let's give it some thought. I have a few ideas. Today I'm having lunch with Madeleine and her Julius, at Maxim's, where else?'

'It's their local,' Jean said.

'I saw this Julius fellow yesterday for the first time. Not uncongenial. A great music lover.'

'Like that SS officer Karl Schmidt, the one who wanted to shoot us to the strains of his violin?'

'No grudges, Jean. Very unbecoming. The SS and Wehrmacht are worlds apart. One day the Wehrmacht will wipe out the SS. Julius may not be a Prussian nob but he's a solid businessman. One of his daughters is married to an English banker in London and one of his sons is at Bern, as an attaché at the embassy. All doors open for him – and he can't live without Madeleine. You should see her, dear boy. Your attitude upsets her.'

Jean promised. One day … In the meantime he would arrange a meeting with La Garenne. Palfy wrote down Blanche's name.

'A Rocroy? That rings a bell. I'll do some research. By the time I meet her I'll know everything about her family. What a performance! You'll see. Come on, come to lunch at Maxim's, both of you. Madeleine will be so pleased.'

'Will there be black pudding?' Jean asked.

'Black pudding at Maxim's? You are joking, dear boy.'

Jesús felt as Jean did.

'I am like 'im, I wan' black puddin'. They 'ave it in a little restauran' …'

Palfy shrugged.

'You're pathetic, the pair of you. I'll leave you to it. See you soon.'

He was already halfway down the stairs.

Everything worked out. Very well. La Garenne, whom it cost nothing, suggested an address to Michel du Courseau. A gallery offered him hanging space. For a modest fee. Jesús was unsurprised. According to him, the ascetic nature of the paintings and their religious inspiration made them powerfully prophetic pictures in wartime. They would show the French how to suffer, now that they were without bread and butter, cheese and meat, and going through their own Passion. Their natural masochism would find an outlet in Michel's display of suffering.

'Your uncle 'e's very talented,' Jesús said approvingly. 'You're no' nice to 'im. Et look like 'e bore you.'

It was true. Michel bored Jean enormously. Not a word he spoke rang true, despite his sincerity. The excessive self-confidence he had always felt spilt over into his art. All around him he saw skilful mediocrities trying to establish themselves in the general confusion. Once he had obtained what he desired, there was no question of his showing his contemporaries any indulgence. Jean who, in reality, barely knew him, so divided in enmity had they been in their childhood, discovered that behind his humble exterior Michel maintained a view of himself that was so superior that no one else actually existed – an idea intensely comforting to a young person aspiring to genius. Even the failure of his first exhibition in spring '41 – a failure that was unjust because even though there was nothing new in his sombre, passionate approach to his subject, it was still a revelation of a painter brave enough to go against fashion – even that failure was a source of pride to Michel. In the essentially biographical idea he had of what counted as glory, a failure was one more 'proof', a necessary expiation that would help him make a name for himself.

But if we occasionally proceed too slowly as far as Jean is concerned, we ought not to go too quickly with the characters in his life. We have scarcely reached the end of 1940, and here we are already talking about Michel du Courseau's exhibition of religious paintings from spring 1941, just before Hitler sets his Panzer divisions on the Soviet Union; about the death of the prince, also in '41, in the course of that summer; and a year later about the death of Albert Arnaud. Our only excuse is that our real preoccupation is the unexpected and hasty departure of Claude Chaminadze, shortly before the first Christmas of the occupation. We therefore request that the reader return with us, for a moment, to the three days that followed this dreadful blow to Jean's existence. He felt he had returned to the aftermath of the departure of Chantal de Malemort in that same building in Rue Lepic where they had lived together so carelessly and happily. With Chantal, however, the disaster had been definitive and complete at the instant of its discovery. With Claude, hope remained: an explanation might be forthcoming that would return their life to what it had been before. Jesús commented, perhaps shrewdly, that Michel du Courseau had the evil eye. Had it not been at the concert he had given in 1939 at the Pleyel that Chantal had run into Gontran Longuet again? Now Michel had reappeared and Claude had vanished. Jean did not believe in the evil eye, but he listened to the Andalusian's grumbling ruminations and they distracted him from his anxiety and pain. It was Jesús's belief, in any case, that women went up in smoke several days a month. They returned transparent, as immaterial beings. In reality they no longer existed: it was a proven way for them to rest and not get older, an old trick they had exploited ever since they arrived from that unknown planet to cause us anxieties that only a real, open friendship between men could attenuate ... Jesús did not deny that these absences had something magical about them, but refused to explain them to himself in those terms because Spaniards and certainly not Andalusians did not believe in magic. Magic was a Lapp invention at best, or a Scandinavian one at worst, a migratory invention whose effects were most noticeable at the start of winter, when the days shorten and night closes in. Fairies do not exist in hot countries, where the sun wipes out imagination.

So there were three dreadful days when, like an automaton, Jean listened to La Garenne shouting for all he was worth and then mysteriously – La Garenne, most sceptical of men – allowing himself to be dazzled by Palfy, who simultaneously conquered Blanche with his extensive knowledge of her family tree and information about several new international branches of the family that she knew nothing about; when he listened to Michel who thought of nothing but his exhibition; and to Jesús who talked non-stop simply to make sure his friend was not left alone with his thoughts. At last, on the fourth day, the telephone rang at the back of the gallery and, picking up the receiver, without even having heard her voice, he knew it was her. And it was all over. She was waiting for him. He would be there as soon as he could after the gallery had closed. And when she opened the door Cyrille ran at him and threw his arms around his neck.

'Why didn't you come and see me at Grandma's?' he said. 'I was really bored.'

And so he discovered, for the first time, that he had been deprived of the little boy as much as of his mother, who offered him her cool cheek and whose light eyes were unreadable with some unexpressed emotion. All Jean could take in at that moment was that she had left Cyrille, her little guardian, behind for three days and gone off, alone, heaven knew where. This realisation cast a shadow over the joy of the reunion. They had dinner together without being able to speak, because of Cyrille. Eventually she put him to bed and came back to where Jean was waiting for her. He put his arms around her.

'No,' she said. 'Not tonight. You'll understand when I explain it to you.'

'Explain it then.'

She sighed.

'If you love me, just a little, you'll give me some time. One day it'll all become clear. For now, I don't know myself. All right … I wanted to get away, to breathe again, and then for us not to part any more.'

'It wasn't me who left you.'

'No, it wasn't you. And it wasn't me who left you either. You have to believe me.'

She smiled through her tears and kissed him on the lips, very quickly. He wanted to take her in his arms again. She stopped him.

'No. I told you: not today.'

'Then I'm going.'

He thought: for good, and he honestly believed it. She misunderstood his words.

'You're a good man. There aren't many good men. In fact I think you must be the only one and perhaps that's the reason I love you.'

'Do you love me?'

'And you're also very silly because you doubt it when I say so.'

'I don't know where I stand with you.'

'Nor me.'

He left her early and climbed back up to Montmartre on foot in the blackout. Figures loomed out of the darkness on the same pavement and stepped aside as he went past. He realised he was walking at an intimidating, brutal pace through the shadowy closed-down city. Opening the studio door, he heard a scuffle and a woman's cry. A single low lamp lit Jesús's bed, where he was lying with the girl he had sent away the evening he and Jean had had dinner.

'Sorry!' Jean said foolishly.

'Can't a man 'ave a fuck now and then!' Jesús murmured with unexpected shyness.

'I'll come back later.'

He returned just before the curfew and found Jesús alone in a dressing gown.

'I'm getting in your way,' Jean said. 'I'd better find myself a room.'

'Listen, Jean, you gettin' on my nerve. You is too little to live alone. Now tell me: what is with Claude?'

'She's here.'

'And she explain to you?'

'No. And it doesn't matter?'

'*Aïe!*'

'What?'

'You is really en lov'.'

'Do you think so?'

Jesús held out his arms and swore it was so, on the Madonna of the Begonias.

'How often does it happen in a lifetime?' Jean asked anxiously.

Jesús assured him that certain men never experienced what it felt like to be in love, and that others in contrast fell in love with every girl they met. He personally had never been like that. No feverishness or sweaty palms, ever, and as soon as his passion was satisfied, an irresistible desire to chuck the girl out. He could not remember having made love to any girl twice. He tried to remember their names, tried to recall a moment of sweetness or tenderness that they might have spontaneously shown him. He couldn't. He inspired sweetness and tenderness in them as little as they did in him. Jean commented that in that case, deep down, he was still a virgin. The Spaniard protested. He was not a virgin, he suffered from an ailment. His blood possessed an antibody that destroyed love. Jean, on the other hand, was in the grip of a virus and his love affairs made no sense to him unless they felt as if they were for ever.

'Is always the lov' of your life!' he said with a despairing expression. 'I canno' keep up with you.'

'Claude is the love of my life.'

'You is twenty years old!'

'Twenty-one.'

Jesús roared with laughter. The difference was, of course, vast. In fact it demanded celebration. They opened the magnum of champagne that Madeleine had brought. The bottle had been cooling on the window sill and they drank it from tooth mugs. Jesús's unmade bed gave off the scent of the woman who had been in it an hour before. On the bedside table lay a silk scarf she had left behind. Jean pointed at it.

'She'll be back for that tomorrow.'

'Tomorrow? No. I will no' be 'ere. You too.'

'Why?'

'We are 'avin' dinner with Mad'leine.'

'I didn't say yes.'

Jesús had said yes for him. The situation was becoming untenable.

Madeleine was deeply offended. One day or another they would need her, or to be more specific her Julius, whom it seemed everyone in Paris had fallen for. Without him, women would go naked, and the theatres and film studios close for lack of costumes. The Germans made Jesús as anxious as Fu Manchu. Yet what real reason did he have to keep out of their way? He was a Spaniard and could not give a damn whether they had won or lost a war, because it was not his war. Julius could not be as bad as all that. He did a thousand small favours, handing out travel permits, clothing coupons, fuel coupons for heating, cigarettes, liquor. At home his door was always open to fashion designers and fashionable young hairdressers, and on certain evenings, mixed up haphazardly with his suppliers, writers, poets, actors, dancers, art critics and film directors. As for Jean, the thought of going without Claude for a whole evening made him more reluctant than the bad memories he had of the Germans from his participation in the brief battle of France. He admitted as much to Jesús, who pretended to tear his hair out and called him a very sublime moron. What was he talking about? Claude disappeared in a puff of smoke for three days, and he hesitated to stand her up for a single night? If he went on that way, she'd start thinking she could behave however she liked! A man who was really and truly in love could not behave more stupidly. Jean did not know what to say.

Madeleine lived on Avenue Foch in an imposing panelled apartment whose owner, a Jew who was also a great art lover, had taken refuge in the United States as soon as the Germans had attacked. Julius kept up the same staff: two hoary manservants, two maids and a butler whom he had had freed from a POW camp to resume his old post. There were rumours that, under the guise of a requisition, the Jewish art lover and Julius had come to a working agreement: a luxury apartment in return for an assurance that the treasures on show would not be subject to any confiscation. Although he had been forewarned at length by Jesús, Jean was nonetheless dumbfounded to find Madeleine in the new role she had created. He tried to remember her the way she had looked two years earlier, standing in a peignoir on the landing of the building in Rue Lepic, taking refuge with him and Chantal one morning when Jesús had nearly set fire to his apartment, and again in 1939 when she had played the ambiguous part of Madame Miranda at Cannes, a little more polished than before but still retaining some of the gestures of the humble streetwalker she had once been. Refusing to colour her hair, she had a fine head of grey hair that softened her tired-looking expression. The make-up artist's skills had turned a previously vulgar mouth into a worldly pout and smoothed the first signs of crow's feet. Palfy's lessons had borne fruit: the suburban accent had gone along with most of her mispronunciations. In short, to all intents and purposes – though she still did not know who was who – she could be mistaken for a woman of the world, even in the rare letters she wrote, in which there were so many spelling mistakes that nobody believed they were not deliberate. As time went on Palfy, who was a bit fogeyish about such things, urged her to give up writing altogether, and she, more than happy, concurred.

'I thought you were avoiding me,' she said, kissing Jean. 'And why haven't you brought your divine lady friend?'

'Divine' was a word much in vogue, which the fashionable young hairdressers with whom she spent a couple of hours every day in order not to look as if she had been to the hairdresser – oh subtle accomplishment of long toil! – used to describe the least of their amazements.

'She's not divine,' he answered. 'She's just a woman with a little boy she can't leave on his own in the evenings.'

He tried not to feel he had been right to hesitate to come and allowed himself to be led towards a group surrounding a bald, plump man with a scarred cheek. Julius Kapermeister had none of the cold, condescending distinction of a Rudolf von Rocroy. The son of a solid line of Dortmund industrialists, he certainly possessed a more than modest opinion of himself, but concealed it beneath an unctuousness that was excessive, particularly if you knew the extent of his official functions – and even later, when you learnt what their objective was. Unused to Germans, Jean had a feeling of unease he found hard to shrug off. Julius spoke precise, heavily accented French, but we shall spare the reader a phonetic transcription of his words. One is enough, and Jesús will for ever chew his French into a sort of pidgin, while Julius had already made considerable progress in less than a year and could express himself relatively fluently in correct French.

'So here you are, Jean Arnaud!' he said with affected surprise. 'I've heard so much about you from Madeleine, yet never seen you. I was beginning to think you were refusing to meet us! There are one or two French who, it must be said, are rather stubborn – though in one sense I forgive them – they're reluctant to understand …'

Taking Jean by the arm, he steered him to a sideboard covered in bottles of champagne, whisky and vodka. The dozen or so other guests present looked at Jean with mingled curiosity and envy. Who was the badly dressed but rather good-looking young Frenchman whom Julius was favouring with a private word?

'What will you have?' Julius asked.

Jean chose a glass of champagne and Julius served him. A white-gloved servant passed around trays of sandwiches and *petits fours* that had survived the guests' first famished rush. Jean refused.

'Ah, I see, you're the sporting type!' Julius exclaimed, clasping his biceps with a firm hand. 'Which sport?'

'I sell pictures!'

The German laughed loudly.

'I know, I know! A very good profession at the present time. The Germans have brought metaphysics, history and music. The French are teaching us taste, good taste, art! And *cuisine*. *Cuisine*, Monsieur Arnaud, is the gift of the gods. Have you read *Is God French?* by our great Friedrich Sieburg?'

'No,' Jean said. 'And I'd be fairly likely to answer the question in the negative.'

'You mean you think God is not French?'

'If God exists He must have slipped away for a bit, and it seems to me He doesn't have a lot of time for us French.'

'Come, come, come,' Julius said, wrinkling his pink brow. 'Do you mean the French lost a war they started because God wasn't on their side but riding on our tanks instead? I suppose it's possible. We must talk about it again. It looks to me as if our friend Jesús is looking for you. Such an extraordinary young man and so profoundly original, yet he's lost the moment he sets foot outside his den. A very shy lion. I say, who is that impressive person following Constantin Palfy? I don't know her.'

'Madame Michette, Marceline Michette. Her husband's a prisoner of war. A former infantry sergeant-major, who re-enlisted in 1939.'

'I see, I see ... We must look into that. And what did Monsieur Michette do in civilian life?'

Jean looked squarely at Julius, to see whether he would raise an eyebrow.

'The Michettes run a well-known brothel at Clermont-Ferrand. Perhaps the best in the Auvergne. If the Michelin Guide was fair, it would give them three stars. Excellent appearance and morals, perfect service ...'

'What a remarkably interesting person! I suppose she has many political friends ...'

'Not many, I don't think... local officials perhaps ...'

'You may be forgetting that the capital of France has moved. It's no longer Paris but Vichy, and from Vichy to Clermont is a mere stone's throw. And what is she doing in Paris?'

'You'll need to ask Constantin.'

Julius moved towards the singular couple, whom Madeleine had already greeted, and Jean found himself on his own next to a servant who was passing round caviar on squares of toast. He took one and the servant asked, 'Monsieur is only taking one?'

'Is it rude?'

'Oh no, Monsieur, but it's not what people usually do here.'

A young woman with very white skin and very dark eyes walked over to him. He knew the face and tried and failed to put a name to it. The woman smiled at him and picked up a bottle of whisky, half filling her glass. It was not him she had wanted to meet; she had just been on her way to the sideboard. She did not look embarrassed to be seen filling her glass, and as Jean made a vague gesture she stopped.

'Have we met somewhere?'

'I have a feeling we have,' he said.

'I don't.'

'I must be wrong, then.'

'I wouldn't lose any sleep over it,' she said, almost rudely. 'You don't know me but you've seen me. Somewhere. In a film.'

'It's a long time since I've been to the cinema.'

She shrugged and turned away. He was alone for a moment and stood watching the guests. Apart from Jesús, Palfy and Madame Michette he knew no one. At a similar occasion in London he would have been able to put names to at least two or three of the faces. Stendhal would have considered it a desperate situation for one of his heroes, greedy to experience the world. What would Julien Sorel have done in his position? He would have had an advantage over Jean, dressed in the black of a future cleric, attracting people's attention by his combination of good looks, outward reserve, and aggressive conversation. But aggression did not come naturally to Jean. The only way he might be provoked into it, he reflected, was if he started thinking about Claude, the evening he was missing with her, and what she would perhaps have started to confess to him if he had not given in to Jesús's entreaties. Not that Jesús craved the high life. He wanted to please Madeleine but had refused to go so far as conforming to the conventions of a formal dinner, arriving in his usual suit of heavy corduroy, tieless, shirt open, revealing his thick, curly chest hair and contempt for social niceties, a contempt that might easily have turned him into the hostesses' darling, had he had any leanings towards a social life beyond Rue Lepic.

Madame Michette, abandoned by Palfy, seemed at a loss. Everything was new here: the apartment's luxury, its *objets d'art*, pictures and furniture (she had just run a finger over the marble top of a console table to see whether it had been dusted recently), the servants whose like she had not seen outside the pages of the sagas she read, and the host, a man so powerful that all Paris was queuing up for his invitations. She had had to admire the fact that within a day of her arrival Palfy, apparently waving a magic wand, had led her to this holy of holies at which – supreme revelation – she had simultaneously discovered Madeleine introducing their mutual friend with the title of baron. Why had he not told her? She felt guilty at having sometimes been sharp with him, at having doubted his social standing. Might Jean not be an aristocrat too in that case, despite being less well-dressed and looking profoundly bored? Madame Michette pounced on him.

'I didn't recognise you straight away,' she exclaimed. 'Although Monsieur Michette is always telling me I'm a *physiognomist*. You need that with customers, otherwise you can find people trying it on. *Machosists* for example. I've spotted one or two of those in my time.'

Jean protested that he was not a masochist. Madame Michette exclaimed that he was being very perverse; she hadn't suspected him of it for a minute. It was just a comparison. She picked up a vol-au-vent and popped it between her plump lips, lightly shadowed by a moustache.

'It's just like before the war!' she winked.

He waited for her to add, 'and that's something of ours the Boches will never have', but she was distracted by having to wipe her thumb and index finger, which she had dipped in the sauce.

'I hear that Monsieur Michette—'

She winked again and jerked her chin in the direction of Julius Kapermeister, talking to the film actress, who by now was looking extremely tipsy.

'Yes. Let's hope he succeeds,' Jean added.

'He can do anything. He got us our *Ausvesses*.'

What fantastic, mad scheme was brewing in Palfy's mind? What use was he intending to make of this person, straight from a Maupassant story and more real and larger than life than any caricature? It was quite unlike his usual modus operandi not to school her beforehand for some role in his Parisian ambitions; instead, within hours of arriving, he had thrown her into a milieu that, though not quite possessing the refinement she imagined it to have, was far above the world ruled by a provincial madam, whatever her superiority in her field. The reason was – as Jean quickly realised – that whilst Madeleine had been malleable, Madame Michette would always remain exactly what she was. Her turn of phrase, her colourful mispronunciations, the way she dressed, even her moral sense, not to mention her avowed profession, would fast make a Parisian character of her. When Jean finally managed to speak to Palfy his friend's face lit up.

'Is she not sublime? And you don't know the half of her! She's got ideas about everything. And devoted! You'll have to see it. To get rid of her yesterday, I sent her on a secret mission. She got on the 6 a.m. train to Vernon and from there took a wood-gas bus to Les Andelys, making sure she wasn't being followed. From Les Andelys she carried on in the pouring rain, on foot, as far as Château-Gaillard. What a landscape! Do you know it?'

'No. Then what?'

'Inside the outer wall, having made sure she was alone, she collected three flat stones, placed them one on top of the other, and slipped a note I'd written in code between stones one and two. Child's play, obviously. Afterwards she had to get to Rouen. She stopped a truck full of Jerusalem artichokes, and as there were already five people in the driver's cab she climbed up and sat on the artichokes. At Rouen she went to the main post office where she delivered a sealed letter to a PO box number I'd given her, 109. She was back in Paris that evening, happier than you can possibly imagine. She longs to *serve*! She shall be served.'

'Is it indiscreet to ask whose PO box it was and what was in the letter?'

'Not a bit, dear boy. I haven't the faintest idea who the PO box belongs to, and in the envelope I put a piece of paper on which I simply wrote, "I'm a silly cow."'

Jean spluttered with laughter just as the butler announced, 'Madame is served.'

'You see,' Palfy murmured, 'everyone is served.'

Cards with the guests' names had been laid at each place. On his right Julius had a bloodless-looking woman with a stare like a fish in aspic, on his left Madame Michette. Madeleine placed Palfy on her right. Was he not a baron, the evening's only aristocrat? On her left sat a Frenchman, the husband of the woman with the fish-eyed stare, who, furious at seeing Palfy chosen over him, swallowed his first glass of Graves in a single gulp to get over his humiliation. Jean found himself at the end of the table between the film actress, whose name he finally discovered – Nelly Tristan – and a frail-looking young woman who spoke French with a strong German accent and whose place card read 'Fräulein Laura Bruckett'. He tried to avoid looking at Madame Michette who, quite at her ease, cut herself a thick slice of *foie gras* and kept the silver knife instead of putting it back in the ewer of hot water. At a sign from the host a servant brought another knife and went round the table. Madame Michette had already finished her *foie gras* before the men were served. Julius, with a nod, had the plate brought back to her, and she cut herself another slice.

'What an appetite that woman's got!' Nelly Tristan said to Jean.

'It's not very surprising. Yesterday she had a long trip on a pile of Jerusalem artichokes.'

'Why? Does she sell them?'

'No, she loves travelling.'

Nelly tasted the *foie gras*.

'Not too horrid.'

Julius declared that even if the entire German army were not celebrating New Year with *foie gras* in a few days' time, there would nevertheless be cause for festivities along the new frontiers. Only England was now plunged into the throes of war, at the insistence of that lunatic, Churchill. But Germany's hand was still extended. No one could conceive of a new Europe without the participation of Great Britain, once she had got rid of the bloodthirsty puppets who dominated her politics ... A small man, with a black moustache that detracted slightly from his resemblance to a baby-faced intellectual, agreed with unexpected vehemence. The red and yellow ribbons of the Légion d'Honneur and the Médaille Militaire, a little too obvious in his buttonhole, attested to his past. It did not stop him finding Julius Kapermeister more than a little timid. What were the Germans waiting for? The minute the English saw the first German land on their soil, they'd be on their knees. For six centuries England had been playing the European nations off against each other like pawns and compromising all efforts at peace. Was it not England that had declared war on Germany on 3 September? Yes, there she was, the first! Dragging France in six hours later. England really was the mangy dog of Europe ...

Madeleine spoke.

'It's Julius's fault. He started it. We promised we wouldn't talk politics. We've got a thousand more interesting things to say to each other.'

'Madeleine's very strict,' Julius said. 'She's interested in everything bar politics. She'd like us all to be like her. It's not easy, you have to admit.'

The small man with the moustache, whose name was Oscar Dulonjé, conceded that politics was not women's business.

'What a prick!' Nelly Tristan murmured in Jean's ear. 'Who is he?'

Had Monsieur Dulonjé heard her? He appeared disconcerted and hesitant. He decided to ignore the interruption and Madeleine, keen to salvage the situation, turned to Nelly.

'My dear Nelly, when are you starting filming?'

'Tomorrow morning. But if I carry on the way I'm going, there's a very good chance I may be a teeny bit late at the studio.'

She emptied her whisky glass and then her white wine, and shot the table a charming and innocent smile. Jesús put his fork down noisily.

'I em never goin' to get used to *foie gras*. All this French food is killin' me. Before the war I live' on peanuts. Is much more 'ealthy.'

'Peanuts?' Julius said. 'We must be able to find those. Laura, will you make a note?'

Fräulein Bruckett said timidly, 'I'm afraid it may be impossible.'

Julius came to her rescue.

'If Laura says it is impossible, she knows better than anyone. She's a secretary at the Department of Supply. A pity, my dear Jesús, you will have to wait for the war to be over before you can stop being forced to eat *foie gras*.'

'I haven' anysing agains' the *foie gras*. Is quite pretty on a plate with this little black truffle and the nice white border.'

'You have to be an artist to notice that sort of thing,' Madeleine said.

The husband of the woman with the fish-eyed stare decided it was time to speak.

'Monsieur is a painter? I didn't catch your name.'

'Rhesús! Rhesús Infante!'

'He means Jesús, of course,' Palfy added, his eyes sparkling with pleasure at so much stupidity spread out before him.

'No one is allowed to call himself Jesús!' Madame Michette said indignantly. 'It is … blasphemous.'

'No' allowed! No' allowed!' Jesús shouted, choking.

Jean saw Madeleine looking desperate. Her dinner was going downhill. He rushed to her rescue.

'Madame Michette means that in the Auvergne it's not customary. No one would call their son Jesús. Not even a bishop. But in Spain, and especially in Andalusia, Jesús is a familiar … presence, someone people talk to every day, to praise him, to curse him or pray to him. Is that right, Jesús?'

'Is true.'

Nelly Tristan leant towards Jean a second time and whispered, 'Don't you find a woman who's drunk disgusting?'

A servant was circulating constantly, a bottle in his hand, each time filling up her glass, which, as soon as it was full, she emptied. She was looking paler and paler. Her gaze shimmered with a general, directionless tenderness.

'No,' Jean said quietly.

'I'm not talking about going to bed, I mean in a general way.'

These private exchanges were arousing the disquiet of a fat, fortyish man in a loud tie seated at the far end of the table. He was unable to hear Nelly's words but appeared anxious to avoid the scene he felt was on the point of erupting. It came as a visible relief to him when Nelly stood up, pushed back her chair and, addressing Madeleine in an affected voice, said, 'Where's the little girls' room, darling?'

The fortyish man stood up too and asked Madeleine to excuse him.

'I'll show her.'

'As you like.'

He took Nelly's arm and they left the dining room.

'You know she's amazingly talented!' Madeleine said.

'She is,' Julius said, 'and also very lucky to have a producer like Émile Duzan. He's like a father to all his stars.'

'All the same,' Palfy said, 'I rather think there's an age when daddies stop taking their little girls to the toilet, and she's past it.'

'Very unhealthy curiosity, I call it!' Madame Michette said. 'Now my girls …'

She stopped and looked at Palfy, who smiled back with perfect sweetness, inviting her to go on.

'You have many girls?' Julius asked.

'Quite a few!' Madame Michette said, embarrassed.

'I'm sure they're ravishing!' Oscar Dulonjé said unpleasantly.

'That's not for me to say!' Madame Michette simpered. 'All I can tell you is that they're well brought up …'

The servants changed the plates and the butler carved a joint of roast beef whose arrival monopolised the guests' attention for some time. A young man with a ferret-like profile who had been silent before grasped the opportunity to say a few words.

'Did you know that the Schillertheater is coming to Paris next month? The French will finally have a chance to get to know Schiller.'

'Indeed,' Julius said, 'that's no bad thing. Schiller's a European writer whose reputation has suffered – though no longer – from the disharmony between France and Germany. Alas, I hear they're putting on *Kabale und Liebe*,[12] which is far from being one of his best plays. Franco-German relations deserve a little more care.'

Madame Michette helped herself shamelessly to three slices of roast beef, a liberty she would never have allowed herself at Zizi's table, but in all this warmth and luxury and feeling of being with the right people she was losing her sense of proportion.

'In return,' the young man said, 'you should do Claudel. Apparently he's very good in German …'

'I've never read Claudel,' Julius said, 'but I hear a lot of talk about him. He was a director of Gnome and Rhône,[13] which is working for our new Europe now, and a distinguished ambassador. The Comédie Française has a project it wants my help with. A very large number of costumes. In these times of restriction it's not easy to lay one's hands on the necessary fabric, but we'll do our best. I think the play's called *The Satin Slipper* …'

Nelly Tristan had just come back into the room with her producer, smiling happily, and pounced on the play's name.

'*The Satin Slipper!* It's gorgeous. I've read it – it must be at least ten hours long. I love Claudel. I recited his ode to Marshal Pétain for schoolchildren. Everyone cried. And there was a prayer that reminded me I was one of Mary's children …'

Suddenly there occurred a miraculous moment, which captivated all the dinner guests as Nelly, whom they hardly knew and whom they looked down on with the bourgeois disdain proper towards actresses and kept women – and Nelly was both – as Nelly lowered her voice and in a tone of unexpected and pure emotion recited Claudel's very beautiful prayer:

> *'I see the open church, and must go in. It's midday.*
> *Mother of Jesus, I haven't come to pray.*
> *I've nothing to ask of you, nothing to say.*
> *I've come here, Mother, just to look at you, and not look away*
> …'

Nelly hiccuped and frowned.

'Shit! I can't remember the rest, but it's really lovely. By the end I was crying too. It's good that I've forgotten it, really, isn't it? What's this? Roast. Madeleine darling, we do stuff ourselves with you. I adore you, and Julius too. You know, if you and Julius weren't having this big thing together, I'd be your girlfriend just like that …'

Émile Duzan was squirming on his chair, pink and embarrassed.

'Listen, Nelly, just stop drinking, will you?'

'Poor love, I'm making him uncomfortable. He's such a sensitive flower.'

'I like it when people are honest!' Madame Michette said.

'I'm flattered!' Julius declared.

'Me too!' Madeleine added.

'Can I have the mustard?' the woman with the fish-eyed stare asked.

They gave her her mustard and she said no more for the rest of the evening, except as she was leaving, when she said goodbye and thank you in a tight-lipped way. The remaining guests wondered why she had been invited, and if she had even been aware of being at dinner with other people, whose wandering conversation never actually appeared to reach her, even when her husband raised his voice to say, 'My wife and I ...' The rest of the dinner passed off in the same way. Jesús had a spat with the ferret-faced young man when he expressed his scorn for modern painting, and Oscar Dulonjé and Émile Duzan discovered with equal emotion that both had joined the same political party on the same day, the party whose great objective was France's entry into Hitler's united Europe.

In the drawing room, where they returned after dinner, Palfy elaborated an interesting theory concerning the curfew and the rise in the birth rate, despite two million men being confined in stalags and oflags. Julius became embarrassed and attempted to change the subject several times; Palfy took no notice. Jean was probably the only guest to discern, behind his friend's salacious speculations, the ironic and mischievous sense of humour he had cultivated in England during his brief period of splendour. As the hours went by Madame Michette became redder and redder, victim to the high blood pressure she suffered from every time she mixed white wine, claret, champagne and Alsatian cherry brandy. But that was what people had come for: to drink and eat and turn their back on daily hardships. They had drunk and they had eaten. Now their fear of missing the second-to-last Métro and the last connection was beginning to be all-pervasive; Nelly, who, having sobered up once, was well on the way to getting drunk again, provided the last event of the evening. She snagged her stocking, and it ran. Madeleine immediately brought her a new pair and, beneath the concupiscent gaze of the male guests, she hitched up her skirt and changed them. There was a glimpse of frothy white lace knickers, of the sort worn by French cancan dancers.

'They're a present from Émile!' she said. 'He likes them. It's a fixation of his. There are worse ones.'

She had good legs. Oscar Dulonjé, forgetting politics for a moment, confessed that he found them 'very shapely'.

'Shapely?' Nelly replied. 'I trust your willy's just as shapely, in that case.'

Émile Duzan coughed until he choked. Dulonjé blushed. Jesús had got to his feet, and people noticed that Fräulein Laura Bruckett, who had stayed in the background for most of the evening, had succeeded in attracting enough of his attention to have a fair chance of spending the night with him. Regulations forbade her gaze to linger on a Frenchman. As a Spaniard, Jesús had neutral status. Julius took Jean aside for a moment in the hall.

'We must meet again. I'm sure you're getting bored in that gallery of yours. And this La Garenne is a disreputable character. You're a young man with a future. Europe needs new men. Your friend Palfy interests me a great deal.'

'I'm not bored at the gallery,' Jean said. 'It's a good place while I wait—'

'Ah, you waiters! There's a choice to be made. The workers who turn up at the eleventh hour won't be the most welcome.'

After Julius, it was Madeleine's turn to pull Jean into her bedroom. She had got a parcel ready for him, wrapped in pretty paper and tied with a gold ribbon.

'You told me she has a little boy, didn't you?'

'Yes.'

'How old is he?'

'Four.'

'They're still sweet at that age. He must be going without a lot of things. I thought you could put this underneath his Christmas tree.'

Jean kissed Madeleine, who suddenly had tears in her eyes.

'You can count on me,' she said. 'But I understand you're reluctant … Julius is very good, very generous. He likes the French.'

Madeleine, once so suspicious, had discovered a world of good intentions.

'I don't doubt it. How does he know so many things about me, about all of us?'

'Yes, it's strange. He knows everything.'

They went back to the others, who were wrapping themselves in furs and scarves to face the freezing December night. A bicycle-taxi was waiting for Nelly and her producer. They separated at the Étoile: Palfy and Madame Michette were staying at a hotel in Avenue Victor-Hugo, Jesús, Jean and Laura got into the second-to-last carriage of the Métro.

Just before Concorde Jean said, 'I'll carry on to Châtelet. See you in the morning.'

'You don' 'ave to.'

But Jesús did not protest and got off, holding Laura's arm.

The lights were out on Quai Saint-Michel. The concierge let him in after a peremptory 'Who is it? Where are you going?' Jean rang Claude's bell and she opened the door, clutching the collar of a quilted dressing gown to her throat.

'I'd given up waiting for you,' she said.

He bent forward and kissed her cheek.

'You're freezing. I can't light a fire, I haven't got any more wood. Cyrille is sleeping with two jumpers. Do you want to sleep here?'

'Yes.'

'I've only got one spare blanket.'

'It doesn't matter.'

He sat on the couch that had given him so many sleepless nights, listening to the city's sounds, peering through the shutters for the dawn that would awaken a slumbering Paris.

'Why didn't you come?'

'I was invited to dinner. Madeleine gave me this parcel to go under Cyrille's Christmas tree.'

Claude sighed.

'I felt so badly about not having anything to give him. Who is this good fairy?'

'She's not a fairy.'

Claude sat down next to him. He put his arms around her, squeezing her with a strength that made her anxious.

'We mustn't leave each other any more,' he said.

'No. Not even for an evening.'

'Not even for an evening.'

Claude shivered. Jean picked up the blanket and they wrapped it around themselves, huddled against each other. Just before drowsiness overcame them, Claude murmured, 'You have nothing to fear from me.'

'I hope so.'

Cyrille woke them at the crack of dawn.

'Jean, Jean. Don't you even take your coat off to sleep with Maman?'

How we would love to follow Madame Michette on one of her top-secret missions, and see her employing the most varied methods of propulsion to travel the highways and byways of occupied France! Never will she remind us more strongly of Madame Belazor, paramour of Pancrace Eusèbe Zéphyrin Brioché, alias Cosinus the scientist.[14] Palfy himself, like the scientist, does not leave Paris. From his hotel room in Avenue Victor-Hugo he directs his agent's escapades, while she is driven on by the sheer force of her romantic folly. But the pursuit of Madame Michette would soon leave us breathless, and divert us too from our subject: the unconsummated, yet so perfect love that binds Jean Arnaud to Claude Chaminadze. All the reader need know, then, is that Madame Michette's zeal will not falter and that Julius Kapermeister has promised that, by February or March 1941 at the latest, Sergeant-Major Michette is to be released and leave his camp in a contingent of fathers of large families. Does he not have eight industrious girls waiting at home in Clermont-Ferrand? The alert reader will naturally have asked themselves another question: who does Madame Michette think she is working for? She does not know. A secret within a secret makes an endless hall of mirrors, in which Madame Michette only sees her own face repeated in ever diminishing reflections. When she seeks reassurance, Palfy demurs: the golden rule of counterespionage is that agents are acted on, not acting. He assures her that her missions will remain without risk so long as she speaks to no one about them, and that, at present, it is vital for her to stay in training before more serious operations. Despite the suspicion in which female agents are held – 'their flesh is weak,' Palfy notes mirthlessly – she is already held in high regard by his superiors. From books purchased at second-hand booksellers' on the banks of the Seine, she learns the basics of operational work. Hers is an exhilarating adventure. Let us allow it to take its course without exposing Palfy's intentions too soon. Does he himself know what they are? In all honesty, now he is just having fun, yet with the impressive instinct that has guided him so well in his exploitation of human foolishness he strongly suspects that Madame Michette may one day be genuinely useful to his ambitions. We shall see his suspicion proved right. Meanwhile he has concluded that there is nothing to be gained from a man like La Garenne, a second-division fraud and insatiable overeater, a slob taking advantage of the times but already behind them. True, the gallery's turnover is continuing to rise, but it is really nothing to do with Louis-Edmond. Let us be honest and admit that Palfy is right: La Garenne has been overtaken, failing to realise that, by dint of his greed and ever-present meanness, he has become dependent on Blanche de Rocroy (whose cousin Rudolf has reappeared, wanting to get hold of some Braques and Derains), and dependent too on Jean, without whom Jesús would refuse to paint either his erotic nudes or the forgeries from which the fat man is piling up a fortune. Ever impatient, from time to time La Garenne buys a fine picture from Jesús at a price that seems madness to him, and one day will turn out to have been absurdly low. The canvas joins the others in a cupboard whose contents no one will think to examine until the war is over and peace has been declared.

Yet a little light has also been shed on the mystery of La Garenne. Blanche, sweeping up and dusting before the gallery opens, selling unspeakably bad pictures with rare refinement, ironing her employer's trousers and from time to time providing him with oral relief, also deals with the book-keeping and tax returns. Thanks to a document left lying on the table, Jean has learnt that the gallery in fact belongs to a woman named Mercedes del Loreto, of no known profession, living in Rue de la Gaîté, in Paris's 16th arrondissement. We should say straight away that at first the name meant nothing to him. He thought it sounded attractive and romantic. But Palfy, whose knowledge, at least in this particular cultural sphere, was vast, was startled by the news.

· 'What? She's still alive! She must be a hundred if she's a day. Everyone thinks she's dead. She wasn't exactly a spring chicken when Edward VII had his way with her, just after Félix Faure. Don't you realise? Mercedes del Loreto is a truly historic figure! Historic!'

She had modelled for Toulouse-Lautrec (Albi museum still had his portrait of her) and been both high-class courtesan and variously lover and fleeting mistress to a wide circle of rich men. If she owned an art gallery, it raised questions. Palfy set Madame Michette on the trail. Staking out Rue de la Gaîté, she soon discovered La Garenne's hideout, the den to which he disappeared at night and certain hours of the day: an apartment under the rafters, opposite the Bobino music hall. Allow me to romanticise Madame Michette's somewhat dry reports a little, while not failing to do justice to their key points.

A dark and sticky staircase filled with choice odours from the toilets on each floor led to the top landing and a single door fitted with security locks. There was not even a concierge to provide the smallest titbit of gossip! The postman left the mail in zinc letterboxes. One of these bore, handwritten, the grandiose name of Mercedes del Loreto. After two days of watching, Madame Michette had initiated a conversation with a little old lady stepping downstairs with her shopping bag in one hand and a cigarette between her lips, her face whitened with powder and grey hair curled with tongs.

'Ah, Mercedes del Loreto!' the old lady had said. 'Of course I know her. It must be fifteen years since I saw her in the building. But she's still up there, still with us. Only yesterday I heard her shrieking. As if there was a sea lion up there ... You know' – she waved her arms and blew out her cheeks – '*arrh, arrh ... oowowoowow* ... What would you say to a quick glass of white at the *tabac* on the corner? You wouldn't have a cigarette, would you? A proper one! I say, things are looking up. Oh, they're German. You won't find the black market flooded with those. The Fritzes keep an eye on things. Plays by the rules, their army.'

They walked to the nearest bistro and stood at the counter.

'Two medium-dry whites, Amédée. Anjou, please.'

The barman raised his eyebrows.

'Madame Berthe, I don't know if you've noticed ... there's a war on. Shortages. Anjou is hard to get hold of.'

'Oh, do stop pretending. Get the bottle out. She's a friend.'

The Anjou appeared. Madame Berthe sipped and clucked with her tongue.

'She moved in in 1920. I know because I was a *diseuse* at the Bobino then. Did you see me?'

'No,' Madame Michette said, 'I wasn't living in Paris. You can't be everywhere.'

'I quit in 1925. Went to Gaston Baty. Do you know him?'

'Gaston who?'

'Baty. Théâtre Montparnasse, you know.'

'And you're a *diseuse*?' Madame Michette repeated worriedly, a provincial who had no idea what a *diseuse* was.

'No, I'm a dresser now. Marguerite Jamois, I dressed her. I did. Oh, there were plenty of actors who couldn't do without me: Lucien Nat, Georges Vitray. There wasn't a button out of place in *Maya*, in *Simoom*, in *The Shadow of Evil*. That was great theatre, Madame. What's your name?'

'Marceline, Marceline Michette.'

'If you told me you were from the Auvergne it wouldn't surprise me.'

'I am.'

'Like him. Monsieur Baty's from Pélussin. Do you know it?'

'No, I'm more from Montaigut-le-Blanc.'

'Don't know it. Anyway, it can't be far. What do you want from old Mercedes?'

'It's for a newspaper.'

'Journalists, I'm used to them. Always hanging round me, waiting for gossip. I suppose everyone's got to live.'

Madame Michette ignored the jibe. What would this stupid old woman have said if she had found out she was talking to a secret agent?

'Mercedes has paid the price for her adventures. Hasn't gone out since 1925. In the beginning you'd hear her walking on her peg leg: knock, knock, knock ... Just like Sarah Bernhardt. She was at Saint-Gervais when Bertha sent over one of her big ones.[15] Bang ... no more leg. A terrible thing for a lady who liked to lead the men a merry dance,' she giggled, knocking back her white wine, 'and then she took to her bed. Been there for fifteen years. There's a chap who lives with her. Some say he's her last husband, others that he's her son. As disreputable as they come, I can tell you. One evening I found him pissing on the stairs; it was running all the way down. He looked very sheepish. Don't say anything, don't say a word, he begged me. He was afraid I'd tell the old girl, his old girl ... I don't know. He goes up to feed her every night and every lunchtime, and if he's late she starts shrieking: *arrh, arrh ... oowowoowow ...*'

The barman, washing glasses behind the counter, grinned.

'All right, Madame Berthe, still doing your impressions?'

'My dear Amédée,' the dresser said, 'you're such a peasant. I'm not doing an impression. I am Mercedes del Loreto; I do her better than she does. By the way, your wine is watered down.'

She had drunk her half-glass in a single gulp. Madame Michette bought her another. At the end of each mission she provided Palfy with a list of her expenses, which he signed and passed on to higher quarters. When peace was declared she would be reimbursed.

'They haven't got any facilities up there,' Madame Berthe went on, 'so he empties the chamber pots. He does it very discreetly, but I've seen him. He's devoted to her. He's not a bad lad, deep down. People aren't all good or all bad, generally. There's degrees. What did you say your paper's name was?'

'It's published in the unoccupied zone.'

'Oh, down in the free! Some folk think they're clever, but it's six of one and half a dozen of the other wherever you go. We're free here too. We're chatting, aren't we?'

'We are,' Madame Michette said.

'So that Mercedes del Loreto, she had a fine old time, I'll say. Bankers and princes. All right, fine ... but in the end we're all the same ... same pussy, up and down, not side to side ... even the Chinese. Then one day a wooden overcoat ... That chap who lives with the old girl, there's one or two who knew him around here. Before the war – I mean the 14–18, not the last one; that was a joke. Yes, he used to hang around the cafés at Montparnasse. Did caricatures. Went from table to table with a sketch pad and pencil. Portrait? he'd say. People let him get on with it. They called him Léonard Twenty-Sous. That's all I know.'

So La Garenne ceased to be a mystery. He was Mercedes del Loreto's son, and at one time in his life had felt he was an artist. All that was left of his ambition was the way he dressed and an unrelenting meanness from his hungry years. Jean told Jesús. He was unexpectedly moved. La Garenne a failure? The old shit had at last won his sympathy. Jesús vowed not to insult him quite so coarsely in future. Palfy also appeared to be touched.

'The thought of him emptying his mother's chamber pots makes me want to cry. I wouldn't have done as much for mine. Let's leave him to his little rackets. He'll never hit the big time. But you, my dear Jean, it's about time you stood on your own two feet. In the space of a few months you've learnt most of the tricks of the most crooked trade in Paris. You should open a gallery.'

'What with? I don't have a sou.'

'Our dear Marceline will provide for you. She's from the Auvergne. A saver.'

'Precisely. She's from the Auvergne, so she's not stupid.'

'To do her duty as a patriot she'd happily hand over every franc. I'll take care of it.'

In barely two months Palfy had gathered together what he continued to call the best capital there was: contacts. Almost nightly his place was laid at Avenue Foch, in an apartment that had become one of the most sought-after destinations in Paris. Soon after midday he was to be found at Maxim's or Lapérouse's or in one of those bistros at Les Halles whose doors were only opened to a select few. Paris could no longer do without Julius and Madeleine, and they could no longer do without Palfy. Thanks to Julius, the theatres effortlessly managed to get hold of the cloth and materials they needed for their costumes and sets, which, with unconscious competitiveness, had never seemed quite so sumptuous. Stagehands, judged to be indispensable for the resumption of the economic life of the country, were released from their POW camps. Sergeant-Major Michette was freed as promised. His brief period of captivity had transformed him. Glimpsed as he passed through Paris, he was greatly slimmed down; like Samson losing his hair, in losing his paunch he had lost his authority. Madame Michette was pitiless: she kept him for a few days, then sent him back to Clermont-Ferrand alone to look after the running of the Sirène. She had no use for a clod like her husband in the giddy exhilaration of her Parisian existence and her secret missions. He belonged to another epoch, a bygone era. She explained the situation to Palfy.

'I can't concentrate with him here. He's only interested in himself. He's like a horse with blinkers on, he only sees what's in front of him.'

Hadn't she read in a work describing espionage for the general public that a spy must be asexual? The truth was that, being very used to the sight of human unhappiness and its several forms of relief in her 'establishment', she felt repugnance for the practical matters to which Monsieur Michette attempted to draw her back after his extended state of celibacy. She intended to remain chaste, convinced that in 'high places' close attention was being paid to her slightest actions prior to her selection for her great mission. The rigorous morals she had imposed on the girls at the Sirène, the attention she paid to their futures when they grew too old, matched a need in her to be respected for the work she did. Hadn't she dismissed two girls who had confessed to falling in love, one with a soldier, the other – worse still – with a town councillor who was a freemason?

Through the offices of Blanche de Rocroy, Palfy had befriended Colonel von Rocroy in the course of mutually flaunting an exchange of entries from the *Almanach de Gotha*. In the belief that he had found someone from 'his own world' Rudolf had explained his Paris mission: to protect works of art abandoned by their owners when they had fled abroad. A mission to be performed quite disinterestedly by the Great Reich, which desired to maintain order in the new Europe, plus a redistribution of its riches among those who deserved them. Hadn't Napoleon (who remained one of Hitler's historical role models) acted very similarly in the creation of his own Europe? Rocroy had been put in charge of a depository at Boulogne-Billancourt where paintings and furniture were stored. He also happened occasionally to buy the odd contemporary master for himself and a few close friends, excellent investments at the exchange rate fixed by the victorious power.

Yet again Jean's eyes were opened by Palfy. He was gradually becoming less easy to surprise, now seeing La Garenne's small-scale frauds as amusing trifles in comparison with the rackets of Rocroy and Kapermeister. The difference lay in their manner. Léonard Twenty-Sous would never have their style, despite his mother welcoming princes to her bed. The deep disgust that sometimes overcame Jean might have pushed him to an extreme solution if he had not had Claude and the few hours they spent together at Quai Saint-Michel and occasional nights when he slept on her narrow couch. Since the night they had spent wrapped in each other's arms, shivering and sad, not daring to take their caresses further, a new intimacy had grown up between them. He had accepted that she could not tell him a secret that was not hers to share, and took what she offered him with a sincerity that was completely genuine. Despite feeling sad, even gloomy sometimes, he asked for nothing more. Jogging back to Montmartre alone at night or daybreak, trying to stay fit, he felt rocks of despair falling on his heart and crushing it. Then, a few hours later, he felt Claude's hand on his face, stroking his cheek, and heard the voice he loved most in the world say to him with a sweetness that instantly revived him, 'No other man would put up with what you put up with. I feel ashamed. Will you forgive me?'

'What for? I come here and I breathe fresh air. I'm not giving up. The truth is, I've never been so happy, and I've been a lot more unhappy.'

The apartment was no longer heated. Claude had installed a stove in the sitting-room fireplace, and with Cyrille she scoured the banks of the river and the Luxembourg Gardens for kindling. Jean arrived with logs Jesús had given him, himself generously supplied by the daughter of a coal merchant in Rue Caulaincourt. They ate dinner in front of the roaring stove and Cyrille fell asleep between them on the couch. Claude scooped him up in her arms and carried him to the double bed where she covered him up to his chin so that only his blond curls, his eyelids with their long, heavy lashes, and his nose, pink with cold in the morning, were visible.

'I can never sleep on my own again,' she said. 'He's my little man. Almost not my son. Since he started talking I don't need to go to the cinema or theatre any more – he acts for me all day long – or open a book, because I feel I'm writing one with him in his head, with the names of the trees, the flowers, lessons about things, stars and fairies. I'm just afraid he likes you too. Too much …'

Jean understood without her spelling it out. When Georges Chaminadze came back Claude would say nothing, erasing Jean from her past, but Cyrille would talk. She hid her face in her hands.

'It's terrible not to know what's going to happen. At this moment, I can tell you, I find it unbearable, absolutely unbearable.'

One evening, when she started to cry, he put his arms around her and kissed her tears away. He had discovered her weakness, so well masked by so much courage and warmth.

'I want to take you away somewhere else,' he said.

'Yes, maybe, somewhere else.'

At the end of May 1941 Cyrille could not shake off a bout of flu. A doctor prescribed a period of convalescence in the Midi. But how could they get out of the occupied zone? Within hours Madeleine had obtained three travel permits. Jean bought their tickets for Saint-Raphaël. La Garenne made his displeasure felt.

'You're really in tune with the times, aren't you! Holidays? You think now's the moment for holidays? With two million prisoners of war and a hundred thousand dead? London and Coventry are ablaze, and Monsieur Arnaud's going on holiday. I'll be a laughing stock if I say yes. Look at Blanche! Three years she's worked for me, and not one day off! People are starving. Hostages are being shot. But Monsieur Arnaud doesn't care. He's off to the land where the oranges grow. Dear sir, you would die of hunger if I let you swan off to the Midi. You're behaving like a silly romantic girl.'

'Bollocks.'

'I beg your pardon?'

'Bollocks.'

La Garenne reddened, then went pale with fury. He had the vicious look weak people have when their anger makes them forget their physical wretchedness and cowardice. Jean thought they might come to blows, which would have been laughable.

Blanche wrung her hands, begging, 'Louis-Edmond, please …'

Some customers in uniform were waiting. They left with some drawings and a sheaf of photographs, the last pictures of Alberto Senzacatso, who had been arrested at the request of the Italian authorities. (He had not been taken into custody for his modest photographic output but for political ideas that he had long since abandoned in favour of his definitive study of Mannerism. A visitor to the gallery and admirer of his, always dressed sombrely in plain clothes and afflicted with a strong German accent, had expressed sympathy for the photographer's predicament and promised to look into his case.)

Watched by his customers, La Garenne swept into the 'bosom of bosoms' and shut himself inside. His no was final. Jean took the money he was owed from the till. Blanche kissed him, genuinely moved.

'I'll sort things out,' she said. 'Go away and don't worry. The important thing is for your friend's little boy to get some colour back in his cheeks. Nothing else matters.'

'I'd appreciate it if you didn't sort anything out. I'm not worried; I've got enough to live on for three months. To be honest, I never want to see La Garenne again.'

'I know he exaggerates, but deep down he's a generous man! It's just that he's so proud he doesn't want anyone to see his noble feelings …'

It was a mystery why Blanche persisted in such a grandiose view of this person whose only attractions were his madness and the secret of his ancient ex-courtesan of a mother, now bedridden and snorting like a sea lion: '*Arrh, arrh… oowowoowow …*' But it would have been cruel to rob Blanche of her illusions.

At Gare de Lyon they boarded a second-class carriage on a packed train that left an hour late and stopped repeatedly to let Wehrmacht transports through. Matériel and men were rolling back northwards, carriages full of blank-faced young soldiers eating and smoking, their jackets undone; artillery and tanks under tarpaulins.

They were eight in their compartment and no one spoke. Cyrille had a reserved seat. A fat man was so close to squashing him that Jean and Claude sat him on their lap rather than protest. The travellers watched each other with sidelong glances in an atmosphere that was suspicious rather than hostile; each clutched on his or her knees a basket or an attaché case too valuable to be put up in the luggage rack. A young couple facing Jean held hands without saying a word. Their appearance was so similar – the same yellow, gaunt complexions, the same big black eyes and full lips – they might have been taken for brother and sister, but their intertwined hands bespoke a deep and anguished love. In the seat nearest the corridor an old woman with wizened cheeks plunged her hand repeatedly into a basket from which she pulled out bread, apples and biscuits which she chewed slowly, her gaze deliberately vacant so as to ignore the covetous looks of her travelling companions. Cyrille was fascinated by her. After watching her for a time, he held out half a bar of chocolate that he had been nibbling.

'Are you hungry, Madame?' he said.

She took the chocolate with a delighted smile and mumbled her thanks, then, unable to avoid the astonished looks around her, felt she needed to justify herself.

'The food coupons we get, we old ones are in a lot more danger of kicking the bucket. It's all for the young these days …'

No one reacted, and she closed her basket and fell silent.

At Tournus, at the line of demarcation, people's faces stiffened as they did their best to give nothing away, despite their anxiety. They all knew that no one's papers were ever entirely in order, and that each day some of those who hoped to cross the line after weeks and sometimes months of effort to do so would be refused. The *Feldgendarmen*, huge, in gleaming helmets, with steel plates hung around their necks on chains, wearing brown wool gloves and giving off a strong smell of leather and homespun, blocked the corridors and pushed back the sliding doors.

'*Papiere!*'

They examined the *Ausweise* one by one, comparing the identity photograph with the traveller's face, then passed the permits to a man in civilian clothes, a file in his hand. A glance at this, and the Gestapo inspector returned the permit. Or he kept it and the *Feldgendarme* ordered the traveller to collect their luggage and get off the train. As they had feared constantly since they left Paris, the man and woman who had been holding hands were called out of the carriage and ordered onto the platform. They were seen entering an office with a German inscription on the door. A sentry stood guard. Jean felt sure he had seen another emotion besides resignation on their faces, almost an expression of relief, like the one articulated two years later in Paris by Tristan Bernard in an admirable phrase when he was arrested: 'Until now we were living in fear, from now on we shall live in hope.'

After a two-hour wait the train set off again, at a snail's pace. Through the windows passengers glimpsed the blue uniforms of French gendarmes, policemen wearing képis at a rakish angle, even a squad of soldiers in khaki on their way to relieve their comrades. The travellers put their packages in the luggage rack, and the fat man spread his backside further across the space left by Cyrille. The old woman with wizened cheeks said dismissively, 'They were Jews!'

The fat man, biting into a sandwich, stopped with his mouth full.

'It's understandable that the Germans are angry with them. The Jews have done so many bad things to them! You should have seen what Berlin was like after the Great War. The cess pit of Europe ...'

No one reacted. With the line of demarcation behind them the passengers had succumbed to nervous fatigue. At Lyon-Perrache some of them got off. The old woman who couldn't stop eating disappeared down the platform in search of food. She returned with some cakes made from millet flour, which she dusted with sugar.

'Will you give me one, Madame?' Cyrille asked.

'Oh, little boy, they're not very good. It's millet, you know, those little seeds you used to give to the birds.'

'What do the birds eat now then?'

'They get by. They eat worms and usually think they taste better. You don't need to worry about them.'

'Worms? If they're so good, why don't you eat them?'

She shrugged and stared out of the window at the badly lit platform, the busy railwaymen tapping the bogies with their hammers, soldiers and police, travellers in search of their carriages, their shoulders sagging from the weight of their cheap cardboard suitcases. Three pushed their way into the compartment, cramming their belongings into the luggage racks, trampling on Jean's feet and claiming that Cyrille had no right to a reservation. A conductor had to be called. At last the train steamed off into the night. Cyrille fell asleep, his head on Claude's lap, and she dozed off leaning against Jean. Dawn light awoke them just outside Marseille. Two years earlier Jean had covered the same route with Palfy, travelling in comfort on the Blue Train. Flashing through most of the stations without stopping, it had connected Paris with Saint-Raphaël, Cannes and Nice in a matter of hours, usually spent drinking and eating in the dining car. On that occasion he had not known where he was going and had let himself wallow in the pleasurable wretchedness that had been gnawing at him since Chantal de Malemort had run away. Each turn of the wheels, carrying him further from his too hurtful memories and useless regrets, had broken his heart a little more, proving how painful we find it to abandon the things that hurt us most. Now the same monotonous rhythm was taking him further from Paris again, but also binding him a little closer to Claude, whose simple, calm, sleeping face reflected her tiredness after the last twenty-four hours on the train. He did not move for fear of waking her. Her hand held Cyrille's, the little boy still sleeping, pale and open-mouthed. In her corner the wizened old woman opened her basket and bit into a sandwich, her gaze once more vacant. The compartment stank of soot, cold food and the passengers being prodded from their stupor by the first glimmer of daylight, with their unshaven cheeks and strong breath. It was cold, and rain lashed at the dirty windows. Beyond Marseille they glimpsed the Mediterranean, as grey as the English Channel. At Saint-Raphaël the rain was pouring down in an icy deluge that streamed through the gaps in the badly maintained platform awning. A horse-drawn carriage took them to the port, where they found a room with twin beds. A cot was brought for Cyrille. The restaurant had just closed and would not be serving food until seven. Jean went out to look for a corner shop and came back with a loaf of bread and three oranges. The rain would not stop, and gusts of wind tore across the surface of the port between bobbing helpless yachts, bending the tamarisks double along the empty quayside. The storm went on for two days. They shivered in their icy room. The hotel had no extra blankets to offer them. Every room was occupied. Claude took Cyrille into her bed. He had started coughing again and stayed with his forehead resting against the window, watching the boats rolling and pitching all along the harbour wall. A screen concealed the washbasin. Claude was first up and splashed herself with cold water. From his bed Jean watched her, naked, in the wardrobe mirror: her fine ankles, her maddeningly lovely bust, her womanly hips and, at the base of her back, a downy softness so sweet that he had to close his eyes, unable to bear it. On the second day, glancing in the mirror, she realised that if she could see Jean in the wardrobe glass, he must be able to see her behind the screen.

'Why are you spying on me?' she asked.

'Why shouldn't I spy on you?'

Wrapped in a towel, she pushed the screen aside and sat on the edge of his bed. Cyrille was still sleeping, and they had to talk in low voices.

'What if he wasn't here?' Jean said, pointing to Cyrille.

She thought about his question with the seriousness and concentration she showed every time they discussed their unusual relations.

'I wouldn't be so strong.'

'He wasn't there to protect you when you went away for three days.'

'Do you still think about that?'

'Now and then.'

Stretching out his arm, he held her ankle, squeezed it hard, ran his hand up her shin to the knee he loved so much and stroked her thigh, exposed by the towel.

'No!' she said.

'When?'

Her eyes glistened with tears.

'I want it as much as you do,' she whispered. 'But not here. Not here. Not now.'

'You're right, it's horrible here. And we came to find the sun. I hate this place, I hate the wardrobe, the colour of the curtains, the violet carpet, that embroidered armchair. Let's not stay. I'll telephone Antoine.'

'Who's Antoine?'

'My grandfather, but he doesn't know it and I'm not going to be the one to tell him. He lives at Saint-Tropez.'

It was not Antoine who answered, because he was out fishing in his rowing boat as he did every morning, but Toinette, whose cool voice and singsong accent brought back the last delicious summer before the war, the cruises on Théo's 'yacht' and a way of living in the moment that now seemed lost for ever. The hotel was shut, she said, and her mother and father were in the 'village', but her mother would phone back before lunch.

It was Théo who telephoned at lunchtime.

'What's all this, Jean, your rain from Paris you're bringing us? We're going to send you and your miserable storms straight back, you know. And what the hell are you doing at Saint-Raphaël? It's the middle of nowhere. Antoine and me've decided you're coming here. I'll pick you up in the truck at three, if I can get the gas generator going.'

'I'm not on my own, I've got a friend with me, a girlfriend.'

'Saints … Toinette didn't say nothing about that. I hope she's good-looking, at least.'

'I think so.'

'That's all right then. We got to take life as it comes ... we've been making do ever since we ran out of petrol ... What was the war like? We got plenty of time, save it for later ... I'll pick you up at three.'

The rain stopped just before Théo arrived, and a radiant sun daubed the houses in fresh colours and lightened the ochre mass of the Maures, sending up a bluish mist in the new sunshine. Théo assured them that wherever he went, the sun followed him. His truck smelt of fish.

'I never make a trip for nothing. I've brought them two hundred kilos. They don't know how to fish at Saint-Raphaël. I'm taking chickpeas and rice back. That's all they have here. Put your bags on top.'

He showed no surprise at seeing Cyrille. He stroked his cheek and peeled him an orange.

'Nice boy. A bit pasty. We'll fix that.'

Théo had not changed. The odd grey hair at his temples, but his face had stayed young, enlivened constantly by the winks, pouts and comical expressions that punctuated his indefatigable chatter. He had sold his 'yacht', which had sailed away, laden with English passengers, just after the armistice. His truck now satisfied his hunger for mechanical toys. The gas generator was not perfect, but by fiddling and coaxing, the truck could be made to start. Antoine had looked very happy at the thought of his friend Jean coming, having not seen him for so long. Of course ... very happy was putting it too strongly. Being a Norman, a man of the north, he didn't show his feelings much, and spoke less and less. Fishing was the only thing that interested him. He was getting very good at it. He kept the house well supplied. Toinette was seventeen now. A real angel. She helped her mother. Oh, yes, Marie-Dévote was well too. He'd find her a bit thinner than before ... yes, true, Jean hadn't met her ... Well, some said she was better-looking like that. He, Théo, he'd liked her skinny, and with a bit of flesh on her, and even good and round, and he loved her the way she was now because there was no other woman on earth like her.

The road followed the curve of the gulf. After three days' torrential rain the rivers were pouring the red earth of the Maures into the sea, staining the waves. Cyrille sounded the horn as they went round the bends.

'I tell you, Jean, this little chap's going to send both of them dotty, Marie-Dévote and Toinette. You don't see blond kids around here much. They'll be crazy about him! Cyrille, you say that's your name?'

'Yes, Monsieur.'

'And polite too! Dotty! Dotty's what they'll be, I tell you. They won't want to give him back! My word on it.'

They were arriving at Saint-Tropez, outside the shuttered hotel. Théo hooted furiously and Toinette appeared at the door in trousers and a sweater, her long chestnut hair falling over her shoulders, instantly reminding Jean of the delightful, unspoken complicity between them during the short summer of 1939 and the deliciously sweet letter he had received at the camp at Yssingeaux where he and Palfy had done their basic training. He could have recited by heart the few lines she had written, to which he had never replied.

Dear godson, I send you my best warm wishes and a muffler. I hope it isn't dangerous there, where you are. Don't catch cold. Uncle Antoine sends you a thousand affectionate thoughts. He says you are his only friend. He kisses you, and I shake your hand. Toinette

Marie-Dévote appeared next, as they were unloading their cases. Jean had not seen her before and he was struck by the richness and maturity of her beauty. She had kept her soft skin and her fleshy mouth, like a Provençal nectarine. Rationing had made her lose the ten kilos excess that had weighed down her hips and bust. She was no longer the scornful girl, the wild fruit who twenty years earlier had beguiled Antoine, but almost another creature, fully in control of her body and its gestures.

'Antoine's waiting for you inside,' she said. 'He's quite choked up at the thought of seeing you again. He hasn't talked much about you, but we always knew you were his friend from way back.'

Turning to Claude, she said, 'I'm Marie-Dévote, and this is my daughter Toinette. What's your little boy's name?'

'Cyrille. And I'm Claude.'

'Cyrille's my pal,' Théo said. 'I'm kidnapping him. We're going to check over the boat. Like boats, Cyrille?'

'Oh yes.'

He took Théo's hand and followed him.

'The hotel's shut,' Marie-Dévote said, 'but we have friends come down now and again and we give them the bungalow over there. There's one big bedroom. Toinette will bring over a cot for the little one. Come on, Monsieur Jean, Antoine's waiting. I'll sort everything else out with Madame Claude. It's women's work.'

'Where's Antoine?'

'In his little place over on the beach side. It's his retreat. Nobody but him's allowed there. You might find he's changed from when you saw him last. To me – to us,' she corrected herself, 'he's still the same.'

Antoine could not have failed to hear the truck hooting as it arrived. Seated on a stool, he was checking the weights on a line he was coiling into a wicker basket. He looked up as if someone he saw every day had come to disturb him, put down the line, and got to his feet. He too had lost several kilos as a result of rationing, and his faded red cotton trousers and rollneck sweater flapped around him, but at sixty-seven, his face scarcely wrinkled, he remained the same solid Antoine, with the same deliberate step.

'I'm so pleased to see you again, Jean! A few days ago I was telling myself I'd probably never see anyone from Grangeville again. Deep down I was convinced I'd left it all behind, but this morning when Toinette came to tell me you'd telephoned I suddenly couldn't wait; I wanted you to be there at once. Come and kiss me. We're old friends – and I've always considered you as my son. Like a second son, one who might have loved me a little ... because ... the first ... Oh, let's not talk about it. It's of no interest ... See, I've become quite chatty, haven't I? Spending four or five hours every morning in my little boat, all alone, I tell myself stories and when I set foot on dry land it all spills out. Then I shut up again. What are you looking at? Yes, it's my garage, my workshop, my shed. I've got my nets, my lines, my tools ... and there's my last love – you'll remember her ...'

At the back of the garage a waxed tarpaulin covered the shape of a car. Antoine pulled on a rope that ran through a block and the tarpaulin rose, revealing the 3.3-litre Bugatti 57S in which he had driven away from La Sauveté.

'Obviously she's not really presentable, except to those in the know. I greased the chromework and the chassis's up on blocks, so the wheels hardly touch the floor. I know it spoils her lines, but the tyres won't rot so quickly. I've covered the inner tubes with talc. Twice a week I start her up ... Wait ...'

He sat behind the wheel and tugged the ignition switch. The engine started instantly, perfectly on song.

'There,' Antoine said, 'a little treat for her. She'll have started three times this week. Can't afford to spoil her like that too often. I've only got two hundred litres of petrol in cans to last till the end of the war. You know that with the 57S you can do the same trick they do with a Rolls-Royce ...'

He took a bronze two-sous piece out of his pocket, opened the bonnet, and balanced it on its edge on the cylinder head. The coin stayed upright for several seconds before a stronger vibration of the engine made it fall over.

'Obviously,' Antoine said, 'that wouldn't happen if it wasn't on blocks.'

The tarpaulin descended, covering the Bugatti again.

'They tell me you're not on your own?'

'No,' Jean said. 'Actually I left Paris to come here with a friend whose little boy badly needs some sun.'

'Is she divorced?'

'Not yet. Her husband's in London.'

'I look forward to seeing her.'

He said it with the indifference of a man happy with the few friends he had.

'I haven't got a lot of news to tell you,' Jean said. 'Antoinette's written. Michel is in Paris. Last month a gallery on the Left Bank had an exhibition of his pictures.'

'So he really wants to be an artist? It's a case of spontaneous generation in our family.'

Antoine sat down on his stool to carry on winding his line. The lead weights lay on top of each other, and in the middle of the basket the line coiled up like a lasso.

'I'm not bored,' he told Jean. 'I like this kind of work. You need two or three hours to get a line straight again, and then a few seconds for it all to uncoil into the sea. Time was, I had about thirty trawlers all working for me and never felt the slightest urge to go on board any of them. Now I fish on my own, grandpa out in his boat, and it gives me more pleasure than you can possibly imagine. I didn't know it, but this was the life I always wanted. I don't need anything, which is perfect because I don't own anything, except for my lovely Bugatti that may never go again. There's a risk that this war will last as long as the first one. It's not my business … or hardly … Were you old enough to be called up?'

'Yes, I enlisted in September 1939.'

'I don't suppose your father thought much of that. How is he?'

'Fairly well, I think … I haven't seen him since then. He works for Madame du Courseau. Antoinette sends me news.'

'I say your father … it's a manner of speaking, obviously, as we're never going to know whose child you really are.'

'I've found out.'

'Ah!'

Antoine stood up and reached for a meerschaum pipe, carved in the shape of a Moor's head with a silver lid, from a rack above a tobacco jar. He filled it with tobacco.

'I'd be wiser not to smoke,' he said. 'Tobacco's getting scarce and Théo, who keeps me supplied, must be paying a small fortune for it. You don't smoke?'

'Not very often.'

'That's good.'

Jean hesitated. Was he going to tell him? Here in this shed, with its door open onto a wide beach of sand soaked by the last few days' rain? The sea was quieter now, and empty. Order reigned inside the shed: nets meticulously tidied, oars leaning against the wall, every tool hanging in its place. A three-horsepower diesel motor, well greased, was hooked onto a trestle. Antoine followed Jean's gaze.

'A good little motor. I made do with it very nicely before the war. Now there's no more fuel. I stripped it down to wait for happier days. It doesn't have reverse, so the trick is to cut the throttle at the right moment. You can brake with the oars too, of course. Now I row with all my might and have a lateen sail. I never go far, but I usually come back with about ten kilos of fish. We keep what we need and Théo exchanges the rest for olive oil and sugar. We have everything we need …'

'Aren't you curious to know whose son I am?'

Antoine relit his pipe.

'The annoying thing about the tobacco you get on the black market is that the smugglers sell it by weight. So they soak it. The first thing you have to do is dry it. You're left with about half what you paid for … You want to know if I'm curious to hear whose son you are? Perhaps. Is it someone I know?'

'Yes.'

'Ah! Come with me. Let's walk along the beach a bit. I like to stretch my legs. I'm almost always sitting down, in my boat or in my shed.'

They heard Marie-Dévote calling from the terrace of the hotel.

'Antoine!'

He cupped his hands to his mouth.

'We're going for a stroll, we'll be back.'

She gave a gentle wave and watched them go.

'She's a woman of complete, perfect goodness,' he said. 'A man as clumsy and demanding as me could have spoilt her, ruined her. She's stayed the way she was when I met her. Better still, she's improved. She had a good head on her shoulders and I didn't even notice it. I only saw her body, only heard her lovely singsong accent.'

Jean was surprised to hear emotion in the voice of this man who had so rarely shown any. It was love: Antoine had stumbled on love, and love had not let him down. They took their shoes off and walked across the cool sand. The tramontana was shooing the last clouds towards the reddening horizon.

'You know, it's such a joy to walk barefoot, Jean. I learnt that here …'

He fell silent until they were at the far end of the beach, near a large grey rock.

'Let's go back now,' he said. 'So whose son are you?'

'Geneviève's.'

'Are you sure?'

'As sure as I can be.'

'To tell you the truth, I had my suspicions, but I found it hard to believe that Marie-Thérèse would hide it from me. Idiotic woman! She kept us apart. In the name of what, I'd like to know! Propriety?

Morality? Because of what people would say? It's a disgrace, you know; I loved Geneviève. She led her life the way she wanted to, and so she should. Does she know you're her son?'

'She might have her suspicions too. I'm not sure. I have a feeling she might have decided, once and for all, that she never had a child.'

'And where is she?'

'In Lebanon.'

Antoine laughed and hung on to Jean's arm. They were approaching the shuttered hotel.

'So, in a nutshell, you're my grandson. Do you know, I'm almost disappointed. I thought I'd found a stranger to love, someone I'd chosen consciously, a long way from all those family ties – I mean the compulsory sort of love people cultivate within the family circle – and now I discover we have the same blood in our veins. In 1939, back when you met Théo and Toinette, I made up a story for my own amusement: Jean, that nice, straight, honest boy, would be the ideal match for my Toinette … She used to blush when she talked about you. At least we've avoided a catastrophe …'

'Toinette's your daughter.'

'Is it very obvious?'

'Yes.'

Antoine sighed.

'I'm proud of her. I adore her. We all adore her.'

'What about Théo?'

'He can't have children. You have to take him as he comes: talkative, sly, always with an eye to the main chance, but with a heart of gold. He likes mechanical things. At least we have something to talk about when we're not talking about Toinette.'

Marie-Dévote had made tea in the kitchen. A cup of hot chocolate for Cyrille, a herbal tea for everyone else.

'We don't have any proper tea left,' she said. 'We make an infusion with the herbs from the mountain. It's good for you ...'

Jean, watching, compared Claude and Marie-Dévote, the young woman and the older, one reserved and fragile, the other outgoing and in the full bloom of her fairly commonplace beauty; yet a link had instantly united them: the blond child sitting in a high chair (Toinette's when she had been small) with a napkin around his neck, drinking mouthfuls of hot chocolate and observing, without speaking, these strangers bending over him one after another with an anxious tenderness, because he had coughed twice as he walked into the kitchen. Jean liked the fact that Claude was not an over-anxious mother, with a suffocating tenderness towards her son. Whatever she did for him she did rapidly, skilfully, without words, and if he were honest, it might have made him jealous because she already loved Cyrille like a man, intelligently, not wanting to crush him. The only difference he noticed in Marie-Dévote's kitchen was that, for once – and perhaps so as not to disappoint Marie-Dévote – she fussed a little more over her son, wiping the corners of his mouth and his hands covered in chocolate.

'So lucky, you are,' Marie-Dévote said. 'Me too, I'd've liked to have a child.'

Antoine roared with laughter.

'Marie-Dévote hasn't had a child. She's only got a daughter.'

Toinette smiled. Perhaps she, too, felt, without bitterness, that boys were the only children. Théo protested.

'If a girl isn't a child, then the world really has gone mad. In any case Toinette, as you see, wears trousers. And I take my orders from her: Papa, go and deliver the fish; Papa, get some wood for the stove; Papa, wash the truck because it's dirty ...'

*

The weather held. Théo was delighted. In his mind it was always raining at Saint-Raphaël and always good weather at Saint-Tropez. Cyrille had stopped coughing and wandered on the beach like a little naked god, watched over by Marie-Dévote while Claude and Toinette bathed, joined before lunch by Jean, back from fishing with Antoine. The fish he caught were only good for the cat; Antoine mocked him. Fishing is a gift. In the afternoons Théo took Jean out in the truck, whose wood-gas generator struggled on every hill. Armed with his movement permit and well in with the gendarmes (to whom he distributed their share), Théo devoted himself to some discreet black-marketeering, delivering fish to Grimaud, Ramatuelle, Cogolin and Gonfaron, returning with vegetables and firewood for the kitchen stove. Under the firewood there was often a calf hidden, or a kid or a sheep, ready skinned. The risk was small, but Théo liked to put on secretive airs and take precautions, though the evening visits of Sergeant Thomasson made them pointless. The sergeant never left without a leg of lamb or some chops in his haversack.

After dinner they listened to the news, first from Vichy, which taught them nothing, then Radio-Paris which reported Germany's dominance in the Mediterranean, the fall of Crete and the British Army's rapid withdrawal to Sfakia. Théo curled his lip. The Mediterranean, German? He opened the window onto the empty sea, the placid shore and the sound of the waves whispering on the sand and lapping against the pilings of the jetty where Antoine tied up his rowing boat. Later on they picked up Radio-Londres, where there was small cause for comfort. The bulletins' emphasis on secondary operations – raids on the Ruhr, the attack on Syria, the overthrow of Iraqi rulers sympathetic to the Axis – could not hide the way things were going. Their heart was not in it. Although he did not like the Germans Théo admired their 'sense of organisation', and though he did not like the English either he acknowledged their 'bravery and coolness'. Antoine refrained from comment, unless he was genuinely indifferent, which was more likely. He listened with half an ear, busy with a pile of old cigar boxes, making model ships like the ones Jean had seen his uncle, Captain Duclou, making a hundred times on the long evenings of conversation in his parents' kitchen at Grangeville. Marie-Dévote, Claude and Toinette knitted with rough wool Théo bought from a farm in the Maures where the old women had taken up spinning again. Cyrille would lay his head on the table and fall asleep and his mother would put him to bed. A little later Jean would join her, allowing everyone to think they were lovers, although their relations were still at the point Claude had sworn to herself never to go beyond, even if now she often walked around naked in their bedroom, a freedom Cyrille reproached her for one day.

'Maman, you mustn't show your tummy to Jean.'

'It's all right with him; he's a very good friend.'

Cyrille no longer spoke about his father, who was already half forgotten, his face replaced by another that he saw every day. Claude never left his side. Perhaps she felt she would not have the force to resist Jean without her innocent guardian. Even when he was fast asleep in his cot, Cyrille was watching over her. But if her hand slipped outside the sheets, another hand, from the bed next to hers, would grasp it, squeeze her fingers and stroke her wrist, and she had no need for words to understand the meaning of the gesture.

One morning Jean said, 'Cyrille's right. Don't walk around naked in front of me any more.'

She covered herself up, and immediately Jean begged her not to pay any attention to what he had said, to behave as if he didn't exist. She was turning a warm amber in the summer heat, and her swimming costume left a line at the top of her thighs and above her breasts. She made Jean desperate. There were moments when she realised it and they fell into each other's arms and wept in silence. Sometimes at night, obsessed and unable to sleep, he got up and slipped out of the window, crossed the garden overlooking the beach, ran to the sea and swam in its phosphorescent water. When he came back he found Claude sitting on her bed, waiting for him.

'Where were you?'

'I went for a swim.'

She would touch his damp shoulder and wet hair and kiss his salt-tasting lips.

One night as he left the bungalow, he bumped into Antoine walking across the garden.

'I can see something's not right,' Antoine said, 'and I don't like not offering to help. But I'm a selfish man and it's probably wise if I stay that way. If I don't sleep, or not much – and badly at that – it's because I'm getting old. But at your age you shouldn't be having sleepless nights. Come into my shed – I've got a bottle of grappa. It's not quite calvados, but you'll get used to it.'

Antoine shut the door behind them and switched on a feeble light after drawing a curtain across the only window.

'No lights at night on the coast. One evening I came in here and was looking forward to some odd jobs, and suddenly the gendarmes turned up. There's a rumour that English submarines are landing spies. It could be true and it's nothing to do with us.'

He took a bottle and two glasses from a cupboard.

'This reminds me of our last night at La Sauveté. Do you remember?'

'I haven't forgotten.'

'A house emptied by termites and removal men. It made me melancholy for a minute or two. Everyone has their weak points. You didn't drink. In training, weren't you?'

'Yes.'

'One day I saw you sculling at Dieppe Rowing Club. It gave me a lot of pleasure. Now?'

'I drink a bit. To be honest, it doesn't do anything for me.'

'You mustn't get too fond of it. It's hard to stop if you do. I don't know how our dear abbé Le Couec keeps going ... I suppose there's always another parishioner who needs his help … These stools are really dreadful … Let's sit in the car.'

He pulled on the tarpaulin, uncovering the Bugatti, melancholy-looking in the light of the single bulb. Jean sat next to him as he placed his hands on the steering wheel and turned it right and left.

'The steering's a bit stiff. Bugatti always wanted cars that would turn on a sixpence. But first you had to learn to drive them. By the time the war's over I won't know any more.'

'Do you think it'll last long?'

'I fear so.'

Antoine emptied his glass and refilled it from the bottle between his knees.

'Well?' he asked. 'What's wrong? You love each other, you're together, and no one's bothering you.'

'We don't make love,' Jean said in a moment of recklessness.

'Ouch! That's serious. Is it you?'

'Oh no! I'm fine on that front.'

He could have told him about Antoinette, Chantal, even Mireille Cece, whom they had shared without knowing it.

'Then it must be her.'

'I don't know why. It's a ridiculous situation. It makes me desperate and there are times when I just can't go on, I feel like bursting.'

'I can't be any help to you. I've been lucky all my life. It's true I had money. But when all the money was gone, Marie-Dévote stayed just the same. Of course now I don't jump on her every five minutes, but I'm very happy, I've got lots of memories … Do you like the smell of leather? They won't upholster cars with hides like this again. You'll see a whole epoch vanish. If I hadn't detached myself from everything, I'd find it a hell of a struggle … Tell me, did Claude still love her husband when you met her?'

'I suspect not.'

'Do you think she's ever had a lover?'

'She swears she hasn't.'

'One man in all her life! Good Lord, that's not something you come across every day. Personally I'd look for the answer with her husband.'

They went on talking for a while longer before getting out of the car, which Antoine then covered up again with its tarpaulin.

Climbing through the window, Jean heard two bodies' regular breathing. Claude and Cyrille were both asleep. He got into bed and lay there, gripped by the idea that Claude was obeying a pact agreed with her absent husband. What had it meant, then, when she disappeared for three days?

The noise of knocking at the door woke him. It was bright daylight. Théo had brought news that shattered the lethargy of the false peace.

'It might interest you,' he said, 'to know that Monsieur Hitler has invaded Russia. Bang! Away we go. Some'll be happy about it, others not at all. Uncle Joe isn't going to be in a good mood this morning. Not like Antoine. He's already out fishing. And Marie-Dévote says it's no reason for us to go hungry. *Brékefaste* is served …'

In the days that followed, the radio broadcast place names no one had heard before. From the Barents Sea to the Black Sea the German offensive gathered pace. Thunder rumbled across Europe, and the beach in front of the hotel remained as calm and empty as before. Cyrille played in the sand, Antoine went fishing, Claude and Toinette swam out until their heads were small specks, and Marie-Dévote, beauty and forty-year-old matron, put a chaise longue out on the beach and knitted. Cyrille would have the best sweaters in all Paris that winter and Claude a wool overcoat. Jean drove away with Théo and they came back laden with olive oil, beef lard that they turned into lavender-scented soap, fresh fruit, goat's cheese and big, round country loaves. At the wheel of his wood-gas truck Théo was in his element. Jean learnt from him that Antoine had spoken to Marie-Dévote. She, too, now knew that he was the grandson of the visitor from Normandy who had brought prosperity to their seaside café. He also learnt of the pictures Antoine had bought from painters who had passed through Saint-Tropez in the period between the wars. When the Italians attacked in June 1940 Marie-Dévote had prudently locked them away in one of the hotel's cellars. They showed them to Jean, and he was astonished by Antoine's taste. He, who had declared himself amazed to have a son who was a painter, had not bought a single bad painting.

'With those in her trousseau,' Théo said, 'Toinette's never going to be poor.'

'But who knows you've got all these?'

'Well … everyone who came here. People used to ask for the room with the Picasso or the Dunoyer.'

'So you don't know that the Germans are making off with every bit of French art they can find?'

'The Germans? We're still waiting for them. Right now, they're going the wrong way. Saint-Tropez's not on the road to Moscow …'

Watching Toinette as she hovered, fairy-like, discreet and silent in the background, it struck Jean that he might have found happiness there if … How many 'ifs' there were! He understood Antoine, his escape from Grangeville, his leaving everything behind. He had decided to grow old at Marie-Dévote's side and, despite the situation's ambiguity – Théo's semi-acceptance, Toinette whom they shared without a mean thought – he had built himself, without really intending to, an ark of happiness that nothing could destroy. It had been his own wish no longer to have a penny to his name. Arriving at Saint-Tropez in the late summer of 1936 at the wheel of his 57S, with a cheque in his pocket representing all he possessed in the world, which he immediately handed to Marie-Dévote, he could – as one-time sugar daddy, the man who had paid for the hotel and much else besides – have been shown the door or offered a shack and ignored. Such a fate would have corresponded to the unflattering opinion he held of humanity and its gratitude, but Marie-Dévote had accepted the cheque and him, a man who asked for nothing apart from a new family, people who understood him and opened their hearts to him. Peace reigned at Chez Antoine, the renowned hotel, halted temporarily in its rise to fame. Marie-Dévote ruled the roost, in spite of Théo's pretensions to the contrary. Her understanding of life, for all her mature warmth and sensual attractiveness, was born of a certain harshness. Her personality had developed to the point where two men had not been too many to unbalance her sense of equilibrium: for her dear Antoine she probably felt that vaguely Oedipal love that tugs at every woman's heartstrings, and for Théo a kind of loving indulgence that fulfilled her maternal aspirations. Her ambitions satisfied, she had at last ventured to show her real generosity. That she might still be a desirable woman never crossed her mind, and she stretched out on her chaise longue in all innocence, hitching up her skirt to bare her long brown thighs which had first caught Antoine's attention twenty years earlier, when she used to bring him his *pan banias* and cold carafe of Var rosé. She would have been astonished if you had told her that she could still tempt a man. Who? She never went out and had never been to a big city; twice she had refused to accompany Théo to the Paris boat show. Her curiosity had never even led her as far as Marseille, let alone Nice, which she considered a foreign country, where the English ruled on their promenade. What can you learn outside your four walls if your passion for your family is all you need: your love for your daughter, your husband, your old lover, and a hotel that was the fruit of so much hard work? Nothing.

She never invited anyone, not out of stinginess but out of politeness, feeling that people were always happier at home than with others and that invitations embarrassed their recipients, who did not know how to refuse them without giving offence. It was Théo's job to maintain external relations. He brought back, on his own, all the excitement and noise she needed. She would say to him, 'Théo, when the war's over, let me know at once, so that I can get the rooms ready and do a bit of cleaning. I'll ask the Swiss boy to come back and run the reception again. Poor boy, in his snowy mountains he must be very cold and lonely.'

Théo shook his head and feigned despair.

'There's millions of men dying, a worldwide cataclysm, towns burning; we could die of hunger—'

'Don't exaggerate!'

'Well, maybe not, thanks to me, because I take care of things, but what about the others? The poor, the unemployed, the pensioners, the invalids? ... You don't know, do you? They can all cop it, and all you think of is reopening your hotel.'

'When they're dead, we'll have to make peace.'

'You've got no heart.'

'Yes, I have. Just not for everybody.'

Marie-Dévote reduced the world, the war, the future, the peace to simple problems. She represented vitality and harmony and the selfishness without which, in the midst of tumult and strife, nothing would survive. Jean, being Antoine's grandson, belonged to this selfish family circle. With Claude it was possible to see Marie-Dévote being more circumspect – 'Who is this stranger who's not from around here?' – but she acknowledged her qualities as an attentive mother, a good cook, serious, and inspiring Toinette's admiration. Cyrille's presence incited no such reservations. Cured of his cough, he was turning brown under the Midi sun, and his gaiety and laughter enlivened an atmosphere that might otherwise have been too staid.

In mid-July Claude received a postcard from her mother, asking her to return. Was it a summons, or merely a request? It was hard to say, with the dryness of the printed card which left room for only single words in response to pre-prepared questions, expressing little. At the same time Jean had a telephone call from Saint-Raphaël.

'Hello! It's Marceline …'

For a moment the name meant nothing to him, nor the husky accent.

'… I'd like to see you. I have a message from the baron for you.'

The baron? He remembered the title Palfy had adopted almost by accident and now used shamelessly. Madame Michette! He should have recognised her from her mysterious tone.

'Can you hear me?' she asked anxiously.

'Yes, yes, I can hear you.'

'We need to meet.'

'Well, come to Saint-Tropez.'

'It's not easy.'

He remembered that she had not been averse to travelling on top of a truckful of Jerusalem artichokes. Théo, who was going to Grasse that afternoon, could pick her up on the way back. They agreed a meeting place. She would be outside the station, carrying a copy of *Paris-Soir*, in a grey suit.

'A suit? In this heat?'

'I've come straight from Paris.'

At four o'clock that afternoon they saw her walking up and down, her eyes hidden behind dark glasses, brandishing her newspaper.

Théo had been briefed by Jean.

'So, Madame Michette, you're one of those who hug the walls and dress in grey …'

Put out by this newcomer broadcasting her secret, she stared quickly around her. No one was watching.

'Don't talk so loudly, please! Enemy eyes are listening.'

'Ah well, that's all right then. Jump in!'

She sat between Jean and Théo and they headed for Sainte-Maxime. She stared hungrily out of the window.

'It's pretty here!'

'Haven't you been before?' Théo said.

'I always spend holidays with my family. And my family's from the Auvergne.'

The new life Palfy had conjured out of the air for Madame Michette had not changed her. Jean reflected that if she went back to her former profession, she would still lead her girls to the Bastille Day celebrations or to confession with the same authority. She accepted her humble clandestine missions from a sense of duty. 'I'm doing my bit,' she said. Her arrival was impatiently awaited at the hotel, as if everyone wanted to be part of Palfy's huge practical joke. Marie-Dévote offered her 'herbal tea' which she tasted cautiously, her little finger crooked, after dissolving a saccharine tablet in her cup.

'It's better for your mood than sugar,' she said. 'Sugar gives you *choler sterol*.'

Eventually she asked Jean to step onto the terrace, where she gave him a sealed letter.

Dear Jean,

Between men such as ourselves one doesn't use the post, one uses a messenger. The divine Marceline is perfect for our purpose. She hides her messages in her bra, where of course no one's going to go looking. Actually, I've got nothing to tell you except that things are going well, so well in fact that I'm rather annoyed you're not here to be part of it. You're dozing down there … Wake up. Now's not the time to be bleating about love. Come back before the war is over. There are opportunities here for the taking. Tomorrow it'll be too late. Give our heroine a note and let me know the day of your arrival. I'll pick you up

*at Gare de Lyon. I have a car and driver. And that's just the
start. Tibi, Constantin*

Jean went inside to write his reply. Palfy was right; he had to
go back. When he returned he found Madame Michette talking to
Antoine.

'You know,' she said, 'Monsieur sold his house to someone I know.
Monsieur Longuet. It's such a coincidence. Madame Longuet is an
absolute saint.'

'So our priest says.'

'What a small world.'

Antoine agreed without protest. Madame Michette drank a large
glass of grappa, which reddened her cheeks without distracting her
for a moment from her mission.

'I must go!' she announced.

'How?'

'By train.'

'You ought to rest,' Marie-Dévote said, unsettled by this obsession
with travelling.

'Later! I'll rest later.'

'"Later" never comes. Life's for living now.'

Madame Michette disagreed. Our lives did not belong to us.
Superior forces allowed us a few years, provided that we returned
them one day, in good condition and with the interest due. The tone
of the discussion rose. Madame Michette believed in destiny. Marie-
Dévote did not know what it was.

Théo drove her back to Saint-Raphaël where she caught the evening
train. Jean felt sorry for her and found himself thinking: why did Palfy
play his pranks? So that the august figure of Madame Michette, who

had lived behind closed shutters for so long, discovered a meaning to life? But Palfy was right: he had to get back to Paris. He'd had more than one reminder that his too-happy existence rested on fragile foundations. That night he found his grandfather in the Bugatti. They had run out of grappa, so they drank champagne.

'Not marvellous!' Antoine said at the first mouthful. 'I've never quite managed to educate Marie-Dévote on the subject of champagne. She used to order hers from passing salesmen who'd palm her off with the vintages they couldn't sell to anyone else. They're back now, but they're not selling any more; they want to buy up our reserve instead. I soon put a stop to that!'

'I'm not as fussy as you. Anyway, being here's what counts.'

They had left the door of the shed open, and through the windscreen they could make out the sea and its swell silvered by the moonlight.

'Let's give ourselves a treat,' Antoine said. 'I'll turn the headlights on, and we'll hope the gendarmes don't jump out of the bushes and nab us.'

He started the engine and switched on the headlights, which lit up the bushes, the beach and the mother-of-pearl surface of the water. After a moment he switched the engine off again.

'So you're off?'

'Yes. I think it's the right thing to do.'

'No change?'

'No.'

'It's the first time I've ever met a woman I didn't understand. Until now their intentions have seemed so obvious to me that I had a tendency to simplify them, to reduce them to their appearances. Is it really possible there are complicated ones too? I'll have to revise all my theories! But I'm too old to backtrack now. I'd rather go fishing.'

They finished their two bottles of champagne and went their separate ways before daybreak. The decision was made. In any case, Jean's money was running out. Every week he gave Marie-Dévote a small amount to cover their board and lodging. But the biggest reason was that he could not go on. He had become obsessed by his desire. Whether Claude covered herself up or walked around their bedroom naked, she had everything he wanted – except openness. He could only look, and see the grace in her movements, her voice and her words. He had begun to slip into bad moods with her. She had accepted them resignedly. The person we love must sometimes suffer, for obscure reasons that are also the mark of a passion grown too intense. Wounded by her distance, Jean could not forgive himself for causing her pain.

One afternoon, when Toinette had taken Cyrille for a walk, he found himself alone with Claude as she undressed in their bedroom. As she took off her shirt, he felt a hunger so violent he thought he was going mad. Did she see the look in his eyes? She stood rooted to the spot with fear, naked to the waist, exposing her lovely breasts, almost untouched by motherhood, pale, soft, trembling fruits that made him want to throw himself to his knees each time she uncovered them.

He grabbed her by the shoulders, ready to hit her, stun her in order to satisfy his desire for a body that would at last be defenceless. She stiffened.

'I'll never forgive you.'

'I'm sorry.'

He let go of her naked shoulders, which a moment before he had wanted to bite until they bled. His fingers had left white imprints on her tanned skin. Tears were rolling down her cheeks.

'You're the only one I love!' she said.

'I'm truly sorry.'

'We'll never part, and I'll never forget these two months.'

'I want to know.'

'It's impossible.'

'Is it always going to be impossible?'

'No.'

'When, then? When?'

She threw herself into his arms, pushing her head into his chest, and he smelt the fragrance of her hair and caressed her bare neck.

'I promised Georges that I'd wait till he came back before I decided.'

'Where did you promise that?'

'I can't tell you that.'

He could not persuade her to say any more. She had gone as far as she could. So Antoine's conclusion had been correct. Jean would ask no more questions. Claude slid to her knees, still holding him. She pressed her cheek against his legs with such unselfconsciousness that he felt hope, for a moment, that one day they would throw aside their clothes and come together. He let himself slide down beside her onto the tiled floor, and they became like two children, kissing each other's lips and face with as much wonderment as fear.

On the wall of Palfy's office a map of Europe bristled with red and black flags.

'You'll get the idea straight away,' he said.

He picked up a ruler and drew a line in the air between the black flags in the west and the red in the east.

'The war has entered its final phase. Leaving the fools aside, who thankfully are legion, for the rest of us the outcome is clear. The Wehrmacht is on the brink of taking Odessa, Kiev and Smolensk, and is approaching Leningrad. Its advance is irresistible. The Baltic is already under Axis control. By the end of October we can look forward to a German Ukraine and Moscow encircled. There are three million Soviet prisoners that no one knows what to do with, dying of starvation and wretchedness. The USSR is losing its bread basket. Its lines of communication are cut, its high command in chaos, Stalin no longer trusts anyone. So what does he do? He purges, purges and purges again to forget his own blindness. You have no idea of the panic in the Kremlin. Neutral representatives are sending back reports that leave no room for doubt. They have understood Hitler's plan: to establish a line from Arkhangelsk to Astrakhan beyond which, from his armchair, he will use his air force to annihilate the Siberian industrial complexes, leaving Chiang Kai-shek a free hand in Mongolia and eastern Siberia. It's as clear as day, as elementary as two and two make four.'

'What about England?'

'She'll win the last battle, as she always does. It's the one thing we can really be certain about.'

Palfy's assurance beguiled and deceived. Jean felt baffled.

'So who will win?'

'Stalin, of course.'

'You seem to be saying the opposite.'

'You're not listening to me.'

'You said the outcome was clear.'

Palfy shrugged his shoulders. His office windows overlooked the Champs-Élysées, where the Sunday crowds were queuing outside the cinemas. Jean could see the enormous letters on an advertisement for one of the cinemas on the far side of the avenue: '*Nelly Tristan in* The Girl and the She-wolf'. Palfy followed his friend's gaze.

'Remember her?'

'Yes, at dinner at Madeleine's. Absolutely legless.'

'Highly successful at the moment. We'll be having dinner with her shortly. Your handsome Midi tan is bound to please her.'

'We're changing the subject … You were saying that the Germans have won the war …'

Palfy raised his arms heavenwards.

'You haven't been listening. I said, "clear outcome".'

'Excuse me, I haven't read Clausewitz or Liddell Hart.'

'Stop trying to be clever. I'm not talking about Clausewitz or Hart, I'm talking about Napoleon. I hope that name means something to you!'

'A bit.'

'Well then, like the soldiers of the Grande Armée, the Germans are advancing everywhere. They would already be at Moscow now, at the end of July, if Hitler hadn't coveted the Ukraine like a greedy little boy. Guderian warned him not to, but Hitler doesn't listen to anyone. He's already finished.'

'You wouldn't think so to look at him,' Jean said.

'If you'll allow me, I shall enlighten you … Have a seat …'

In his room with its large bay windows overlooking the middle of the Champs-Élysées Palfy had assembled an elegant desk and some Louis XVI armchairs, an admirable Lancret, and in a bookcase a complete collection of the reports of the Fermiers Généraux.[16] The company name displayed on the door, 'La Franco-Germanique d'Import–Export (FGIE)', had little outward connection with the interior's Louis XVI style. Is it necessary to spell out what was taking place here? That, without going into details, the so-called FGIE was a cover for the substantial commercial dealings to which Julius Kapermeister and Rudolf von Rocroy were key?

Jean sat.

'Hitler,' Palfy said, 'is a genius. His pan-Germanic socialism is a psychological weapon as effective as the idea of liberty that preceded Napoleon's armies. Everywhere he is greeted as a "liberator", like the soldiers of year II.[17] The sad thing is that this shy impulsive man does not think he is loved, or perhaps he cannot accept that he is loved. So he crushes, exterminates, imprisons. In the Ukraine they were expecting a saviour and they got Attila the Hun, bombing the triumphal arches prepared for his victorious arrival. Not a very effective way to make yourself loved …'

Palfy raised his index finger.

'He could have half the population of the USSR with him if he wanted: the Byelorussians, the Don Cossacks, the Muslims in the Caucasus, the Balts … Alas, this oversensitive, sexually inhibited vegetarian teetotaller prefers to be alone, like a god. In addition to which he possesses an unfortunate array of physiological defects which cannot help but eventually have a deleterious effect on the situation. Of course you're aware that he is pathologically flatulent. Not one of those ordinary farters we all remember from our classrooms at school, but a truly high-powered professional – despite not, so far as I know, amusing himself by blowing out candles, like the famous Pétomane at the Alhambra. The awful thing for him is that he simply can't control it. Imagine – you who are such a sensitive boy – the anxiety of the Führer at Nuremberg, stepping forward to address tens of thousands of men, to exalt the Third Reich – and suddenly, in the middle of a superb flight of oratory, the microphone amplifies a triumphant fart, echoing through the loudspeakers to every corner of the rally! No dictator could live down the gales of laughter, the ridicule. He has always had a problem with gas, ever since he inhaled ours on the Western Front, but in the last few years it has deeply wounded his self-esteem and dignity. He has found only one remedy that works: strychnine pills. Pitifully ignorant as you are, you nevertheless know that strychnine taken in regular doses is a poison that causes burning in the stomach wall. So there is our Führer, caught between two ills: ill-timed effusions of gas and intolerable cramps. But just at that moment, nothing less than a miracle occurs! A certain Doktor Morell arrives, a magician whose services are in great demand in Berlin society. He tampers with pharmaceutical products and cures incurable patients with cocktails of his own invention. He has been charged several times with quackery, but powerful figures have had the charges dismissed. Emma Göring is one of his protectors. What does Morell suggest to Hitler? A modest white pill and a daily injection. The cramps subside and the gas is tamed. Hitler is reborn and full of good cheer again. He can speak to the crowds without fear of public ridicule. Doktor Morell becomes his personal physician. He accompanies the Führer everywhere. Naturally the prescription has to be gradually increased: two, then three and four pills a day. At this stage we are up to five pills and two injections to stop him falling asleep. Morell is with him constantly, syringe in one hand, pills in the other. Three times a day he takes his baby's blood pressure. The leader of the eternal Reich is so perforated he's turning into a sieve! Needless to say there are those around him who try to put a stop to this madness. Nothing doing. The Führer no longer farts. That's all that matters to him. Unfortunately the active ingredient of the heaven-sent pills is methamphetamine, a euphoric and stimulant whose chronic use is known to cause Parkinson's disease-like symptoms and episodes of psychosis resembling schizophrenia. Which is why, despite appearances, despite the admirable achievements of von Brauchitsch, von Rundstedt, Rommel, Guderian and a few others, all of them true military geniuses, the divine Hitler will not survive an extended campaign. And all because of his farts! Human nature is truly a petty thing! There's nothing to laugh about. Germany deserved a leader with better health. Amen. Having said that, in the light of this ultra-secret information, we need to row our boat intelligently while the German rearguard – including those souls on the somewhat tipsy Paris gravy train – continue modestly to celebrate their victory. I know a number who are already looking forward to ordering their caviar and getting their boots polished for the big review on Red Square. Let us not rain on their parade. When a man feels the euphoria of victory, he is open to interesting offers. He can be a gentleman, so long as it doesn't cost him too much ...'

'I still have a question to ask you.'

'I know what it is. How do I know all this? Well, my dear boy, there are one or two realistic soldiers left. It happens. I suppose you also want to know how I heard about Doktor Morell? From the same sources. Some believe that this shady character with a dubious past is actually an agent of British military intelligence or the American OSS. What a wonderful thought! There would never have been a war if those two organisations of espionage and counterespionage had possessed the slightest intelligence. A plan like that would have been brilliant. Just as if the German Sicherheitsdienst had managed to supply Churchill with his daily bottle of whisky ...'

The summer night was falling. The avenue with its blue lamps was fading into shadow, pierced by the occasional headlights of a car. A Light 11 – Palfy apologised: there was really nothing but Citroëns to buy at the moment – was waiting at the entrance. The chauffeur got out, took off his cap and held the door open. The day before, he had been waiting for Cyrille, Claude and Jean at Gare de Lyon, where he had piled their luggage into the boot: a mute figure with a pear-shaped head and a bovine expression, happy to drive a privileged individual while the unhappy populace crowded into the Métro.

Dinner was in a bistro that had a notice on the door: 'Closed on Sundays'. They made their way down an unlit side passage and Palfy knocked twice, and twice again. A door half opened and a bald man with a plump red face appeared in the gap.

'Ah, Baron, please come in! You're the last to arrive. And late! Fortunately the *petit salé* can wait …'

'Louis, this is Monsieur Jean Arnaud.'

'Monsieur Arnaud, our friends' friends are our friends.'

He moved aside to let them pass through into what must have been the back room of the restaurant, a small room that opened into the kitchen, wallpapered in a design the colour of mud. The ceiling light, which had a tasselled lampshade, lit a round table around which, already seated, were Madeleine, Marceline Michette, Nelly Tristan and as always, her producer, Émile Duzan, and Rudolf von Rocroy. Madeleine kissed Jean.

'You're a deserter. We never see you. But your complexion reassures me: the sun suits you. Julius will be sorry to miss you. He left for Berlin yesterday. He'll be back tomorrow …'

Rudolf had sufficient good manners to recognise the young salesman from the Montmartre gallery whom Blanche had told him about: 'He's a very honest and intelligent boy. He'll do well.' We shall spare the reader the details of the menu. They will have already guessed that in this den of initiates the cuisine was considerably above the usual Paris standard for the time. Louis, a former café owner, and his wife, a skinny, raw-looking woman from the Auvergne, cooked for a select clientele: *foie gras* from the Landes, *petit salé* with lentils, cheese and *nègres en chemise*.[18] A proper wartime menu, with champagne to go with the *foie gras*, a 1929 Bonnes-Mares for the *petit salé*, and a modest

Anjou with the dessert. Seated between Marceline Michette and Nelly Tristan, Jean would have had a boring evening if it had not been for Nelly deciding, several glasses into the *petit salé*, to pick a fight with Rudolf von Rocroy. Émile Duzan cringed in shame and fear. Rudolf thought she was teasing him and laughed heartily at her insults, not understanding them. Palfy scribbled a note and had it passed to Jean. 'She says everything I think about him. Isn't she divine?'

Divine? Jean found it hard to see her in that light. The summer had brought no change to Nelly's almost sickly pallor, her black, glistening eyes and mouth of an exquisite natural pink that opened to reveal perfect teeth. Innocence was the only possible word to characterise her features, framed in her medallion-like face. But then the face spoke and became animated, and her lips, designed to eat cherries or nibble shyly at a shoulder, poured out a string of obscenities. It was a gripping performance, and one could understand why Émile Duzan waited anxiously each time to see what she would come up with. Despite her producer's mute pleadings, she laid down her knife and fork, clasped her pretty hands under her chin, and said to Rudolf with an angelic smile, 'Let's play the truth game. Do you know it?'

'Yes! Viss great pleasure.'

'All right. I would like to know whether all of you Teutonic warriors, Prussian squires, Baltic barons and Austrian bastards aren't really, I mean deep down, secretly poofs.'

The German would rather have been cut into little pieces than admit that he did not understand a word in French. What should he make of 'poof'? Should he not be reassured by Nelly's smile that it could only be a very positive epithet?

'Ach, let us not exacherate. There are some who are, more or less.'

'I think, dear Rudolf,' Nelly said, leaning her head on Jean's shoulder despite the furious stare of Émile Duzan, 'I think, dear, handsome Rudolf, that it's all a question of stoicism. The first time one is sodomised, it is really very painful.'

'Fery painful,' he agreed.

'Afterwards it becomes quite pleasant.'

'Fery pleasant!'

Madeleine interrupted.

'Nelly darling, I'm not sure this is a terribly nice conversation. I much prefer it when you recite something. You're so different ... so ... how shall I put it ... possessed by what you're saying, you make me shiver.'

'What do you want? Some Valéry?'

'I don't know. Everything you do is so lovely.'

Nelly put her hands up to her face and, in a transformed voice that was hardly audible, recited 'The Steps'.

> *'Your steps, offspring of my quietness.*
> *Placed so slowly, and so saintly,*
> *Towards the bed of my sleeplessness*
> *Proceed, stonily and faintly.*
>
> *Purest one, shadow divine*
> *With what restrained, soft footfalls you with me meet*
> *Gods! ... all the gifts you have made mine*
> *Come towards me on those bare feet ...'*

Nelly stopped, took her hands away from her face, and poured herself a glass of wine.

'The rest next time,' she said. 'So, handsome Rudolf, do we like French poetry?'

Jean observed with pleasure that the young woman's poise and versatility had such an impact on the German that they robbed him of his facility and his fatuous air of a man of the world. Rudolf assured her that he adored Paul Valéry and read him every day. But it turned out that Nelly had not done with her previous subject, and she began to go into detail. Madame Michette frowned and interrupted.

'At my establishment such matters are never spoken of,' she said with barely controlled indignation. 'If a customer wants that sort of thing, we make him pay extra!'

Palfy puffed on his cigar and blew smoke rings. Jean understood that he was at his absolute happiest, savouring with profound relish the disarray being produced in the wake of this euphoric dinner. Louis brought out a bottle of Armagnac, as a welcome diversion. Nelly's leg was pressed against Jean's, and he thought about Claude: she was having dinner at her mother's with Cyrille tonight. She would be coming back to Quai Saint-Michel by the last Métro. They had parted that morning, unhappy, indecisive, hesitant about seeing each other again, yet certain that they could not avoid doing so. He liked Nelly's perfume and he liked the refinement and grace of her profile and her shirt open to reveal her braless breasts. She was a devil, and he had made no sacrifices to the devil for too long.

When Émile Duzan told her the bicycle-taxi was waiting, Nelly refused to go with him.

'I really can't bear to see another single one of those tandemists with his fat bum aimed at me. Who'll see me home?'

Rudolf, Palfy and Madeleine all offered. Each of them had a car. She chose Palfy indirectly, taking Jean's arm. Duzan tried to display his authority.

'I'll wait for you to ring the bell. You don't have a key.'

In the commotion it was difficult to hear her ungracious response, inviting Émile to stick the key in an unnameable place. The reader will be aware that he was not about to comply and he took such offence that he declared it was all over between them. Nelly gave a deep sigh.

'At last!'

Rudolf kissed her hand and promised to telephone her.

'But please do, dear Rudolf.'

Sitting between Palfy and Jean in the back of the Light 11 as they drove down Rue de Rivoli, she yawned.

'Where shall we have our last drink?'

'At my place,' Palfy said.

'What about my little Jean?'

'He lives with me. From now on we shall never be parted.'

'You're not poofs by any chance, are you?'

'Nelly darling, it's becoming an obsession with you.'

Since the beginning of June Palfy had been living in Rue de Presbourg, in a superb apartment furnished with as much taste as Julius's. The owner was in Spain, awaiting better times. He was fortunate that his *objets d'art* would not find their way into the public domain. As for Jean living there, it was true. He had wanted to go back to Rue Lepic, but the key was no longer under the doormat, where it had always been. Palfy claimed to know what had happened: slowly but surely, Fräulein Laura Bruckett had got her claws into Jean's friend Jesús. He had softened and, now sharing the rations of his rapt German admirer, was currently thought to be in the Chevreuse valley, where he and Laura had been on a honeymoon for the past fortnight in a small farm filled with butter, cream and smoked hams. She was stuffing him with cakes. His waistline was expanding. How fast everything changed! In two months at most. At the Galerie du Tertre, La Garenne did not know what to do: no more paintings, no more drawings. Fortunately Alberto had been freed and resumed his photographic business. Blanche had gone to find Palfy to beg him to bring Jean back ...

Nelly took her shoes and stockings off before having her last drink.

'You mustn't think I'm drunk,' she said. 'I'm just so bored stiff. Life is no fun. I've got to get rid of Duzan. He's hopeless. He promises me Hollywood when the war's over but he's never set foot there. And he's never got any money; he borrows, gets into debt, doesn't pay me – he's so mean I could scream – and as for *The Girl and the She-*

wolf, what a dud! For that I'll never forgive him. You know … I feel crushed by something as bad as that. But people will watch anything, and everyone knows there's a sweet little scene with me in the bath. Duzan lives off my tits …'

She pulled open her shirt and offered them to the two men's gaze.

'I quite agree, they're very pretty indeed,' Palfy said politely, pouring himself another drink. 'I find it reprehensible that Émile Duzan makes his living by showing them to the general public.'

'Find me another sugar daddy then! A real one. And I'll stop drinking! Where's the toilet?'

Jean showed her to the bathroom adjoining his bedroom. She shut the door as the telephone rang. Palfy told Duzan that Nelly was already asleep and that it would be best to leave her where she was. Were there not two of them there to look after her? No, no, she hadn't drunk anything since they left the restaurant. All Jean could hear was a distant gurgling: the producer's furious, desperate voice demanding and then imploring Nelly's return. All day long this man terrorised his employees, and in the evening snivelled over a girl abandoning him for a night. He hung up eventually, half convinced by Palfy, but he must have called Madeleine to complain to her because shortly afterwards she telephoned in turn, anxious about the consequences and begging them to drive Nelly back to Duzan's. The best jokes were the ones where you knew when to stop, she said. Julius liked the producer and would take his side. Palfy reassured her: nothing bad would happen to Nelly and they would take her back if she showed the slightest inclination to go. At present she was locked in the bathroom, standing in front of the mirror and thinking about the ravages that alcohol would soon wreak on the smooth skin of her lovely face. Madeleine agreed that was a good thing. Yet Nelly was not an alcoholic. While she was filming, not a glass of wine passed her lips. Alcohol was simply a means of forgetting her boredom when she was not working and her panic when she found herself in a room with more than two people. Palfy convinced Madeleine that they would take care of her. She sent her love and begged them to have lunch with her tomorrow at Avenue Foch. Julius would be back and there would be a very interesting Pole whom they really ought to meet. Palfy promised.

'Obviously,' he said to Jean after he put the phone down, 'you have little idea of the nest of vipers in which we are operating. Julius is officially in charge of overseeing all textile production in France and requisitions everything that appears on the market. Less openly, he is also the boss of the Abwehr's economic intelligence service and in open warfare with the same department of the SS. Duzan is his key person in the film industry. We therefore have to move carefully in order not to offend him … Listen, go and check your girlfriend hasn't fainted in the bathroom.'

Nelly's skirt, shirt and underwear were spread over the bedroom floor. Naked under the sheet she had pulled up to her chin, she was already asleep, her angelic face lying on the pillow, lit by a bedside lamp.

'A Greuze to the life,' Palfy murmured. 'Night, dear boy. What a brilliant return to Paris this is! I'm happy for you. Let me repeat, in case you've forgotten, that she's also talented, immensely talented. Ask her to recite the telephone directory and she'll move you to tears …'

'I'm not going to ask her to do that tonight.'

'No, evidently not.'

'Where am I going to sleep?'

'Idiot!'

Shutting the door, he disappeared. Jean bent over Nelly's face. Her dark eyes gave a bluish tinge to her fragile eyelids. Her face was like that of a child without sin. Only complete candour could have inspired such a pretty nose. He turned away to look out of the open window at the warm, black night swept by the beam of a searchlight. In the East the butchery was continuing, and the rattle of death filled the red sky, while Antoine, at the wheel of his jacked-up Bugatti, drank champagne or grappa and from time to time switched on his headlights to light up the expanse of the Mediterranean. Toinette too was sleeping, another angelic face. He should have stayed with them, jumped at Théo's invitation to share their life and wait out the end of the war there, as Palfy had predicted it. Claude might perhaps have stayed too. She had adapted painlessly to the Tropezians' careless, immature existence. But would she have resisted her mother's imperious demands, resisted what bound her to Paris? There was no convincing that categorical creature once she had said 'no'. He imagined her, across the rooftops, in her apartment on Quai Saint-Michel, sharing her bed with Cyrille, a woman both weak and strong, suffering a torment she could not overcome and to which she too awaited the end in anguish. If their thoughts, as they stood or lay awake that night, were not alike, then they were no longer of any help to one another in this world.

Nelly turned over in bed, offering her other profile. Jean switched off the light and lay down beside her, not daring to touch her. The hours passed and a greyish gleam rose behind the roofs. A German car engine disturbed the silence in the street, followed by pedestrians talking in loud voices, their footsteps ringing on the pavement. Jean moved his hand to Nelly's hip and she shivered, sighed and snuggled against him. She stroked him and he buried his face in her neck and hair. She lifted her head and pressed her lips to his cheek, roughened with his beard, in a childish kiss.

Just as they concluded the last of their amorous exercise, Palfy knocked at the door. He was pushing a trolley covered in china and silverware.

'My butler stayed in London, I'm afraid,' he said. 'I do hope poor Price is saving my honour and paying my debts. I asked him to come, but he refuses. He's like those island birds that die if you change their climate. He prefers to spend his nights in underground shelters. A man without imagination, a sheep.'

Nelly jumped out of bed stark naked, kissed Palfy, ran to the bathroom and shut the door.

'I must say,' Palfy said, 'she spends a lot of time in that little room.

It doesn't make her any less charming, not at all, and one does prefer the clean sort of person, completely clean. As for you, you look a real sight. About a hundred years old, I'd say ...'

'I am.'

'You must fight it. Age is a serious handicap. Look at that child; she woke just like a rose. What an exquisite creature! Keep her for a few days. I'll disconnect the phone and tell the concierge to admit no one.'

'Thanks, but I'm letting her go.'

'I despair of you. It's in infidelity that the strong measure the greatness of their love. I hope you're thinking of that at this moment.'

'I wasn't, actually. Thanks for reminding me.'

Nelly came back, wrapped in a bath towel that left her shoulders and thighs bare. Jean closed his eyes. One morning Claude had sat on the edge of his bed in the same way. Their two bodies had something in common, with something more finished and calm about Claude's. Nelly lifted the lid of the plate warmer, served herself eggs and bacon, and ate greedily.

'Émile hasn't telephoned yet, has he?' she asked with her mouth full.

'Last night. I didn't want to disturb you. You were already asleep.'

'Was he making a fuss?'

'It can't be said that he was happy.'

'I don't care. I don't want to make films any more. I'm going back to the theatre. Oh, not to see his face ever again!'

'Love doesn't move you?'

'Mine does, of course. Not others'.'

She leant towards Jean and kissed him on the forehead.

'Go and shave,' she said. 'We'll go for a walk. I'm giving myself a holiday.'

'We have to have lunch at Madeleine's,' Jean said timidly.

'Oh God, eating, always eating! That's all we'll remember about this occupation. Why don't we go into the country instead and see your friend, the great Jesús?'

*

What they did that day is of little importance. Did they go to see Jesús or did they have lunch at Madeleine's with the aforementioned Pole, who was actually hardly a Pole at all and more a stateless Jew like the already famous Joanovici and, like him, a supplier to the Germans, plundering France in their name and amassing a fabulous fortune? Yes, it hardly matters, because what matters, as the reader will have guessed, is that Jean has tripped up and in doing so renewed, after long abstinence, his acquaintance with the pleasure women offer and begun a period in which the vanity of an affair, even a chaotic one, does not transcend his self-disgust and remorse at being unfaithful to Claude and seeing her suffer. He does not even need to lie. She knows, yet when he misses an evening with her and returns the next day without an excuse, hardly a shadow is visible on her face.

Nelly could be delightfully provocative. That is to say, she possessed many ways to please. Jean discovered her talent, of which he had so far had only glimpses through a fog of alcohol. When she was not swearing at the imbeciles who surrounded and exploited her, she could awaken a lover by reciting softly in his ear:

> 'Our weapons are not like enough
> For my soul to welcome you in,
> All you are is naive male stuff,
> But I'm the Eternal Feminine
>
> My object's lost amid the starry trail!
> It's I who am the Great Isis!
> No one has yet peeled back my veil
> You should think only of my oasis ...

If my song offers you any echoes,
You'd be quite wrong to hesitate
I murmur it to you as no pose
People know me: this is my womanly state'

Jean listened to the voice, which spoke only to him. Nelly, naked, opened the window wide and exclaimed, 'What are we doing, always fucking when there's life outside, just waiting for us?'

'Who's that by?'

'By me.'

'No. Before.'

'By Jules.'

'Jules who?'

She shrugged her shoulders and skipped into her bathroom, where he followed to see her covered in soapy foam.

'You don't know anything. You make me feel like an old woman who's teaching a schoolboy a thing or two.'

'Jules who?'

'Jules Laforgue.'

She splashed him with foam. Ten minutes later, fully dressed, she left for the studio where Émile Duzan was waiting for her, having rapidly abandoned her vague resolutions to quit the cinema. Between scenes she telephoned Jean, whom she now called Jules-who, and if she reached him it was always to beg him, 'Please come, Jules-who. I really cannot cope with these pricks any more. I love only you.'

He did not believe a word of it. She still occasionally slept with Duzan, who endured torments, hated Jean, and offered him a job in his studio, in public relations. Palfy urged Jean to accept.

'It's an ideal job for you. You get out. No being stuck in an office. In six months you'll know everybody.'

'And every morning I'll see Duzan's ugly mug! No thanks!'

'He's not a bad person. His being in love and being bashful about it proves it. Anyhow, he likes to suffer; it gives him the feeling he exists.

He just wants to keep his executioner close.'

Faced with the difficulty of finding anything else, Jean eventually said yes. He earned double what La Garenne had once begrudged him. And in any case a catastrophe had befallen the gallery on Place du Tertre, to which Blanche had beseeched him in vain to return. One afternoon two inspectors had arrived and introduced themselves, asking politely, but brooking no refusal, for the director to open his flies and show them his member. Terrorised and struck dumb, La Garenne had complied. Faced with this graceless object, the inspectors had nodded and requested La Garenne to follow them. Blanche had been nonplussed. She had run to Palfy, and from him had an explanation. Since June they had been taking a census of Jews, and anonymous letters had been flooding in to the Préfecture and the Kommandantur. Apparently the former Léonard Twenty-Sous was not called La Garenne but something much less sonorous, despite its being one of the most celebrated tribes of Israel, to which the Virgin Mary had belonged. Several telephone calls established that Louis-Edmond was being held pending confirmation of his identity. Once he was released, he would no longer have the right to run a business. Blanche still could not understand what had aroused the suspicion of the inspectors. Palfy tactfully explained to her the mysteries of circumcision. Blanche, who had never known another organ besides La Garenne's, discovered how far the parents of an otherwise worldly girl might neglect her education, in the name of outdated modesty. She burst into sobs.

'He's broken my heart! And he claimed to be the descendant of a crusader! Why did he lie to me? I would have put up with everything from him. He's a man of quality.'

Palfy, uncomfortable at this paean of lyricism, took her out to lunch, where she drank more than she was used to, which had the unexpected merit of bringing her back to her senses.

'With the gallery closed and Louis-Edmond in prison, I'll be on the street.'

'No, I think I may have just the job for you.'

'I don't know how to do anything. Without him, I'm nothing.'

'The important thing, as I repeat endlessly to Jean, is not to know how to do anything. You're the ideal person.'

So Blanche became Madeleine's companion, warmly recommended by Palfy and Rudolf von Rocroy – but before finding her in that role, let us not forget in passing Mercedes del Loreto. It was three days after Louis-Edmond's arrest that Jean remembered the investigation carried out by Marceline Michette. Louis-Edmond had not even been allowed to go to Rue de la Gaîté to collect a toothbrush, which in any case he did not possess. What had happened to the poor bedridden old lady, whose sea-lion shrieks regularly shook the building? He dashed to Montparnasse with Marceline. Madame Berthe, the dresser, was propping up the bar of the café-*tabac* where the waiter was pouring her third glass of lunchtime medium-dry Anjou. Madame Michette took matters in hand, displaying a sudden authority that months of Palfy's petty ultra-secret missions had been stifling.

'Madame Berthe? Do you recognise me?'

'Ah, the journalist. How are you? You'll have a glass with me, won't you? Is this your son?'

'No, a friend.'

Madame Berthe winked.

'Perhaps you're in the press too? Photographer?'

'No,' Jean said. 'In films …'

'Films! Pouah!'

'We'd like to know if there's any news of Mercedes del Loreto.'

'It's funny you should mention that: this morning I was just saying to myself that it's been a good two days since I last heard the old lady's "*Arrh, arrh… oowowoowow …*"'

*

The police station gave them the address of a locksmith, and a policeman went with them to the top floor of the building.

Sitting up in bed, supported by cushions on either side and resting with a pillow behind her head, her hands clasped on the sheet, her stiff hair dyed with henna and held in place at her temples by a pink ribbon, and her eyes, a viscid blue, wide open, she was waiting for them. One might have thought that her relaxed lower jaw, laying bare a few last teeth, the yellow colour of old ivory, that poked up out of shrunken, rotten gums, was that way because she was about to complain bitterly, with sea-lion cries, of their neglect. But she was still. The wrinkles on her face covered thickly with foundation, her bituminous eyelids, the crazed, bright-red lipstick, were frozen for ever. The room's sour-sweet stench – a nauseating mixture of things left to rot, face creams and dead flesh – left no doubt. Mercedes had risen to the occasion of death with her sense of theatre undiminished. Her pot of foundation sat open on her bedside table, and on the floor – it must have slipped from her hands after a final inspection – lay a cheval glass, on which was written in greasepaint, 'Down with the Jews!' Yes, unintentionally she was berating her unknown visitors, the chance witnesses of her death – Marceline Michette, Madame Berthe, Jean Arnaud, an anonymous locksmith and a policeman (no. 2857) – for the mirror's message was meant for the person she had waited for in vain, her whipping boy, the deplorable Louis-Edmond upon whom she had heaped infamy since the day he was born. At that moment Jean felt sorry for him, however odious and ignoble he might be. What an ordeal his life must have been, caring for this mother he had loved, admired, cosseted, washed and spoon-fed, whose chamber pot he had guiltily tiptoed out to empty daily in the WC on the landing, and whose reward, as the ineluctable proof of her brief affair with a banker, had been to be showered with insults. The banker must have acknowledged the child, then abandoned it after one tantrum too many

223

from Señora del Loreto. The story did not seem hard to reconstruct, and one could picture the hell of these three rooms, with Mercedes hating Louis-Edmond for being the symbol of an ultimately failed career. What horror, and what a stench! The smell was unbearable, yet no one dared move, as if, pinned down by embarrassment, not one of the five witnesses could take another step. Agent no. 2857, who had already come across plenty of horrors and whose strong spirit was ready to confront more in this long, dark period, was the first to come back down to earth. He opened an attic window that no one had touched for centuries. The catch came away in his hand and a rod clattered down, freeing two panes thick with grime that smashed on the parquet floor. For the first time fresh air blew in with the sounds of Rue de la Gaîté: a newsboy selling *Paris-Soir*, a horse neighing. Madame Berthe stifled a theatrical sob.

'Madame del Loreto! Madame del Loreto!'

The policeman felt he should pick up the broken glass but rapidly gave up. Potato peelings, cigarette butts and newspaper cuttings were scattered thickly over the floor. Instead he moved to the bed to touch the scraggy arm that emerged from a lace nightdress that was grey with dirt.

'She's cold!' He nodded. 'And stiff!'

A doctor was summoned, who confirmed the death and signed the death certificate.

'It'll be difficult to straighten her out,' he said. 'But that's the undertaker's problem.'

Madame Berthe took things in hand.

'I'm a friend. Her son has been arrested.'

The policeman feigned mild interest.

'Has he committed a crime?'

'No. They say he's a Jew.'

'Everything's possible.'

She began searching through the three rooms. A wooden leg fell out of a tottering wardrobe.

'Just like Sarah Bernhardt!' Madame Berthe exclaimed. The theatre was in her blood.

A chest of drawers released a cascade of lace underwear.

'That's worth something!' Madame Michette said, acquainted with both the tastes of men and the lace of Le Puy.

The second room was a sort of kitchen with a stone sink overflowing with dirty plates and empty tins. The third was clearly Louis-Edmond's, if you could call a cupboard lit by a lead skylight a room. The dim light fell on a child's iron bedstead where he could only have slept curled up. Straw poked out of the torn mattress. La Garenne slept under a horse blanket that was full of holes. On a table there was a spare wig and some sketchbooks filled with pitiful caricatures, relics of the impecunious years of Léonard Twenty-Sous around La Coupole and the other cafés of Montparnasse. His cape hung on a hanger, and in a cardboard suitcase open on the floor there lay black ascots, celluloid collars and long johns of grey jersey.

At the sight Jean felt as if he was intruding so odiously into a man's privacy that he turned and left, taking Marceline Michette with him.

'We'll have seen a few things by the time this war's over!' she said. 'People sitting dead in their beds! Mercedes del Loreto! What a woman she must have been! And him? What a chap! Devoted and all ... And that old bag of bones, mustering the energy to insult him one last time before she snuffed it. There's no thanks for the charitable!'

The rest of the story belongs to the undertaker and to Louis-Edmond, who was released for a reason as obscure as the one that had got him arrested. The only people present at the funeral were him, Jean, Madame Berthe, Marceline and, in the background and so discreet his shyness was almost touching, an old gentleman in a hound's-tooth suit and white spats, his grey bowler hat at an angle, and in his buttonhole a red carnation that he threw on top of the coffin. Who was he? No one ever knew. He disappeared as he had come, between the graves of Montparnasse Cemetery, on a muggy morning at the end of August beneath a sky heavy with clouds that burst that afternoon, drenching Paris. Only Madame Berthe cried, out of theatrical habit, while Louis-Edmond remained dry-eyed, his face frozen, pasty from the days he had spent in custody, in the shadow of the Dépôt.[19] On the same day the Wehrmacht entered Dnepropetrovsk.

Anna Petrovna crammed a sugar cube into her mouth, drank her cup of tea and declared, 'The Germans will never take St Petersburg. The Russian people will force them back into the sea.'

Jean looked at her uneasily. He had said nothing which could have provoked this declaration of faith. In fact he had said barely a word after having arrived without warning at Quai Saint-Michel and found himself face to face with Claude's mother. Cyrille had thrown his arms around Jean's neck.

'Why don't you come every night any more? I'll tell you a secret when we're on our own, just us.'

Anna Petrovna had pretended not to hear, although her pale-blue eyes were scrutinising Jean with enough intensity to make him feel genuinely embarrassed. Claude had done her best to dispel the awkwardness.

'Maman has brought us some real tea. Do you want a cup?'

'Yes, but I shouldn't, it's so precious.'

Claude had poured him a cup and Anna Petrovna had launched her attack, as if what Jean had said somehow cast doubt upon the fighting qualities of her Russian compatriots.

'*Muzhik* or *tovarishch*, it's one and the same. When he's roused he'll defeat the world.'

Thinking of Palfy's theories, Jean almost smiled. Palfy foresaw a similar outcome, for more Gallic reasons. Deep down Anna Petrovna was suffering at the thought of the Russians' defeat, Russians she had so hated when they had driven her from her country.

'They'll allow them to reach Moscow, and Moscow will burn.

They'll only have ashes left. Stalin doesn't care. He's Georgian. To him the Muscovites are yellows.'

'What's yellows?' Cyrille asked.

Anna Petrovna shrugged. She spoke with a strong Russian accent, and even though Claude herself had no accent, their intonations were similar. Like many people at this time she had grown thinner and her face, a year ago still attractive, full and smooth, had sagged suddenly. New lines dragged at the corners of her mouth and eyes, destroying the remains of a beauty that had certainly been great, greater than Claude's with her regular features, her calm and reflective face. Anna Petrovna stood up.

'I must go. Good evening, Monsieur.'

Jean hoped that she had guessed everything and loathed him, not because of the way he looked, but because he was upsetting Claude's life. Cyrille hardly paid attention to his grandmother's departure and ran to fetch a building set Jean had brought him. Anna Petrovna swung a sealskin coat across her shoulders that looked tired, very tired despite suiting her very well. She drew Claude out onto the landing and Cyrille whispered, 'Jean, Maman cried when you didn't come three days in a row.'

'You mustn't let her cry. You have to make her laugh.'

'What were you doing?'

'I was working.'

The lie instantly weighed on him. You didn't lie to a child. Claude came back.

'We missed you,' she said.

'Spare me your reproaches.'

'I have no right to reproach you.'

'No. None at all.'

'Are you talking or playing?' Cyrille asked.

'I'm playing.'

Claude crossed the room.

'Are you eating with us?' she asked. 'I'm afraid it won't be much of a dinner.'

'I'm taking you both out to dinner.'

'Everything's so stale in restaurants these days. Let's stay here.'

'No, I insist.'

Cyrille clapped his hands.

'Let's go to the restaurant, I really want to!'

'You see!' Jean said.

Claude stood in front of him. He was tempted to jump up, take her in his arms and wipe everything out in an embrace.

'Are you playing then?' Cyrille repeated in an exasperated voice.

They played, then had dinner in an oriental restaurant at La Huchette. Cyrille was asleep in Jean's arms by the time they climbed the stairs at Quai Saint-Michel and Claude put him straight to bed. Jean tidied the building set away.

'You're too nice to him!' she said. 'By the time you've finished spoiling him there'll be nothing left for me to do.'

He stopped and took her hands.

'If we have to talk as if we don't mean anything to each other, it's better we never see each other again.'

'Never?'

'At least let me cure myself.'

'Cure's not the word you're looking for. Actually it's a ridiculous word, all right for an injury or for a bout of flu, but not for love. Love's not a sickness, love's a very healthy thing, despite what you say in its name or the qualities you give it. It's our own anaemia that makes it dangerous: I mean that when we feel defenceless or depressed and lonely, we're more vulnerable. Truly, cure is not a word for a man of twenty-one ...'

'Twenty-two!'

She smiled, losing her seriousness.

'I do beg your pardon ... yes, you're very young, you've got luck on your side, and Paris is a city where you can happily lose yourself. Where I can change my address tonight and you won't ever find me again.'

'I'll post Madame Michette's girls at every crossroads. They'll track you down.'

'At Clermont-Ferrand, perhaps, not here ...'

He took her in his arms and kissed her without letting her finish. Was that Nelly's fault? Was it she who had got him used to such an easy manner so quickly? He was being more direct than he had ever been. Claude gave a little moan and slipped to the floor.

'No,' she said, 'no. You promised me.'

'I didn't promise anything.'

'You know that I promised.'

'Who to?'

She shook her head and he took it between his hands to draw towards him her open, confused, almost innocent face ... almost, because if Nelly's innocence was powerful in its attraction, he found Claude's paralysing.

'You're my only friend,' she murmured.

He crouched next to her and they sank to the carpet together, hand in hand, mute, so filled by a desire that was rising in both of them in waves that they found themselves in each other's arms, their faces damp with tears.

'I love you,' he said.

'I love you too. I'd like you so much to take me far away from here, with Cyrille, the way you did to Saint-Tropez.'

'Let's go back there.'

'No. Marie-Dévote and Toinette don't like me.'

'You're talking nonsense.'

'It's something men don't see. They think I make you unhappy.'

'It's true.'

Claude sighed.

'It's true and it's false. They want you for themselves.'

'I've never been as happy as I was there. You used to walk round our bedroom with no clothes on.'

'I shouldn't have.'

'When we came back I was unkind. I lost interest for a while. I was annoyed.'

'I know …'

Jean would have liked to admit everything, but could not find the words. If he had been able to, perhaps he could have freed himself from Nelly that evening. Concealed, she continued to exist, and her power was great. Named, she would have been diminished, reduced to what she was: someone who had seduced a still weak young man who does not know how to say no. But the happiness that Claude represented had returned, with her anxiety, her demands, her moments of euphoria and the immense burning unhappiness he felt at not possessing this beautiful, luscious body that had no secrets for him. He spent the night at Quai Saint-Michel and returned to Rue de Presbourg at dawn. Palfy was furious.

'Your bitch of a girlfriend phoned ten times in the night to check whether you'd come home. Call her.'

Jean did not have to dial the number. Nelly rang for the eleventh time.

'Is that you, Jules-who? Where were you, you pig? I was worried sick. I phoned all the hospitals to find out if you'd been run over. I even called the Gestapo. They weren't very nice … Where were you?'

'With some friends.'

'Listen, Jules-who … You're a sweet boy and I like you a lot, but you're not allowed not to be there when I need you …'

'And when you don't need me?'

'You can do what you like. Come now.'

'I can't, I have meetings at the office.'

'Then when you've finished, come and pick me up at the studio. Tonight you're mine. Big kiss.'

She hung up. Palfy was drinking tea in his dressing gown.

'Jean, three-quarters of your life is taken up with women.'

'Once, at least, that suited you.'

'When?'

'In London.'

'That's true; I'd forgotten. What a terrific scheme that was! Do you remember?'

'It was a complete cock-up.'

'The best-laid plans of mice and men ... This time I've got it all worked out.'

'Like you did at Cannes?'

'No, you fond foolish boy. At Cannes I was just playing games.'

'You lost everything.'

'I picked up a barony.'

'Yet another theft.'

'You steal what belongs to someone else. Not what belongs to everybody. In any case you can't overlook the way your friend the prince and his faithful chauffeur ruined my plans ... Speaking of which, now would be a good moment to open the famous letter.'

'I promised not to use it unless I absolutely needed to.'

Palfy made a careless gesture.

'Oh, let's not wait for absolute need. We'll call it a random act. Anyhow, it's a little late for that.'

'Why?'

Palfy pulled the letter from his dressing-gown pocket. The envelope was open.

'You really are a bugger!' Jean said.

'Yes, and your life's too much of a mess. You should be admiring my tact. I'm saving you from any remorse.'

Jean had little choice but to hear him out.

'It's fairly childish, and to be honest I doubted if it would contain anything valuable anyway, but I wanted to know the final recipient: an interesting character, rarely discussed, except by the brothel owners whose names were on the list in the first envelope.'

'So who is it?' Jean asked impatiently.

'You know him.'

'Me?'

'Yes. It's Longuet, whose charming son Gontran you had a fight with and who took Chantal de Malemort from you. Yesterday in the *Journal Officiel* I saw that henceforth he has the right to call himself Longuet de La Sauveté. Soon it will be just Monsieur de La Sauveté, which will be a fine monicker for his little Gontran. I rather foresee another baron in the French peerage. What's most interesting is discovering how powerful this person is. Yet again we find the mafia of the white slave trade deeply mixed up with politics and the police. Here, take your letter, dear boy. It could be useful to you one day. And go and shave. You've spent the night with your Claude and it does you no good, ever.'

We shall not linger on Jean's life in his new capacity. It would be pointless to be any more interested in it than he is himself. There is too much passing trade, faces coming and going whose outlines and voices are immediately forgotten, so that Jean numbers them to remember them more easily. Paris at the close of 1941 is far more captivating. After months of despondency, courage has returned, though events are scarcely conducive to optimism. Who is lying, who telling the truth? No one knows that the Wehrmacht, having become bogged down in the autumn mud, is now freezing at the gates of Moscow. Paris has resumed its role as the fun-loving and intellectual capital of Europe. The theatres have never been fuller, there have never been so many books read, and the film industry, so in the doldrums before the war, is basking in a new golden era. No thanks to Duzan specifically: he is content to follow in others' footsteps, to jump on bandwagons and benefit from the gap in the market left by the dearth of Anglo-Saxon films. Nelly Tristan's star is rising, she has been signed for three films that she will eventually not make. She will make others later, when the war is over, all equally bad until the day she finally meets a proper director.

But Duzan was vain enough to like having her under contract and, from time to time, to warm his bed. It was a vanity that came at a price: Nelly had a gift for exposing it in public by treating him like a doormat. Humiliated, he complained to Jean, who wondered whether the producer wasn't employing him to be sure of keeping Nelly. He would storm unannounced into Jean's office.

'Do you know what she's just done to me?'

'No.'

There followed a tale of some joyful prank of which he had been the wretched victim.

'She's impossible. Yesterday evening, at the end of shooting, she was drunk, completely drunk—'

'It's nothing to do with me.'

'When you're there she doesn't drink.'

'I can't be there all the time.'

Jean felt contempt for Duzan. How could a crook such as he was be so feeble and snivelling as soon as a fragile woman came on the scene? Not for a second did he imagine that Duzan was in love and that, however embarrassing his love for Nelly might be, it was nevertheless an emotion that deserved sympathy. He thought Duzan old – over forty! – mean and stupid. The only things that mattered to him were a passion for money rapidly earned and the misplaced pride of being a producer. And what was he looking for when he came to Jean, if not the trace of Nelly's perfume and the magic formula of the man to whom she gave herself for nothing?

'Yes,' Duzan said, 'I know everything. I forgive her. She had an unhappy childhood. She tries to forget …'

Jean, unkindly, decided to give him something to think about.

'You forgive her because she's the devil.'

'The devil?'

Visibly more anxious than privileged to have been sought out by the devil, Duzan left his office and did not return for three days. Nelly considered Jean's idea excellent. Wasn't everything permitted to the devil?

'Now and then, Jules-who, you're a genius. Here I am, cleared of guilt, forgiven, and seduction itself. And somehow you've flattered that idiot. The devil doesn't go out of his way for just anyone.'

She lived near Place Saint-Sulpice in a studio apartment filled with books, set models and signed photographs from her friends in the theatre. That was how he learnt she had won first prize for comedy from the Conservatoire for a scene from *The Widow*.

'The Widow? Who?'

'I love it when you say "who", you scrumptious little Jules-who. Whose widow? Pierre Corneille's. Listen to Clarice:

'Dear confidant of all of my desires
Beautiful place, secret witness to my disquietude,
No longer is it with my sighing fires
That I come to abuse your solitude;
Past are my sufferings
Granted are my longings
Words to joy give way!
My fate has changed its law from harsh to fine .
And the object I possess in a word to say,
My Philiste is all mine ...'

Jean was discovering that this careless and chaotic woman possessed a feeling for poetry that was genuinely harmonious. She truly loved the music of words, and Palfy had not been exaggerating when he declared that she could have made an entire auditorium weep by reciting the telephone directory. She was Dr Jekyll and Mr Hyde rolled into one, or at least with such a brief interlude between the two that it was frightening. Absorbed in *La Jeune Parque* while the lighting was being readied on set, she would awake from her reverie and, seeing Duzan hiding behind a camera, yell, 'Get him out of here!'

'Nelly, he's the boss!' the studio manager would implore her.

'The boss is an arse ... Everyone repeat after me: The boss is an arse... the boss is an arse ...'

Duzan left, pursued from the studio by the shouts of the technicians and the actors. When the scene had been shot, was in the can, and on its way to the lab, Nelly called him.

'I'm waiting for you! You and your bicycle-taxi bum! You surely don't think I'm going home by Métro?'

Duzan ran to her. He felt like weeping, but instead took her out to dinner in a restaurant where he hoped everyone would recognise her.

'It's Nelly Tristan!'

And his assurance would return as she recounted her day to him, her tiffs with the other actors, or complained at length about the screenplay's excessive vulgarity. Then, if he was too high-handed with the waiters, she would summon the head waiter or the restaurant's owner.

'Pay no attention. He's very spoilt. He's just playing at the producer-taking-his-star-out-to-dinner.'

To Jean, when she saw him the next day, she admitted, 'He's never loved me as much as he has since I've been cheating on him with you. I need to cheat on him much more. What a bore! Because then you'll start getting jealous.'

'No. Not a chance!'

'Oh well ...'

She was not at all put out. She knew Jean had another love.

'Is she kind to you?' she asked.

'Very.'

'What's her name?'

'Claude.'

'Is that a woman or a man?'

'A woman.'

'Are you sure she's not a transvestite?'

'Absolutely sure.'

'Phew!'

If Claude had dinner at her mother's – which seemed to be happening more frequently, as though Anna Petrovna, apprised of the danger her daughter was running, was doing her best to take her in hand – he stayed the night at Nelly's. Sitting on a deep-pile carpet in front of the fireplace where a wood fire crackled, she would question him.

'What have you read, then?'

'*The Thibaults.*'[20]

She shrugged.

'Average. What else?'

'*Remembrance of Things Past.*'

'Better. Who's your favourite poet?'

'Before I met you, I didn't know anyone who knew how to recite poetry.'

'What do you want to hear?'

'Whatever you like.'

She closed her eyes, suddenly absent again, and her voice rose, so poignantly that it enveloped Jean.

> *'My heart beats only with its wings*
> *I can follow no further than my prison wall*
> *Oh my friends, lost beyond all recall*
> *It is but your hidden lives I'm listening to ...'*

'Who's that by?' he asked.

'Reverdy.'

'I don't know him.'

'You scrumptious boy.'

When they were alone together, she did not drink.

'With you,' she said, 'I don't need to be unbearable in order to exist. You're kind. You're actually extraordinarily normal. Not *machosistic*, as old Madame Michette would say, not machosistic for a second. I might be unhappy for a few minutes the day you leave me.'

'Who says I'm going to leave you?'

'Me. I know you are. And deep down I don't care, just like I don't care about you. You're not irreplaceable.'

'I know. What about Duzan?'

'Dudu? Oh, he's for life. I'm his Omphale.'

'He's not Hercules.'

'No, he's not … but I've told him he's an arse so often that he believes it.'

'He told me you had an unhappy childhood.'

'Me? Not for a second. I love my papa and maman. He works on the railways, she's at home. Stationmaster at a little village in the south-west. He'll never get another promotion and he doesn't mind a bit. Ever since he was a child he's written poetry, and all his poems are as bad as each other, but he doesn't know that. He's a member of the Société des Gens de Lettres and he thinks it's something very similar to the Académie Française. He's kind and generous and has always got his head in the clouds. A poet, you see. He's had several near-misses changing the points. Otherwise he's a very good stationmaster. One day we'll go and see my parents. You'll see my mother look at me wide-eyed. She says I'm like my father, artistic. He adores me because I'm his revenge on the people who don't understand him. When a magazine rejects his poems he's unhappy and shouts at everyone at the station. Otherwise he's awfully nice. One in a million. I tell myself it's from him that I have inherited the little light burning in me, that makes me not like the other actors around me, and him not like the other railway workers around him.'

*

Jean should have been torn between Claude and Nelly and he felt confused not to be, failing to grasp, in the happy surprise of it all, that the two women complemented each other and left him no freedom whatsoever. He went from one to the other as if to two different pleasures. Claude's beauty had the appearance of tranquillity, yet was anything but tranquil. Nelly's was that of a charming, false muddle. One was half hidden behind a stubborn secret, the other was open and laughed and glittered like diamonds. He could not have borne Nelly without Claude, and without Nelly he would not have been able to put up with the kind of relationship Claude offered him. Nelly was visible to everyone. Claude remained hidden. That was why he did not want Palfy to see her again or want Madeleine to know her. He thought about Jesús and decided that he was allowed.

Earlier it seemed to us unimportant for this account of Jean's life to know whether he went to the Chevreuse valley with Nelly the day after their first night together. This was a mistake. In fact it was extremely important, and let us say here and now, having made enquiries, that they didn't, giving in instead to Madeleine's pleading that they should come and meet her Pole, another key individual in the Germans' organised plunder of France. But Jean felt that Jesús was one person he wanted to introduce Claude to. He wrote to him. From Paris, where she returned to work every day, Fräulein Bruckett telephoned Jean's office. They would expect him that weekend.

'That's good timing,' Nelly said when she heard the news. 'I was about to feel bad about leaving you on Saturday and Sunday. Dudu's taking me to a château whose name I've forgotten. Some people he swears aren't in the least bit annoying. Go to your friend's. A bit of fresh air will do you good.'

*

Jesús was waiting for them at the station at Gif-sur-Yvette. He had got fatter. Not in his face so much, but his waistline had thickened. He carried Cyrille on his shoulders for the two kilometres to the farm. Laura came home early every evening, and left again at dawn in her little car. She was the vital force of their house. As soon as she arrived she would shed her field-grey uniform, put on a pair of corduroy trousers and a sweater, and cook, dust and pickle vegetables. Jesús had turned a barn into his studio. Jean saw immediately that he was working for himself, feverishly and with a pleasure that transformed him.

'You see, Jean, I'm on my way again. I'm paintin', do you hear, I'm paintin'. No more bollocks. I am an artis'! No' a clown for La Garenne. You know 'e came to see me?'

'When?'

'Yes'erday.'

The previous day, in fact, La Garenne had turned up at the farm, puffed out from the two-kilometre walk, brandishing a piece of paper.

'I've got the certificate, I can reopen my gallery! Jesús, you can't leave me now. All this nonsense has cost me a fortune. Not counting my mother's burial. She wanted it all first-class, the organ at Saint-Sulpice, six horses, mountains of red roses and invitations for all of Paris society …'

Jean disabused Jesús. Louis-Edmond had conducted his mother to Montparnasse Cemetery with the least possible pomp. As for the certificate, it was yet another fraud. A Professor Montandon, a so-called ethnologist approved by the Commissariat of Jewish Affairs, had certified on official notepaper that the subject of his examination had been circumcised in his youth for medical reasons. La Garenne had sworn that his name was unimpeachably authentic, that he was indeed the descendant of a crusader, and that because his true father was not in a position to recognise him he had had him adopted by a proxy. So yes, he was officially called Levy and had suffered for it since childhood, because he could not stand Jews.

''E disgust' me,' Jesús said. 'I 'ave chucked him out. In Spain is no Jews! We is all a lil' bit Jewish, thanks to thee Inquissición. Yes, all converted an' good Christians. If you 'ad seen him! He was cryin' … Get out, filthy antisemite, I tol' him. Laura drove him back to the station …'

The studio looked out onto an orchard whose trees were bare with the approach of winter. Beyond the orchard a line of poplars bent in the wind. Jesús took no notice of the gold and grey Île-de-France countryside. His easel stood in front of the window, and he painted the Andalusia he knew, the Mediterranean, its skies purged of all content by the noonday heat. Jean wondered if Jesús really was a great painter, a marvellous force of nature exploding into colour.

'Wha' do you think?' Jesús asked, anxious at his friend's silence.

'Very beautiful.'

'Then don' say me anythin' else.'

Laura appeared before nightfall. She brought a suitcase of food and a present for Cyrille, a model car made of painted wood. Jean would not have recognised her if he had met her in the street. Physically small, a brassy blonde, she was as insignificant as a woman can be. Despite her strong accent and timid voice, she spoke excellent French. This nondescript person had had the wit to keep Jesús, to isolate him so he could work, feed him properly and divert him enough at night so that he didn't go looking elsewhere. Under her spell, he had forgotten his theories on love. He had spent far more than two nights in a row with Laura – six months of nights – and settled into the well-considered comfort she had organised around him. Every evening she brought back from Paris food she was able to obtain as a result of her post in the Department of Supply for the occupying army. Jesús, with the help of a carpenter and a stonemason, had refurbished and installed the big kitchen, his studio and two bedrooms. Each morning he pushed down the pump handle three hundred times and the pump, connected to the well, pumped water into a tank in the attic. He strongly recommended Jean to have a go himself: the exercise would transform him from a weakling into a bodybuilder. Sawing wood for the farm's fires and stove also helped Jesús stay fit, because the rest of the time he was in his studio, working without a fire, in shirtsleeves. An Andalusian is never cold. It was only people in the north who complained of the cold and people in the south who complained of the heat. A world government endowed with a modicum of common sense ought to organise, in the near future, when the war was over, massive migrations to make people happy once and for all. Jesús was convinced that if ever he returned to live in Spain one day, he would paint nothing but the landscapes of the Île-de-France, or Rue Norvins in the snow.

Cyrille was playing with his car, crawling across the flagstones of the kitchen. Laura was lighting the stove and getting dinner ready. Claude was setting the table. The two men had their feet up in front of the fire, glasses in hand. Outside the wind whistled. A passing hailstorm pattered on the windows. Jesús said carelessly that, despite being not the slightest bit bothered by the cold, he would rather be inside a house with walls a metre thick than outside in the open countryside.

'Not everybody has your good fortune,' Laura said gently.

She was thinking about her brother, an infantry lieutenant in von Bock's army. The previous day in a letter he had begged her for socks and sweaters. The Russian winter was starting and the Wehrmacht had still not taken Moscow. A thousand leagues from that turmoil Jesús painted and gave La Garenne the boot, and tonight was welcoming his friend Jean. An unknown small boy was playing on the kitchen floor. Laura and Claude seemed to be getting on, busy around the stove. Apart from the hail that came to beat on the windows for several minutes, the rest of the world might not have existed. Jesús was not even aware that Laura was closing her eyes and, far from her office where she spent her day balancing figures, doing her best to forget the war. It was enough for her to know that he was working enthusiastically on a picture of which she understood little but which could only be beautiful. The future? Was there one? She didn't believe it any more. Death struck swiftly and often. Those she spent her day with and the man she spent her nights with belonged to two different universes. She didn't confuse them or forget them. Jesús was beginning to tell himself he no longer needed anything, that he had had enough of other women and Laura was what he wanted now, and he had seen enough of other artists' paintings not to feel curious any longer. The moment had come to create a vacuum and only exist for himself, to discard all theories and send all the professors home, in order simply to be himself. If he went exclusively in his own direction, he would go further. Money? He would not have less than if he were working to fatten Louis-Edmond de La Garenne. In any case Laura had money. She was ready for anything. For an artist it was not a right but a duty to be a pimp. Pimp for a woman, for a society, for the wealthy. It was the greatest honour you could pay them.

After dinner Claude put Cyrille to bed and Laura started to clear away. Her voice had scarcely been heard during dinner. If she spoke, it must have been to Jesús when he was alone with her, or when Jean was not present. The two men resumed their conversation before the fire.

'So,' Jesús said, 'is this the one? I thought she would be more of a bomb. But not at all. She is perfec'. Round. Without angles. You wan' to marry 'er?'

'She's married already.'

Jesús remarked that Jean had a taste for complications. He was in love with a married woman *and* sleeping with an actress who was all over the place. He was heading for endless problems if Nelly, by some accident, were to fall in love with him.

'I judge that possibility to be extremely unlikely,' Jean said.

Jesús suggested to his friend that he settle in the countryside with him if he did not want to be consumed by the capital. He described an idyllic life, divided between everyday activities – they would raise rabbits and hens, plant a kitchen garden – and the art for which both of them had been put in the world.

'You want me to be like you, dear old Jesús, but I don't have a gift for anything. Everything is easy for you, now that you've discovered you can live outside society. This is your vocation. Mine is to live inside it, and if it suffocates me, tough luck. I'm rather less brilliant at the role than Palfy is. Just think: the bloke that I met on a road in Provence, disguised as a priest and stealing cars and collection boxes to pay for the trip, must be about to pass his first hundred million. I don't know what his racket is exactly, but he's found an opening and he's amassing a fortune. He'll lose it in the end, with his usual elegance, the way he lost the others. Really and truly it's the risk he enjoys. He's got Kapermeister and Rocroy in his pocket …'

Jean turned round, conscious of having uttered two names he should have kept to himself. Laura was putting the glasses away. He was sure she had heard everything. Claude appeared. They clustered around the fire together, until there were only embers left. At ten o'clock Jesús yawned and stretched.

'In the country you 'ave to rest,' he said in an exhausted voice. 'Tomorrow we'll talk again about that …'

Cyrille slept in a sleeping bag on a sagging couch next to the double bed that nearly filled the room, apart from a wardrobe and a shelf for the chamber pot. Outside the wind whistled in the trees and wrapped itself around the groaning roof.

'Take Cyrille,' Jean said. 'I'll sleep on the couch.'

'No, I want to sleep with you.'

'Do you realise what you're asking me?'

'Yes. And I am asking you.'

He switched the light off and they undressed in the dark and lay down in the icy bed.

'I'm cold,' Claude said.

He hugged her and stroked the small of her back through her nightdress.

She shivered. The timbers creaked at a gust more violent than the others. Jean felt Claude's warm breath on his neck.

'You don't love me as much as before,' she said.

'How do you know?'

He did not feel he loved her less. He even thought he loved her more, but in the darkness of the bedroom he could just as easily have been stroking Nelly, who in bed suddenly became as tender and modest as Claude.

'I don't know why you carry on seeing me. You should leave me alone, let me go, and then I'd keep on hoping I'd see you again when I was free.'

'You really think you'll be free one day?'

'Yes.'

'Then I'll wait. Stay where you are.'

The wind dropped and she fell asleep. Cyrille woke them up.

'Jean, I want to go into the forest.'

He had drawn back the curtains, letting in the red glow of the winter sun. The frost-covered fields rose gently towards a birch wood. In the courtyard Jesús was pumping the handle of the water pump in shirtsleeves. Through the floor they could hear kitchen sounds: Laura was prodding the stove into life, putting bowls on the table. Jean went down first and took over at the pump. He quickly ran out of energy and realised how unfit he was. He no longer jogged across Paris; instead he ate too much in black-market restaurants and too little when he was with Claude. The cold air stung his cheeks. He came back in, breathless, with Jesús, who had already sawed a couple of dozen logs. Cyrille was drinking a big bowl of hot milk.

'You know, Jean, it's *real* milk. Jesús fetched it for me from their neighbour. She has cows that give *real*, real milk.'

He shook his head as he said 'real', charmingly, his eyes shining with pleasure. Jesús seemed to notice for the first time the grace of this child to whom, in his pleasure at seeing Jean again, he had hardly paid any attention.

'After breakfas' I'll draw him,' he said.

'Can you draw?' Cyrille asked.

'A little.'

'Why do you speak with such a funny accent?'

'Me? An assen'? No' at all. Is you who is an assen'.'

Cyrille thought this was tremendously funny. He burst out laughing. Laura turned round and smiled at him and her gloomy face lit up for an instant, revealing more than she usually showed. Jean decided that she was alive but had suppressed her own existence, so as only to live through Jesús. At that moment he was sure she envied Claude's happiness in having a lover and a child, a happiness she felt to be more complete than her own. Apart from Jesús, who loved himself enough not to need anyone else, they all believed in everyone else's happiness. Laura wanted a child with Jesús but the circumstances were not right, and Jesús showed little or no interest in children, although it was true that several of his theories had gone up in smoke in the last six months: he had the same woman in his bed, and he had noticed Cyrille, bringing over a sketchbook and starting a series of sketches of the boy, eating, drinking, laughing.

Later all five of them went out. Cyrille, as tubby as a bear cub in his suit and hat knitted by Marie-Dévote and Toinette, skipped along the path that went through the birch wood to the Yvette, exhaling clouds of white vapour. The sun clung to the last golden leaves of autumn and from the fields on the other side of the river there rose the same white vapour, a veil of delicate gauze that shredded in the cold light as they watched.

'We are 'appy!' Jesús shouted.

He was, without reservation, and it was visible in his face, which was usually a little tough-looking because of the way his beard, even when he had just shaved, left a blue shadow. A woodcock flew up in front of them and two hares sped away. They met nobody. The countryside was enjoying its Sunday rest and one might have thought it deserted, hibernating in the cold. Cyrille returned to the farmhouse with cheeks like red apples. He wolfed down his lunch and curled up to sleep in one of the armchairs in front of the big fireplace.

At four o'clock, just before nightfall, Laura drove them to the station and they boarded a train crowded with passengers returning to Paris, loaded down with heavy suitcases full of the results of their plundering of the countryside. At Gare de Luxembourg a barrage of police awaited them, filtering the arrivals and ordering them to open parcels and suitcases. Jean went through without difficulty, taking Claude and Cyrille with him. Newsboys were announcing a special edition of *Paris-Soir* all the way up Boulevard Saint-Michel. The headline filled the whole front page: 'US PACIFIC FLEET DESTROYED BY JAPANESE AT PEARL HARBOR.' Passers-by grabbed the paper and read the short bulletin as they walked to the cafés.

'What's going on?' Claude asked.

'The Japanese have declared war on the United States.'

'What does it mean for us in Europe?'

'The USA is at war with the Axis powers.'

'So there's a hope it might all be over quickly?'

'Maybe.'

Claude grasped Jean's arm and was silent. Cyrille held her hand, dragging his feet, exhausted by his day in the open air that had so disoriented them all that they felt like foreigners in a Paris both dark and hectic. At Rue de la Huchette four German soldiers occupied the width of the pavement. Other pedestrians were stepping into the road to avoid bumping into them. They were young and neither hateful nor arrogant, weighed down by their green uniforms and probably dumbfounded by the city's peacetime Sunday air. Jean sensed that Claude was about to refuse to step off the pavement. He squeezed her arm.

'Don't waste your energy on pointless protests.'

She followed him, her head down, and they skirted round the soldiers.

'I don't like them,' she said.

'No one likes them.'

'You have dinner with them.'

'Not many. What else can I do? They're everywhere.'

'Yes, I know. Laura's kind and yet I felt uncomfortable being with her ... I can't explain it, it's as if she were hiding the truth from me.'

'It wasn't her we went to see, it was Jesús.'

'That's true.'

She said nothing more until they reached the door of her building, where she hesitated.

'Do you want to come up? I haven't got anything I can offer you for dinner. I think I've got one egg left for Cyrille.'

'Come on,' Cyrille said. 'Come, and carry me. My legs feel all wobbly. You can kiss me good night.'

He lifted Cyrille onto his shoulders and climbed the four flights. As she opened her door Claude snatched up a square of white paper with 'G' written on it, poking from under the doormat, and slipped it into her bag. Jean realised that he was not to notice anything. Cyrille ate his supper. He looked worn out, his cheeks still pink and his eyes already dreamily unfocused. Claude put him to bed and he instantly fell asleep.

'You need to go,' she said to Jean as she came back.

'I suppose I do. Who are you afraid of?'

'No one.'

'It's not true.'

She begged him.

'Jean!'

'Yes.'

'I'll tell you everything.'

'When?'

'Soon. Let me be on my own tonight.'

She kissed him on the lips and pushed him towards the door. He felt as though his strength had deserted him, that he was helpless before her anxious and beseeching face. She merely added, 'Don't forget that I love you.'

'No. I won't forget.'

It was all too rapid, too brutal. He went down the four flights of stairs, oblivious, and out past the door of the concierge who spied on him, noting his comings and goings. For a moment he thought he would stay on the *quai* and, from the shadows, keep watch on the building. It would have been a betrayal of Claude, of the trust she had placed in him. He set out along the empty *quais*, seized by the sadness that Paris reserves for lonely souls.

At Rue de Presbourg he found Palfy sitting over a radio set. An intermittent crackling masked a distant voice whose affected English accent could just be made out. The interference rose in volume and the voice disappeared. Palfy fiddled with the knob.

'This is exciting. What do you think?'

'About what?'

'Pearl Harbor. Don't pretend you haven't heard.'

'I read a bulletin.'

'It's world war now. Don't you find that much more interesting?'

'To be honest I find it vile, and I'm beginning to understand my father. We live in a shell here.'

'The Japanese have just shattered the Americans' shell. The Pacific will be Japanese within two or three years. It's the end of the white man in Asia ...'

But Jean could only think of one thing, of a G on a slip of paper hastily torn from a notebook. There was no longer any doubt. Another war was beginning this evening, a war that interested him far more than the war in the Pacific, an ocean apparently of infinite expanses of blue water sprinkled with ravishing atolls encircled by coral reefs that was really not like that at all.

Palfy handed him the telephone. He had his cup of coffee in the other hand and *Le Matin* open on his lap, screaming in banner headlines the destruction of the US Pacific fleet. The Japanese were landing in Malaysia and the Gulf of Siam.

'Someone is asking for you. A charming Russian accent. Perhaps it's Moscow. Stalin's private secretary.'

Jean took the receiver and immediately recognised Anna Petrovna. Her voice was strained.

'Hello? I need to see you. At once.'

'Is there something wrong?'

'I can't tell you.'

'Where do you live?'

'I'm not at home. I'll be at your office at ten o'clock.'

She hung up and he heard the click of a public call box. She was probably phoning from the post office.

'How is Uncle Joe?' Palfy asked.

'Don't joke. Something's happened. It's Claude's mother.'

Palfy stopped smiling.

'Is it serious?'

'It must be serious for her to call me. I've only met her once and she made it very clear that I'm not her favourite person.'

'What do you think's happened?'

Jean thought again of the square of paper with a G on it that Claude had found under the mat the previous evening and of the way she had asked him to leave after putting Cyrille to bed.

'I'll come with you,' Palfy said. 'You know nothing. I can help you.

We're going into a stage of this war where those who are on their own will be defenceless. Appalling things will happen. They are already …'

Anna Petrovna had arrived early and was waiting in the secretaries' office. Her pallor and the sharp, almost hateful look she gave him struck Jean.

'I'm with Duzan. Call me when you've finished,' Palfy said.

Anna Petrovna's gaze followed Palfy with a suspicion she made no attempt to hide.

'Would you like to come into my office?' Jean said.

She stood up. Her lips were trembling. He took her elbow and guided her.

As soon as they were alone she said, 'Claude was arrested last night.'

Two tears trickled down her face, which was puffy with fatigue and which, for the first time in many years, she had not bothered to make up. Jean, unable to say a word, seized her hand and squeezed it hard. He had hoped it would be something else, perhaps the threats of a mother who no longer wanted him to see her daughter.

'Where is Cyrille?' he said.

'With my son … He's asking for you. It was him who gave me your telephone number. You're stealing my daughter, and now you're taking my grandson from me too. I would like you to know straight away that I hate you, but I have nowhere else to turn. I know you have … *powerful* friends in Paris.'

'You're wrong.'

'On Saturday you took my daughter to see a German!'

'No, to see a Spanish painter. He has a mistress who's German. He's within his rights. His country's not at war.'

She looked disconcerted for a second and wiped away the traces of her two tears.

'When was she arrested?' Jean asked.

'Yesterday evening at eleven o'clock.'

'Who by?'

'Plainclothes inspectors.'

'French?'

'It seems so. But they'll hand her over to the Gestapo. You don't know them!'

It was true, he didn't know them. Until that day he had managed to avoid the drama that was endlessly being played out. Now the noose was tightening. To begin with it was insignificant characters like Alberto Senzacatso, then La Garenne. Today it was Claude's turn. The words 'arrest', 'police', 'interrogation' suddenly had a meaning. Laura Bruckett, Rudolf von Rocroy, Julius Kapermeister – even if they had nothing to do with Claude's arrest – were on the side of this invisible authority that claimed the right to put an end to the freedom and even the life of beings he loved.

'There has to be a reason for it, all the same,' he said.

'You know it as well as I do.'

'Her husband?'

Anna Petrovna shrugged her shoulders contemptuously.

'Yes, Georges. Even if they were going to divorce, he's still her husband.'

Claude had never mentioned divorce. Jean lowered his head, gripped by a wild hope and a vast joy that lasted as long as a lightning flash before becoming no more than an intolerable anguish.

'I suppose he's in France.'

'They were too late for him last night. They won't catch him. They'll never catch him.'

'It's not the first time he's been to France?'

Anna Petrovna's features closed up. She did not deign to reply.

'All right,' Jean said. 'The situation's becoming clearer. Wait here for me.'

She jumped to her feet.

'You could have me arrested too!'

'Don't be stupid.'

'I shan't let you!'

'You can't let me do anything or stop me doing anything. Sit down.'

He found Palfy with Duzan and took him into the corridor to tell him what had happened.

'Hell!' Palfy said. 'We have to act quickly. I'll go straight to Rocroy.'

'Why not Kapermeister? He seems more powerful.'

'You don't know how it works. Julius is Abwehr, the army. Gloves, honour, gentleman spies. Rocroy is from the Reichssicherheitshauptamt, the Reich's central security agency, the SS, the Gestapo. We need to get to her before she falls into their hands. You look after the mother. Send her back home. Above all tell her not to move. If she starts shouting from the rooftops that they've arrested her daughter, she'll never see her again. The most important thing is that the machine isn't set in motion. I'll ring you as soon as I can.'

He turned to walk away. Jean caught hold of his arm.

'If you do this, I'll never forget it.'

'I'll be glad if you do, because I'm sticking my neck out here, and for them that means there'll be a big favour to be returned …'

'Why are you doing it?'

'You stupid boy … I'm thirty-four years old and it's the first time in my idiotic – though by no means boring – life I've had a friend.'

He was gone, leaving Jean alone in the corridor lined with photos of Nelly Tristan – full-length, head and shoulders, diving into a pool in her swimming costume, on horseback, in a headband and driving a racing car, being presented with flowers as she stepped off a plane, dressed in crinoline or as Jeanne Hachette,[21] her long and beautiful legs shown off in tights.

Anna Petrovna was sitting on the edge of an armchair, as though despite her tiredness she was determined to show that she was there merely for a few minutes and was now ready to leave. Her anxious features, however, betrayed a naive optimism that asked for only a word of reassurance to turn hope into reality.

'Well?'

'I have a friend who knows an important German. He has gone to see him immediately.'

'The man with whom you arrived?'

'That's none of your business. Now there's just one thing you have to do: go home and say nothing.'

'You're telling me that? When I have only one desire: to scream that my daughter has been arrested!'

'In that case, make sure you restrain yourself!'

She burst into tears, embarrassing Jean to the point that he did not know what to do. He knew her loathing for him was reflexive, an almost natural reaction for a mother who judges by appearances the man her daughter has told her she loves.

'Go home!' he said. 'And stay with Cyrille.'

On a piece of paper he wrote in large letters, so that the boy could read easily,

Cyrille, I send you a big hug. I'm looking after your maman. Keep calm. We're going to be happy. Your friend, Jean

'Give him this from me.'

Anna Petrovna took the piece of paper, read it and dried her tears.

'You also need to know,' Jean added, 'something else: that I love Claude and that, despite appearances, I am not her lover in the strict sense of the word. Having said that, I want you to be certain that I have only one desire: to become her lover one day, when she'll have me.'

'I don't believe you.'

'It's not me you have to believe, it's your daughter.'

She folded his sheet of paper and put it in a crocodile handbag so ancient that the leather was split and the clasp gaped. Her worn-out sealskin coat was a further reminder of happier times, already many years in the past. Despite such details giving her away, there was no doubt that she had once been an elegant, even fashionable, woman. He put her at around fifty, and well preserved, but felt she was likely to age very fast from now on.

He was walking her back down the corridor as Nelly appeared, her face pink from the cold and wearing an astrakhan hat like a stage Cossack.

'Hello, scrumptious boy!' she said.

And lightly as she passed she planted a kiss at the corner of his lips, before sweeping into Duzan's office.

Anna Petrovna, her mouth tense with disgust, said, 'Even if you save Claude I shall do everything in my power to make sure she never has a relationship with a man like you.'

Jean felt so deeply wounded that he could not think of a reply, and then Anna Petrovna was gone down the stairs, clinging to the banisters with one hand, still quivering with hatred and humiliation, and perhaps crushed by anxiety too. But he did not hate her and he admired the pride she had shown, despite her distress. Why had she not sent her son instead?

Could he work in such circumstances? There was no question of it. He cancelled all his meetings. His office window looked out onto Rue François 1er. Across the street a nightclub employee was taking in the dustbins. Next door, the Café des Artistes, where the *quartier*'s producers gathered, was just opening. Bit-part actors always loitered there, with the stand-ins and impoverished old actors looking for a picture. The *patron* was a former Tour de France rider. Five Tours! Highest place: twelfth. He had always given his wheel, broken his rhythm, abandoned a sprint to support the champion. Jean remembered his name from a breakaway and a stage win at Rouen. When they met they spoke in monosyllables, swapping names and dates like secret agents. Cycling would come back after the war, but it wouldn't be the same. The young ones didn't have the same determination. And no sense of putting others first. They'd all want to win. It would be a fine mess. Toto Passepoil nodded his bald head. Running a bar had thickened his waistline. His waiters called him Tubby Peloton. He came out of the café and studied the dirty pavement and gutter with disgust. With an imperious wave – this was the man who had always been the leader's domestique – he summoned a waiter, who came and swept lethargically. Looking up, he saw Jean at his window and made a friendly gesture, a clenched fist with his thumb raised. It signified everything: come and have a drink, the Germans are done for, the Yanks are out of the race, the Japs eat only rice – or better still, I've got some real coffee and the Beaujolais Nouveau has arrived. Jean waved back. Toto was the one person he could imagine talking to. But to leave the office would mean leaving the telephone. He stepped away from the window. Nelly came in.

'Jules-who!'

'Yes.'

'What a long face!'

'I've got problems.'

'What?'

'Claude's been arrested.'

'Claude?'

'The love of my life.'

'So it's not me. What a letdown!'

'Don't laugh.'

She took off her astrakhan hat. The hairdresser had shingled her hair like a boy's. She was making a film set in 1925, to avoid meddling by the censors. It had given her natural grace an ambiguous quality. All she needed was the long cigarette-holder, the cigarette with the gold band, the sequined dress, bare knees, and shoes with ankle straps.

'I'm not laughing. I like you a lot. And everything you love belongs to me too.'

She had never said so much, and with such gentle honesty, before.

'The Boches?' she asked.

'I don't like the term. But they're not involved yet. Palfy's doing his best to step in before she's handed over to them.'

She sat on the corner of his desk and looked thoughtful.

'You're unhappy.'

'Yes.'

'The ghastly Dudu's on first-name terms with them.'

'Don't get mixed up in this.'

'Anyway he wouldn't lift a finger, not even to help his mother. He's such a creep. Listen, Jules-who …'

'Yes.'

'Would you like me to sleep with Julius or Rudolf?'

'I don't think so. There's enough of us in your bed already.'

'Don't be mean.'

'Sorry.'

'There's you. And sometimes there's Dudu. That's all. It helps me wait.'

'Wait for what?'

'Until I stop. Feeling bored.'

Her lovely dark eyes glistened and her lip quivered. He hugged her, pressing her to his chest. How could he explain that he loved her too, and that in the impasse of a life so pointless for a man of his age she represented a different kind of friendship? Jesús, Palfy, Nelly: he reminded himself of his extraordinary good fortune.

Duzan entered, blushing furiously. He put up with what the eye did not see, but physical evidence was too much.

'In my offices!'

Nelly disentangled herself.

'Listen to me carefully, Dudu. One wrong word and you'll be free of me for the rest of your life, which incidentally is going to be short, because you eat and drink much too much.'

'Drinking too much is rich coming from you! Only yesterday—'

'Your unbelievably ghastly aristocratic friends were driving me mad. I drink when I'm with creeps. Ask Jean. I never drink when I'm with him.'

'In other words I'm a ...?'

The word would not come. Relenting, Nelly came to his aid.

'Yes, you are.'

'Without me, darling, you'd just be some minor thespian doing nothing but rep.'

'Yes, and it would be Corneille, Racine, Marivaux, Cocteau, Anouilh, Claudel and Giraudoux instead of your shitty screenplay writers. My poor Dudu—'

'Don't call me Dudu!'

'My poor Dudu, it's not even smoke and mirrors, what you do. There. I refuse to sign another—'

The producer prevailed over the outraged lover.

'You have a contract!'

'I'm throwing it away.'

'Find a very good lawyer then.'

He went out, slamming the door.

Nelly stroked Jean's cheek.

'Well! That's much better for both of us.'

'Yes, much better.'

She replaced her astrakhan hat and re-applied her lipstick in front of the mirror. A secretary knocked and entered. She brought an envelope and a typewritten letter.

'Monsieur Duzan asked me to give you this cheque. He'd like you to sign your letter of resignation.'

'What about me?' Nelly said.

'He didn't give me anything for you.'

'Shame.'

Jean read the letter of resignation and signed it.

'Shall I throw his cheque back in his face?' he asked Nelly.

'No. Keep it. His money's as good as anyone's.'

Jean put the cheque in his pocket and asked the secretary, if anyone telephoned him, to redirect the call to Rue de Presbourg.

'No,' Nelly said. 'To me. Today I'm keeping you with me. I'm inviting you home for lunch. My Uncle Eugène, who has the incredible good fortune to live in the Vire, has sent me an *andouillette* you'll still be talking about when you're sixty.'

If she had offered him a herring bone, he would have followed her wherever she told him to go. She was there, she existed, she understood everything. He desired her while Claude, under arrest somewhere in Paris, in isolation, was asking herself whether those who loved her had abandoned her. Unless she was not sitting alone on a hard wooden bench but being questioned, slapped, beaten and humiliated into admitting she had met Georges Chaminadze.

They reached Place Saint-Sulpice by Métro. Passengers recognised Nelly. A little girl with a lisp held out an autograph book. Nelly took Jean's arm to cross the square. A man with a red nose who looked numb with cold and had a haversack on his back was attracting pigeons with breadcrumbs. A bird pecked at his palm. He grabbed it by a claw, wrung its neck and stuffed it into his haversack. The other pigeons flew away, then came back. He waited calmly for them, not moving, his arm extended, showing neither pleasure nor boredom. The brim of his homburg hat was pulled down over his eyes. All that was visible was his really very red nose and the stubble on his badly shaven chin.

'I should like to find a poet who talks about Saint-Sulpice and pigeons and people going hungry,' Nelly said. 'But ... it's difficult. Of course there's Ponchon: "I hate the towers of Saint-Sulpice – whenever I see them I piss on them ..." I can't promise that's it exactly, but Ponchon's a real poet.[22] He wrote about black stockings and virtuous maidens. Do you like black stockings?'

'I don't know.'

'Notice that I didn't ask you what you thought about virtuous maidens.'

'I haven't known one. They're a rare breed.'

'That's a shame. If you had, you could have recited Ponchon's excellent speech to her. "Now we know on what a fat purse, Mademoiselle, you mount your horse ..."'

He laughed. Nelly dispensed gaiety. These days gaiety meant hope and courage. She was making the waiting and uncertainty disappear with a discretion he would not forget.

The studio was icy. Jean lit a fire of logs while Nelly changed her dress for a pair of trousers and a roll-neck sweater. But for her slight bust, she would have looked like a beautiful young man. Even her voice could have been a boy's. She chattered incessantly to Jean, to herself, even briefly to a cat slinking across the balcony on the other side of the street. Opening the window she called out, 'Marc-Adolphe Papillon, you shouldn't be out in weather like this. You'll catch cold and your papa'll get worried.'

She closed the window. The cat did not move, staring at her, its back arched.

'Funny name for a cat!' Jean said.

'It's not any old cat, it's Maurice Fombeure's cat. In the morning when Marc-Adolphe comes home, Fombeure tells him:

'My cat coming back from his rambles
He smells of the earth and sun's heat
He smells of Calabria and Puglia
He smells of opossums and feet,

He smells of bollocks and palavers
With hefty and bewhiskered toms

And of the bitter bark of the trees
He smells of Bantus and drums

'So you can see he's not any old cat.'

'Do you know any other poems of Fombeure's?'

'Plenty. But let's go gently. You shouldn't stuff yourself with poets. Very indigestible. I'll teach you to cherry-pick …'

He recounted to her how, as a boy of thirteen, he had met two Breton separatists on the run and how one of them, Yann, had recited Victor Hugo to him in a voice he had not forgotten and how a few hours later the second separatist, Monsieur Carnac, had ridiculed the poet's flight of fancy by quoting the lines that were missing from the stanza: 'Love each other! 'tis the month when the strawberries are sweet.' What had become of Yann and Monsieur Carnac? The Germans, having envisaged backing the Breton Liberation Front, had given up the idea under pressure from Vichy. Were Yann and Monsieur Carnac continuing the struggle, pursued now by the police on both sides? But someone else had offered him a poet too. He spoke of his fabulous meeting with the prince and his chauffeur, the enigmatic Salah who had slipped a copy of Toulet's *Counter-rhymes* into his haversack. The copy had been left behind at his last billet. Jean remembered how, during his long marches, staggering under the weight of his kit, full cartridge belts and the machine gun biting into his shoulder, he had recited to himself, without moving his lips, the thrilling lines that conjured up a naked woman and the fragrance of the Indian Ocean.

'I wouldn't say them well. I'd like to hear you read them.'

On a shelf Nelly had a copy of *Counter-rhymes*. Together they searched, like a pair of schoolboys, for the poem Jean had liked so much for its contrast and the escape it had offered from the stubborn stupidity of army life. Nelly recited:

'You whom winter's hearth inflamed
To a naked carmine

Where the scent of your skin
Your nakedness already framed;

Neither you, of whom a remembered sight
Still captivates my heart
Vague island, flowers' shadowy art,
Oceanic night;

Nor your perfume, violet-filled,
Beneath the cooling hand
Are worth the rose that grows from burning land
And the midday heat compels to yield'

The telephone rang. Nelly sprang to answer it.

'Oh, it's you … No, leave me alone. Listen, Dudu, I'm expecting a very important call. You have to leave my line clear … Yes … of course … I'll see you on one condition … that *you hang up*. And do it now. Jean? Of course he's here. I'm in the middle of photographing him quite naked on a tiger skin. You cannot imagine how delicious he looks. Hang up and I'll see you tomorrow.'

She replaced the receiver and smiled.

'He's not as bad as he seems. You have to treat him a bit meanly. I can't always do it. I'm too weak …'

She made lunch on the table covered with oilcloth in the kitchen, where there was barely room to move.

'I'm turning into my mother. She has a dining room, but it's only for family occasions. Otherwise it's in the kitchen. Near the pans. She claims you eat better with an oven behind you. Papa wipes his knife, fork and glass before he starts. He's never been able to lose the habit. It annoys Maman. He doesn't care. Oh blast, I haven't got any red wine.'

'We'll do without.'

'No, I've got champagne. Julius and Madeleine sent me some Dom

Pérignon 1929. A case. Do you think it'll be enough?'

'I think it'll be enough.'

'Sit down then. And tell me the stories about the prince again. I'm like a little girl. I love princes and fairy tales. You said he was the lover of your real mother?'

'Whether he is or was, I've no idea. When I last saw him in August 1939, before he left for Lebanon, he was dying slowly … I've had no news since then.'

'And of her?'

'None of her either. Why would she send me any? She doesn't know I'm her son.'

'Will you tell her?'

'Palfy says I shouldn't. He feels it wouldn't be good manners.'

'Your friend's awfully funny. I've never met anyone as cynical as him. Don't you like it?'

'Palfy? Of course—'

'No. I mean the *andouillette*.'

'At least as much.'

'Have some more then.'

After lunch they lay stretched out on the rug in front of the log fire, another bottle between them.

'You're not too sad?' she asked.

'Sad? No, that's not the word. I'm waiting. I can't do anything. I'm waiting. It's easier with you.'

She held his hand and shifted closer to him. He wanted to undress her. She stopped him.

'No. Let's keep our clothes on. When you're naked, pleasure goes everywhere. I want you just to be inside me. Everything should happen there. You'll see, it's much more intense.'

She took him out and loosened her clothes just enough. He felt so good when he was inside her that he stopped moving and closed his eyes. Their pleasure intensified, gently, without their saying a word. They stayed like that for a long time, before they finally came together.

*

Later the window let in only a vague greyness. The flames from the logs cast flickering orange shapes onto the ceiling. Books, photos and drawings trembled in the fire's dying light. The building and street were slowly submerged in the darkness. They distantly heard the noisy iron shutter of a shop selling religious objects coming down. The telephone, within reach of their hands on the rug, did not ring. Nelly lifted the receiver to her ear to check the line had not been cut. No. There was a dialling tone. She replaced it quickly. They opened another bottle. The third, or fourth? They weren't counting any longer, and it hardly mattered. Everything flowed over them. They shut themselves away in a patience that could no longer be distracted by desire. Nelly got up to put another log on the sputtering fire. Burning pine added its sweet smell to the room.

'Tell me something else,' she said.

He told her about Chantal de Malemort, the little girl who had taken his hand when they hid in a dark room, the girl who had exercised her horse in the Arques forest, the one who one day in Paris had run away with someone else. Antoinette had written that the hard life at the Malemorts' since the marquis had become a prisoner of war had transformed the delicate girl into a sturdy countrywoman, her cheeks ruddy from labouring in the fields. Like her father. Like three generations of Malemorts who had defended their property without imagination, with a gruff stubbornness. She refused to see Gontran Longuet. She had turned her back on her past, speaking ruefully and scornfully of her former girlish pretensions to happiness. Malemorts looked down on love. Love was for servants. And as servants became harder to find, so did love. One still saw her occasionally galloping flat out through the forest, followed by a couple of hunting dogs, and never acknowledging a friendly wave. For two years she had spoken to her mother only twice a day: once to say good morning, and in the evening to say good night. The Marquise de Malemort suffered in silence.

'You'll see her again,' Nelly said.

'I hardly ever think about her. She's buried under all sorts of old things now, and under new experiences and other women.'

'Yes, but it was love. True love. There are only two sorts: the love you feel in childhood, and love at first sight. The rest is just mucking about, and then you add a bit of literature to make it feel like a dream. Claude is love at first sight. If you lost her, you'd never find anything like her ever again. I hope Palfy can save her. If not, little Jules-who, you're going to turn into – and you'll have every right to – a dreadful cynic just like your friend.'

'I'm already—'

Nelly kissed him on the cheek.

'No. Not with me. You're not cheating on her with me. We're friends. We share everything, even pleasure. And we've no secrets from each other.'

'I've never met anyone like you.'

'Thank you. Now that's a very nice thing to say. Usually men aren't as nice as that and prefer to tell me that it turns out I'm just like all the others, a bitch who'll sleep with anyone.'

'It's stupid we didn't get to know each other sooner.'

'Sooner? Before Claude? Before my first lover? Poor Jules-who, with me you'd have been unhappy straight away. I'm too inquisitive. I always want to know more. I'll never stop. When I'm old and ugly and ruined like Mercedes del Loreto, I'll pay for lovers. I will, I'll have money and I'll pay for lovers. Beautiful boys, novices, half-boys, half-girls. But hung like stallions—'

The telephone rang. She grabbed the receiver.

'Constantin? Yes, he's here … What's happening? Oh, that's wonderful! I'll pass him to you …'

Jean grabbed the phone. He was shaking.

'It wasn't easy,' Palfy said. 'I'll explain. It's better if she doesn't go home this evening ... We could bring her to Rue de Presbourg but that's not ideal either. Nor Madeleine's ... Any ideas?'

'No. Not really. Wait ...'

He turned to Nelly.

'It's better if Claude doesn't go back to her apartment this evening.'

'Tell her to come here.'

'Here?'

'Why not?'

It seemed perfectly natural when Nelly said it. There was a silence, then he heard Claude's voice.

'Anywhere, Jean. Anywhere. I just need to sleep. I can't go on. They questioned me all night and all day. But I'd like Cyrille with me ...'

Everything was settled. The chauffeur would drive Claude to Nelly's. Madame Michette would accompany her. Then the car would take Jean to fetch Cyrille. Things happened so quickly that there was no opportunity to reflect or find Nelly's hospitality unusual. She wanted Cyrille to stay too.

Claude appeared, supported by Marceline Michette and the chauffeur. She could hardly place one foot in front of the other and her face was waxy and she was shivering in her wet dress, her fine ash-blond hair hanging in rat's tails. Nelly hugged her. Madame Michette took matters in hand: a bath, warm towel, rub down with eau de Cologne, and electric hairdryer.

'I've brought some woollens. Now go and get Cyrille!'

She pushed Jean and the chauffeur out of the door. Anna Petrovna lived in Passy, where the White Russians had gathered in exile, in a detached house down a private path overgrown with ivy. She opened the door and started when she saw Jean.

'Well?'

'She's been released.'

'Why hasn't she come?'

'She's exhausted.'

'I'll go to her.'

'No. You won't find her at her apartment.'

She did not invite him in and despite the cold she left the door open. Behind her Jean could see a hall wallpapered in a hideous design.

'I've come for Cyrille,' he said.

'He's with my son.'

She pointed to the side of the building where there was a single room, probably an old garage, with a light in the window.

'But you'll only have him if Claude asks me herself.'

He gave her Nelly's number.

'Come in!' she said finally.

Jean placed his hand on the receiver as Anna Petrovna seized it.

'Wait!'

He lifted the receiver and listened for the telltale click of a listening device. There was no sound.

'You can dial the number.'

Claude was very brief. Anna Petrovna burst into tears. There was no one at the other end when Jean took back the receiver.

'You've taken my daughter from me!'

'I doubt it.'

'When will I see her?'

'Soon.'

She wrapped a shawl around her shoulders and stepped across the little garden to knock on the door of the garage.

'Vladi! It's me!'

The door was unlocked and opened onto a magnificent disorder in the middle of which Cyrille, sitting on the floor, was busy tossing a ball onto a roulette wheel. As soon as he saw Jean he scrambled to his feet and threw himself into his arms.

'Jean, Jean, you came. Where's Maman?'

'She's waiting for you.'

Vladimir looked like Claude, but he had in his expressions something so inconclusive and soft that the second time one looked at him one discovered an entirely different person, a thin and spineless-looking giant, whose hair was too long and whose hands trembled. As for the chaos he lived in, we would need pages and pages to describe it, with the risk of the reader dying of boredom before the end. Let us simply say that Vladimir, who had never managed to pass his baccalauréat, considered himself to be a great inventor, specifically of a rotary engine that could fit in the palm of a person's hand and produce the power of a 200-horsepower diesel engine. The one-time garage had become his workshop and bedroom. Not his bathroom, as he rarely washed, except on the days when he went out to win a little money at a bridge club. In fact it had been a long time since he himself had actually believed in his invention but he continued to maintain its fiction because it concealed his laziness and inaction. The money he and his mother lived on he owed to his card-playing skills, particularly bridge, at which he was first-rate. The war had interrupted a career that had reaped rich rewards on cruise ships, where for the price of a ticket to the Caribbean he had learnt how to clean out all the wide-eyed amateurs in the space of a fortnight. Despite a few unpleasant aftermaths – two shipping lines had blacklisted him – he had been planning to leave for Japan, changing ships several times en route. Now, forced to stay in Paris, he made do with fleecing the amateur clubs of the 16th arrondissement and waited for better days. Jean understood in a flash what Claude had wanted to keep hidden from him and would be angry with him for having discovered.

In his arms, Cyrille hugged him tight.

'Take me to see Maman now, Jean. Good night, Uncle Vladi. Good night, Grandmother.'

Nelly had given Claude her bed and she was resting with two pillows under her head. In the narrow kitchen Madame Michette was fussing and complaining at the lack of room. Organised as always, she had brought food borrowed from Palfy's refrigerator.

'A boiled egg, some York ham, a slice of Gruyère and some stewed apples, that's all a tired tummy needs. And where's the egg cup?'

No, Nelly never ate boiled eggs. All she needed was coffee. Ingeniously Madame Michette decided to serve the egg mashed with bread soldiers. She had everything under control and reigned, maternal and full of authority, treating Cyrille to a tap on his fingers when she caught him picking his nose. Claude lay back with an expression of profound sadness on her face, as if the world from which she had returned by an accident of extraordinary good luck had opened up an abyss underneath her, to which a kind of vertigo kept trying to drag her down, despite her efforts to resist. She smiled at her son, ate because Madame Michette insisted, and wrapped herself back up in her torpor. Nelly kissed her on her forehead and eased a pillow from under her head. Cyrille, already naked, slipped under the covers and pressed himself up against his mother.

'Off you go, the pair of you,' Marceline said to Jean and Nelly. 'I'll stay and keep an eye on them, keep the fire going so they don't catch cold. I've brought my coffee. Count on me, I won't drop off. And there's lots to read anyway …'

She had put on her glasses and was scanning the bookshelves.

'Michaux? Is that it? He didn't go overboard, did he? Just little pieces. I knew a Monsieur Michaux. He was a council worker. Can't be him. Max Jacob? Wouldn't be Jewish, would he? Mind you, I've got nothing against Jews. On the contrary. Now they're persecuting them, I think that's disgusting. Anyhow, not all Jacobs are Jews. I knew one of them too, a Protestant, a real one. He'd never come to the Sirène on a Sunday. Very devout. Oh, but this Max Jacob only writes little pieces too. You do like your writers to leave half the page empty, don't you, Madame Nelly? Oh, look, Corneille! The *Complete Works*. *Le Cid* must be in there somewhere. Dialogue's so much more fun. Don't you worry about me. I've got lots to read. The night will go very quickly. That little lady will be much better after a good sleep.

And if she wakes up, I'll give her another pill. Go on, leave us alone. Go and have some fun, now that the worst's over.'

Nelly offered her some champagne. After studying the label Madame Michette shook her head.

'It's *brut*. I only like semi-sweet. Don't worry. I've brought my little bottle of burgundy. A glass now and then and the night will be over in a flash. Go on, my dears, off you go, off you go …'

Cyrille sang to her, 'There was a lady called Madame Michette, and Madame Michette, she lost her pet …' She wagged her finger at him, pretending to frown but in reality delighted and enchanted by this little boy who ran, whooping like a Sioux, along the paths of the Luxembourg Gardens where the piled-up dead and frozen leaves crunched underfoot. The stone urns on their pedestals looked whiter than usual, as if turned to ice by the cold, and the statues shivered in the frosty air. Like mummies in their sarcophagi the German sentries guarding the Senate in their concrete pillboxes observed the children clustered around the big pond through their aiming slits. The layer of ice on the pond, broken up by stones, allowed the model boats to sail among the yellowish icebergs, shadowed by goldfish in search of bread. The rigid lines of barbed wire did not cut Paris off from a victorious Germany, but cut Germany off from a childish, joyful world immersed in imaginary battles with pocket submarines and sailing boats. The uncertainty of combat remained a mystery for these men who had also once played with model boats or whose children, far away, were doing the same thing in a public garden. Marceline was carrying Cyrille's boat – a Breton fishing boat with red sails, a gift from Jean – while Cyrille collected chestnuts in a paper bag. He already had a bagful in the studio, and in the afternoon she prised the chestnuts from their spiky sheaths and helped him use them to make fantastic characters: beggars, kings, fairies, bulls and ants. Their big project was to make a Nativity scene for Christmas. There was no hessian, paints or gold paper in the apartment, but Marceline had managed to find some at a hardware shop on Rue des Canettes. In one of Nelly's drawers she had found a tube of glue. Clumsily she had sculpted the ox and the ass out of peeled chestnuts, and she was anxious now that her efforts at the baby Jesus and Virgin Mary would be even clumsier.

Cyrille came back to her, his cheeks on fire, cheerfully blowing out a cloud of condensation.

'Look, Marceline, I'm smoking.'

He inhaled from an imaginary cigarette and pretended to hide it behind his back when she scolded him.

'It's very bad to be smoking at your age. Monsieur Michette, who's ten years older than you, has never smoked in his life. That's why he's so well …'

'Is Monsieur Michette the bogeyman?'

'You know, I'm really going to get cross with you.'

'Oh no, I don't think you will. You're too good.'

Marceline's heart turned over: a child was telling her she was good. She had reached the age of fifty without knowing it. Cyrille grabbed her hand.

'Let's go home. Maman will be getting worried.'

They crossed Place Saint-Sulpice. As soon as Cyrille glimpsed the pigeon catcher he started shouting and clapping his hands, running away from Marceline and making the birds scatter. The man said nothing, waiting patiently for calm to return and again holding out the breadcrumbs on his palm. His nose was getting redder and redder. Its luminosity was the only thing people noticed in his obtuse face. They called him Red-nose and told him he was a nasty piece of work.

Claude was regaining consciousness, but hazily and so confusedly that for most of the day she seemed absent from her own life. Getting up late, she had mainly sat slumped in an armchair. Her hand dangled and Cyrille, on all fours, pushed against her apparently lifeless fingers with his head. The fingers caught a curl of blond hair and wound it around them, and Cyrille purred.

'I'm your pussycat.'

'Yes, you're my pussycat.'

Afraid that Claude would let herself be taken away, Palfy and Jean had forbidden Anna Petrovna from visiting her daughter. She had telephoned from a public call box. Claude had affected a lighthearted voice to reassure her. Anna Petrovna allowed herself to be convinced because she was reluctant to leave darling Vladimir, who was in bed with influenza. As soon as she put the phone down Claude relapsed into apathy, from which she only emerged when Jean arrived. As soon as he appeared her face lit up and her voice regained its eagerness, so much so that Marceline, who had begun to develop a literary turn of phrase since spending time among Nelly's bookshelves, exclaimed, 'You're Tristan and Iseult! What are you waiting for? King Mark has gone.'

She took Cyrille out, pretending that there was shopping to be done in the quartier. On her return her trained eye was surprised to see them still sitting apart from each other.

Alone with Claude, Jean spent his time trying to find out what had happened. Each day he extracted from her a few more words that she uttered with infinite reluctance. She spoke of a night in a cupboard, a blinding light, questions that two men drilled into her, a cold bath into which she had been thrown and where she had fainted, and a man with greying hair who had picked her up and carried her to a car and then in the car to Palfy's apartment.

'Please,' she said, 'don't keep asking me. I don't want to remember. You have to say nothing. They know everything. They know more than I do.'

The one certainty was that they had not arrested Georges Chaminadze, who had come from London on a special mission and left again by unknown means. It was his second such mission. On the first, despite orders to the contrary, he had spent three days with Claude, without Cyrille for fear that he would talk. The G was him.

'Do you still love him?' Jean asked.

'No. I love you.'

So why would she not give herself to him?

'I promised him. On Cyrille's life.'

'If he extracted that promise from you, it's because he loves you.'

'No. He doesn't even love me. I'm not explaining anything. We were to divorce. He was living with another woman. But he didn't want me to see anyone else.'

'Then why did you let him force you to make that promise?'

'Oh Jean, you're the one torturing me now ... I really don't know. He's very convincing. He's handsome. He was my husband, my only lover. He's Cyrille's father ... I didn't know I was going to meet you ... I hoped he would come back and that, even if I didn't love him any more, we'd be able to live together, so that Cyrille would be happy.'

Piece by piece the picture of Georges Chaminadze became clearer, a very different picture from the photograph glimpsed in Claude's bedroom of a tall, uncomplicated-looking young man, happy to be alive, racket in hand on a tennis court.

'You have to understand,' Claude said, 'he was terribly spoilt. At the age of five he used to have servants kissing his hand. He's like Vladi, he never wanted to work. And like Vladi he was a natural card player. They often used to team up on international cruises. Both of them spoke Russian, French, German and Spanish almost without an accent. Maman adores him ... Nearly as much as Vladi ... When I said I'd divorce him if he went on living like that, she said I was wrong.'

'That's why she hates me.'

'Yes, she's crazy, but you have to forgive her; she's lost everything and now Vladi's a loser too, banned from playing in all sorts of places ...'

On other days Claude did not speak, answering only yes or no, but from a smile or the pressure of her hand, Jean knew she was happy he was there. He was anxious to know how she had lived until now.

'On very little,' she admitted. 'I don't spend very much, which must be a reaction to Maman. If she ever gets a thousand-franc note she'll go out and buy caviar rather than pay the gas bill. I've sold some jewellery. Very cheaply, but in any case I don't have many needs. And you don't know it, but you helped me a lot. The first time he came Georges left me some money too. It must have come from the expenses he was given for his French mission. He's never been very scrupulous. The police searched the apartment. They took my last two rings and the money I had left. Now I've got nothing …'

She held out two open palms.

Marceline said that if Claude would agree to get dressed she would regain her appetite for living, but by staying in bed in a nightdress or lolling in an armchair in a dressing gown she was wallowing in self-pity. Without admitting it, Marceline had discovered in herself extraordinary depths of devotion. She protected Claude, cared for her, made sure she ate, refrained from asking her a single question, and unilaterally decided to take charge of Cyrille's rather random education. Claude listened astonished to this large woman, built like a wardrobe and with the veins in her cheeks flushed a lively red after a bottle of cheap burgundy, delivering her remarkable course in manners. But what was good enough for the girls at the Sirène was also good enough for a small boy. Cyrille drank his glass of water with his little finger crooked, washed his willy morning and evening, and said, 'Hello, Monsieur Palfy; good evening, Madame Nelly.' Taken all together, his instruction contained many good things, and there would always be time to go back on certain habits. The main thing was that Cyrille trusted Madame Michette, secret agent and woman of action, in a way that did not rule out being cheeky to her.

*

Nelly appeared occasionally. She came back for a coat, a book, a dress. Claude knew she was living with Jean at Palfy's. She did not mind. No one was deceiving anyone. Only Duzan wandered lost through the labyrinth, discovering that he needed Nelly more than she needed him. He was like a fly bumping into a pane of glass. He saw Nelly free and called out to her repeatedly, and she did not hear him. He thought of denouncing her and dropped a hint to Julius Kapermeister who would have shown interest had Madeleine, tipped off by Jean, not intervened. She had taken Jean's side, Nelly's side, the side of the unknown Claude who had been pointlessly tortured. Every day she sent a chauffeur to Saint-Sulpice with some 'treats'. Thanks to her companion, Blanche de Rocroy, she had discovered the part played by Rudolf in spiriting Claude out of the hands of the Gestapo's French auxiliaries: a dangerous role that for the first time had compromised this man of aristocratic demeanour but soft character, who found himself alarmed at the thought of being disciplined and posted to a combat unit for his actions. Goodbye to the black-market restaurants, to his picture-dealing racket and the confiscation of Jewish wealth, not to mention another, even more fruitful business activity, which we shall return to.

Claude had escaped from the French police but they had not accepted that they were beaten and still hoped she would eventually lead them to Georges Chaminadze. Better informed than the police, we can reveal that Georges had already left French soil, probably on board one of those little Lysanders that landed at twilight or dawn, setting down in open fields men and women who melted into the anonymous crowd and often never reappeared. It may sound as if such missions hardly tally with what we know of Georges's character, but that would fail to take into account the fact that, as a born gambler, he found in the secret war the same pleasure he found in squeeze plays at bridge or bluffing at poker. Danger amused him. That this time death might be the endgame was an added attraction. In the same lighthearted way he had disobeyed orders and spent three days with his wife, then tried to see her on the Sunday when she had been in the country. The concierge had informed on him and now Quai Saint-Michel was a busted flush, under permanent surveillance. He had made his wife a hostage with a disregard for her safety that reflected his true personality. In London he had been congratulated on his mission's success, having concealed the fact that by going to Quai Saint-Michel he had been a hair's breadth from a disaster that could, if he had talked, have led to an entire intelligence network being laid waste.

There is, therefore, no longer any Claude mystery for Jean. All is clear. The silence she met him with has been broken in a few sentences. Where his entreaties and insistence came up against a brick wall, the brutality of the police succeeded in a single night. Jean is delivered. But life has taken a dangerous turn and Claude, recovered and returned to normal life, may still be forbidden to him. He is simultaneously happy and desperate.

He would be more desperate than happy if Nelly were not there to entertain him. He discovers her generosity and what she herself calls her volatility. Relieved of Duzan ('It wasn't a weakness,' she explained, 'but a concession to received ideas: an actress *must* sleep with "her" producer. Why make yourself conspicuous? It wasn't my lucky day! I've been punished and found out Dudu's an ass'), relieved of Duzan, she is returning to the theatre. Jean-Louis Vaudoyer has offered her back her old place at the Comédie Française, and Dullin, director at the Théâtre de la Cité, formerly the Sarah-Bernhardt, is tempting her with a part in Jean-Paul Sartre's first play, *The Flies*. But the Comédie Française is promising Corneille. Madame Michette is pushing hard for Corneille. Since she began living at Nelly's studio, her reading habits have broadened and deepened. She is not so keen on comedies. Tragedies are what she finds really exciting. She longs to see Nelly in the role of Chimène, to hear her speaking Camille's imprecations and Pauline's sweet lament. She is discovering the 'greatness of spirit' that the life she has led hitherto has rarely given her the chance to encounter. The result is both a shock and an inspiration. She would like to speak in verse, but doesn't know where to start. There is a lacuna in her education. If only the Blue Sisters of Issoire had not made do with teaching her to read and write, to count and sew and cook! If only they had led her to the heroes of Antiquity! Her life would have been so different. A deep wistfulness wells up in her. The powerful ones of this world have flaws they overcome as an example to us. Now it is we who must follow in their footsteps!

To return to more down-to-earth matters, Jean was without a job. His 'resignation' cheque from Duzan left him enough to live on for a month. Of course the producer was trying every means he knew to take Jean back, hoping he would bring Nelly with him. Even Palfy advised against falling into the trap.

'Ultimately Duzan's a windbag. All mouth. If Nelly doesn't want him, he ceases to exist. Even the German co-producers are refusing to help him. Let him go under. You need to travel light. I suggested opening a gallery …'

'Thanks. After my La Garenne experience …'

'La Garenne's a no-hoper, small fry. I don't want to hear another word about him. He hasn't managed to reopen his gallery and works as a broker now, running from one Paris dealer to the next. To half of them he swears he isn't Jewish, to the other half he swears he is and that the racial laws have ruined him. No, truly, La Garenne no longer exists. I'm suggesting something much more serious, on Avenue Matignon: the Galerie Européenne, a front, an outlet for dealers who can't work openly any more.'

'I don't know anything about painting.'

Palfy, as was his wont, appealed to the heavens.

'I've never come across such an idiot! What about the dealers, the critics, the experts? At least you've got an excuse, being brought up by a gardener and a housekeeper while they were living in houses stuffed with pictures. I don't know a thing about it either, but I pretend. Remember London and how I impressed Geneviève … On the subject of Geneviève, I've got some news for you. She's been seen in Switzerland, at Gstaad, where she's pampering herself. The prince is dead. Apparently Salah has taken over the reins. Why are you making that face?'

However much he had anticipated the news, Jean was still shocked. He remembered his last meeting with the prince, who had shrunk from the light, ruling over a kingdom of a few files in a luxury hotel suite. The prince had shown him kindness without reason and a generosity that might have given a child a false idea of life. As for his mother, Geneviève, he found it hard to imagine what she would do without that protective shadow.

'Would you like to see your mother again?' Palfy asked anxiously.

'Now that I know she's my real mother, I'd say no. A woman brought me up. Her name was Jeanne Arnaud. She was good and not very intelligent. She got over her sorrows with an apple tart or a piece of bread and gooseberry jam. It may sound too simple, but there's nothing better …'

Nelly appeared, beaming.

'Jules-who, kiss me passionately and respectfully. I am joining the Comédie Française. Yes, it's almost a nunnery. I'm giving myself to the great writers for three sous and five centimes. When I want a mink I'll have it off with a sugar daddy – a proper one, a banker, not an ass like Dudu, who lives by swindling people. Kiss me – you'll be my true love …'

True love? It was certainly a more agreeable prospect than being a sugar daddy to someone like Nelly. Palfy assured her that she had done the right thing and that Marceline would be proud of her and buy a season ticket for the classical matinées. They telephoned Madeleine, who was just as thrilled and invited them to drop in at Avenue Foch, where she was expecting a few people that evening.

'I'm not entirely sure who,' she said. 'Blanche has got the list. She promises me it'll be perfect …'

Blanche had always been a shadow: her parents' shadow, La Garenne's shadow, she was now Madeleine's shadow with the intoxicating bonus that Madeleine listened to her and understood her. With some success she taught her to speak in a sort of sibilant accent, a refined voice in a world without an Oxford or Cambridge to set you apart from the crowd. Madeleine was making noticeable progress. She learnt the names in *Who's Who* with childish application and memorised their relations to each other. It would not be long before she was word perfect on titles. She was reading Proust, without always understanding him ('His story's a bit muddled,' she said, 'but there are some lovely bits'), comparing herself to Madame Verdurin (whose common vanity had so far escaped her) and unsurprised to see her end up as the Princesse de Guermantes, an ascent she found perfectly natural for a woman who has encouraged poets and artists. On the matter of whether certain people were genuinely talented or not, Blanche could scarcely offer guidance. At most, all she could do was assert that such and such an Academician was well brought up, such and such a poet kept his nails clean, and such and such an actor had had the manners of a duke ever since he had played Victor Hugo.

A large part of Blanche's time was spent in regulating who secured admittance at Avenue Foch and who did not. She had already eliminated Émile Duzan. She did not care for Oscar Dulonjé and only tolerated him because Julius Kapermeister saw in the former socialist a man potentially capable of leading a French political party of the force and importance of Nazism. Of Nelly she said, 'She's a *titi*.[23] We need some. Kings had their fools who were allowed to mock them to make them forget all their flatterers and hangers-on.' Her remarks about Jean were full of gentle innuendo: 'Illegitimate? Not as illegitimate as all that! There's a little prince hiding in there.' Palfy inspired mixed feelings. He might well be a Balkan baron, no one could tell. He had a certain class, that was not in doubt, but his cynicism was disconcerting: worldly people may be obnoxious or scornful, but rarely cynical.

'Cynicism,' Blanche said categorically, 'is the sign of a vulgar soul. It should be left to starlets.'

Madeleine docilely took it all in. The luxury and wealth that surrounded her but did not turn her head was gradually erasing the distrust she had acquired over years of serving men's more base needs. Blanche was also teaching her to be old-fashioned.

'Only tarts follow fashion too closely,' her companion declared. 'Look at Madame du Chaloir. She's forty-five. She's been wearing the same turban for six years, and she's an elegant woman, one of the most elegant in Paris.'

Madeleine changed her hairdresser and discovered that grey hair suited her, found a new dressmaker, a jeweller and a shoemaker who made thirty pairs of shoes of the same design Madame Chanel had been wearing for the last twenty years. She told Blanche that she wanted to add this new entourage to the guest list at Avenue Foch. Blanche dissuaded her.

'If you like, make a day for them on their own, but don't mix them with your bishops, generals and politicians, and definitely not with the writers, who are most of them as snobbish as concierges. On the other hand, there's nothing to stop you asking Madame Michette. Her mistakes in pronunciation are some of the best moments of a dinner.'

It was true. One evening Marceline was distinctly heard rebuking the Duchesse de Pont-à-Mousson, who was injecting morphine at the table, through her dress to save time.

'Madame, you'll give yourself an abscess. And not just an abscess, but *delirium tray men's*, and not just men's but women's too!'

The duchess, her gaze swimming in morphine, had stared in astonishment at this mysterious person whose voice appeared to be coming out of a thick fog.

'You are a darling!'

Marceline, who was unaware of being a darling, nevertheless realised that her sudden sally had delighted the other diners. Very quickly Paris learnt that there was fun to be had at Madeleine's. Some were envious, others jealous, but their spiteful remarks only enhanced the reputation of the soirées at the apartment of those who by now were known as 'the Kapermeisters'. Julius found life splendid. His private business affairs that, like Rudolf von Rocroy, he took care not to neglect had put him in a very comfortable position, whatever the war's outcome. He had always liked the French. Now he loved them.

'Their frivolous side,' he told Palfy, 'is metaphysical, purely metaphysical, and that's why the Germans like it so much, not having at all the same approach to life themselves. We're here to make sure they don't go too absurdly far on 14 July or the night of 4 August.[24] But one's forced to admit that if the French were not here to distract us, National Socialism would bore us all to death.'

'The French frivolous? My dear Julius, you must be joking. They're simply looking after number one. And to that extent they deserve better than to be treated as clowns by a German army which is in the process of getting a good hiding.'

The table went quiet. Guests studied their plates or took a long swallow of vodka or cognac. Julius gave a forced smile. In private he accepted such judgements with humility, though his deference was sometimes feigned. In public he was less flexible, despite wanting to be seen as liberal, fearing that, if he agreed, his words might be repeated in higher quarters.

'Dear Constantin, you go too far and too fast. The Wehrmacht is organising itself with the thoroughness and care for which it is well known, to resume the fighting after the spring thaw. We have taken Ukraine. Without Ukraine Stalin is powerless. I don't need to remind you that the Ukrainians have come over to our side. They are enlisting en masse in special German units, working in our factories and on our farms.'

Magnanimously, in order not to embarrass him further, Palfy concurred.

'Very well! Let us say that the war's outcome remains unpredictable.'

'For you!'

In truth Julius was convinced that Germany was falling into an abyss, which was an excellent excuse for exploiting the position in which the Wehrmacht authorities had placed him. His wealth was already safely stashed away in Switzerland, Spain and Portugal.

'For my children!' he assured Palfy, to whom he entrusted these missions. 'They find life boring in our dear old Germany. Their futures will be international, and as for me, I love only Paris and Frenchwomen.'

His wife, from whom he had lived apart for many years, had just died. Although neither man spoke of it, it was expected that he would marry Madeleine as soon as circumstances permitted. Hadn't he bought a delightful country house for her at Montfort-l'Amaury?

This agreeable, cheerful, careless reality, so perfectly self-interested, masked another, less light-hearted, for the French who were not invited to the feast. The winter of 1941–2 was hard not just for the Wehrmacht. In France people's reserves were running out, their clothes were wearing thin, and they were dying of cold. Their days, by the German clock, seemed shorter, as if life had shrunk, stifled by darkness. Uncertainty reigned. Posters announced the execution of hostages. People learnt that there were Frenchmen and -women who were disobeying the orders of the occupying power, and that that power was beginning to strike back. The question of where to shelter Claude became pressing. She had suddenly improved, almost inexplicably, and was getting up, dressing, looking after her son again, and wanting to leave Nelly's studio. Nelly assured her that there was no hurry. It seemed out of the question to go back to Quai Saint-Michel, where it was more than likely that the trap was still waiting for her. The Gestapo's French branch must have realised that Rudolf had taken them for a ride and were continuing to try to track her down.

The concierge, warmly congratulated by the police, was revelling in her importance. One morning, as soon as he had seen her leave for the market, Jean ran up to Claude's apartment. Helped by Palfy's chauffeur, he emptied the wardrobes and drawers. He felt wretched, as if he were violating her privacy, sweeping up the knick-knacks she treasured, a photograph album, her underwear, Cyrille's favourite games. It was all stuffed into suitcases and taken down to the car. The question of where Claude could safely stay remained. Jean thought of Saint-Tropez, but she refused point-blank.

'Without you? It's out of the question. I've got Cyrille and you. I can't live so far away.'

Jean travelled to Gif-sur-Yvette one afternoon, when he was certain not to bump into Laura. In shirtsleeves in his icy studio Jesús was painting a hill and a tree where they met the sky.

'Jean, you are kind. You don' forget me. We mus' celebra' that.'

His mood became less cheerful when he heard what had happened. Of course he was willing to look after Claude and Cyrille, but there was the question of Laura. Jesús admitted that he did not know Fräulein Bruckett's feelings. They did not have long conversations and in bed they talked about other subjects besides politics. Nonetheless, he did not think that Laura was, in reality, quite such a simple person as she seemed. An ordinary secretary in the Department of Supply? It was too straightforward. She enjoyed unusual privileges in an administration that was used to calculating very finely. She owned a car, dined at the Kapermeisters' and slept at Gif while her colleagues were billeted in a hotel on Rue de Rivoli. Jesús also confessed that he did not know what she was thinking, apart from the days when she arrived joyfully waving a letter from her brother at the front. None of this bothered him personally because he was Spanish, neutral, and bored stiff by politics. Even so, it was not certain that she could be confided in blindly, as it seemed probable that her modest job was combined with a more important function. Half the Germans were watching the other half, who were watching them too. Everyone was playing hide-and-seek.

'Listen,' Jesús said, 'we'll try. Come tomorrow. It's Christmas. No need fo' explanations. Laura will find that natural. Then, well, we see …'

Nelly was leaving for the south-west to spend the holidays with her parents.

'You know,' she said, 'my dear papa's so happy I'm back at the Comédie Française, he begged me to come. My rehearsals start on the second of January. I shall submerge myself in nature. Maman has made a *confit d'oie* and pudding. We're going to drink some of Papa's reserves of Corbières with a cassoulet. Until you've tasted Maman's cassoulet, you haven't lived. One day, if you're a very good boy, I'll take you with me. This year you have to spend your Christmas with the love of your life, but don't forget your girlfriend. And don't worry about me: Maman warms my bed every night before I go to sleep. No need for a chap at all. No fucking under my parents' roof is my motto!'

Palfy was leaving for Switzerland. Julius and Madeleine were going to Spain and Rudolf was returning to his wife in Berlin. Christmas was separating them all, as it did in peacetime. They were travelling in private carriages, sleeping cars. Madame Michette was the only one travelling third-class. They were preparing a surprise for her homecoming at the Sirène. After so much emotion and so many journeys she longed for a family atmosphere. As for the gallery whose management Jean was finally to take on, it would not open until the beginning of January. He was free.

Jesús was waiting for them at Gif station in the pouring rain. They took refuge in a café, next to a glowing stove. Certain scenes haunt us for a long time, with no explanation, and Jean was not to forget the two hours they spent in the café, its marble-topped tables, its zinc counter, the posters advertising aperitifs and the grubby waitress who refilled their glasses of red wine. Labourers came in, dripping with rain and smelling of wet leather and wool. They shook themselves like dogs and hung up their oilskins on the coatstand, under which a rivulet formed. On the door Jean read backwards

CHEZ JULES

VINS ET SPIRITUEUX

Jules! But he was Jules-who too. The memory of Nelly tugged at his heart. He would have sworn that having Claude back would erase the other's presence so completely that he would not think of her. But Jules-who was thinking of Nelly, and the previous night they had slept together. You can't separate everything. It's impossible. Somehow something is always left behind. Studying Claude as she talked to Jesús, he was surprised by her face's transformation. Her changed features bore witness to the suffering she had gone through, to an anxiety she needed constantly to be distracted from. The smallest thing upset her. Whenever someone came in, an unfamiliar face, she suddenly tensed for several seconds, hugging Cyrille to her as if the stranger had come to take him from her. Jean realised that morning how much she had truly changed. The taut skin of her gaunt face exposed the veins at her temples and the base of her nose. She clasped her hands together to hide her trembling fingers, flinched whenever someone ordered a drink too loudly, and shivered constantly despite being next to a glowing stove. The waitress laid their table and brought soup bowls, a basket of bread and a small carafe of wine. A young woman with coarse hair that was as straight as straw, wearing a black schoolgirl's blouse, collected their food coupons and placed them in an old metal cigarette box. The waitress returned from the kitchen with a steaming pot and a ladle. Ignoring the labourers' banter and complaints, she filled the bowls to the brim. The soup steamed and a silence fell as they sipped the first spoonfuls, after which the men served themselves bread and wine. Jesús started sketching on a drawing book Cyrille had brought with him. Jean put his hand in Claude's and her smile of artificial gratitude revealed to him how far removed from the present she was, how much she was still beating her lovely forehead against an imaginary barrier. During the last two days in Paris she had seemed better, but Jean suddenly gauged the fragility of her recovery: the smallest thing could break her – even the heavy atmosphere of this country bistro might be enough, the smell rising from wet clothes in the room's Turkish bath-like heat, the man at the next table who was pouring a spoonful of red wine into his soup, a ritual that reminded Jean of his own childish disgust when Albert had sharpened his soup the same way, greedily contemplating his wine-laced bowl. The rain ran in sheets down the bistro's windows and there was nothing to be seen of the village except, from time to time, the outline of a hastening figure. The waitress stationed herself behind the counter and opened *Le Petit Parisien*. The front-page headlines announced the British retreat in Malaysia, Japan's attack on Hong Kong, and two battleships sunk in Alexandria harbour by Italian frogmen. The waitress closed the paper again. She only skimmed it these days, since the censors had forbidden the horoscopes because spies used them to exchange secret messages using the signs of the zodiac.

As abruptly as it had started, the rain stopped. Sunshine spread across the street, a white light so intense it was blinding on the other side of the window. Jesús hoisted Cyrille onto his shoulders and was the first to leave, singing. Jean carried a suitcase in one hand, holding Claude's arm with the other, but he did not need to hold her up. In the crisp air her colour and will returned.

'How it's all changed!' she said.

In three weeks the countryside had been transformed, shedding the last of its green. The skeletal trees in the forest stood in a thick carpet of dead leaves of beautiful shimmering gold and dark red. From the bare fields a bluish mist rose like a smoker's breath. The house appeared at a bend in the road, set back, sheltered by an avenue of ash trees whose enormous roots clutched at the leaf mould like the talons of a bird of prey. Jesús had replaced the wobbly front door with one made of oak and two cramped ground-floor windows with a wide bay that let a golden light into the single downstairs room. The fire had gone out while Jesús had been away, and only glowing embers remained. Claude pressed her cheek to the still warm stonework around the hearth, then dropped into a tattered Louis XIII armchair whose springs poked through its torn upholstery. Jesús revived the fire with small pine logs, and flames suddenly rose so intensely that the rest of the room felt glacial.

Jesús wanted to make 'real' coffee. He battled with the wood stove.

'You should help him,' Claude said to Jean, who had sat on the floor at her feet and was playing with Cyrille.

Jean helped him. All through her life Jeanne had battled with a wood-burning stove, refusing in her latter years to switch to the bottles of gas that were taking over on the farms from the archaic stoves that used branches and small logs of resinous, scented wood. So he got the cooker going again, and they heated water for coffee. Claude dozed. Jean lay at her feet, his head turned to her, watching for the slightest movement the face of a woman who still hid the truth of herself from him and whom he had now decided he had to know completely, even if it meant becoming obsessed by her. The leaping flames coloured Claude's features, lessening the pallor of her cheeks and her temples' transparency. Jesús coaxed Cyrille outside.

'We are collectin' mushrooms and pickin' up snails!'

Cyrille let himself be wrapped up and put on the mittens Toinette had knitted for him, and they disappeared into the birch forest. Claude opened her eyes and saw Jean looking at her.

'How long are they going to be gone?' she asked.

'I don't know. An hour maybe.'

She sat up and pushed her hand across her brow.

'I'd like to sleep. Come with me.'

He followed her into the bedroom, which was warm from the fire downstairs but dark, illuminated only by the dormer window that looked out onto the birch forest. Claude undressed and lay down.

'Come,' she said again.

He lay down beside her. She was burning. As he hugged her to him he realised that this time she was ready, that the cruel refusal imposed on her was crumbling, leaving them, at last, face to face.

'I love you,' she said.

Jesús's return dragged them awake. He was tossing logs onto the fire, stoking the stove. Cyrille's piercing voice came up through the floor.

'So are you going to play battleships or not, Jesús?'

They listened, then the Spaniard's resonant voice was raised.

'Cyrille, you are cheatin'!'

'I always cheat with Maman.'

'If you was my son, I would smack you' bottom.'

'Just try it. You're not strong enough.'

There were shouts, puffing and panting and eventually Cyrille's victorious voice.

'Both shoulders! You're touching, Jesús. You lose.'

'It's true, I los'!'

Jean got dressed and went downstairs.

'Where's Maman?' Cyrille asked.

'She's resting.'

'She's been resting a jolly long time, she must be tired …'

They had collected black chanterelles and a few snails, and some sweet chestnuts that they were roasting in the embers. Jesús was putting up a Christmas tree, a young fir, and making cutouts of gold paper in the shape of shooting stars and figures from the Nativity.

'That's the donkey!' Cyrille said.

'No, 'e's no', silly boy! 'E's Sain' Josseph …'

'Or it could be the Virgin Mary.'

'If you don' sink I 'ave any talen' I'll go and 'ang myself up by …'

Cyrille stretched his neck and cocked his ear to hear the end of the sentence.

'By the what?'

'The 'airs in my nose!'

'All right … I thought you were going to say something else.'

Jean's arrival put an end to the argument. Above their heads they heard the floor creak at Claude's footsteps.

'So is she coming?' Cyrille asked. 'What's she doing?'

Claude came down as Laura arrived, laden with parcels. Jesús unloaded the car.

'We're goin' to wisstan' a sieze!' he said.

She had thought of everything, even the candles for the tree, which was transformed under Jesús's skilful fingers. On their earlier visit she had seemed to Jean dull and submissive. What revelation had suddenly changed her, so that this young woman, no natural beauty and charmless with it, should, against expectations, reappear as someone so extraordinary that her entrance was stunning, as though a new being had replaced the old? She kissed Cyrille, then Claude and Jean.

'Tonight,' she said, 'we forget everything.'

'Yes, oh yes … everything!' Claude replied, taking Jean's hand and squeezing it, communicating her joy and her serenity. The pressure of her hand brought back the events in the bedroom and the agreement Jean believed had at last been sealed between them. For a second, in the moment of sadness and dejection that follows pleasure, he had been afraid that Claude's surrender had been a farewell. But she was there, warm, her hip pressing against him, quiet, pacified, finally giving free rein to the tender sensuality she had held back for so long. With a finger he lifted up a stray strand of hair from her beautiful forehead. She caught his hand and kissed it.

'Maman!' Cyrille cried. 'You don't kiss men's hands.'

'Yes, you do, my darling. When it's Jean's.'

Next morning Laura did not come down when it was time to open the presents. Cyrille wanted to go upstairs and fetch her. Jesús caught his arm.

'No, Cyrille. Leave 'er, she's cryin'.'

'Why? It's Christmas!'

'Yes, and as you are a big boy, I'm goin' to teach you somethin' you'll remember all you' life. Yes'erday, before she came 'ome to us, she found out that 'er brother 'ad died in Russia. She didn' say nothin' because she didn' wan' to spoil our party. She's very brave.'

'What is "died"?'

Jean felt Jesús's emotion, his inability to explain.

'It means,' he murmured, 'that she'll never see 'im again.'

'Never ever?'

'Never.'

'What did he go to do in the war?'

Jesús, his voice breaking, said only, ''E was an officer.'

'German?'

'Yes.'

'We have to kill all the Germans, that's what Uncle Vladi says. And Grandmother wants to see them all dead too.'

'Be quiet, Cyrille!' Claude cried, so pale she looked as if she might faint. 'Be quiet, my darling.'

'But Uncle Vladi knows those things.'

'Be quiet.'

'The Germans are making war on Holy Mother Russia.'

'There's no mo' Holy Mother Russia!' Jesús said. 'There's no' one country that is holy any mo'.'

'That's very sad. So why did he died?'

Jean put his arms around Cyrille and lifted him up the way Albert had once, long ago, lifted him.

'For nothing, for nobody. And remember something else, Cyrille: the men who've died don't have a country any more. They're all brothers.'

'So everything's all right at the end. Then ... can we open the presents?'

For a long time the men of my generation were taught that to obtain too quickly and with too little effort the object of their desire would provide no satisfaction, not even to their self-esteem. Worse, they would find themselves tiring rapidly of the object in question. Subsequent generations have felt an instinctive suspicion for such traditional morality. Instinct – I mean the instinct of the moment, with everything wild and intuitive that that implies – instinct tells them that the desired object or person loses its desirability in the course of waiting, and so becomes devalued or degraded. In us, likewise, spent desire is robbed of its spark of energy. How can it stay alive when it is subject to fragmentation and dilution in a sea of temptation? When women were not easy (I'm talking about yesterday, not the day before yesterday, for, as we are too apt to forget, morals go through fashions of rigour and laxity in a way that ought to make us more modest in our claims about the extent of our victories in the name of liberty), when women were not easy, the gift of one of them inspired in him who possessed her a feeling of satisfaction and pride that contributed greatly to the perfection of pleasure. We speak here of love. We could be talking about houses, cars, horses, books or jewellery. In a society where temptation is all around – not a consumer society – as the overused phrase has it patience is the virtue of fools. To practise such a virtue is to be defeated from the start. Youth swiftly grasps this, by a special grace it is given. War and its repercussions, or rather the miseries of war and their repercussions, have a tendency to break the fragile bonds that linked us to our long-term desires. Tomorrow belongs to no one, and today demands thrilling, fleeting pleasures that rarely touch the heart and never the soul. Every satisfied desire is wreathed in the glories of a farewell. It is a gauntlet thrown down. And as it is bound not to be picked up, the gambler wins or feels he has won. There is no time to reckon gains or losses. Victory is already past, its traces rubbed out. For sensitive hearts, a poignancy and sadness remain. Some detect in all this a proof of the existence of God, arguing that the act of procreation, even without the intention of giving new life, is an act of faith and a gift. But does God not feel a deep and enduring bitterness, after having created us so little and so ill in his image that the best one can say is that He's no artist? Possession is no longer the highest aspiration of an existence, the affirmation of a personality whose guiding principle we would like to pass on. Possession is merely a fleeting desire that, once satisfied, leaves barely a trace. What? Was that it? Once more, we speak here both of love and of life's playthings: houses, cars, horses …

Jesús was cutting wood. With his foot on the sawbuck he lengthened his saw strokes, enjoying his power, the use of his strength. He finished splitting each log with a kick of his heel. His body, fit and taut with effort, steamed slightly. Like an athlete in training he paced his breathing, brushing a rebel strand of curly hair from his damp forehead with the back of his hand. His rolled-up sleeves exposed bare, hairy, tensely muscled forearms. Jean offered to help him.

'Go for a walk,' Jesús said. 'I'm sawin' in half the fellow who killed Laura's brother. Is my business.'

Claude was making lunch and Cyrille was colouring a book of printed drawings. Jean walked down the path that led through the birch forest. The pure icy light of Christmas Day sharply outlined the leafless branches against the sky, with the naive clarity of a Japanese painting. It might have been titled 'The clear morning and the dew' or 'The dream of the trees in the breath of the earth' or even 'The sun discovers a landscape that belongs to no one'. The path climbed uphill. At the top rusty bracken was colonising a clearing where tree trunks, blackened where they had been cut, lay on the ground like octopus tentacles. The sharp scent of bracken and the sweet smell of leaf mould saturated by ice-melt assailed Jean so violently that he stopped, feeling he was intruding on sleeping nature. There was a crossing of four paths here. Behind him was Jesús's farm, a building of sturdy grey stone whose slate roof reflected the light. It looked like water spangled with silvery glints. From the chimney there rose a vertical column of smoke that the cold air dispersed immediately. The rasp of Jesús's saw reached Jean like the rhythmic buzz of an insect, now quick, now slow because Jesús had hit a knot or got his blade stuck in green wood. There was no need to see him to picture him clenching his teeth, setting himself angrily to avenge Laura.

Ahead of Jean the ground fell away steeply among bracken, broom and brambles down to a river whose iridescent reflections winked back in Morse code at the slate roof. He walked down towards the water, which ran between well-defined banks. In fact it was not a natural river but an abandoned drainage canal. A log bridge spanned it. As Jean arrived two moorhens flew up and hid themselves in a reed bed, disturbing a couple of mallards which rose so swiftly against the light that they disappeared in its glare. Had they ever been there, had they really flown away into the milky-white sky where their plumage – at least the male's, the female being more discreet – should have sparkled like a firebird's? After they had gone a near-silence fell, broken only by the water flowing between the canal's black banks, and Jean made out the quicksilver gleam of trout flicking and darting against the current.

He remembered the Marquis de Malemort pushing up his sleeve and plunging his hand into the reeds or under a rock to feel for and grab a trout that he would toss onto the bank where it would flop, gasping, and die. Jean regretted not having learnt to poach when he could have done. Around Grangeville the woods were too formal. You encountered the hunt and, on calm days, the hinds and their wet eyes. Or Chantal exercising her mare, which would sneeze in the morning mist. Further on, a plantation of young firs made a green wall in the bruised forest. It was practically impossible to get through the wall and Jean decided to walk along its edge as far as a hedge that the winter had thinned out. Hawthorn and brambles seemed to have been pruned to leave just a circular gap at eye level. The track skirted round an octagonal hunting lodge with Louis XIII windows in which waxed paper covered the broken panes. The place could have been delightful, in the midst of a huge clearing of beeches that stretched out their gaunt branches, but it looked somehow tainted by a scorn for the lodge's prettiness, by a contemptuous neglect and indifference that were so manifest it was only suitable for a passing vagrant. A checked shirt was drying on a line next to a pair of long johns and, oddly, a patched coat, an old rag better suited to scaring birds. The carcass of an old car was being used as a henhouse. No smoke rose from the chimney. The person living in the lodge disdained the use of a fire, and it seemed likely that he disdained most things. The forest encircled him in his small clearing and would end up stifling him. Young growth was pushing through everywhere, probably pruned the previous autumn. Someone hoped to see them growing fast.

One day soon, with the clearing shrunk to the size of the lodge itself, the trees would force their way under the eaves and the roof would fall in. Two beeches, dead from old age, were rotting inside their bark, the wood yellow, their mangled branches overrun by ivy. No one had thought to cut them down and they stood there, collapsing little by little into the loose earth, blanketed in moss, seething with woodlice, like the ancient image of giants struck down, brandishing their black roots like horrible fingers.

Jean skirted the clearing that had distracted him from his exploration of the forest. The path led into an undergrowth of fragile ash saplings, tangled and shooting in all directions yet poised and graceful in their wild growth. A subdued light lit the ground, carpeted with leaves of a fine bronzed brown. Jean stopped to listen to the forest's rustling, a sporadic music, discontinuous, now whispered, now repeated to the point of insistence, impossible to locate among the branches or underfoot. He disturbed a hen pheasant that flew skilfully to cover and landed a short distance away in front of some brambles into which it waddled and disappeared.

The undergrowth descended gently towards a pond of black water. Jean was back at the drainage canal, which emptied here into the bulrushes and reeds. The forest opened up to his scrutiny like a flower whose pistil he had finally reached. He stopped, startled by the encounter, so simple and so captivating, when all he had done was wander at leisure, and realised that unless he retraced his footsteps he might find himself lost before this placid mirror in which the outlines of yellow and ochre-coloured trees trembled. The world had perhaps looked like this at its very beginning, and beneath the waters of the pool there crouched in their lairs giant animals, monsters with long necks and tiny heads, fearful and shy, threatened and devoured by otters and badgers, bedecked with leeches.

It moved him to see the forest revealing its intimate self, its melancholy secrets, caught off guard in its innermost heart. Jean would have liked to console it in its neglect as well as its beauty. Sitting on a black rock crowned with white lichen, he wondered whether it was not a blessing that the forest had been forgotten by men. They had not burnt it or cut it down or shredded it with their bullets and shells. They had not hidden there in order to kill each other better. Elsewhere, over in the East, in other forests muffled by snow, soldiers slipped through the trees and shot each other like enemy game while the white sky hummed with invisible planes that blindly released their sticks of bombs, unleashing fire and death.

At his arrival he thought he detected a sort of hesitancy in the waters and the tall bulrushes, unruffled by any breeze. Everything seemed to him preternaturally silent, as if in his presence the trees and muddy grass at the pool's edge had suddenly fallen quiet to observe him. He had not moved for several minutes when he noticed, coming from among the reeds, two ripples disturbing the sleepy surface. A pair of teal, followed by another, emerged from their hiding place and set out across the pool, the males with their heads of maroon browny-red, flecked with green, the female flecked with brown. Coming towards the bank on which he stood, a little to his right, they could not fail to see him. He remembered their arrival in Normandy when he was a boy, at the end of autumn when, after a long migration, they rested on the beach at Grangeville for a few hours before flying on inland. It was impossible to imagine a more suspicious bird, or one quicker to put itself beyond reach. That was what made it incredible to see them out in the open, swimming unconcernedly and quacking enthusiastically. Jean followed them with his gaze. They were heading purposefully for the bank. Only then did he glimpse, half hidden among the reeds and standing up to his thighs in the water, a man, or rather a scarecrow covered in sacking, a brown hat on his head, so still he looked like a statue, like one of those objects one leaves for years in hard water and that harden like stone without losing their colour. He had been there before Jean arrived, blending into the vegetation so well that he would have stayed invisible if the teal had not swum in his direction. When they were no more than two metres from this outlandish figure, an arm came out and lobbed a handful of some kind of pellets that floated. The teal rushed to them, gobbled them up and took off, skimming across the water to hide again in a clump of bulrushes. The man clambered onto the bank. He was wearing black waders and the sacking had been stitched together with some skill to make a rough overcoat that he must have put on over his head. He rubbed his hands, protected by woollen mittens, and pushed back his hat, an old round homburg camouflaged by more sacking. Until that moment all Jean had seen was a black beard. Seeing the rest of the face, he was surprised to find it younger than he had expected. The man came closer, walking stiffly in boots still caked in thick mud. Yes, the face was that of a man of barely forty, with shining, dark eyes beneath thick eyebrows, and a slender nose. The beard hid three-quarters of his face and concealed its thinness and hollow cheeks, their cheekbones reddened by cold.

'Good morning, Monsieur,' the man said. 'I must say I thought because of you they wouldn't come.'

'They're winter teal, aren't they?'

'Ah, so you know your ducks! That's unusual. To know the names of things is a remarkable sign in a world that generally talks about thingumabobs and whatchamacallits.'

The voice was distinguished, without affectation. The get-up was at odds with the tone of the man, who turned towards the pool and pointed towards the reeds where the teal were concealed.

'Nervous, aren't they? You'd need centuries to tame them … and we have so little time. You don't smoke, I hope?'

'No. Well, hardly at all.'

'But you drink alcohol!'

'So little too that it's hardly worth mentioning.'

'That little is still too much.'

The man shook himself and Jean was caught unawares by the smell he gave off, a mixture of grime and manure.

'Yes, still too much,' he went on. 'Humankind's committing suicide. But I suppose there's nothing new in that. It's been going on for three thousand years.'

'Humankind's a suicide victim who's doing fairly well, all things considered.'

The man scratched his beard, half amused. The tips of his fingers, poking out of his mittens, were appallingly dirty, covered in scales of filth and with black nails.

'You think I'm repugnant,' he said. 'And I am. Beyond measure. But solitude makes one indifferent. To tell you the truth, you're the first person I've spoken to for nearly two years. Oh, of course I've vaguely seen human beings moving in the distance. Sometimes they came so close I heard their blah blah blah. Apart from their clothes – about which they display unbelievable vanity – you can only distinguish them from animals by their lack of instinct. When I saw you appear here you surprised me. You watched and you stood still. I could have sworn you were enjoying imagining the presence of a monster in this fetid pool ...'

'I was.'

The man scratched his armpit. Jean thought he must be infested with lice.

'That's the great problem: where have all the monsters gone? There's one here. I've seen its tracks. Animals aren't innocent. No more than men are. They're nasty, brutish and cruel. We have to teach them.'

Jean was stirred: a few moments before he had pictured a monster lurking in these depths, and now this man was talking about it as if it was a reality. Between his beard and his eyebrows his eyes shone, sharp, mad, amused.

'What do you feed your teal on?' Jean asked.

'I collect worms in the mud and mould them into balls.'

'So really you're encouraging their carnivorous tastes.'

'Not bad! Not bad! Well thought through. No doubt about it, I'm a lucky man: the first human I've spoken to for two years is a thinker. He thinks! A miracle! Yes, Monsieur, it's true, I sacrifice worms to teal, but the teal are innocent. You ... you are not.'

'And you?'

'Me? You won't be surprised: I was falling apart before I hid myself away in the forest. By the way, where are we with the war? Is Danzig still a free city? Has Poland pulled through?'

He scoffed and held up a hand to forestall an answer Jean hesitated to give him.

'Don't disappoint me! Don't disappoint me, Monsieur!'

'I shan't disappoint you,' Jean said. 'Danzig remains a free city.

Poland is free, Austria has expelled the Germans. The Sudetens booed Hitler at a parade and, because they annoyed him, he gave them back to Czechoslavakia, which has returned to being a fine, proud republic with a socialist government. Italy has put good King Zog and his pretty queen Geraldine back on the throne of Albania. Mussolini has offered his apologies to Haile Selassie and given him back his throne at the same time as Victor Emmanuel renounced the title of emperor. General Franco has opened his borders to the remaining Republican army for a festival of reconciliation. Oh, I forgot to mention that Hitler has stepped down as Chancellor of the Reich to devote himself full-time to oil painting. The great dealer, Braun-Lévy, has signed him up exclusively for his first exhibition, which will take place this spring.'

'Marvellous! I did well not to get involved and I was right to run away from these neighbourly disputes. I'd have been a complete spare part. I bet no one's even noticed I've gone.'

'It's true; no one's said a thing to me.'

The man smiled indulgently and sat down on a tree trunk mouldy with slippery brown mushrooms that squashed beneath his backside.

'What's your name?'

'Jean Arnaud.'

'Arnaud with an "l"?'

'No, without an "l".'

He looked disappointed and subsided into a reverie that lasted two or three minutes, while Jean waited unmoving, the better to observe him. The man scratched himself and tugged on his beard with his thin and dirty fingers. It would have been interesting to see him shaved and his face revealed.

'And my name is Pascal. Blaise Pascal. Does that mean anything to you?'

'Yes, but you're not Blaise Pascal.'

'What do you know about it?'

'You don't look like him. He was clean-shaven and neatly dressed.'

'You're talking about my physical appearance. What about his soul? I've run into his soul here, Monsieur, wandering in the damp woods of the Chevreuse valley, lingering by the noisome waters of these pools. I have merely given it a body, my own. His soul is warm there; it no longer wanders cold and alone, and I'd go so far as to say that it's enjoying itself. I grant you it's not inventing wheelbarrows, problems of geometry or pulley systems to draw water from a well, but it has other amusements. We discuss grace and the world's folly and talk to the animals.'

He stood up and raised his hat, revealing his baldness and a dirt-encrusted scalp.

'It's been my pleasure, Monsieur Arnaud.'

'Mine too.'

He took three steps and paused.

'That's not just a figure of speech. I have greatly enjoyed our conversation. Perhaps I've exaggerated to myself the inanity of intercourse with my fellow men. Where do you live? Oh … don't worry … I've no intention of visiting … Purely curiosity.'

'A Spanish friend has bought an old farmhouse behind the birch forest. He's a painter.'

'Are you talking about that tall hairy fellow always in his shirtsleeves? I've seen him sawing wood. A painter? Now that's interesting. I find art to be window dressing. I mean the art of today. I once had a collection of paintings, can you imagine? And you have no idea how easily one can do without. Adieu! Or perhaps au revoir. Who knows? If you're passing my house – a delightful Louis XIII hunting lodge – tap on one of the few remaining window panes. I'll always be happy to see you. You have a pleasing face. We'll talk of those "gentlemen", of Mother Angélique[25] and Saint-Cyran[26] … What formidable intelligence! And we'll speak ill of the Jesuits … I hope you weren't raised by them …'

'No. I was cast in the ordinary mould of village primary school and lycée.'

'I detest the Jesuits. Well, cordially detest them.'

He made a comical gesture with his arms as if he was about to strangle the entire community. His laughter followed him as he plunged into the wood, where the hessian of his sacks camouflaged him instantly.

Jean clapped his palms together. The teal took off and spiralled up above the pool before hiding themselves again in the reeds.

Jesús was sawing the last log.

'One hun'red! And Chris'mas mornin'! I am the only man in the worl' who 'as sawed one hun'red logs today. Come inside. Lunch mus' be on the table. The boy came to find you three times.'

Laura did not join them. Jesús said she did not want to make their lunch gloomy. She was not hungry. She had not cried but sat still in an armchair, next to the window, her eyes full of images. When he bent over her he could see her brother there, playing with her as a boy, a garden, a wide meadow where there stood ricks of hay that they sprawled on, a sandy Baltic beach, bordered by a curtain of mist hiding the boats whose anxious foghorns sounded at regular intervals. Jesús told himself that when she had reviewed these images she would feel quieter. They were her prayer for the dead, for a young infantry lieutenant buried beneath the snow.

Jean told the story of his encounter that morning. Cyrille wanted to talk to the scarecrow who did not scare away the teal. Jesús had never seen him, but knew of his existence. At Gif, in the cafés and shops, they discussed the man in the woods as if he was a legend. A few walkers had glimpsed him fleeing at their approach. A search by the gendarmes had produced no results. They had entered the hunting lodge, which was a true pigsty. Yet the man existed, and Jesús had sensed him one day outside the front door, invisible in the bushes, spying on him. A sensation more than a certainty. A madman, without a doubt.

'He's not mad at all!' Jean said. 'Very sensible, actually, apart from the fact that he thinks he's Blaise Pascal.'

'Blaise Pascal?' Cyrille said. 'I know him. He plays every morning in the Luxembourg Gardens. He's a little boy. He wears red. He's got a submarine.'

'So there are several Blaise Pascals. Why shouldn't the man in the woods be one of them?'

Jesús admitted he did not know Blaise Pascal and that, being wholly ignorant of his personality, he did not see why the teal hunter should not call himself that. For one thing, the little boy in red with the submarine claimed that was his name and nobody thought he was mad, since they let him carry on playing in the Luxembourg Gardens.

'What's even more interesting than his name,' Jean said, 'is what he lives on. He doesn't smoke or drink, and boasts about it, which would seem to indicate that he must once have smoked and drunk a lot. He also claims to have once possessed a collection of paintings …'

'I can do him a drawing,' Cyrille said. 'Jesús showed me how.'

'If you like I'll take him one, and perhaps he'll rediscover his taste for life when he finds out it's the work of a small boy. Then I'll know who he really is.'

'I want to go and see him now.'

Jesús promised Cyrille he would take him.

After lunch Claude bundled up her son and he went out with Jesús. Jean stayed behind, standing warming himself at the fire. He watched Claude clear the table. She had not said a word during lunch.

'Come here. I want to be alone with you.'

'We are alone.'

'No. The way we were yesterday.'

He took her hand and drew her to the stairs and then into the bedroom where she stayed standing by the window.

'Take your clothes off,' he said.

She did as she was told, indifferently, almost as if she was not there, and her nakedness felt all the more shocking to Jean.

'Do you want me?' she asked, her face pale, her eyes feverish.

'Completely.'

She got into bed and he joined her. She was neither wanton nor reticent, just outside time. Then, as he caressed her, she seemed to come back to herself and wrapped her arms around him. Later she said again, 'I love you.'

He felt like crying. He wanted to clasp her to him all his life, to never let her go more than a metre from his side. All of their misfortunes came from their not being able to live together.

'I love you too,' he said.

She kissed his neck. He stroked the back of hers. Their legs were intertwined so tightly that their desire, satisfied moments before, revived without a pause. Jean said nothing. He carried on holding her tightly, deferring until later, for ever, the questions and answers that would make him so unhappy that they might not see each other again. Claude fell asleep. He bent over her face, which still wore the traces of recent days. Her private suffering made her features, usually so peaceful, even more beautiful. Jean did not recognise her. An immense tenderness gripped him: it was a face full of pathos. Her courage had left her; she had surrendered. He realised that from now on he would have charge of her as she, for nearly two years, had had charge of him without his noticing, so discreet and restrained had she been in helping him to survive. It was thanks to her that from now on he would be a man and through her that he had known a happiness, before they made love, that no other woman would ever be able to give him again. He knew too that Claude's deep generosity caused her problems and that mean spirits would always be tempted to do her injury. It was a time to remember that he had wounded her himself on at least two or three occasions, and that he continued to wound her by his affair with Nelly. He looked for excuses. They were all too easy.

The front door slammed. He heard Cyrille's voice and got dressed. Claude curled up under the sheets. He went downstairs.

'Where's Maman?'

'She's asleep.'

'We didn't see Blaise Pascal but we saw his house. It's not nice.'

Jean realised that Laura was in the room, dressed and with a travelling bag standing ready by the door.

'Where are you goin'?' Jesús said.

'To Paris, to ask for leave to see my parents in Germany.'

Jesús looked helpless at the idea of having to live without her.

'Will you come back?'

'Of course. My life is here now, nowhere else.'

Jean was struck by her choice of words, at odds with her forced smile.

'Are you going away?' Cyrille said. 'That's sad. Then I'll stay with Jesús and make him feel better.'

Laura crouched down and held out her arms. The child ran to her. She raised her eyes, filled with tears, to Jesús.

'A little boy is so sweet!' she said.

Jesús did not answer. He had abandoned many sententious ideas about women but he still stuck to a number of firm resolutions about fatherhood, or at least was unwilling to admit that a crack was starting to show.

'I'm goin' with you to Zif. I'll walk back. I need the exercise.'

'You've just had some with me,' Cyrille observed.

'No' enough! Cheeky boy!'

'No, stay!' Laura said. 'It's better to say goodbye here.'

She kissed Cyrille, then Jesús, and went out, her travelling bag in her hand. They heard the car's engine as it came out of the barn and turned down the rough track. Jesús poured himself a large glass of cognac which he drank in quick mouthfuls, facing the fire. Simply and without boasting he explained to Jean that until meeting Laura he had led a marvellous life. Nothing touched him; everything was like water off a duck's back. But she had skinned him, and now he felt everything with an almost painful acuteness. He had learnt the anxiety of waiting, the sadness of going away, and on the nights he was alone, it grieved him not to make love. Everywhere she left signs for him, those small signs of care a woman lavishes on the man she loves. How do these things happen? he demanded. Who was trying to get at him through Laura, who wanted to destroy his artistic solitude? His voice broke.

'Jesús,' Jean said, 'you're talking nonsense. You're drowning in words. Be careful or you'll start to believe it … And I know you won't believe it, but you're going to listen to me tell you again that Laura has demolished your fixed ideas in order to uncover the artist you really are. Since she came into your life you've been painting for yourself, you've shown La Garenne the door, and you've started signing your pictures Jesús Infante, which is an exceptionally fine name for a painter. It makes me happy, Jesús, that you're unhappy when Laura goes away. It's good for you! In the past you were mostly getting away with a generous tip and a kick up the backside. You shoved all those girls unceremoniously out of the way to make space for Laura.'

'You think so?'

'I'm sure of it.'

'An' who decided all that?'

'That's the big question.'

Cyrille had gone upstairs to see his mother. He was coming back. Halfway down the stairs he called to Jean.

'Yes.'

'You have to come upstairs, Maman's crying.'

Jesús looked reproachfully at Jean. Claude was crying and someone or something was behind it, even if one accepted the notion that women easily became sad. The Spaniard shrugged. Jean met Cyrille on the stairs.

'Leave me with your maman. I can cheer her up better if I'm on my own.'

Cyrille for once obeyed without protest.

Her head buried in a pillow, Claude was sobbing. Jean covered her bare shoulders and moved his hand towards her neck, which cried out its innocence, almost a child's neck attached to a lovely woman's body. He told himself that a man could fall in love with Claude just by glimpsing that soft space of downy skin under her hair. A vulnerability was hidden there, but it was also the secret of her graceful way of carrying her head. For the first time he felt its tension, contracted by fear, by a quivering terror that only subsided when he placed his lips at the hairline of her ash-blond hair. She turned over and sat up in bed, her cheeks shining with tears, with such a sudden intent in her eyes that he was afraid in turn and stepped back.

'I'm getting up,' she said. 'I'll get dressed and go down. Tell them to wait!'

He held her by the shoulders and shook her.

'No. I'm here.'

She smiled and did not stop him when he bent forward to kiss her unfeeling lips.

'Jean, are you certain that Lieutenant Bruckett's dead? Over there. In Russia. That he'll never rise up from the snow and curse us with his frozen arm? You have to tell Laura it wasn't me who killed him.'

'No, no, it wasn't you.'

'The Russians kill all lieutenants. Cyrille's never going to be a lieutenant. Promise me.'

'I promise you.'

His heart aching with a deep and terrible anxiety, Jean released her shoulders.

'Darling, get dressed. It's cold.'

'You know they held me down in a freezing bath?'

He hugged her tightly to stop her seeing his own tears and begged her, 'Wake up!'

'But I am awake!'

She pushed him away and made a pout of reproach as though he did not understand her.

'Oh Jean, Jean, don't leave me, I love you, I love you …'

She laughed through more tears, tears of happiness now, like a lover choking with joy at the beloved's return. Night was filling the sloping-roofed room, but neither thought of lighting a lamp.

'Where's Cyrille?' she asked.

'Downstairs with Jesús. Perhaps we should join them.'

He picked up Claude's underwear from the floor, her corduroy trousers and the sweater she had worn at lunch. She ignored her underwear.

'Aren't you putting anything on underneath?' he asked.

'No, it's nicer being like this.'

They went downstairs. Jesús was drawing on a big piece of paper. Cyrille, sitting on the table, was watching him.

'Maman,' he called, 'Jesús is doing the man in the woods for me, the way Jean saw him this morning. You're not crying any more?'

'No, my darling. You can see I'm not.'

'Then why were you crying?'

'I can't remember.'

He lost interest in the question and leant over towards Jesús.

'Is Laura still in her room?' she asked.

'Laura's gone to see her parents.'

Claude threw two logs on the fire and slumped into an armchair. Jean opened a book he had borrowed from Nelly's shelves. Where else? The people he spent time with didn't read. Even Claude possessed only Russian authors she hadn't opened for a long time. Palfy was happy with his newspapers and Madame Michette devoured spy novels. Only Madeleine was deep into Proust, but she hired her

Proust from a reading room, the idea of buying a book having never occurred to her and Blanche de Rocroy not being the type to suggest it to her. He opened the book Nelly had lent him and heard her cheeky, husky voice.

'You want a book, Jules-who? Why? You won't read. You don't read when you're in love. Take this anthology. You can recite some poems to yourself and try to hear my voice. If a poet bores you, try another one, then another one, till you've found the one who talks to you best about yourself. Then you'll be much happier than with a big fat novel about an illicit love affair between a man on the night shift and a woman on the day shift ...'

It was a thick volume in a sandy-coloured binding that called itself an anthology of new French poetry. He opened it at random.

> *To you, Germans – with my mouth at last released from military reticence – I address myself.*
> *I have never hated you.*
> *I have fought you to death with stiffly unsheathed desire to kill very many of you.*
> *My joy sprang to life in your blood.*
> *But you are strong. And I wasn't able to hate in you that strength, the mother of things.*
> *I took pleasure in your strength ...*

The date of the poem was 1917. The author was called Drieu la Rochelle. Jean turned to Claude; her lips were quivering. She stared at him.

'Do you think they'll punish them?' she asked.

'I'm sure they will.'

'That's all right then.'

He took the hand she had let fall. For an instant he recalled the blissful moments, gathered one by one, before Claude had been his. How could he get them back? Stroking her knee in the train that had brought them from Clermont-Ferrand, the way they kissed on the cheek every time they met or parted, her dressing gown falling open to reveal her breast, her nakedness in the mirror in their hotel room at Saint-Raphaël. Did all that have to lose its meaning, just because they had made love? Did a single act reduce to childishness all the feverish, intense emotions that had fired your imagination? From the age of thirteen until he was twenty he had written down in an oilcloth notebook his reflections and impressions of the life that was opening up before him. The notebook had got left behind in the tankette they had abandoned in the village square. Monsieur Graindorge, the surveyor, had doubtless picked it up and had a good laugh reading it. Jean felt he would have liked to add another entry to his old notebook that evening: 'One sort of love, the most beautiful and the only really precious sort, comes to an end the moment you sleep with the woman you love for the first time. The stolen kisses, her half-glimpsed body, become childish things. An enormous, superb, intoxicating but obscene adventure begins. An immense amount of tenderness is needed to stop it degenerating into debauchery. Only in idealised romantic novels is the act of love portrayed as a marvellous levitation, the earthly flight of two bodies. The reality is not so magical, and that less magical element makes everything scary. Two bodies fall to earth, suffering the vertigo of emptiness, the return to oneself, a moment of appalling indifference. Sounds, smells, precautions can ruin everything. I'd be wiser never to make love to the woman I most care for, and instead to do it very often with women I'll never be attached to. If I'm honest, the most balanced period of my life was the time between my first night with Nelly and my first afternoon with Claude. I didn't realise it. Now I know it. My pleasure with Nelly may be over for good. With Claude, it's perhaps the start of a long and difficult road to the prize …'

Claude's hand squeezed his hard, as if reminding him to protect her, but her gaze remained turned to the fire.

'Jean … There's someone watching us.'

'There's only Jesús and Cyrille.'

'No, someone else. Behind my back.'

Later – wrongly, because she was right – Jean remembered that it was this fear of Claude's that had aroused his first suspicions. Before, she had (he thought) just been talking nonsense, floating in a semi-comatose sea of sedatives.

But Jesús looked up, stared at the window, and leapt to his feet to run to the front door, which he threw open. The fire crackled, spitting a ball of smoke.

'Maman, it's snowing!' Cyrille shouted.

Jesús came back in, holding a whitish form tightly by the arm, a man covered in snowflakes. Claude wailed and threw herself into Jean's arms.

Jesús closed the door behind the figure, who shook himself and took off his hat, leaving the top of his head and upper part of his face free of snow.

'Why was you spyin' on us be'ind the window?'

'I am sorry, so sorry. Deeply sorry, Madame.'

There was nothing frightening about him: he was more comic than anything else, twisting in his hands (in white leather gloves) a silk-brimmed hat of the sort known as an Eden. Jean recognised him more from his voice than his dress. The man from the woods had gone to considerable trouble. The melting snow already forming a pool at his feet revealed him dressed for polite society: a soberly elegant pinstriped navy-blue suit, black pointed shoes and in his hand a cane with an ivory knob.

'Maman, Maman!'

Cyrille was crying, clinging to his mother's legs as she, shaking convulsively, hid her face on Jean's shoulder.

'It's nothing!' Jean said. 'It's just a visitor.'

'Yes, I came to wish you a happy Christmas. We're neighbours, are we not? I had no wish to disturb you. Having lived as a savage for some time, I've rather lost the habits of society …'

He must have made an effort to wash himself and to run the scissors over his beard and hair, but the smell of dirt still hung around him, a tenacious tramp's smell. He was so outlandish and unexpected that Jean would have burst out laughing if it had not been for Claude's trembling. He gently pushed her down into the armchair so that her back was to the visitor. Cyrille, regaining his courage, peeped at him.

'Jean, is it the man in the woods?'

'Ah, so I am known to this young man!'

Blaise Pascal – it was he – coughed to clear his throat, hoarse with emotion. The hand clasping the knob of his cane went to his beard to restrain possible germs.

'Why was you lookin' in the window?'

'Ah, so you're the Spanish painter? Your friend told me about you. There was a time when I was very interested in painting. Would those two landscapes on the wall be yours?'

'Oh, the boy could do jus' as good ...'

'Don't you believe it, dear Monsieur. I know that modern painting claims to have rediscovered, via a complicated detour, the genius of childhood, since – as they declare – all children possess genius, except for child prodigies. But allow me to tell you that your painting – in so far as I can judge from these two pictures – displays the very opposite of childishness. You know everything and you have had the strength to harness your ability. Trust me, Monsieur, I am happy to inform you, if no one else has already done so, that you are a great, a very great painter.'

Dumbfounded, Jesús stared at him. It occurred to Jean that this pure spirit with the frame of an ox knew nothing of deceit, and he felt greater faith in the bearded stranger's measured speech than in La Garenne's self-interested paeans. Jesús would accomplish his work in solitude, far from sycophants and the most articulate of admirers; in truth, all he needed was friends and love ... Claude turned to look at the figure whose pleasant voice, with a nuance of vanity in its assured tone, seemed to have calmed her attack of nerves.

'Come and get warm!' Jean said.

The snow had all but melted from the visitor, but he stayed standing in his pool of water, embarrassed, trying to please by his refined politeness.

'I would not wish to frighten you, Madame.'

'I'm not afraid of you,' Claude said.

'You'll excuse me for having spied on you at the window for just a moment. The truth is that I couldn't decide whether to knock at the door or not. You made a delightful, delicate picture. The child is very handsome. Is he your boy, Madame?'

'Yes, he's my son.'

'Come and get warm,' Jean repeated.

The man did nothing, not from discretion but because he had developed a habit of not accepting any invitation.

'You're all wet!' Cyrille said.

'Very true, my boy, but I had no umbrella. When I left two years ago I took only this cane with me ...'

'You left your house two years ago? What does your maman say?'

'I haven't got a maman any more.'

'Show me your cane. Is it a swordstick? My father gave me one before he went away. If any thieves come, I'll kill them.'

'Now that sounds very brave to me!' Blaise Pascal said.

Leaning his cane against the wall, he placed his Eden hat on the table and pulled off his gloves. He had washed his hands with their caked fingernails, but greyish traces remained in the places where his skin was cracked from chilblains. These details were at odds with his elegant appearance, or nearly elegant, since his wool suit was flapping around his emaciated body and his grey Eden had yellowed considerably. Somehow the man radiated kindness, perhaps because he was secretly revelling in his hosts' astonishment or, better still, because after months of loneliness he felt a pleasure that amazed him to find himself among human beings again.

'As you suspected,' he said to Jean, 'my name is not Blaise Pascal and I do not share his genius. The name was a homage to a product of the Port-Royal schools. As I told you this morning, I live very much with him inside me. The *Pensées* is one of the ten books I took with me when I went into my exile. You are familiar with the parlour game of which ten books you would take with you to a desert island? I actually did it. You know one of them. If we get to know one another a little more, I'll tell you the others ... But I have arrived at a bad moment ... You were perhaps about to have dinner?'

'Stay with us!' Jesús said.

The man made an embarrassed gesture.

'You know ... I've lost the habit of eating meals ... You can do without them very easily. There are blackberries, mushrooms and sweet chestnuts ... and I'm forgetting watercress, watercress all year round. Very healthy, especially with a few potatoes that I grow. The human organism has no need of abundance.'

Claude got up and walked across the room to fetch some potatoes, which she put to bake in the embers. She had regained her calm, but her fine features still bore a trace of the violent emotion that had overtaken her. More and more, Jean thought, she was closing in on herself. She could be brought back to earth by squeezing her hand, or stroking her hair or cheek. Now, having overcome her fear of Blaise Pascal, she did not give him a second look. As she crossed the room, she brushed past him and he had been profuse in his apologies but Jean wondered if she had actually *seen* him. In any case the man saw her and could hardly take his eyes off her. He spoke for her benefit, caressingly, measuring his words' pleasure.

'For a man who lives alone you do a lot of talking,' Jean said, mildly irritated.

Blaise Pascal's eyes lit up.

'You're so right, Monsieur. I should have unlearnt the power of speech. It might even be fun to see me walking on all fours and barking. That was the pitfall. I foresaw it and I left this world with a mirror. I talk to my mirror and my mirror answers me. Alas, its answers do not satisfy me. As Cocteau puts it so nicely, a mirror should reflect before it offers a reflection.'

Jesús did not understand. Jean had to explain the play on words to him. Blaise Pascal was delighted.

'Monsieur—' he began.

'My name is Rhésus Infante!'

'Monsieur Jesús—'

'There is no Monsieur Rhésus. The French, they say little Rhésus, I am the other, not the big, the Rhésus and that's it ...'

'Shall I make an omelette?' Claude asked.

'Yes, Maman! Can I break the eggs?'

She let him break them into a bowl. He only missed two of them, which broke on the tiles in front of the oven.

'What I wanted to say is that your time has come!' the man said to Jesús, finally moving closer to the fire.

His clothes steamed, and a smell of disinfectant pervaded the room.

'Excuse me,' he said. 'This suit was going to lie in mothballs until peace was declared.'

'Who says it wasn't declared long ago?' Jean said.

Blaise Pascal smiled.

'Monsieur—'

'My name's Jean Arnaud.'

'Yes, without an "l". Am I to call you "Jean"?'

'It would be simpler, Blaise.'

'Well, Jean, I've been drawing my own conclusions. I go as far as the road and I hide there. There are no cars, apart from one driven by a nice-looking woman, which has a German registration.'

'That's Laura,' Jesús said.

'Her brother was killed by the Russians,' Cyrille said. 'She's gone to bury him. The Russians are killing lots of Germans.'

'Be quiet,' Claude said. 'Go and wash your hands.'

She laid four places at the table. Jesús opened a bottle of wine, poured a glass and offered it to Blaise.

'Thank you, no,' Blaise said. 'I don't drink. Loneliness and alcohol don't go together. There are no half-measures. Either you don't drink or you drink like a fish. I chose abstinence, although, believe me, I wasn't always that way disposed.'

Claude served the omelette.

'Does your diet exclude eggs?' Jean asked.

'No. I even owned two hens and a cock. Two months ago they disappeared. I suspect a fox had them. You will object that eggs are not vegetable. You would be right.'

He raised his finger to ensure their attention.

'But by eating an egg I am fighting in my own way against overpopulation. By the year 2000 there will be four billion earthlings. Malthus was right. Limit the number of births and you'll have no more need of wars to mop up the consequences of an ocean of sperm.'

'Of what?' Cyrille said.

'Forgive me, my boy, I forgot you. It's a scientific word.'

'Sit down,' Claude said, seeming to pay no attention to the man or his chatter.

She served them in silence and sat with her own empty plate in front of her. For three weeks she had eaten almost nothing at all, making do with a glass of water here, a piece of bread there. Trousers and sweaters concealed her new slimness, but when Jean had hugged her to him in the bedroom that afternoon he had been surprised by how thin her body, once so moving in its shapeliness, its secret harmony between flesh and frame, had become. Her failure to eat had already blighted her face, making her eyes more protuberant and her cheekbones more prominent, the avatar of a beauty that had once been placid and simple and was now impenetrable. Her looks were changing as much as if she had put a mask over her face, and her fixed expression concealed, from anyone who did not know her, a sadly etched image of fear …

Jesús, whom the visitor had so surprised as to leave him speechless, regained his composure at dinner. He had been so carried away by the compliments about the only two canvases hanging on the wall that for a moment he had been unable to assert himself. But one did not condemn a man of Jaén to silence as easily as that. Nor, at Jaén, was there any shortage of hermits. His uncle, Antonio Infante, had shut himself up in a Saracen tower on the edge of the town, on the Bailén road, at the beginning of the civil war. It was an old tower with solid walls, but its upper platform had collapsed. Antonio had walled up the outer door and moved in with a guitar. Every morning he tossed a rope over the wall to which a box was tied, full of bread, water and some fruit. He sent the box back with some trifling ill-smelling objects that were buried elsewhere. Except at midday precisely, he was always in the shade. When it rained he opened his umbrella, and on icy winter nights he wrapped himself in a quilt. One day Jesús brought a ladder that reached the battlements. His uncle was dozing, his guitar beside him. He had grown a long black beard, like Tolstoy's. He had become much thinner in his dust-covered clothes. Sometimes he was heard singing, accompanying himself on the guitar. At the end of the war he had emerged from his retreat to shave and get married. He had two children already, had announced his intention to have another one every year until 1950, and led a modest life running a haberdashery.

'Human foolishness knows no limits,' Blaise Pascal said, put out that Jesús dared to steal his thunder with such a picturesque anecdote.

'That's exactly wha' I sink of you!' Jesús answered calmly. 'You don' do anythin'. You are simply afraid. And fear is no' pretty.'

'But you also—'

'Me, señor, I don' make somebody else's war …'

'What do you mean? It's always somebody else's war! I've only ever understood one war, and that's civil war. At least one knows why one's beating and killing one's brother. But the Germans? Why? I don't know them. I wouldn't go and live with them for anything in the world. Their philosophy bores me. Musicians? Well, yes, certainly. Alas, I'm not fond of music. Their women? I'm sorry, I like – or rather I used to like – petite women with brown hair. You see, I've no reason to be angry with them. They leave me cold. That's all!'

Jean tried to catch Claude's eye. He sensed that she was not listening and was overcome by tiredness. Her eyelids were heavy and her head kept slowly sinking then starting up suddenly. He leant towards her.

'Do you want to go to sleep?'

She answered so quietly that he could hardly hear her.

'Yes ... but you will fuck me, won't you?'

Neither Jesús nor Blaise Pascal seemed to have heard. He took her arm and went upstairs with her, followed by Cyrille, who got undressed on his own and snuggled into his sleeping bag.

'Will you both kiss me, please?'

Claude, sitting on the edge of the bed, smiled and blew him a kiss.

'Go to sleep, darling.'

Jean kissed him. The boy was dog-tired.

'He's funny, the man in the woods, don't you think, Jean?'

'Yes, he is pretty funny.'

'Will he come back tomorrow?'

'I suspect he probably will.'

Rising from the ground floor, the muffled voices of Jesús and Blaise Pascal were still audible.

'Jean, undress me,' Claude said.

'All right.'

He laid her down on the bed. Cyrille turned over.

'Good night.'

Claude did not even appear to hear him. She raised herself fractionally to let Jean take off her trousers and sweater, then murmured something so indistinctly that at first he hardly heard her and was then shocked as he understood.

'Be quiet,' he said.

The Light 11 stopped at the entrance to Allée des Acacias. Palfy got out before the chauffeur had a chance to open his door. He spread his arms wide, inhaled a lungful of cold air and, catching sight of Jean waiting for him, turned to the chauffeur.

'Émile ...'

Jean hated him calling a man Émile whose real name was Jean ('You understand,' Palfy had said, 'that I *had* to unbaptise him, *because of you*').

'Émile, no need to stay with us. I'm just going to the Cascade and I'll be back. You can switch off the engine ...'

Turning to Jean he said, 'Émile is a splendid chauffeur. My mother called hers "my mechanic". In those days chauffeurs knew how to keep their cars on the road. Modern engines have killed off the enterprising mechanic. I doubt if Émile knows how to change a spark plug, but he's like a father to me. Let's walk, shall we, I could do with some exercise. We'll talk in vapour bubbles like the heroes of comic strips. But if we meet anyone else, they won't be able to read them. They'll be written in invisible ink.'

He wore a fur-lined coat with a black astrakhan collar, and a soft grey hat. His tanned complexion was a sign of wealth in an era of pallor.

'Where did you get your tan?' Jean asked. 'I thought you were in Switzerland.'

'I was. In the mountains. Wonderful sunshine. Snow and the simple life. Gstaad is a little paradise, despite meeting mostly people who are waiting for the end of the war. Anyway there weren't only people like that there. I also met a very charming woman and we talked about you.'

'Don't make me laugh. I don't know a charming woman: if I did I'd remember her ...'

'What about Claude?'

'I'll tell you later. But you didn't meet her at Gstaad.'

'No, you smart alec. I met your mother.'

Jean was silent. An image from the past suddenly came to him: the yellow Hispano-Suiza on the quayside at Cannes. Geneviève, the prince in a wheelchair, and Salah getting out. They were deserting Europe. Geneviève, in a pale dress and wearing a beret, a light coat over her arm and carrying her jewellery bag, had turned to glance at the families and curious onlookers crowding around the landing stage. Jean remembered the sadness on her hardly made-up face. She was already missing Europe, her friends, her sparkling, clever London where she had been so happy. She was leaving, resigned but not yet convinced of the necessity of her going.

'The prince is dead,' Palfy added. 'Geneviève is finding it difficult to obtain a residence permit for Switzerland. But with money everything can be worked out ...'

The reader has the advantage over Jean of having known this piece of news for a long time. He or she also knows that Albert Arnaud will die the following summer at Grangeville, during the Dieppe raid. The state of war, Europe's isolation, and within Europe the isolation of every nation forced back onto its own hardships and hopes, the censorship that weighs on every letter as much as on the press, muddle our chronology. The past, discovered so long after the event, is as hard to understand as the present. It is already hedged around with forgetting, with resignation. Its freshness is suspect; its emotion has lost its savour. It possesses almost no surprise, and to some degree it is not hard to think of it as an importunate interloper, reminding you indiscreetly of his existence. The saddest news comes so late that it is already consigned to history, minor, insignificant, cold, overtaken. The anguished longing to know what tomorrow will bring pushes yesterday back further than it should be. Trifling distances, which yet seem unmanageable, deaden the horror. No one spills old tears. They hold them back with little pity. Life expectancy numbs the most acute notes of the funeral march. The survivors take pride in still being alive when the weakest and unluckiest have vanished. It would not take much for them to accuse the victims of cowardice.

At the moment of hearing of the death of the prince who so influenced his own life, Jean is too obsessed by Claude's state to feel more than a swift stab of sadness. As for the news of his mother being in Switzerland, it leaves him cold. He has decided that Jeanne was his mother, the housekeeper at La Sauveté, the person who gathered him up in his Moses basket, adopted him, loved and protected him. Geneviève, whatever he feels, is a mother like the one a child creates in a burst of romantic invention: beautiful, charming, intelligent, loved by everyone and more or less virtuous. When they had met in London he had fallen a little bit in love with her, and she too had probably fallen a little for him. It was nothing. Something that did not count, and yet had had some magic and that afterwards – when he had known that she was his mother – he had enjoyed mulling over like the sort of incest to be found in a popular romantic serial.

'I hope,' he said to Palfy, 'you didn't tell her I was her son.'

'You and I had already decided that it would be out of place. If she finds out, it won't be from us. In any case, it would age her overnight. I suspect she has decided that she'll always be thirty. An excellent age that she's right to stick to. She hardly looks it. The mountains suit her fragility. She's remarkably lovely.'

'I'm wondering how you managed to find her.'

'It wasn't too hard. I had dinner one evening with a Lebanese banker. I talked about her to him. He supplied the key: Gstaad. A little bit of heaven on earth!'

Allée des Acacias was almost deserted, its trees frozen, cold and grey on this January morning. Palfy liked this walk. It reminded him of his childhood Sundays, of his father and mother driving there in their Renault open tourer. The car would roll down the avenue, crowded with residents from all over the 16th: young girls in wide-brimmed hats, bare-headed boys, riders and a few remaining carriages conveying old ladies, their faces caked in cream and powder, their laps covered with real or imitation sable. He even claimed to have seen, on one of his last outings around 1921 or 1922, Mercedes del Loreto. His Sunday mornings belonged to the past. The only people to be seen now were women dressed like tramps, in worn greatcoats, stooped, shuffling, grey-faced and guilty-looking as they collected firewood, or riders in uniform, sitting stiffly as if at riding school, their boots black and gleaming. One greeted Palfy with a discreet movement of his hand.

'You know all the Germans in Paris,' Jean said.

'No. A modest few. That was Captain Schoenberg, the blue-eyed boy of one of the generals. He won't go to Russia. He's been given the job of overseeing the national stud farms. Pleasure can't go completely by the board – the French would revolt. By the way, while we're on the subject, Rudolf von Rocroy's got problems. The one time he's ever shown any courage – to help your Claude – and they're threatening to send him to the Eastern Front. It's mayhem. Don't worry, he won't talk. I've got him under control. In any case he only needs to dig himself a tiny bit deeper into his racket to be forgiven …'

Claude. Jean hesitated. He had come to meet Palfy to confide in him, but Palfy's blithe self-assurance silenced him.

'It's bizarre, I can tell you, how far one feels from all that at Gstaad, even though Switzerland's the only place where rationing is actually enforced. No strawberries and cream. Meat twice a week. The restaurants are quite inflexible and the Swiss are very disciplined. But I didn't go there to eat …'

'What did Geneviève say?'

'She's bored. She's rented a floor of a country hotel, brought in a gramophone, made a place to read. She reads all the time when she's not listening to music. The hotel's stuffed with foreigners, who play cards while they wait for the motor shows and carnivals by the sea to resume, the selfsame world they knew before the war. In one sense, Geneviève's isolation and loss of her little train of admirers has done her good. I found her a bit less of a bluestocking. You don't feel you're taking an exam every time you talk to her these days. And we talked … oh yes, non-stop. In her room, out walking, or on the sleigh. Ah, the sleighs of Gstaad! I never suspected I'd fall for their romance. A fat driver with a red nose and a leather apron tucks you in like babies. The horse wears ice shoes and trots as if there weren't any ice. I had the great pleasure of holding Geneviève's hand to keep it warm …'

'That's the first time I've seen your lyrical side!'

Palfy looked embarrassed.

'Listen, my dear boy, I can only say this to you …'

'Are you telling me you're in love with Geneviève? Don't make me laugh. You'll never love a woman …'

Jean was mistaken. If Palfy was not yet in love he was soon going to be, and at the age of thirty-five, just when he thought he was safe, his whole life, his unusual sense of right and wrong and his cynicism and scorn were about to be changed for ever. We can sense just how incredible this transformation is. Palfy himself cannot foresee its repercussions. He imagines one can let oneself be attracted to a woman like Geneviève while remaining as one was, and will find out – with a mounting sense of wonder – that, on the contrary, to love

325

and be loved by her one must become more like her. That is how one deserves her. It is no longer a matter of surveying life with a cold and sarcastic eye, with the gaze that has so long served him as judge and defence; it is a matter of being worthy of Geneviève. Palfy cannot yet see where this metamorphosis demanded of him will take him. He will not be a second prince, for his contempt for humanity is of a lower quality, and in particular more greedy and opportunistic. The prince never experienced the vulgar temptation to become rich, for the simple reason that he always was rich. On the other hand, despite his generosity, he did not throw away his fortune and, however wise and unusual he was, it is doubtful whether he would have accepted his ruin with the elegance Palfy has displayed on several such occasions.

Palfy is still looking for that pedestal from which he can defy his critics. He knows that once a certain level of success is achieved, impunity follows. Doors open wide, respect is blind. He has been admitted to this privileged circle two or three times. Without his appetite for risk, he might have stayed there. Deep down he loves starting again from nothing, disconcerting those who have believed in him. As we now see him on this January morning in 1942, in Allée des Acacias in the Bois de Boulogne, walking briskly, his arm in Jean's as if the better to persuade him of his sincerity, Palfy knows nothing of what awaits him. An inexpressible joy that he finds hard to contain, indeed is allowing to brim over, has taken possession of him. We have already guessed that he – the Palfy who has never felt a single moment's tenderness – will shortly reproach Jean for not devoting his life to the delights of love. He believes his task is to be intelligent and insensitive. Geneviève will convince him that he is not as intelligent as he thinks he is and that he is almost bursting with sensitivity.

Such a revelation, naturally, is not the work of a day. It will need many journeys to Switzerland, many sleigh rides and, that summer, a visit to Lake Lugano during which they will witness from a balcony Italy falling apart on the far bank. Geneviève will not tell him her life story; she has no need to. It will be his job to tell her his, and entertain her. Revealed, stripped naked, he will be in her power. He will be jubilant as he relinquishes his old self. For a moment he will lose his poise, that marvellous passport that has helped him so much in his life. Geneviève will smile. She will have won, and as the price of her victory she will give him back – albeit attenuated and civilised – the confidence in himself that he lost in an upsurge of passion.

I'll say it again: nothing can astonish us more than this metamorphosis. It is so unexpected that it surprises us as much as its victim, whose destiny seemed preordained. We had already interned him when France was liberated, ruined him, thrown him out on the street and, since his boats had been burnt all over Europe, watched him leaving to attempt some fabulous new fraud in South America. Indeed, that was certainly what awaited him, and in a sense Palfy's good luck had always been his bad too, compelling him to resort to his genius for mystification. We are delighted to announce instead that this time, at last, Fortune is on his side, and not, as one might crudely think, Geneviève's fortune of which he has no need, but that ravishing figure, her form barely veiled beneath a transparent tunic, who awakens those infants slumbering incautiously on the coping of a well. The tiny wings on her back do not allow her to fly to the aid of everyone. She must choose her targets. Seductive and seduced, she attaches herself to those who will not let her go. Why should it surprise us, then, that in her generosity to a few, she is cruel to the greater number? She will desert Salah and only much later pay any attention to Jean Arnaud, after he has endured those tests inflicted by Sarastro on Tamino in *The Magic Flute*.

For the moment we are still on Allée des Acacias, where it is necessary to walk briskly to keep out the dry cold of the winter of '41–'42, which marks the decisive turning point of a war we have spoken little about, since it is happening far away and its impact on the majority of the French population is mainly the problem of finding enough to eat.

'By the way,' Palfy said, 'how is your beloved?'

'Not well.'

'A cold?'

'No. A breakdown. I've managed to get her admitted to a psychiatric clinic in the Chevreuse valley.'

Palfy stopped and gripped Jean by the shoulders.

'Good heavens! Do you think …?'

'I'm sure of it. Those twenty-four hours were too much for her. She cracked. It has all gone downhill very fast in the last few days.'

'My dear, that is what is called a trial.'

He resumed walking, still holding Jean's arm tightly.

'How did you notice?'

'There were certain warning signs I should have paid attention to sooner.'

'What signs?'

'I don't want to talk about it.'

They walked as far as the Cascade without speaking. Jean's memory filled with episodes from Claude's illness, whose progression had remained confused to him until the final crisis. Episodes that had in an obscure way heralded Claude's gradual deterioration: the awful emptiness of her gaze, her indifference towards Cyrille, her periods of silence, as though she was speaking privately to someone not there, the rapidity with which she moved from formality to informality, her sudden shedding of her defences and the fevered pleasure she took in lovemaking – lyrical, elated, carried away by frenzy – followed by a deep torpor, as if only sex gave her burning body the fathomless rest she craved. That she had not been stupidly, fussily modest during their long period of unconsummated love had pleased Jean. Unable to reveal everything, she had offered her only truth, a physical one. It has not gone unnoticed – and perhaps been exasperating – that she let Jean come close to her on so many occasions without letting go. Let us say again that she loved him, and probably loved him more than he loved her. Jean was sowing wild oats and slow to mature, though several women had already been clear about their wish to hurry him. Claude had been ahead of all of them by a long way, with her seriousness, her thoughtfulness, the understanding she had had, even in their passion, of the consequences of her acts. We might possibly have wanted her to be less thoughtful, more susceptible to passion, but we cannot remake her. That is how she is. Or more precisely, how she was, for now, abruptly, she is quite different, no longer on her pedestal, transformed in a sense as radically as Palfy, in reverse. And so Jean must learn through her, as through his friend, that there are no beings who stand still and that it needs only a meeting or an upheaval for a secret truth to be born. Claude had broken down. If Jean had resisted – but heroism has its limits after such a long wait – she would perhaps not have given way as she had. He could not reproach himself. It was too late. Since their first afternoon she had thought of nothing else but making love, casting aside all modesty, disregarding Cyrille's presence asleep in the bedroom, murmuring streams of obscenities that froze Jean's desire instead of fuelling it. That these words had come out of Claude's mouth seemed monstrous. Jean had felt he was back with Mireille Cece, the sex-mad bistro keeper of Roquebrune. He felt a deep revulsion, not for Claude but for himself. A great hatred rose in him at the same time: monsters of cruelty and dishonour had destroyed the woman he loved. They were all-powerful. There was no defence against them. Jean reflected on his earlier indifference to war. It had, at last, dealt him a blow, sweeping away an image of beauty that, however pointless it seemed in the prevailing horror, mattered more to him than anything else. He had been superficial, careless, preoccupied with his own life, and now Claude lay in a clinic, stupefied by sedatives that smothered her obsessions.

*

They reached the Cascade and saw the Longchamp racecourse with its bleached turf, long sweep of stands and winter trees that hid the Seine. The roofs of Suresnes glittered in the blue morning. A large Mercedes sped past them.

'General Danke,' Palfy said. 'The best he can hope for is to be shot, or he might even lose his head. He's convinced Germany has lost the war in the East. He's what they call a traitor in his country and a man of honour here.'

'You see! You do know them all.'

'No, only one or two. The important ones. It's better to be prepared. Let's go back to the car. We must do something for Claude.'

'What? There's nothing we can do. Except look after her. I haven't enough money to keep her in the clinic, and if she goes into hospital she'll die. They warned me: the Germans have ruled mental patients to be useless mouths to feed.'

'Dear boy, now you're being stupid. I'll help you.'

'You've always helped me, but now I need money.'

'I never lend money. I've offered you a job, the gallery …'

'And I've accepted it, but it's idiotic: I don't know anything. I'll fall flat on my face.'

Palfy looked thoughtful. The walk had put colour into his yellow complexion.

'I've got an idea, but there are risks. In any case, take the gallery. It will serve as cover …'

'I don't mind risks.'

'Oh, at the moment they're non-existent … But later … when Germany collapses. You'll have to be ready for some score-settling.'

Jean was surprised, and we may share his astonishment. Yes, the Wehrmacht had failed to take Moscow, but it still held Europe and its army remained intact. Everywhere else it was racing from victory to victory, and the United States, grappling with Japan, had so far made no more than symbolic gestures towards Britain. It is easy today to have a character in a story which, to many, will seem made up, announce in 1942 that Germany will lose the war, since we know that it subsequently did. Yet well before that date Palfy had realised it would happen: he was one of the few witnesses of this period to judge events clearly. He will not be wrong. He has coldly assessed the situation, seen there is no way out and has his plans ready: first, to exhaust the immense possibilities offered by this difficult period, and then to prepare his withdrawal. His most important task is not to give himself away. One word too many carries an enormous risk. Already, even with Jean, he feels he may have said too much. Yet he will help him, because of Geneviève.

'I'm going to give you a single piece of advice. Do not trust anyone.'

'Not you?'

Palfy shrugged.

'What did I just say to you?'

'Not to trust anyone.'

'I cannot say it any more clearly.'

Jean rebelled. Trusting by nature, by naivety or from lack of an alternative, he found deception hurtful and dismal. The idea of living with suspicion put him off. Palfy, by contrast, was a born deceiver, anticipating traps with an instinctive pleasure, almost regretful when he encountered loyalty, as if the world was trying to steer him away from his natural infamy.

'But you'd still trust me?' Jean asked.

'Yes, reluctantly, and perhaps because there are times when I wonder about your naivety. I just can't believe it's feigned.'

Jean smiled. Nelly had said something similar: 'Dear Jules-who, your naivety is your poetry.' His trials were curing him, but slowly. So Palfy was right, and Jean saw himself compelled by necessity still to turn to him.

'In that case I have no alternative but to accept.'

'Honestly, you are a most royal twit. In Paris alone there are ten thousand fellows a lot less fussy than you who'd jump at the chance, and here you are holding your nose.'

They had reached the Pavillon d'Armenonville, where their car was waiting. Émile jumped from the driver's seat and stood by the rear door.

'Come and have lunch tomorrow at one at Maxim's,' Palfy said.

'Who with?'

'Wait and see.'

'Julius?'

'Yes.'

Émile drove towards Porte Maillot. Palfy was silent, perhaps regretting having revealed more than he should.

'Can you drop me at the Étoile?' Jean said.

'Of course. Where are you staying?'

'At Nelly's. But not for long. Jesús is lending me his studio in Rue Lepic. I'm moving back next week.'

He did not admit that he could have moved in immediately, and had returned to Nelly's as much because he was unable to be miserable on his own as because he still found Nelly physically desirable.

'I'm not sure I entirely understand you,' Palfy said.

'I'm not sure I entirely understand myself.'

'Notice that Nelly has the gift – rare in women – of never being boring. She and Geneviève are the only ones I know who fall into that category. Having said that, don't fall into her clutches. She's rather a tough nut.'

Jean did not doubt it. On that point at least he had no illusions. But he loved Nelly, as a sort of incestuous sister who displayed such an appetite for life that one forgave all her inconsistencies.

They turned off before Place de l'Étoile, which was blocked by a line of police. A regiment was about to parade down the Champs-Élysées, led by its band. Émile stopped in Rue de Presbourg, outside Palfy's building.

'Can I offer you lunch?' Palfy asked.

'No thanks. I'll see you tomorrow at Maxim's. I'll walk back. I need to walk.'

He had walked a great deal in the last few days, as a way of thinking and trying to understand what was happening. He was tired out by the time he reached Rue Saint-Sulpice and sat down to wait for Nelly. From there, at least, he could telephone the clinic. The supervisor answered irritably. Once, he had been put through to Claude, who had begged him to come, but the supervisor had come back on the line and repeated the doctor's orders: no visits in the immediate future …

Beneath Pont des Invalides two men were sitting on the river bank, fishing. The other problem was Anna Petrovna. Cyrille would be unhappy with her. But what could he do? Jean had promised to take him to the zoo one day. More generous towards animals than mental patients, the Germans kept the zoo well supplied. When Jean had phoned the previous evening Cyrille had also implored Jean to come and fetch him, and Anna Petrovna had taken back the receiver and might even have smacked Cyrille. Two prison guards were denying him contact with the people he loved.

Coming off Pont de la Concorde to turn in front of the Chamber of Deputies, a bicycle-taxi took the corner too fast and overturned. The cyclist was thrown against the kerb and split his head open. Blood began streaming down his white face, its features drawn with exhaustion. A woman was calling from inside the canvas cabin. She crawled out, revealing her legs as far as her stocking tops. Passers-by ran to the scene. They sat the man on the pavement. He gestured to say he was not hurt then, wiping his hand across his forehead, brought it away covered in blood and sat still with his mouth open, staring at the young woman who was weeping with rage and pointing to her stocking, torn above her knee. She was young and pretty and held a crocodile handbag tightly to her side, repeating, 'What about my silk stockings, what about my silk stockings, who'll pay for them?' People looked at her pretty legs, exposed by her rucked-up skirt. Jean swore to himself that he would never travel in a bicycle-taxi. Being propelled by another human being offended the idea of basic dignity he continued to maintain. At a pavement table at the Café du Flore he noticed Picasso, his wide eyes gleaming with mischief, and in front of the church of Saint-Germain-des-Prés saw Sartre shuffling along, his nose red, a thick scarf around his neck, huddled up in a coat two sizes too big for him. Nelly had read *The Flies*, which was in rehearsal at the Théâtre Sarah-Bernhardt (now Aryanised as the Théâtre de la Cité).

'For an intellectual,' she had said, 'it's not bad to have written a play like that.'

In Rue des Canettes he bought their bread ration and two slices of pâté without coupons, and at the wine merchant's a bottle of vintage Bordeaux over the counter that cost four times the price of *vin ordinaire* and was not worth it. Nelly's mother sent *confit d'oie*, *pâté de foie* and truffles from the south-west by means of a network of railway workers that ended at Gare d'Austerlitz, where Jean collected the parcels. Her daughter was exasperated rather than grateful.

'What's she thinking of? I could get that from any of my admirers if I asked for it. What I need is steak and chips. There's no steak, no potatoes, no fried food. What are we going to eat her truffles with? Swede?'

Unusually Nelly was waiting for Jean at her studio, when she should have been at the Français.[27] Wrapped up in woollies, she was drinking a hot toddy.

'Jules-who, you are making yourself desirable. When you're not here it doesn't suit me at all. I get impatient. When you're here too, unfortunately. I have to conclude that sometimes, only sometimes, I love you. A bit. Where were you? I nearly died. You wouldn't even have been here to hold my hand.'

'What's wrong with you?'

'I might be getting flu.'

'And you call that "dying"?'

'What about my voice?'

He had not thought of that. She kissed him on the cheek.

'Oh lovely, you've brought bread and wine. And pâté!'

She tasted it.

'Utterly disgusting. Let's dunk our bread in the wine instead.'

'I prefer it in soup.'

'Oh yes, I forgot, a peasant boy at heart. Like me. No soup without bread.'

She opened her pretty red mouth wide. Her uvula quivered delicately. She said, 'Ah, ah ... I've got a throat infection, haven't I?'

'Yes, give it to me.'

He shut her mouth with a kiss.

'That's all you think about!' she said happily.

'No, but I'd like to—'

'Here? This minute?'

'No, I mean, I'd like to think only of that.'

Nelly swallowed her toddy in one.

'I drink to forget that you're unfaithful to me. I get drunk with work for the same reason.'

'Then you're not so ill.'

'Listen, settle yourself peacefully in a corner and be quiet. Dear old Michette's coming to go over my lines with me.'

'What are you talking about?'

'Yes, the dear thing's become passionate about Corneille. She'll play Stratonice. With her Auvergnat accent she'll be wonderful. Corneille must have written the part with an Auvergnat girlfriend in mind.'

They were dunking their bread in the wine when Marceline Michette rang the bell. The cold had given her ruddy cheeks, making her look more like a lady of good works than the *patronne* of a brothel. She, like Palfy, was at a turning point in her life, on the brink of a less profound but equally lasting transformation. She had become enthralled by the theatre since meeting Nelly and spending a fortnight in the studio looking after Claude and Cyrille. And she had embarked on another adventure too, a real one and a secret one, outlandish and yet plausible at this time. Yes, Marceline Michette really had become a secret agent. Don't laugh! There were few more devoted to the task than she was. How had it happened? It is difficult to be sure. Probably thanks to her often mysterious demeanour, someone had noticed her, sounded her out, tested her. And gradually, smoothly, she had begun to work as a messenger for what people were already referring to as the Resistance. She was a good choice: was the *patronne* of a brothel not a person above suspicion, accustomed to remain as silent as the grave? In churches and Métro stations, booking halls and cinemas, Marceline received and handed on documents the meaning of which she knew nothing. She operated with relaxed courage. In this regard the reader will allow us to admire Palfy, who had only sought to amuse himself with her, who had played his cards randomly and purely on the basis of his fondness for mystification. With Marceline he had turned over an ace. Through her he began to prepare his exit plans. It seemed to be a stroke of genius, though in fact it was unpremeditated and the result of sheer chance. His luck had started to turn at last. The Croix de Guerre Marceline will receive soon after the Liberation will help Palfy to get himself off the hook and return to France after a prudent period of exile. Meanwhile, she was giving Nelly her line:

'*For you Polyeucte feels no end of love ...*'

Jean fought back his giggles. But in Marceline's wake came Nelly's golden voice.

'*An honourable woman can admit without shame*
Those surprises of the senses that duty does tame;
It's only at such assaults that virtue emerges
And one doubts of a heart untested by its urges.'

He heard his own heart beating. He had been put off Corneille in his French class at school but, like Marceline, shivered for Pauline embodied with such grace and fervour by Nelly.

'I loved him, Stratonice; and he full deserved it.
But what befalls merit when no fortune preserves it?'

When Marceline had left for one of those meetings that now punctuated her days, Jean found himself alone again with Nelly.

'I wonder if I'm not going to fall in love with you. Hearing you speak those lines is wonderful. You're someone else.'

'Oh Jules-who, you are talking codswallop. I've warned you before. I can love you, but you mustn't love me. You're nowhere near solid enough for someone like me. One day you will be, and then you'll see that being an actress's lover isn't a good idea, not a good idea at all. If you let yourself go with me, I guarantee I'll break your little romantic, and somewhat divided, heart. Stop it now, darling, and telephone your Claude. I'm unhappy about what's happened to her too. She's the love of your life. The only one.'

They made love, and afterwards Jean called the clinic. Madame Chaminadze was sleeping. The supervisor told him she was slightly better. He hung up.

'You see,' Nelly said, 'I'm useful for something. You couldn't be on your own. It would be unbearable.'

It seemed to Jean that Julius was welcoming him more warmly than usual, which made his earlier reticence all the more expressive. Thanks to his elocution lessons, Julius now speaks practically without an accent. He has Frenchified himself far more by taste than necessity for the milieu in which he moves. Madeleine, meanwhile, continues to benefit from Blanche de Rocroy's social skills. She can no longer be confused by those little details that tripped her up a year ago. She is in a period of transition nonetheless, and, conscious of what she still lacks, has lost her early assurance and not yet acquired the self-confidence she will be recognised for later. To put it another way, she is going through a timid phase, wholly understandable given the task she faces: to consign to oblivion the weary, pessimistic prostitute who would have foundered without the encounter with Julius. Julius adores her. Does he know where she comes from? Palfy thinks not. As foreigners do, Julius has accepted what he is offered at face value. He brims with that German generosity that finds everything good. When a German sets about being good, it's enough to make a cat cry. Julius, in the grip of love, has transfigured Madeleine. He never noticed her suburban accent, and her newly refined speech has only just struck his ear. He marvels at her distinction and finds nothing too good for her. He has put in Madeleine's name the property he bought recently at Montfort-l'Amaury, a ravishing little village which is not yet fashionable but whose fame Madeleine will contribute greatly to after the war. In reality, Julius is a man of simple tastes: all he wants is to live in France, in the country, in a reasonable house within striking distance of Paris so that they can come up to the theatre in the evening or to meet friends. In his eyes the outcome of the war has little to do with these plans. Should Germany win, its union with France will become closer, leading on to a golden age. Should it lose, France will find itself as it was before, immersed again in easy living. Julius has done enough favours for those around him to hope that after a brief period in purgatory he will be welcomed back with open arms. He loves Paris, its theatres and concerts, French fashion, the outrageous, superficial and amusing conversation at grand dinner parties. And how can one live without going to Maxim's two or three times a week? The mirrors, the rococo decor, the service from Albert, a head waiter one might think had come straight out of a play by Édouard Bourdet,[28] those tables where everyone knows everyone else, exchanging kisses and secret phrases, have little by little become a second home to this man overflowing with human warmth. So it's here that he deals with his increasingly important personal affairs. What else would such a perennial optimist be doing but preparing for life after the war?

In this happy atmosphere, this oasis of luxury and gourmandise, Jean found out what was expected of him, which was simple and required only his discretion, complete discretion. Little by little we shall find out, as he does, exactly what that means, and to be honest it hardly matters: needs must when the devil drives. Each week he has to pay the bill at the clinic, which is predictably exploiting him like a character in a Victor Hugo novel. It is a wretched business, though we can be reassured: Jean will not be forced to sell his teeth and hair, as Cosette's mother is, to pay for Claude's keep. Yet again in his short and already colourful life, he is facing temptation. We shan't claim, hypocritically, that he succumbs to it. He grabs it by the scruff of the neck. Julius is blissful. Madeleine has not understood, or pretends not to understand. She nods, and the sommelier, quick to turn the slightest sign into an order, brings another magnum of champagne. Julius draws attention to the date: 1929. An exceptional year, and a good idea to drink it rapidly, before the army's technicians get the idea of transforming this sublime liquid into a fuel substitute for their tanks.

'Talking of the German army,' Julius adds, immediately regretting his subversive sally, 'the front has stabilised. All necessary matériel is being delivered to the lines in preparation for the spring offensive ...'

Palfy is in a good mood. He does not contradict him. Why should he? The battle grinding on in that icy hell does not concern them. Julius believes himself as safe as he can be, having reconciled politics, the war and his own affairs. Everything is in place ... So which was Liane de Pougy's table? Ah yes, that one opposite. And Boni de Castellane's? In the room at the end. Julius is not one of those superficial Parisians who don't know their 'little history'. He would have liked to live at the time of Toulouse-Lautrec, Jane Avril and Chocolat. He drops their names the way one might drop illustrious titles of the nobility. Madeleine, who has only known the Moulin Rouge as a dance hall where girls found themselves lonely and impecunious lovers, refrains from joining in the conversation. She has discreetly passed Jean a packet of sweets for Cyrille and two pairs of stockings for Claude. She adds in his ear, 'If you're going to open that gallery for Palfy, you should see Louis-Edmond. He has contacts, but he's going through a bad time at the moment. You have to help him.'

'Was it Blanche who told you?'

'Yes.'

'Does she still see him?'

'She more or less has to. He pursues her, rings her constantly, weeps down the phone at her, begs her for money, disappears for ten days and then starts all over again. Do something!'

And she slips him a piece of paper with a telephone number at which La Garenne can be reached, at the apartment of a painter he is looking after.

'La Garenne's never looked after a painter in his life. He's always exploited them.'

'No, I assure you. Blanche is positive that he's taking care of this Michel Courtot ... or du Courtot admirably ...'

'Michel du Courseau.'

Madeleine is briefly embarrassed. Everything would be all right if she didn't mangle people's names. With ordinary people it didn't matter, or was all to the good, but if it was an aristocratic name an error became a faux pas, and a faux pas made her look silly. It would be less embarrassing if she made Madame Michette's sort of howlers. Everyone expected them and was unspitefully amused. They had become an essential part of the dinners Marceline was invited to, even if she was unaware that she was singing for her supper. Jean perceives Madeleine's discomfort.

'Anyone could mix the two up. I just happen to have known Michel since he was a child.'

'Is he famous?'

'No, not yet. One day perhaps … When I say I know him, he's my uncle … I mean he's my mother's brother.'

He explains. Madeleine is delighted. Nothing pleases her more than discovering who is related to whom and adding them to her collection.

'La Garenne sold me one of Michel du Courseau's paintings. I haven't put it up yet. I'm waiting to hear what you think.'

Jean reassures her: Michel has talent, a great talent even, though he is prickly and difficult.

'You should invite him to dinner,' Julius says.

'I thought of it, but La Garenne assures me he doesn't go out.'

'What does one do with people who refuse to have dinner! They're savages,' Palfy says.

Madeleine does not know the answer. By issuing invitations to dinner, she has cultivated a circle of friends. Without these gatherings she would be merely Julius's mistress. At least Rudolf von Rocroy is a man who dines.

'I fear he's doing penance at this moment,' Julius observes. 'I doubt Dr Schacht has summoned him to eat *foie gras* and sip champagne …'

And so Jean learns that Rocroy is involved, and that he has been unwise. The Finance Minister of the Third Reich is not the joking kind, and if he agreed to turn a blind eye to the smuggling of Reichsleiter Reinhard Heydrich, it was strictly on condition that no scandal resulted. Rocroy has made the mistake of drawing attention to himself … General Danke makes his entrance into Maxim's. He has left his heavy overcoat in the cloakroom and appears squeezed into a uniform designed for officers kept trim by battle. General Danke eats and drinks too much. It is part of his duties. He dazzles and reassures. The prefect whom he has invited today is at Maxim's for the first time, a special day in his life. By the time dessert is served, he will agree to whatever is asked of him. Danke greets Julius with a discreet hand gesture; Julius, though in mufti, straightens and nods formally. Jean suppresses a surge of hatred, which is unjustified as Danke has no police powers and it would be stupid to hold him responsible for Claude's torture. He is, Palfy has assured Jean, an enlightened man and a friend of France. The only question to be asked is why all these great friends of France seem incapable of procuring peace for it.

'Jean,' Madeleine says in a low voice, 'you look uneasy. Do you still dislike the Germans?'

He shrugs.

'Madeleine, that's not a proper subject of conversation.'

Michel du Courseau was renting an apartment on the floor below Alberto Senzacatso, the photographer fascinated by Mannerism. After a short spell in prison Alberto had regained his freedom, for which he continued to pay with occasional pieces of information to the vice police. In his studio Michel was working on a four-metre by two-metre canvas of Christ surrounded by children. Alberto – whom he had given up the idea of informing on – provided him with models. The canvas, which was to cost him a year of gruelling work, was destroyed on the eve of the Liberation by Michel himself in the course of an acute attack of mysticism. He has spoken so many times in interviews since then about the painting's destruction that it is unnecessary to revisit it. Spiteful tongues insist that the devastation was an essential sacrifice to a reputation that Michel wanted to be immaculate. Jean followed the work's evolution without being able to show the enthusiasm Michel sought from his infrequent visitors, but was nevertheless struck by the anxious tone in which the painter said to him one day, 'I'm worried that I'm taking too much pleasure in it.'

In his mouth the word 'pleasure' sounded so obscene that no one could doubt its meaning, and yet Michel merely intended to indicate how much the slightest distraction harmed his sense of himself as a Christian artist. Jean no longer had any illusions as to the state of mystical constipation in which his youthful uncle lived, but his complex personality, afflicted by some internal curse, and his increasing sanctimoniousness, combined with a talent that was going from strength to strength, made this unusual artist a subject for contemplation by Jean in his gradual understanding of his fellow human beings. At heart he felt that the distinction between Palfy's cynicism and Michel's unctuousness was minimal, and if he preferred the Palfian outlook by a long way, it was only because of its innate sense of humour. Between Michel and Alberto there orbited, like a Cartesian diver, the figure of La Garenne, whose gallery on Place du Tertre, reopened by an Aryan of impeccable credentials, now sold sunsets over beached fishing boats, cows drinking from a pool, unequivocal subjects that everyone could respond to. La Garenne, half tolerated, lived a marginal existence selling Alberto's pornographic photographs on the sly, extracting small commissions from the distribution of copies executed by his company of painters down on their luck, fencing the odd picture here and there, keeping for himself a few rare works offloaded by real or phoney policemen who pillaged abandoned Jewish-owned apartments, and amassing, by means of loud lamentation, tears and hands clasped in despair, a fortune that he will never be able to enjoy. A multimillionaire at the Liberation, within a week he will find himself imprisoned at Drancy while the FFI empty his hiding places and distribute among themselves the gold, Picassos and *objets d'art* piled up in his garret in Rue de la Gaîté. In short, and even though he scarcely counts as a footnote in such a murky era, natural justice will take its course for La Garenne more harshly than he really deserves, making a scapegoat of him, without pity.

When he first encountered La Garenne at Michel's studio, Jean wondered what could have brought together two such radically different beings. The truth was that Michel, disoriented by his move to Paris and hardly knowing his way around, had taken up with La Garenne as a guide, knowing nothing of his racketeering. The dealer had summed him up at a glance, put him in touch with Alberto by renting the apartment beneath him, and steered him towards a gallery that guaranteed his new agent a percentage.

'I'm working for the future!' Louis-Edmond had told Jean. 'Your friend is greatly talented. I shall help him, even if I have to ruin myself in the process.'

He was not ruining himself, but at present was making little profit from Michel, who still had a provincial's sense of thrift. So either at Alberto's or Michel's La Garenne would find a couch and a screen where he could lay his weary body in privacy when his long expeditions around Paris took him far from Rue de la Gaîté.

'He's repulsive, I grant you,' Michel said to Jean, 'but he has ideas, and Christian charity requires that we must not abandon him at such a time. There is no soul that is completely lost. He sometimes asks me extraordinary questions about salvation and grace. I sense that you're hostile because you knew him at a time when he was brought low by a woman. This Blanche has been the great curse of his life. Without his mother whom, alas, I didn't know, a real angel of mercy, of kindness and pity, whose name alone is sublime – Mercedes del Loreto; Loreto where the angels transported the humble abode of the Virgin Mary – without that sublime being he would have sunk into utter wretchedness. Beware women, Jean. There are Blanche de Rocroys everywhere. I don't need you to tell me that you have a tendency to give yourself up to the pleasures of the senses. You should tread very carefully. A man can only be fulfilled in chastity …'

And are the boys provided by Alberto Senzacatso part of your scheme of chastity? Jean wanted to ask. But he did not. Michel, wrapped in himself, would have been so discombobulated by the question that Jean preferred just to listen to him, with a hypocrisy equal to that of Michel himself. In any case, who cared! There was no doubting his sincerity when he sermonised like this. Despite their past and their childhood when they had hated each other, Jean retained a scrap of affection for the du Courseaus, who had had such a profound influence on him; and remained fascinated too, like an entomologist, by that insect La Garenne and his breathtaking nerve, fooling everyone so completely for a time. Poor Blanche! And she was still trying to help the scoundrel who, not content with humiliating her, was now dragging her name through the mud.

*

In March Antoinette came to Paris for a few days. At twenty-seven, in the eyes of the world in which she lived, she was already an old maid, only fit to be married to a widower with children who would accept her for her dowry if there was one and would close his eyes to a scandalous past. Antoinette brought butter, two chickens killed the previous day and some pâté made by her mother for Michel. Of the gaiety and carelessness that had once enlivened her face, there was no longer any trace in her insipid features. Dressed in black and wearing the sort of felt hat beloved by ladies of good works, she looked older than her years. Her mother had imposed mourning on her for her Mangepain uncle, suddenly departed after an excessively good meal with the Germans, to whom the former radical socialist and freemason had been a most faithful vassal in an obscure pact of collaboration. Oppressed by an absurd observance that meant nothing to her, Antoinette's youth had vanished. Jean hardly recognised her, yet their last meeting had only been in 1939, two and a half years earlier, an interval that at their ages should have meant nothing. Perhaps at Yssingeaux, when she had come to tell him that he was Geneviève's son, he had already noticed the first signs of her vitality fading. That day he had desired her, but everything had become impossible with the sudden shift in what was right and wrong, and they had gone their separate ways, sad and disappointed in each other, frozen by inhibition. Antoinette's arrival in Paris in March 1942 was a serious shock to him. The restraint, humility and awkwardness of the provincial woman in a capital city that frightened her, despite its state of calm and near torpor, robbed him of the happy images of his childhood, of the discovery of love, the scene at the cliff when she had shown him her pretty, plump bottom and the melancholy, tender last night in a Dieppe hotel before his departure for England. He could not believe that this woman in flat-heeled shoes, cotton stockings, and without make-up had inspired in him the first passion of his life. Close to her, he sought in vain the smell of the beaches where they had caressed each other, the barns where they had kissed and fumbled, and the dream of their first night together, when they had made love in almost every room at La Sauveté. Life had swiftly worn Antoinette down, leaving its mark on her once irresistible features. She had started to look like her mother, though she would never inherit Marie-Thérèse du Courseau's character. Women's lives and men's march to the beat of different drums. Beauty – strictly speaking, Antoinette had never been beautiful but she had radiated health and a love of pleasure – beauty fades too fast and exposes its blemishes, while in men the same blemishes are taken for signs of character. Jean had felt none of time's ravages. His discovery of its hold over Antoinette in the space of just a few years was sudden and disagreeable.

The news she brought from Grangeville seemed to come from another country. Albert Arnaud, ill-resigned to growing vegetables, was dragging his leg and grumbling more than speaking; his cousin, Monsieur Cliquet, with whom he was still living, was conducting (with such a mysterious air that it was transparent) a secret campaign on the railways, where he had gone back to working as an interpreter-auxiliary for the German railway workers; Captain Duclou had built a home-made radio and hidden an aerial in the anemometer in his garden to receive the BBC's French service broadcasts and pass on their news to the village; the Longuets increasingly believed themselves to have been born de La Sauveté; Monsieur Longuet, having reinvented himself as a civil engineer, had signed a contract with the Todt organisation to build bunkers up and down the coast. Thanks to him, there was not a man left unemployed in the neighbourhood, although work appeared to be far from the chief ambition of his son Gontran, who had just married a Mademoiselle de Beausein (the 'de' was as doubtful as it gets) from the Rouen bourgeoisie; she had already had visiting cards printed bearing the name 'Baronne L. de La Sauveté'; the Marquis de Malemort, released from his oflag with a group of other farmers and outraged by this act of usurpation, had insulted Gontran after Mass; the gendarmes, acting on a complaint from the Longuets, had threatened to send him back to his prison camp but he had thrown them out with such aristocratic finality that nothing more was heard of the affair; Chantal was working with her father – Jean wouldn't recognise her: heavier all round, ruddy, foul-mouthed as a trooper, the last of the Malemorts downed her calvados with all the assurance of the marquis; and the abbé Le Couec, more destitute than ever and fed by the measured charity of his farmers, travelled the countryside on foot, dispensing the one asset in which he was rich, a saintly generosity: people said he was a member of the Breton Liberation Party but at the same time hid Allied airmen shot down over France and guided them to a secret organisation that repatriated them to Britain.

Jean wondered whether, apart from what concerned his adoptive father and the dear abbé, these pieces of news still had any meaning for him. That world was no longer his, and never would be again. He had bid it farewell the day he had challenged it and fled to Paris with Chantal de Malemort. He no longer had a refuge there and he was sufficiently wise now not ever to want to see Chantal again. Even Antoinette bored him a little by reminding him of the milieu in which he had lived. He found her drab and lifeless, far from his own preoccupations; he took her to the theatre where she was mystified by Giraudoux, and to the Opéra where she fell asleep during a ballet. They talked about Michel, whom she admired as a man about Paris, without a hint of irony. He became annoyed with her for her awkwardness that tarnished his picture of the past. Yes, he was shedding his baggage or, to put it another way, he was discovering his solitude, the daunting wasteland in which he would have found himself if it had not been for Nelly. He would have liked to talk to Antoinette about the young woman who had given his life so much colour, about Claude who had sunk so deep into the darkness. But it was easier to say nothing, and those withheld confidences separated him from the woman who had been his first love.

He went with her to Gare Saint-Lazare. On the platform neither of them knew what to say. Antoinette put her cardboard suitcase up in the luggage rack and rested her arms on the open window.

'I'm happy to have seen you again, looking so well,' she said awkwardly.

'Same here.'

'You won't forget?'

'We don't forget anything.'

She still hesitated.

'I do! I forgot to tell you I met one of your old friends, Joseph Outen. He's been released from his stalag. He asked for news of you.'

'What's he doing?'

She put a finger to her lips. Jean knew she had not forgotten to tell him about Joseph. She had not dared. German soldiers smelling strongly of leather and coarse cloth passed behind him, looking for their reserved carriage. Antoinette followed them with her eyes.

'Come closer,' she said.

He went closer, and she held out her hand. He squeezed it.

'He's full of odd qualities,' she added with unexpected warmth. 'He's interested in all sorts of things. He's learning English at the moment ...'

'He was learning Chinese once too.'

'Oh, that's all over ... A youthful mistake. English is more useful for what he's doing now.'

She put on a knowing look. The platform staff were slamming the doors.

'It looks as if the train will leave on time. Monsieur Cliquet will be happy.'

'Yes,' she said. 'I'll tell Joseph I've seen you. He was worried about you. He's always saying how talented you are and that you were the best oarsman at Dieppe Rowing Club. He told me to tell you that you should take up yoga, like him. I don't really understand what all the exercises are about, but apparently it helps concentrate your mind ...'

At the last minute she was confessing what she had not dared to admit since she had arrived: that in Joseph Outen she might have found a last hope. Jean was moved and reproached himself for not having helped her.

'You should come to Dieppe,' she said. 'You get on so well together. He has big plans …'

All his life Joseph would have big plans, which would fail one after another. Now it was Antoinette's turn to be on the receiving end of his fervour. Her face lit up because she was talking about him. He was probably waiting for her at Dieppe, where they saw each other in secret. Antoinette would only ever have guilty love affairs. The finger on her lips, the knowing look meant that Joseph had got himself involved in clandestine activity, that he was riding a new hobbyhorse. But he was not up to it, and it would beat him the way he had been beaten by his previous enterprises. Poor Antoinette! The widower and his children would be waiting at the end of the line.

The train began to move.

'I'll come,' he said. 'This summer. Definitely.'

He walked beside the carriage. Antoinette was smiling and crying at the same time. Their fingertips touched. Jean stopped and soon saw only an arm and a hand waving a handkerchief. The reader already knows that there was no return to Dieppe in the summer of 1942, when the Canadians landed. Jean did not see his adoptive father again. As for Joseph, it is the author's turn to know more than the reader and to anticipate the story. The former bookseller, who has had no further impact on Jean's life after being his first mentor, has resurfaced in his mind almost by accident, one afternoon on a station platform. Yes, he is Antoinette's lover. Flimsy, furtive encounters that only bring them, because of their blindness, a brief elation that disguises a reality both mediocre and without a future. Lacking any experience, Joseph has set up an intelligence network that he has christened, with some pomp, Light and Truth. The network is composed of amateurs whose best weapons are faith and naivety. Each day Monsieur Cliquet provides a breakdown of the German convoys bringing equipment and troops to the Normandy coast. The Allies will take no account of this information that summer and find themselves massacred quite unnecessarily. Aside from Monsieur Cliquet, transport expert, the network's other members know no more than Madame Michette, but Marceline is supervised, used by professionals whom she obeys as only women who wield authority themselves know how to obey. Joseph's team, knowing nothing about secrecy, take grossly innocent risks that for six months produce a number of results. With the disaster of the butchered Canadians, Joseph learns his lesson. The Allied high command has refused to listen. In disgust he decides to dismantle his network. But it is too late. A woman has been arrested by chance. Within minutes she provides the names of the entire Light and Truth network.

Monsieur Cliquet dies in the carriage taking him to Germany and Joseph is deported with his companions, apart from the woman who so kindly betrayed them and who is then turned to work for the Sicherheitsdienst. As he already speaks German and knows the conditions in the camps, Joseph survives; the only one. At the end of May 1945 he is repatriated and parades through Dieppe with other former prisoners in their striped uniforms under a banner that reads, 'Never again!', a declaration all believe in, until the moment the world is covered in new concentration camps which humankind's finer feelings this time forbid it from describing in such terms.

But Joseph has come back too late. The scramble for the spoils is over. The gluttons have scoffed the lot; the jobs are all taken and Antoinette has married Pierre du Gros-Salé, a squire from thereabouts, a widower as we foresaw with six children who need to have their arses wiped and their noses blown and be brought up without, of course, displaying a scrap of gratitude. Joseph is a decent man. He will not bother her. His consolation prize is a post as tutor at Dieppe's lycée. For a moment he believes himself to be a guide to young souls to be moulded, but rapidly discovers that they are frightful brats who like to mock his skeletal thinness, imitate the lisp he acquired when the Gestapo knocked all his teeth out and which he cannot afford to fix because he has no money for dentures, and make fun of his ugly demob suits and hollow, hacking cough. So he leaves, for black Africa where he has discovered that his status as 'resistant and deportee' is enough to earn him a headmastership. Here he feels for a time that he is contributing to the radiance of France and introducing its values to the young and awakening intelligences of his pupils. It does not take him long to realise that this too is a mirage. The 'young, awakening intelligences' are only interested in kicking him out, him and his radiant France. He will die stupidly in Douala in 1956 from a scorpion bite, mourned by his companion, a pretty Fula woman with copper-coloured skin who has given him a daughter they christened Antoinette. Exit Joseph, whose life is remarkable in one respect, that it is as touching and insignificant as it is a failure from start to finish. In short, he is one of those beings from whom those of a superstitious bent do well to keep their distance: he brings bad luck, and worse, poor man's bad luck. He himself realises it in the few minutes before he dies, in one of those dazzling visions the grim reaper apparently allows, like a condemned man's last drink. Lucid at the finish, he is relieved to slip away. His daughter, his honey-coloured baby, is brought to him and he smiles at her but refuses to kiss her, for fear of contaminating her with his bad luck. His precaution is wise: at the age of twenty, named model of the year in New York, Antoinette Outen will marry Peter Kapp III, heir to the fashion stores that bear his name. At the time of writing, after three months of marriage she has divorced and is making her first film. There lies the proof: Joseph Outen's life was not completely pointless.

I hear you say that this is a long digression about characters who, in this second part of Jean's life, no longer play any part. Yet a tree only grows if one prunes it. Two branches have been cut. Jean is still not truly free, he still has new steps to take, but he already knows the value of these symbolic separations. When one is no longer tempted to lean on anyone, the future takes on a sweet taste of adventure. Driven by necessity, he has set out on a hard path, and that is our subject now. Do I mean the gallery in Rue La Boétie? No. We shall barely refer to that any more than the production company where Jean spent a few lacklustre months working for Émile Duzan. He has a handsome office and two salesmen, both experts on the Impressionist period. His clientele is mainly composed of a particular group of *nouveaux riches* that in times of scarcity thrive on other people's misery. The black market is the only economic force in France. It controls everything. But money earned too fast by those who have been hard up burns a hole in their pocket. No one is taken in by the fiction of price controls. The new rich no longer keep the money launderers in business. They invest in haste in reliable commodities: paintings, gold, *objets d'art*, jewellery, property. Easy to dupe and flatter, like those drunk with rapid social success they step delightedly into an antique dealer's or a private gallery, talk headily in hints and whispers with a moneychanger, or visit a chateau for sale. You see them driving in cars, taking the sought-after places in the few sleeping cars still operating on the main lines, lunching and dining in restaurants whose supply chains the economic police turn a blind eye to, because the other half of their clientele is German. In fact a large-scale and still hardly noticeable revolution is taking place. France is being transformed because wealth is changing hands; a class of owners is disappearing, gradually ruined, selling its traditional possessions, lovingly amassed and preserved from generation to generation, and another class is taking its place, vast, infatuated, its pockets filled with cash, over-made-up, its women dripping with costume jewellery. There wafts around this new category of French citizens an atmosphere of happiness and self-confidence that provokes endless supplicants to line up and cadge a favour or money. Jean sees it all, indeed had observed its beginnings before the war at the time of Antoine du Courseau's sale of La Sauveté to the Longuets. He watches and says nothing. It is not his job to mix with the customers. If he were to listen to them, he would be unable to stop himself from throwing them out, these philistines snapping up a Bonnard because the subject is a nude next to her bathtub ('for our bathroom, darling, don't you think, over the bath'), a Matisse ('it'll amuse the children'), a Renoir ('for my wife, she does love her roses'). He has been put there to certify transactions that benefit a clique whose names he affects not to be aware of. At its head stand Palfy, Rudolf, Julius. He lends his name and will be the one who pays if anything goes wrong. He knows it, but at the end of the month there is the cheque that just covers the bills for the clinic where Claude lies sedated. We shall return to Claude. She is there, she exists, from time to time Jean can see her, gaze back at her heavy, imploring eyes, kiss her warm mouth. She does not know, she will never know, he swears to himself, what he has got himself involved in to bring her back to life. Before we do, we must speak of the other business proposed by Palfy, and of Jean's first journey.

Rudolf von Rocroy was pacing up and down the platform at Gare d'Austerlitz, less aristocratic in a suit than in his colonel's uniform. The war, even though he has done his best, successfully until now, not to get mixed up in it, was what gave him his brilliance. His return to a synthetic flannel suit, tasteless tie and starched collar was a reminder that the officer in gleaming uniform concealed a gentleman of slender means who had difficulty making ends meet and then not always in a dignified manner, for he too belonged to a doomed class under Germany's National Socialism. His cowardice and dishonesty had been the price of his survival. Jean found him pitiful and inexcusable. Rudolf caught sight of him and turned his back, the sign they had agreed. They had reserved seats in the same compartment of the same carriage of the Paris–Irun express and no longer knew each other. Rudolf buried himself in a French book. The other travellers were of no interest. Jean watched through the window as the landscapes of a France he had never seen before slipped past. Where was war or occupation to be found in these green contours of Touraine, Limousin, Charente, Bordeaux? He could only see the peace of fields and woods, the promises of springtime and hamlets warmed by the beautiful day's sunshine, the little roads that wove a network of friendship between farms and villages. The blitzkrieg had left no wounds here, or if it had they had been dressed: reconstructed bridges, roads cleared of the endless detritus of an army fleeing the enemy. Only the mainline stations and their German railway workers in their curious caps proclaimed the poignant reality: at its nerve centres France was no longer itself. An insidious shadow shrouded it.

Between Bordeaux and Bayonne he fell asleep. He opened his eyes in the Basque country, awakening in him thoughts of Paul-Jean Toulet, whom he had discovered thanks to Salah on the eve of war. Between banks of rhododendrons he caught sight of Guéthary, where the poet had died. If Nelly had been with him, she would have recited his lines on Bayonne:

> *Bayonne! A walk beneath its arches,*
> *No more need one bear*
> *To leave one's inheritance there*
> *Or one's heart dashed in pieces.*

After the war he would find Salah again and take him to hear Nelly. But what did 'after the war' mean? No one had any idea when it might be. And where was Salah living, now that Geneviève was alone in Switzerland? When he heard about her liaison with Palfy, which was now official, there would be fireworks. The unusual Nubian was the prince's executor, managing the fortune Geneviève had inherited. Incapable of adding two figures together, she had had to put herself entirely in his hands. Jean imagined Salah's cold rage. He would try to destroy Palfy. But this time Palfy was forewarned. He would not allow it to happen, and there was no doubt that he was of that breed that always knows how to put a former servant in his place.

At Irun, long checks delayed the train. *Feldgendarmen*, French police, Gestapo and customs officers went through the hundred or so passengers with a fine-tooth comb. Rudolf was to spend the day at San Sebastián. Despite his rank and the fact that his mission documents were in order, he was subjected to almost as rigorous an examination as Jean. With their papers stamped, they still needed to present themselves to customs. This time Rudolf's curtness had an effect. Jean was searched, but the suitcase, which at that moment belonged to neither of them, remained in the luggage rack, untouched. Jean grabbed it and carried it to the Spanish train, where he had a sleeping compartment reserved. The hardest part was over, and he was surprised to have been so calm and indifferent, even wondering if an arrest and interrogation wouldn't have troubled him less. Rudolf disappeared. He was alone. Spain as seen from Irun station hardly aroused enthusiasm. He remembered his arrival in Italy a few years before, the intense pleasure he had felt at crossing the frontier, and he would have liked to encounter Spain in the same fashion, with a haversack on his back and a bicycle, but his adolescent passions were out of time and he was not entering the country to visit it with his Théophile Gautier in his hand, the way he had visited Italy aiming to follow in Stendhal's footsteps. It was a dismal beginning: at the sight of his French passport the Spanish police had become even more unpleasant, and now the train was delayed for an unknown reason. Travellers who had counted on the delay kept arriving, running along the platform with parcels tied up with string in their hands. Night fell. The station lights went on. They were wretched and yellowish, but the effect was like a party after France in the blackout. At last the train rolled slowly through the town, its suburbs and industrial estates, and plunged into a long tunnel before speeding up slightly and panting along an uneven, jolting track. The ancient engine could be heard labouring at the front, puffing a plume of golden flecks into the night. There was a dirty, smoke-filled restaurant car that stank of cooking oil and served cold omelettes and rancid biscuits. Jean sat down at a table. Three Spaniards sat around him, voluble and self-assured, swallowing the unspeakable tortilla without blinking, ordering bowls of coffee and smoking foul cigarillos. The train toiled on through a mountain pass. Several times it seemed as if it would run out of breath and stop, and then with a last effort it was over the top, and descending in a hellish squeal of steel.

Jean slept and woke up at Burgos. He had had to shut the window to keep out the coal dust, and when he opened it the icy air of the Castilian plain rushed into his compartment. The Civil Guard, their bovine faces blue with stubble, kept watch on the platform as the same late passengers started running again, carrying their parcels tied up with string. A little old woman, spruce and with her hair in a bun, walked along the carriages carrying a clay pitcher and chanting, '*Hay agua, hay agua!*' Hands stretched out, grasped the pitcher and tipped it up. Jean walked to the restaurant car, where the same travellers seemed to have spent the night smoking their rank cigarillos. There was weak coffee, stale bread and bars of chocolate on the menu. The train moved off again, and through the window he glimpsed old Castile at last, a landscape set ablaze by cold light and dotted with motionless villages beneath ochre-coloured roofs among the bare rocks. From time to time a Roman belfry, a tower, a fortress-like farm broke the deep, dignified monotony or, looming out of nowhere to startle the watcher, a peasant in black on his grey mule next to the track. Antiquated and breathless as it was, the train jarred as an absurd anachronism in this marvellously preserved landscape. Jean studied it greedily. Since the previous day, his appetite for travelling had come back to him, an appetite smothered by defeat, which had shut men like him up as if imprisoning them. He felt again something of the feverish pleasure that had quickened his spirit on his first expeditions outside France: the secret excitement he had felt in London, the sense of marvel in Italy. The lost war had closed his country's borders to everyone except the privileged and those willing to risk the hazardous adventure of a fishing boat in the Channel or a crossing of the Pyrenees. A forgotten feeling came back to him, that there is no imagination without movement. It struck him that he could stay in Portugal. Palfy was taking a risk in sending him out of France. In short, he had trusted him … Jean smiled to himself at the idea of beating Palfy at his own game. Never, ever would Palfy have the right to criticise him for doing so, without contradicting himself. Jean walked back to his compartment. The attendant had folded the bed against the partition, put the seat back straight, and vaguely tidied up. Jean locked the door and opened the suitcase he had exchanged with Rudolf. It contained, in denominations of ten and twenty, three hundred thousand pounds sterling. Obviously it would be deadly dangerous to walk away with the suitcase's contents and not take them to the bank where they were to be deposited. Palfy had warned Jean that Lisbon was teeming with OSS agents, the Sicherheitsdienst and MI6. As soon as he arrived he was expecting to be followed, his every move watched and noted. The vastness of the sum and of the operation put it in a different class from everything he had been used to. His percentage more than satisfied him. He shut the suitcase and began to daydream: from Lisbon he could reach England and America. He could go back to London, to graceful Chelsea and the black Thames. How he had loved London! The daydream slipped away: he was not free. Claude was surviving at her clinic because of him. If he stopped paying, they would move her to an ordinary hospital and she would disintegrate, and Cyrille would starve at his grandmother's. Palfy had taken every aspect of the situation into account. He was not afraid. Jean would fulfil his mission and come back. One day, later …

He closed his eyes to summon an image of Claude in her barred room. Her treatment had swollen the clear, fine features that had expressed the nobility of her beleaguered soul and dulled the gaze that had once been so calm and balanced. She spoke slowly, with deliberation, and several times had implored him to take her away, to rescue her from the nurse and doctor. For a time Jean had wondered if he still loved her, knowing it was a dreadful, pitiless question and blaming it on his bitter disappointment. You cannot love someone the same way when they have a breakdown – it was as if the obstacles and barriers that that person put in the way to defend themselves were the spice of love. In fact he still loved her as much as ever, but seeing her made him miserable. The ordeal of every visit took several hours to get over, before he could salvage yet again, intact, the perfect feeling that had brought them together. Alone with her in her blue room, whose barred window looked onto a kitchen garden and a road, he did not know what to say. One Sunday, as he had walked away towards the station, she had shouted from the first floor, 'Jean, Jean, don't leave me.' Her bare arm had reached out between the bars, her hand extended with her fingers spread as if she was putting a curse on him. He had turned and seen her desperate white face, so white she looked nearer dead than alive. The nurse had dragged her away from the bars, closing the window on her cries …

In the late afternoon the train, after spending hours unmoving in dismal stations, stopped at Fuentés de Oñoro on the Portuguese border. The Lisbon express, having tired of waiting, had left an hour earlier. The delay, the stormy exchanges between Spanish and Portuguese railway workers, and the confusion of officials allowed Jean to get the case through without difficulty. The most hazardous part of his mission was over and he saw himself stuck in an insignificant Portuguese town, about to spend twenty-four hours in the station waiting room, when a young man in a grey suit and a black felt hat approached him. In good French he offered Jean a lift in his car to Guarda.

'There's an excellent inn there. You'll get dinner and a bed for the night. It's better than spending a day and a night in a station.'

He had a pleasing, open face. Jean accepted this stroke of luck.

'I didn't see you on the train,' he said.

'I wasn't on it. I work at this station from time to time … I might as well tell you straight away that I belong to the PIDE. I believe you call it the Sûreté in your country. I hope I'm not alarming you?'

He smiled. He had an old Chrysler waiting outside and took the wheel with assurance. The road climbed up to Guarda. He drove cautiously, asking the sort of banal questions one usually asks a stranger.

'Is it your first trip to Portugal?'

'Yes.'

'I hope you'll like our country.'

'There's no reason for me not to like it.'

It did not sound from the man's tone as if he was interrogating him, but Jean, certain that behind the banalities the young policeman was gathering information, decided to be open with him.

'Exit visas from France are rare,' the man said. 'It's a great shame. Portugal would open its doors to all those who seek asylum.'

'Oh, there's nothing secret about my reason for being here! I jumped at an opportunity one of my uncles offered me: he's very well in with the Germans. I have to see his banker. If he came himself he'd arouse suspicion. I'm just coming and going straight back. It's good to breathe free air for a change.'

Guarda was an austere, handsome town: the pearl of the Serra da Estrela. The policeman dropped him outside the hotel.

'I'll probably see you tomorrow,' he said. 'The Lisbon express leaves at six in the evening. If you're interested I'll show you around. I'm free tomorrow. The dinner at the inn is good. The cook is excellent. Ask her to make you a fish pie. There's nothing better …'

Jean's bedroom looked out on the Praça Luís de Camões. He froze for much of the night in a huge bed. The morning market woke him.

Men in thick cloth jackets with fox-fur collars strolled among the crouching vendors, black mummies of whom all he could see, apart from their headscarves knotted beneath their chins, was their angular profiles. They held out eggs, herbs, butter, or a plucked chicken. After France's obscure misery and Spain's rancid version of the same misery, a Portuguese market was lavishness itself. Jean was astonished that the suspicious buyers, with their ascetic faces and measured gestures, were not falling on these most rare products like wild animals.

A small maid in a lace apron and starched collar, with a sallow serious face, entered, bowed as she murmured, '*Com licença,*' and placed coffee, a jug of milk and toast on the table. She indicated by gestures that a *senhor* was asking for him downstairs. She meant of course the PIDE official.

'I hope you slept well. I forgot to tell you my name: Urbano de Mello ...'

'And mine's Jean Arnaud.'

'I know. I saw your passport ... You might like to know that I've had a telephone call from Lisbon. I have to go there this afternoon. I'll be driving, and if you like I can take you.'

Jean was no longer in any doubt that someone was particularly interested in him. The important thing remained to get to Lisbon. There was no safer way of getting there than with the young policeman.

The Chrysler laboured through the Serra da Estrela. Its valves clattered painfully.

'Our petrol's very bad,' Urbano said.

He drove unhurriedly along narrow roads edged with mimosas and Judas trees in bloom, commenting on the sights.

'It's a shame we don't have more time. There are churches and some beautiful palaces I'd like to show you. Have you heard of Coimbra?'

'There's a university there, isn't there?'

'Dr Salazar taught political economy there before taking over as head of the government. He's a quite remarkable man. He has saved

361

the country from ruin and anarchy and this time once again he has kept us out of the conflict. Peace is an incalculable asset.'

Jean did not doubt it. While Spain, even glimpsed from a train window, seemed barely to have recovered from its exhausting civil war, Portugal radiated a prosperity and sense of easy living that the rest of Europe no longer knew and might never know again.

They stopped at a restaurant at Coimbra, near the university. Students in frayed black gowns were talking animatedly, crowded together around several tables. Urbano declared that they served the best salt cod in all of Portugal here. He went on to elaborate a multitude of different gastronomic approaches to cod and ways of serving it. Jean listened to him, amused, wondering how, after playing cat and mouse with him for twenty-four hours, he planned to keep up his surveillance in Lisbon. Whatever happened, there was no doubt that in the capital Jean had been judged sufficiently interesting to assign him a bodyguard who would not let him out of his sight.

'Seeing these students makes me feel young again,' Urbano said. 'I studied law here myself once.'

Jean no longer wondered whether Urbano was more than a simple border official stamping passports. An older student than the others came into the restaurant, slumped at a table and suddenly caught sight of the man from the PIDE.

'Urbano!' he called. 'What the devil are you doing here?'

The two men thumped each other vigorously on the back.

'I see, João,' the young policeman said, 'that you're still not in any hurry to finish your exams. How much more have you got to do?'

'Why should I be in a hurry? I like life in Coimbra. If I fail a few more exams I can probably stay here till I'm at least thirty.'

Some students who had finished eating crowded round them. Urbano explained that Jean was a Frenchman passing through. They sat, keenly interested, bombarding him with questions: what was life like in Paris, in the free zone? What did the French want to happen?

Had the universities reopened? Jean responded to their thirst for information as best he could.

'It's a shame we have so little time,' Urbano said. 'We'll have to come back. Portugal is a friend to France.'

'France has few friends when she's on the winning side, but she's lucky enough to have plenty when she finds herself in the shit.'

João burst out laughing.

'Shit! Shit! And they taught me at school that French is a refined language, the language of diplomacy! You're right, but we all cried in 1940 when Marshal Pétain requested an armistice. But he did well. They say here that he's distracting the Germans while General de Gaulle – his favourite pupil – is preparing, alongside the Free French, to drive them out of the country …'

The other students protested that they did not share his view. Dropping out of French, which they spoke well, they began an excited discussion that would have been interminable if Urbano had not called an end to it.

'We need to be in Lisbon this afternoon.'

João ordered a bottle of wine that they drank standing, to France's health.

'I hope,' he said, raising his glass for the last time to Urbano, 'that they were lying to me when they told me you'd joined the PIDE.'

Not missing a beat, the young policeman raised his glass in turn.

'They were lying to you, João. I'm a civil servant. That's all.'

'Then,' João said, 'long live the Republic and long live Coimbra!'

For the first time Jean heard France being talked about from outside the country. The perspective was very different from what could be said in Paris. Urbano was especially keen to know what Jean thought of a confused situation, to which optimists attributed a Machiavellian intent (unfortunately non-existent). For his part, Jean was shocked that Urbano had lied about working for the PIDE. As they left Coimbra the policeman sought to justify himself.

'I didn't lie, I dissembled,' he said. 'As I'm sure you'll appreciate, no student likes the police, and it's not my job to shout my credentials from the rooftops. Many ways are open to me to serve my country. I chose this one. It's not the least interesting by a long way …'

They spoke little for the rest of the journey. On the outskirts of Lisbon Urbano suggested he drive Jean to a small hotel run by a friend of his.

'Not too expensive and very comfortable. She'll give you a good room. The hotels are full … there are so many refugees, people waiting for a ship to America.'

Jean assured him that he was not short of money. His 'uncle' had given him enough for any eventuality. Anyway he preferred big hotels. You could come and go unobserved. Urbano laughed.

'You sound as if you think I want to keep an eye on you!'

'But you do. Admit it!'

'Not exactly. And Lisbon's a big city. You can disappear for twenty-four hours without the PIDE catching up with you.'

'I don't see why the PIDE should be interested in me.'

Urbano did not look embarrassed.

'Oh, I won't deny that you interest us. Foreign powers are exerting pressure on us to keep spies under surveillance.'

'I'm not a spy.'

'I'm sure you're not. Even so, admit it, it's hardly usual for a man of your age, living in a France occupied by Hitler's Germany, to get hold of a visa for Portugal on the pretext of paying a banker a visit.'

'It's true that it's not very likely.'

They were coming into Lisbon. It started raining heavily and the old Chrysler had to slow down, its worn tyres skidding on the wet asphalt. Urbano stopped at a large hotel and accompanied Jean to the front desk. Contrary to his prediction, there was a room available. Jean thanked him, convinced that the policeman had taken the opportunity to point him out to the doorman. His movements would be watched. He did not care. In any case they would not be able to stop him being at his meeting with the bank the following day. He was delighted to have been so unmysterious. There was nothing so calculated to disconcert the police or, if not the police, then the foreign service for which Urbano laboured discreetly to augment his modest salary.

The next day Jean kept his appointment with the banker whose name he had been given in Paris. He was introduced to a cold, offhand individual whose expression was hidden behind sunglasses and who spoke to him at first in German.

'No,' Jean said, 'I'm not German. I'm French.'

The banker fell silent, took off his sunglasses and cleaned them with a silk cloth. His eyes were bloodshot.

'I suffer from conjunctivitis,' he said. 'Before the war I was treated by an ophthalmologist from Leipzig. He's in Russia now, amputating frozen feet.'

Jean commiserated but did not smile. The banker put his sunglasses back on. He was no longer the same man with the wet, blinking gaze.

'You understand,' he said, 'that we'll have to make some checks …'

'I realise that. When will you give me an answer?'

'Tomorrow morning.'

Jean left with a receipt in his pocket. He set out on foot through the city. He did not feel he was being followed and he was disappointed. It would have been fun to keep on intriguing Urbano and his superiors. Perhaps they had lost interest in him. The thought mildly annoyed him. He walked around Lisbon as, when he was much younger, he had walked around Rome and London. To be a stranger in an unknown city for the first time is a marvellously heady feeling. You lose yourself in the name of discovery, and your head is filled with a new world in which you are the savage. Jean knew nothing about Portugal. He could, like Valery Larbaud, have shut himself up in a hotel room and learnt Portuguese ferociously in a week, but he much preferred the distance that separated him from a warm, well-lit city in which the sound of people's voices surprised him and reminded him at every moment of his difference. He admired the attractive, soft gaze and amber-coloured skin of the women, and the asceticism of the masculine faces. He wandered the streets and strolled around the museums. From the Castelo de São Jorge he surveyed the terraced city and the *mar da palha* crisscrossed by small, heavy lateen-sailed boats. He liked the *aʒulejos* of Estrela, the Manueline doorways and the marvellous way the Portuguese had of covering the exteriors of their houses, which they kept closed to the light, with flowers. He would certainly come back to share this jewel of peace and grace, but who with? In the last three months he had despaired of ever seeing Claude seize hold of reality again, and if she did there would still need to be peace for them to be allowed to leave and forget everything. Nelly? Even if she enlivened life and quickened it with her generous spirit, he didn't think he could count on her company to spend hours wandering around a beautiful city. She loved poetry and the theatre because they sprang from words; over the rest she cast an indifferent gaze. Besides, what good was dreaming? He could see nothing in front of him except, if he was utterly honest, complete uncertainty. In the evening he went to Estoril. At the casino a crowd that talked in many tongues pressed around the gaming tables with an eagerness that defied the rest of Europe at war. It was a euphoria he did not share.

The banker confirmed the sterling purchase at the advertised Lisbon rate. A numbered account was opened. Jean had another opened for himself and deposited his commission. He would leave it there until the war was over.

'You're very sensible,' the banker told him. 'The escudo is a healthy currency that will weather the storms of this devastated world well. I had rather expected a young man of your age to stuff his pockets and spend it all on parties.'

'I don't feel like that.'

'In a way I know what you mean.'

They shook hands. Jean went back to his hotel and did some sums: he had never had so much money at his disposal. He was surprised not to feel any pleasure, any heady feeling. The telephone operator had a call for him from Urbano.

'Good morning, Monsieur Arnaud. I have an idea that you're about to leave us.'

'Yes, this evening.'

'I hope you liked Portugal. You forgot to visit the Jerónimos.[29] You must come back.'

Jean could no longer doubt that his every step had been followed since he arrived.

The hunting lodge was deserted. In its current dilapidated state it was beyond habitation. Wind, rain and hail had torn down the waxed paper that had covered the broken panes. A yawning hole in the roof exposed blackened beams. In its neglect, postponed no longer by a clumsy handyman, the lodge had acquired a kind of smashed grace more in keeping with its past of hunting meets in the forest, and the halt of tired horsemen after their pursuit of the stag. Jean glanced inside, putting to flight some rats nesting on a mattress. He circled the building. Foxes had scattered the rubbish left by the kitchen door. He was surprised to see empty bottles of spirits, mouldy bread covered in fungus, empty tins. Before he left, Blaise Pascal, nature lover and vegetarian, had regained his appetite for intoxicants and processed foods.

On the way back, from the path that led out of the birch forest, he caught sight of the tall, well-muscled figure of Jesús still sawing wood in the courtyard. With his torso bare in the sunshine, the Andalusian woodcutter exiled to the Île-de-France cut a fine figure, his brow glistening with sweat, his hairy upper body gleaming in the light.

'I am workin' for the winter,' he said. 'The famous General Winter who wins all the battles, who will eat Hitler up. 'Ave you been for a walk?'

'Just to Blaise Pascal's lodge. The man in the woods isn't there any more. Have you heard anything of him?'

'No' much. I think 'e 'as returned to normal life.'

Jesús picked up an axe and started attacking a trunk. Chips flew around him.

'Did you see him again?'

'Yes, a few times. 'E started washin'. 'E didn't smell so bad.'

Laura stood in the doorway in an apron.

'Lunch is ready.'

She had returned to her place at Jesús's side, driving from Paris each evening and staying on Sunday when Jean spent the day with them before going to the clinic to see Claude. Since her return from Germany she had not talked about her brother or her parents, but Jean had a feeling that she had also made a resolution she was keeping to herself, one that profoundly affected her internal life. Everything seemed to be a secret to this introverted woman with her closed features, wholly absorbed, it appeared, in her love for the bristly devil whose extravagance and bohemian character she had domesticated, and whose artistic life she had succeeded in ordering without smothering it. It was possible that she liked Jean, but he was unsure, or perhaps she tolerated him in a diplomatic way, because after having isolated Jesús so that he could work, it made her anxious to see him so alone during the week, dwelling perhaps on regrets of his life of joy and pleasure that he had left behind at the studio in Rue Lepic. In fact she was wrong: Jesús did not regret anything and gave himself so totally to his painting that he aspired to nothing more, apart from a little friendship with Jean and his nights spent with her, nights that he talked about with his customary fierce lyricism. For with a disarming naivety and amnesia for his expedient philosophy of the past, Jesús had turned himself into an apostle of monogamy, expatiating solemnly on the months and months needed for a man and a woman to perfect their pleasure in each other. He was so sincere in his naivety, and so ardent in his proselytising, that Jean kept to himself the sarcastic quips he might otherwise have directed at his friend. And wasn't Jesús ultimately right? His lyrical way of expressing himself might have masked a bald truth, but bald truths also have a hidden meaning we cannot ignore. Jean's own memory of lovemaking with Claude was awkward and remorseful. He remembered only an exasperated pleasure too quickly taken, too sudden, the kind a young man feels at his first experience of sex. Had he satisfied her? No, he couldn't have, in the unbalanced state she was in. Then it was a failure, ridiculous, yet another mistake after such a long wait, a shattered mirror in which, looking at each other, they would only see their disfigured images. Yet if he compared Claude to Nelly, he felt he had honest excuses. Nelly approached pleasure with a romantic tenderness he had hardly expected from her cheeky, inconstant character. They knew each other well now and were connected by a delightful bond that was impossible to classify. In each other's arms they rediscovered both the solemnity and the sudden giggles of childhood. Jealousy, lies and hypocrisy were unknown to them. They were open with each other and never talked about tomorrow, not from reluctance but simply because they didn't imagine there would be one or, rather because they were both too young to commit themselves when life was so rich in splendid uncertainties.

'I didn't know,' Jean said to Laura, 'that Blaise Pascal had come back again. Actually I'd almost forgotten him, our troglodyte of the forest. He amused me.'

'I don't like him,' she said.

'You don' like anyone, excep' Jean and me.'

'So what?'

'You're right.'

Laura seemed to want to say more about Blaise Pascal, but she waited until Jesús was busy uncorking the bottle of champagne Jean had brought.

'I know what was wrong with that man,' she said.

'What?'

'He was afraid. He hid in the woods because he was afraid of the war, the bombs, the bullets. He's a coward. And to lie to himself he invented a philosophy of the nature lover who hides in the woods, which is a lot nobler than fear. I won't deny that after a while he probably ended up believing in his philosophy, but in the beginning it was all about fear.'

She spoke tersely, with a rancour surprising in someone so shy. Jean was sure she knew more than she was saying and was refraining from saying it because of Jesús.

'You're exaggeratin', Laura. He knows abou' paintin' …'

'He's a sycophant.'

Jesús turned to Jean, opening his arms to show his impotence.

'She is stubborn.'

'I nearly forgave him because I thought he was Jewish,' Laura said, 'but he isn't.'

'How do you know?'

'I made some enquiries about him. He's moved to a country hotel near here under his real name. He's shaved off his beard, cut his hair, and plays backgammon and belote with the people in the village.'

Jesús exclaimed, 'She knows everythin'. Absolutely everythin'!'

He admired her with such sincere enthusiasm that it was touching. Jean told himself that reciprocal admiration was also a form of love, and not the least nor the most foolish. These two beings carried each other. Realising it, he envied them and loved them more. In truth he had only them and Nelly, forsaking all other friendships, so much did the world he lived in inspire instinctive distrust in him. He nevertheless suspected Laura of creating a void around Jesús while Jesús himself, at his best, loved the whole world. Did he have to pay such a price? He doubted it.

'I ask myself,' Jesús said with his mouth full, 'why you aren't livin' at Rue Lepic. My studio is empty …'

'I will, I will, but not now. When Nelly chucks me out.'

Jesús scolded him for defeatism. You don't let yourself be chucked out. You leave first.

'It isn't that,' Jean said with a frankness that surprised him. 'It isn't that … The truth is, I'm very bad at being on my own. It's a sort of panic. When I was a boy I borrowed three books from the library at the lycée by Camille Flammarion, the astronomer: *Where Do We Come From?*, *Where Are We?* and *Where Are We Going?* I've worked out where I came from. I still need to find the answers to the two other questions, even if I half know the answer to the third, since death is obviously where we're going ...'

'Listen ... you know nothin' about thir' question neither. When the anarchists of the POUM launched an attack durin' the civil war, they shouted, "Viva la muerte!" 'E's not so stupid. Death is the other life, the beautiful one, and I believe in my death and in all those people who will think me an 'andsome genius when I am dead.'

'You, yes. Not me. I won't leave any paintings or sculptures behind, not a page, not a child. I've only got one life, and at this moment I feel I'm using it up. And Claude's still mad.'

Laura got to her feet to cut more bread and said, 'She can still get better.'

Jean no longer believed it. In the afternoon he walked over to the nursing home. Each week he both looked forward to and recoiled from the visit, which upset him even though he could not do without it.

'She's better today,' the supervisor told him, taking out her pass key to unlock Claude's room.

'In that case why is she locked up?'

'It's Sunday. I look after the whole floor. We have to take precautions.'

'There are patients walking unaccompanied in the garden.'

'During the week she goes out, but, as you know, her little boy comes to see her on Sunday. She's unpredictable after he leaves ...'

The door opened. Claude was sitting on a chair next to the barred window, looking at the kitchen garden and the road. She turned to Jean, her face serene.

'I've been waiting for you,' she said, offering her cheek.

'Shall we go for a walk in the garden?'

The supervisor protested. Jean took no notice and led Claude downstairs. They walked along the path that bordered the lawn. Residents were strolling on the grass or reading under the trees. A number, in perfect mental health, were paying dearly to remove themselves discreetly to a place of safety from the new racial censuses. An arbour in the shade of a copse of young copper beeches had benches where two men were reading newspapers. A young woman, her face ravaged by nervous tics, was rummaging in an overnight bag, pulling out rags, folding them and replacing them in a jumble to start again.

'She's crazy,' Claude said. 'Pay no attention.'

They sat on two chairs, facing the sprinkler watering the lawn. The flowerbeds were full of lettuces.

'Did you see Cyrille?' he asked.

'Yes, this morning with Maman. Poor darling, he gets bored here, goes round and round in circles. Maman scolds him all the time. I asked if I couldn't have him with me. They could put a small bed in my bedroom …'

'And the doctor said no?'

'He says no to everything.'

A man in his sixties, in white trousers and a shantung jacket and wearing a panama, raised his hat politely as he passed them. Claude gripped Jean's arm and murmured, 'All that man thinks about is raping me. He's tried to several times.'

'I'm sure he doesn't. He's harmless, I promise you. I've talked to him. He lived in the Far East for a long time … He's not a pervert.'

'But you don't know him. When you're not here, he shows me his—'

He interrupted her.

'No, Claude, no. Think about something else.'

'If I can't tell you, who can I tell?'

'Nobody. When you say those things you start to believe them. So don't say them.'

Her eyes filled up with tears.

'You don't love me the way you used to.'

'I love you more than ever.'

She turned her mouth to him and he kissed her lightly.

'Everything's better when you're here,' she said. '*They* don't dare come.'

'There's nothing for you to be afraid of any more.'

'Maman says they can find me here.'

Anna Petrovna's stupidity exasperated Jean and he began to despair. What he had hoped was an ordinary depression, in his relative ignorance of mental illness, was turning out to be a deep, painful wound that was probably incurable. Claude's illness, or possibly an overuse of sedatives by her doctors so that she left them and the nurses in peace, was altering her looks. Her face had become expressionless and her blank stare reflected her constant indecision. She seemed at the mercy of the last person to speak to her. How could he fight it?

'You haven't told me what you're doing,' she said.

'I'm running a gallery.'

'Are you enjoying it?'

'Not really, but it's a living and it means I can help you.'

'Do you mean you're paying for me here?'

'Yes, you know I am.'

She looked thoughtful for a long time.

'I've got an idea,' she said. 'If I leave the clinic, you won't need to work any more. We'll take Cyrille to Saint-Tropez, to your grandfather's. I'm sure Marie-Dévote will have us. You can go fishing with Théo and help him with his delivery business. Cyrille's very pale. He needs sunshine.'

He was amazed how at certain moments she could reason with such logic and imagine practical solutions to the situation they found themselves in. There was no doubt that Marie-Dévote and Antoine du Courseau would welcome them with open arms. He had thought of it himself. But Claude's mental fragility made it too great a risk.

'We'll go swimming,' she said. 'The sea's always blue and warm. Cyrille can play on that lovely sandy beach. Your grandfather can start up his Bugatti, and at night we'll make love, lots. I'm dying to make love to you, Jean. Here I dream you're inside me, everywhere inside me, and then I wake up crying because I'm empty …'

She squeezed his hand with the force of desperation. The man in the shantung jacket stopped in front of them and raised his panama.

'What a glorious June we're having, don't you think?'

'Glorious,' Jean said.

'Not too hot, not too cool. The Île-de-France is paradise. Our kings should have left it at that. Why make it bigger? Ambition is the mother of all misfortune. Napoleon should have stopped at Austerlitz. He'd beaten the two emperors of Russia and Germany, taken forty thousand prisoners, including twenty Russian generals, captured forty flags and a hundred cannon. Why go on? He was master of all Europe … I bid you a very good day.'

He went on his way, panama raised.

'You see …' Claude said. 'Now you understand.'

'I didn't hear him say anything rude.'

'Because you're here …'

A maid appeared at the doors of the home pushing a trolley laden with a tea urn and cups. There was no need to summon the residents. They had seen her. Leaving their benches and interrupting their strolls, they converged on the trolley, producing momentary confusion around it.

'Don't push, don't push,' the woman huffed, as if she were talking to spoilt children. 'There's enough for everyone.'

Claude stayed sitting with Jean. The man in the panama walked past them again, raising his hat and leering.

'There's tart today,' he said. 'It's Sunday.'

The supervisor's head and shoulders appeared at a first-floor window, looking down at the group massed around the trolley. A patient caught sight of her. Word went round and the impatience subsided. Her voice nevertheless rang out.

'Monsieur Trouleau! Don't push. I can *see* you pushing! You'll be served along with everyone else. And you, Madame Chaminadze, you *must* have your tea.'

Claude got up meekly, joined the group and waited patiently to be served with the liquid they called tea. Jean watched her from a distance and tried to rekindle the extraordinary emotion that had swept over him at Clermont-Ferrand when, as the regiment marched past, he had seen her standing between himself and the light. Her body was as firm and willowy as it had been then, but the rough dress she was wearing made her look heavier. The residents dispersed into the garden with their tasteless slices of tart on the rim of their saucers.

The supervisor shouted again, 'And remember when you've finished to *bring back* your cups.'

Claude returned to Jean, smiling, her face suddenly enlivened by pleasure.

'We'll share,' she said. 'I asked for some tart for you, but there's just enough for the residents. The cooking's awfully good here.'

He doubted it, and was startled, too, to see Claude obeying the commands of the virago on the first floor so readily, and docilely parroting the glowing reports the nursing home gave itself. She was in their power and, despite a few timid outbreaks of revolt, had surrendered to the regulations laid down by the management with the distressing resignation of a being who places her life permanently in the hands of a nameless power. She began to talk about going away again, but now with a fearful indirectness.

'They're talking about shutting down the clinic,' she said. 'The doctor wants to go on holiday. He's entitled to a holiday like everyone else, isn't he?'

'Of course.'

'The supervisor and the nurses too. I could come and live with you in Paris. Or at Quai Saint-Michel if you like …'

He had enquired: there was no question of the clinic shutting for the summer. Claude had made it up. The resident psychiatrist lived on the top floor, avoiding patients' families and friends as much as he could. Jean had seen him twice in six months. With each monthly bill he included a medical report couched in sufficiently cautious terms for it to be impossible to draw any precise conclusion. Claude was 'making progress', an ambiguous phrase that was not to be construed as meaning recovery. For as long as they could pay, the patients remained helplessly in the hands of this occult power lurking under the eaves in a book-crammed apartment. His name was Dr Bertrand, and he had been working on a thesis on the madness of Gérard de Nerval for the last ten years.

Claude took her cup back and returned to sit next to Jean.

'You don't tell me anything about Nelly,' she said. 'Do you still see her?'

He preferred to lie, though Claude never showed any jealousy.

'Less than I used to. She's working hard and she was a terrific Pauline in *Polyeucte*. It's a pity you can't see her. We'll go as soon as you're better. She's always asking for news of you.'

'I'd like to see her again. It was so strange living at her place and knowing she was your girlfriend too. Do you still sleep with her?'

'No, of course not.'

The man in the panama paused in front of them.

'How did you like the tart?'

'Excellent,' Claude said.

'Wasn't it? There are so many residents who've come here to treat their nerves, but I'm here to treat my stomach … I'm on a gastronomic cure. The world's going to pieces and we're eating our fill. It's the survival of the fittest. See you soon, I hope.'

He raised his hat and immediately went to sit on a garden chair next to the young woman who was unpacking and repacking her bag of rags. She paid no attention to his conversation, her face tense with anxiety, counting the rags in her long skinny fingers. The man stood up, shrugging his shoulders, and walked back past Jean and Claude.

'She's not normal,' he said.

Claude smiled and whispered to Jean, 'Am I normal?'

'Perfectly. You're just tired.'

'You haven't given me any news of Madame Michette.'

'Oh, she's all right, I think. Always very busy.'

'Cyrille infuriated her.'

'She got over it.'

A cloud covered the sun. Faces looked up and walkers paused as if the mechanism that regulated the peaceful scene and its movement had been thrown out of gear. The supervisor appeared in the doorway, looking up to squint at the sky. The cloud went on drifting, a single formless mass in the infinite pallor. The sun was already coming out again and the cloud was passing. The supervisor walked towards Jean and Claude.

'The doctor would like to see you.'

'Now?'

'If possible.'

He squeezed Claude's hand.

'Wait for me.'

She looked up at the supervisor, who stood watching her and saying nothing.

'Jean, I think I'm going to go back to my room.'

'She's very sensible,' the supervisor said. 'Very. If only all the patients were like her.'

Jean's heart ached. Claude drifted at the mercy of any will stronger than her own. The supervisor's face displayed a kindness and indulgence that froze his soul. Claude followed her, turning at the door of her room to kiss Jean before walking over to her chair by the window. He would have wept, had it not been for her radiant smile as the door closed on his past.

'Is it really necessary?'

'The doctor will tell you, Monsieur. We're responsible for Madame …'

The psychiatrist's apartment was reached by a spiral staircase that ended in a door with double locks. The doctor himself opened it, in shirtsleeves, a man in his fifties whose Freud-like goatee beard failed to conceal the innate cheerfulness of a face whose eyes sparkled with amused curiosity. He wore dark lenses whenever there was a pessimistic diagnosis to be delivered to a patient's relations. Yet, as we have noted, this man was not fond of external contacts, of anything in fact that disturbed his closed universe in the nursing home, and considered the explanations he was obliged to supply in order to keep his patients there as a distasteful chore.

'Monsieur,' he said, 'I've only had the pleasure of meeting you twice, and to be honest, though I know many things about Madame Chaminadze I know nothing about you. Forgive me for asking you up here. I should have come down to my consulting room to meet you there, but it's Sunday – I deserve a little rest too, and I thought an informal meeting in my apartment would be more pleasant and relaxed, that you'd find my curiosity less oppressive and that we might even have a drink together, though my drinks cabinet is very modest: a brandy and water as Mr Pickwick preferred it, or a bootleg pastis the way Marius liked it. What's your choice?'

'Nothing,' Jean said. 'I'm listening.'

He did not like to be talked to, by an intelligent man, in language that indicated he was thought to be an idiot, unable to work out the most elementary aspects of life. Dr Bertrand annoyed him, and Palfy had taught him how to cut short such false chumminess.

'Oh, well … you'll allow me not to follow your example.'

He poured himself a cognac and water. Jean relaxed: there was nothing sinister about this Freud lookalike, he was simply cultivating an attitude, as shown by his evident awkwardness when he was not addressing a mental patient, or perhaps he had got into the habit of considering all his interlocutors as grown-up retarded children, to whom it was necessary to explain the most ordinary facts.

'I know how concerned you are by Madame Chaminadze's condition …'

He had sat down at his desk, piled with documents and files, a sheet of paper half covered in handwriting in front of him. The shelves on the walls were sagging under the weight of books. A voice rose from the garden.

'Monsieur Draguignan, can I remind you that there are *lavatories* on the ground floor. If you don't mind …'

The doctor smiled.

'She's a dragon, I know, but without her the patients would do exactly as they pleased. She's especially interested in your relation's case, you know …'

'She's not my relation; she's the woman I love.'

'Oh, I know, I know, but we are sometimes obliged to maintain a certain fiction. Where the mentally ill are concerned the family are all-powerful and can forbid the visit of someone who isn't a family member.'

'I don't really see how Claude's mother could forbid me to see her daughter. Putting it rather vulgarly, Doctor, I buy the right to see her by paying your monthly bills.'

'I know, I know …'

His embarrassment was growing. He swallowed a mouthful of brandy and put the glass down in front of him. A mad thought crossed Jean's mind: a plan had been hatched against him, and they were going to prevent him from seeing Claude. He was gripped by a terrible anxiety and the thought that he still loved her as much as before, even in her present condition. If he had doubted it in recent months, the threat he faced reminded him of his attachment.

'I'd be happy to have a brandy and water like you, Doctor.'

'Ah, now we're being sensible ... Good sense always wins out.'

As delighted as if he had just won a personal victory and made a wayward patient see reason, Dr Bertrand put on his glasses and fetched the bottle of cognac.

'It's not easy to lay your hands on good cognac at the moment,' he said. 'I had some put by, but it quickly ran out. Fortunately I have relations in Charente. Do you know Charente, Monsieur Arnaud?'

'No, I don't know Charente. War and defeat haven't really favoured my appetite for travel.'

'Fancy that! But I hear you often go abroad.'

'I've been to Portugal three times since the beginning of the year, but not for tourism, for business.'

'You're a very young businessman.'

'I have a feeling it's a profession I'll do well not to grow old in.'

Anna Petrovna was the only person who could have told the doctor, and even she could only have known of his journeys via Cyrille, who Jean had answered carelessly about one of his absences. He began thoroughly to detest Claude's mother, who had clearly mounted an undeclared war against him. Dr Bertrand sat down at his desk.

'Yes,' he said, as though resuming after a digression a train of thought interrupted by small talk, 'yes, I get the impression that your visits, despite the desire she expresses for them, are upsetting Madame Chaminadze. You know that she is suffering from an obsession triggered by physical mistreatment, the nature of which I don't need to elaborate on. She used to be, I believe, according to what you and her family have told me, a balanced person, very much in control of herself. Is that correct?'

Jean, resolved not to come to his aid, nodded in confirmation. Dr Bertrand compressed his lips purposefully. Once more he had let himself get carried away by long phrases that reassured him of his own subtle understanding of psychology, but this laconic interlocutor whose irritated gaze he felt settling on him, this boy whom Anna Petrovna had claimed was involved in shady business dealings, disconcerted him.

'I've been thinking,' he went on, 'that you should space out your visits … Just an experiment, you understand, a simple experiment, but we need to try everything in the case of a sensitive patient such as this, in which science only has formulas to offer, when what we really need are intuition and psychology.'

'If you'd talk to me openly, Doctor, we'd understand each other, and I'd answer you.'

The doctor again compressed his lips, which were full and sensual in his round, happy face. It was a tic that had been commented on sarcastically at his oral examination and he thought he had succeeded in suppressing it, but the slightest difficulty made it reappear. It embarrassed him horribly.

'Nothing is ever quite as "open" as you think, my dear Monsieur. The psychology of a human being who's been disturbed by a violent event is a delicate mechanism that in reality we don't know how to repair, because we know nothing about the brain, the brain being, of course, the vulgar term that scientists use to speak of the soul.'

Jean emptied his glass and got to his feet.

'Thank you very much, Doctor, goodbye.'

Dr Bertrand paled. He could get angry too. He felt wounded by this young man's disrespectful behaviour. He stood up, his two fists on the table, leaning forward.

'I regret to inform you, Monsieur Arnaud, that Madame Chaminadze's mother and uncle wish you to desist from further visits to see your girlfriend.'

'Ah, so Claude has an uncle now? That's news to me.'

'The family, which was decent and united before your arrival, did not judge it necessary to include you ...'

Jean had sworn to himself that he would stay calm. He took a moment to collect himself, glimpsed a possible way out and, deciding to pursue it, smiled.

'Doctor, I respect your profession too much not to consent to your experiment. I agree to abstain from further visits for the necessary period. Nevertheless, if you have any humanity you will understand that that comes at a price. I therefore wish to discuss it with Claude. Perhaps not today. Tomorrow or the day after. Give me some time to think, to weigh my words so as not to disappoint her. I'll confess it to you again: I love Claude. And she loves me. No one is going to separate us: not a foolish mother nor a brother who lives from gambling nor an unknown uncle, nor even you, who knows exactly what I'm talking about.'

'Of course, I entirely understand, even though I'm not certain that Madame Chaminadze is in a fit state to answer you. If you telephone me before you come, we shall arrange matters so that there is no disagreeable meeting with the family.'

'One more thing, Doctor. Up till now I've paid the clinic's monthly bill. I wanted to say that I'll continue to do so.'

Dr Bertrand took off his glasses, revealing a victorious and amused look.

'That won't be necessary. The family has taken the patient into its care. I have been instructed to return your last cheque to you.'

The cheque was ready in an envelope. Jean took it and tore it up. He felt hurt, profoundly hurt, and detested the stranger's interference in Claude's ordeal.

'I'm sorry,' Dr Bertrand said. 'Very sorry … I didn't think you would be so affected. The truth is that I know nothing about you and I'm merely an instrument in a family's hands. That's the law.'

He walked round his desk to Jean, taking his arm with sudden affection.

'You're young; you've yet to discover stupidity and malice. You'll only really be a man when you have a precise idea of what they are. Meanwhile take care.'

He let go of Jean's arm and turned his head to add in a lower voice, 'And fight. I'll help you if I can, even though you don't have a very high opinion of me.'

'Then tell me if you think Claude's curable.'

The doctor emptied his glass and turned back to sit behind his desk.

'Sit down. Please. I won't give you a lecture, but I'd like to give you some insight if I can.'

His tone had changed. It was persuasive, and Jean thought he detected a new sincerity.

'For several years now, to distract me from the atmosphere in this rather confining place, I've been interested in Gérard de Nerval. You'll tell me that literary critics are studying that writer with more talent than I'll ever have. The one difference is that I seek to bring a doctor's diagnosis to bear on Nerval and to imagine how I would have been able to cure him. My thesis is that he *was* curable, where Maupassant was not. The basis of my research is my reading of that coded document, *Aurélia*. No one can deny, Monsieur, that here we have the most beautiful, the most *lucid* testimony of what frenzy is. With this document in my hand I can confidently tell you that Nerval, who was sound in body, was also sound in mind. All that was needed was to persuade him. About Madame Chaminadze I cannot, I'm afraid, say the same thing. A question mark hangs over her case. Volition seems to escape her. She won't regain it here. We have neither the time nor the means to help her. We can soothe her anxieties, that's all. And offer her, relatively speaking, a refuge, since the Gestapo are not yet raiding nursing homes. Is a refuge more important than a mental status quo? That is up to her family to decide. I shan't say what I think. My duty is to keep the maximum number of residents I can, but I'm sure you understand that an empty bed is immediately taken by a new patient. There's a long waiting list. I've told you everything. You must do what you feel you should, and if you try your luck, I shan't blame you …'

*

On the ground floor Jean met the supervisor, sorting out rags, scraps of sheets, torn clothes.

'A lady is waiting for you at the door in her car. It has a German registration.'

'Thank you.'

'Oh, Monsieur, don't look at me like that! I'm collecting rags for Mademoiselle Durand. After a week she gets bored with putting the same ones away every time.'

Behind the closed French window the man in the panama stood drumming lightly on the glass with his hand. The supervisor wagged her finger at him.

'No, Monsieur Carré, it's not time to come indoors yet. Go for another little walk.'

Monsieur Carré waved and turned away to go round the lawn again.

'You have to be firm,' the supervisor said with a smile.

She was not trying to excuse herself, merely displaying her ability to maintain order in the nursing home, to prevent this bunch of lunatics doing as they pleased, and regarded it as proof of the mildness of her system that she was obeyed without question.

'I'd like to see Madame Chaminadze, just for five minutes.'

'Oh, I'm sorry, I'm afraid that's impossible. She was very agitated after you left her and we had to give her an injection. She's sleeping now.'

*

Jean could not summon the will to insist. Outside Laura was waiting in her green car, a book resting on the steering wheel.

'I'd have walked back,' he said.

'I know you would, but I wanted to talk to you.'

They drove through the peaceful village and turned onto the road for Gif, overtaking pedestrians walking to the station, bent double under the weight of suitcases full of food, and cyclists in shorts with haversacks on their back.

'They're hungry,' Laura said. 'The French are hungry.'

'Do you understand them?'

'Yes. The good thing is that they admit it. In Germany no one would dare to … I came to talk to you about Blaise Pascal.'

She was silent. The private unease Jean had felt at his meeting with Dr Bertrand overcame him again.

'Where does he live?'

'Here, in this village.'

'I don't feel very strong, Laura,' he said. 'I really don't want to talk about another mad person.'

'We must.'

She was driving her noisy two-stroke car fast. Going downhill, the exhaust pipe popped drily, misfiring. Laura slowed down in the forest to park in the shade of a side road.

'Jean,' she said, 'we have to clear up some misunderstandings. After Christmas, when I came back from Germany, you left Claude with us for a few days …'

'Yes, I shouldn't have. She was already going off the rails. I knew she needed to go to a clinic, but I was looking, I didn't realise …'

He would have liked to see Laura's expression, but she stared straight ahead as if fascinated by an image emerging from the shadows of the forest, which sloped down gently down towards the Yvette. Golden splashes exposed the undergrowth. He listened to her, wondering why she hadn't spoken earlier, but it was in the character of this unusual woman to reveal herself only after a long personal struggle.

So he learnt that Blaise Pascal – forgive me for not yet revealing his real name and possibly for not revealing it at all – that after the awkward dinner to which he had invited himself, Blaise Pascal, the lice-ridden and apparently mad dandy, had reappeared several times and it required no great perspicacity to realise that it was Claude's presence that had drawn him out of his retreat. Of course he had acted circumspectly, delousing the 'man in the woods', reappearing in much more attractive guise and deploying all his charm before disappearing again. He had even succeeded in making her smile and she had ceased to consider him with dread. Laura was no longer in any doubt that the hermit had re-entered the world as a result of falling for Claude, an emotional change that had fully revealed to him the cowardice and inanity of his withdrawal from the world. He had already decided to give up his hunting lodge before Claude was admitted to the nursing home. Laura surmised that, having assumed his other identity – of a youngish man of independent means, simple, modest and good-natured – he had set himself up in the village next to the nursing home in order to be able to visit her more easily. But things had not stopped there: a fortnight earlier she had seen him with Anna Petrovna and Cyrille.

'So now we know who the uncle is,' Jean said.

He did not want to know any more. They drove back to Gif and the farmhouse, where Jesús was working in his studio. Laura vanished as only she knew how, and the two men remained in the room, which was already growing darker in the fading light. Grey shadows filtered through the trees and spread stealthily, murmuring over the house in the calm of the evening. On a long canvas Jesús was painting flashes of light, a luminous composition of muted gold and silver in the green sunlight of Chevreuse.

'Is no good at all!' he said, despairing, sitting down on a stool. 'I am a useless idiot who 'as no talent.'

He was sincere, believing it fully. Inside his tall, solid frame there lurked a childlike soul that was prone to sudden despairs as magnified as they were fleeting. Jean, who knew him very well, refrained from reassuring him and occasionally even expressed himself in complete agreement, just to incite his friend to react in a spirit of contradiction. To him the painting on the easel looked to be of such dazzling beauty that he no longer doubted Jesús's great talent. He had purged himself of everything, of his false daring, of the old-fashioned academicism to which his skill had long bound him, of the influences that had held him back, and now his painting radiated the force and ardour that a great original artist brought to it. Jean was sure of it: Jesús would be counted among the few masters of his generation when, matured by his retreat, he finally made his way back to the galleries.

'What do you want me to say?' Jean said to him. 'That you've got no talent, you're a dauber and you'd do better as a house-painter, or that you're the artist I like better than all the others, in fact the only one? You won't believe me either way, and you'll spend the next hour boring me stiff with your doubts. Stop it, you're talking rubbish. You're a happy man and it upsets you, and that's entirely normal, because you've always heard that great artists live in a state of permanent torture …'

'Michel du Courseau suffers!'

'He suffers, but not because of his art, which he's totally happy with, to a degree you and I can't imagine. His suffering is about something rather different: how can he reconcile his very real and very sincere faith with his taste for little boys? He hasn't found an answer yet. The day he does, he'll suddenly stop being so repressed.'

Jesús rapidly forgot his own anxieties. He had worked all afternoon with passion and pleasure. The release of tension explained his pessimism and fears.

''Ow is Claude?' he asked.

'The same. It's me who's not well …'

They talked about Blaise Pascal. He sometimes came to the house in the afternoons. He had even bought two canvases, but had not taken them with him. Jesús occasionally found him interesting, and at other times thought him irritatingly pedantic and self-assured. They still did not know who he was, nor whether he had really possessed a collection of paintings before he buried himself in the forest. Jesús was nevertheless aware that he had conceived a sudden, violent passion for Claude. Fulfilled himself and therefore feeling that his own love affair was the only real one, the only one worthy of interest, Jesús assured Jean that what had happened was a stroke of luck for him and would provide him with an honourable means of extracting himself from an impasse. Jean did not reply. How could he explain what he still felt for Claude, and which would never be extinguished, even if she failed to regain her sanity? In short, that he owed her his love.

Shadows filled the studio. Jesús, sitting on a high stool, his feet resting on a bar with his chin on his knees, seemed immense and invincible. He belonged to a world-view that left no room for doubt at a moment when Jean was discovering the depths of human misery, loneliness and the looming approach of a despair that, fortunately, still repelled him. He felt an intense need to see Nelly and rushed his leave-taking.

Laura drove him to Gif station and as they were saying goodbye told him, 'I'll help you, but it's not so easy. We're all being watched and we're all watching each other. You'll have to take her away somewhere. Anywhere. Otherwise … you'll have to give her up.'

She had touched the nerve of a passion that, in the saddest way, was starting to fade just because it did not know how to change. In the train taking him back to Paris Jean realised that the distance, small as it was, and his return to Nelly were beginning to erase Claude from his emotions. Life could not be this love that had no way out.

Night was already falling over the Luxembourg Gardens. He reached the Comédie Française, where the matinée had just finished. Nelly was taking off her make-up in her dressing room, replacing a stage face for one shining with cream that looked tired and drawn.

'I've been waiting for you,' she said. 'If you hadn't come in time, I was never ever going to see you again. I wasn't very good this afternoon and I'm depressed. I wanted to be a genius and it turns out I've just got some talent. That's mediocrity for you. There are evenings when I'm just a sad and unhappy little girl who wants to cry her eyes out. Absolutely the worst thing of all, you horrible Jules-who, is that I'm starting to ask myself whether I'm not in love with you. Undo me, will you?'

He unhooked her heavy, starched seventeenth-century dress, which held her graceful bust in a straitjacket. She emerged, naked from the waist up and cream-skinned, staring at her mirror. She held her pretty, pointed breasts in her hands.

'Maybe these really are my best bits,' she said, letting them go. 'And people are wrong. I have no talent. I just have nice tits. Kiss me.'

Her dresser came in.

'Do you need me, Mademoiselle?'

'No thank you. I've got my undresser. See you tomorrow, Mauricette. I hope I'll be less terrible than today.'

'You were marvellous.'

Nelly was talking to her in the mirror, her face tense, smoothing her eyebrows whose natural arc emphasised her dark eyes.

'And to think I'm a stationmaster's daughter!' she said.

'My brother works on the railways too!' Mauricette replied, folding a scarf.

They walked back to Place Saint-Sulpice together, arm in arm. Before leaving for the theatre Nelly had made a cold supper and they ate it on the kitchen table, he in his shirtsleeves, she naked under her dressing gown. The summer night, silent and heavy, drifted through the window, filling the studio. In bed, Nelly snuggled against him.

'The time for admissions has come,' she said. 'I've been wanting to say it since yesterday. This is the situation, my scrumptious Jules-who: I believe I'm actually in love with you, though you don't deserve it. At the same time I'm also attracted to Jérôme Callot. Why? I don't know. Well, every night we play the most sublime love on stage so convincingly that I suppose some of it's left behind afterwards. But he's an awful dunce; he got married when he was twenty and has two kids and and is never going to leave his bourgeois wife for me. So we say nothing to each other except for the cues Musset gives us, like two old hams. And I hang on to you, like you hang on to me, in spite of your Claude. See? I'm more honest than you. Now let's go to sleep, as if you were Jérôme and I were Claude. Marvellous, isn't it?'

Nelly's skin still had the sweetish taste of make-up and her make-up removers. He could never confuse it with Claude's. She fell asleep immediately, like a child consumed by sleep, her fists clenched, surrendering to her dreams with the same passion as she surrendered to the theatre. Sometimes she lived her dreams so intensely that she slept panting and out of breath, or uttered disjointed phrases that Jean memorised so that he could repeat them to her next morning. But she remembered nothing. Jean tried to summon a memory of Jérôme Callot's face. He had seen him on stage and once in the wings at the Français: his large, leonine head, his curly hair, his superb voice, an assurance borrowed from his characters and, underneath it all, more than likely, an enormous stupidity of the sort that only actors are capable of. Nelly was attracted to him, conscious of his vanity, but knowing he lived in her world and that they shared the same double life, and Jean would never be able to do as much. He was astonished that he felt no jealousy, only a vague fear that was hard to define, possibly the fear of finding himself suddenly alone at a moment when nothing had prepared him to be. But he would always love Nelly, in his way, and an immense affection would bind them that nothing would dislodge. He leant over her and murmured in her ear, 'My little sister …'

She snuggled up tighter.

Jean had gone back to Portugal twice and each time had found Urbano at the border, waiting for him. The young PIDE inspector made no attempt to conceal his surveillance of Jean and had become increasingly friendly.

'You know,' Urbano had said at their last meeting, 'I think you're rather brave. You're running definite risks. You could be murdered on the way; no one would ever try to find out where the shot had come from. With me at your side you're in less danger, so long as my government doesn't arrest you, but, as you must know, I don't only work for my government. It's a matter of material necessity. Dr Salazar is a great man and he intends to keep our country out of the war. Having said that, he's also tightfisted. His prime ministerial salary is just enough for him to live on because he has very few needs, and he feels the servants of the state ought to follow his example. So everyone moonlights. I've resigned myself to it, like everyone else. A foreign power that I shan't name asks me for information. When that information doesn't compromise my country's own affairs, I provide it. My superiors close their eyes, probably because they do the same. So I've been ordered to find out why you come here, and it may be that I know, but because I like you I'm taking this opportunity to warn you. I think it unlikely that you'll complete a fourth journey. You probably won't make it to prison; you'll be liquidated before you get there. Who will protest? Not the Germans, you can be sure. Nor the Vichy government, who'll know nothing about it ...'

They had had dinner at Peniche before reaching Lisbon after nightfall, and this time had eaten not cod but perfect rock lobsters and drunk a *vinho verde* from Minho that had stripped away some of

Urbano's reserve. Jean listened to him, careful not to give anything away. He had been lectured too often by Palfy and Julius to be unaware that a policeman, however charming, convivial and cultured, is still a policeman, and the innocent ways of picking up an indiscretion are infinite. Yet he did not dislike the Portuguese man and it would not have taken much to make him feel friendship for him, especially as Urbano was also a foundling, adopted by a family of minor civil servants. He had finished his schooling with the help of scholarships and learnt English and French on his own. His talents and intelligence had raised him in the ceremonial and complicated hierarchy of Portuguese bureaucracy. One day he would be someone, and he had no doubt of his future.

From the restaurant terrace they watched the fishing boats coming ashore on the tide. Oxen towed them clear of the water and women with baskets on their heads unloaded their catch in an extended Indian file lit by acetylene lamps placed on the white sand.

'It's true that I've taken risks,' Jean said, 'but I'm just the messenger in these transactions. If anyone wants to take me out, that won't make any difference to the people running the show. But … I hear what you're telling me and I'll give it some thought.'

'I haven't made you angry?'

'No, no, not in the slightest. You're doing your job, I'm doing mine. I *absolutely* have to have money … for reasons that might make a jury weep, but not a secret service. So I'm taking the risk. I'm too much on my own to have any other choice.'

'Is it for your parents?'

'No. It's for a woman I love, who the Germans arrested and tortured. They drove her half mad and I've got no other way to protect her and help her get better than by putting her in a nursing home where she's safe.'

Urbano was thoughtful for a moment.

'The rule of my profession is never to believe what people tell me, and I don't know why I believe you. You trust me; well then, I shall trust you, Jean. You must settle your business tomorrow at the earliest possible opportunity and get away without delay. Don't stay in Lisbon a minute longer than you have to. You'll be picked up, and I shan't be able to do anything for you. As soon as you leave the bank, call me from a public phone box on a number I'll give you before I leave you. We'll meet at a place I'll tell you and I'll find a way to drive you to Vila Franca de Xira, where you'll be able to catch the express without being followed. I can't do more than that …'

'You'll be losing a fat bonus.'

'It's too bad. There'll be others. Lisbon is teeming with people with something to hide. Anyway, money isn't everything for me.'

'You've got no reason to behave like this towards me.'

'Very true!' Urbano conceded with a smile. 'But I do a job I don't enjoy every day of the week, so perhaps this evening I'd like to make amends to myself for the bad aspects of my life. You make a good hostage. So I'm not just a policeman, I also have a friend …'

This had happened at the end of May, shortly before the events we recounted in the previous chapter. Jean had taken the card Urbano had slipped him under the table. It could have been a trap; it was like tossing a coin. But the man from the PIDE had been as good as his word and Jean had found himself back in France safe and sound, with a warning that a fourth trip would not be tolerated. Palfy was unsurprised.

'You were lucky, dear boy. I didn't think you'd come back from the last trip.'

'I'm thrilled by your honesty. I suppose you'd have let me rot in prison, if nothing worse happened?'

'I warned you of the risks.'

Jean was reminded of the narrow margins within which he had to exist. The substantial sums he had put away in a numbered account were exactly what his life was worth. Without false modesty, he found the price derisory. He demanded to know the whole story. Palfy told him. For more than a year the Sicherheitsdienst had been producing counterfeit banknotes so perfect that even the Bank of England could not tell the difference. Somewhere in the Reich a printing press was operating. Envoys were selling the notes in Switzerland, Portugal and the United States, everywhere there was a free exchange rate. The funds thus acquired paid the SD's foreign expenses. The Reich's Finance Minister, Dr Schacht, although initially opposed to the operation because it lay outside the meticulous organisation of his own closed monetary system, was aware that he would be sidelined if he did not agree and had turned a blind eye on condition that there were no blunders. Palfy related all this with glee, since in his eyes it resembled an extraordinarily good joke. It filled the pockets of both intermediaries and sellers, while scarcely denting the already inflationary sterling exchange rate. Jean did not, strictly speaking, disapprove. In an appalling war from which he had been excluded it represented a tiny incident: spies and traitors being paid in funny money. In any case he had had no choice: he either accepted, or he let Claude die in hospital. He had absolved himself. It was an era of rotten morality. Bombing a defenceless town was a far greater crime. Neither Great Britain nor the United States appeared overly troubled by scruples. There were worse things than his racket. Even so, he would not go on. Palfy shrugged.

'You're putting yourself in a difficult position. For the sake of our friendship I shall try to extricate you. But if I'm not listened to, you'll only have yourself to blame.'

'The sake of our friendship? You're weakening, Palfy!'

'My life has changed greatly … love, you know …'

He was not being ironic. He was in love. It occurred to Jean that if he revealed the truth to Geneviève, she might no longer see her Constantin in the same light.

'And what if I talked to "Maman" about this business?'

'You won't. You're a decent boy, stupidly honest, a chump through and through, and because you're so fond of the high idea you have of yourself you are, quite simply, incapable of being such a rotter.'

He was right. Palfy's past would remain above suspicion as long as Geneviève kept out of the way of Salah, who knew some of the truth about Palfy, in the shape of the disgraceful Cannes affair in which he had attempted to launch a parallel network of call girls, with Madeleine as their coordinator. But Salah was a long way away and Geneviève remained without a protector. At the same time, however clear-sighted he was about his friend, Jean had no doubt either that Palfy loved Geneviève. She would never make a saint of him, but in any case she could not care less about saints, who made life impossible.

Palfy was quick to guess the nature of any reflections that concerned him and added, abruptly, 'We're going to get married.'

He was trying to hurry things up. Papers were missing. Switzerland was refusing to allow him to stay longer than a month at a time. A highly placed lawyer had promised to solve the problem.

'One is powerless in a country where the law is taken so seriously that they laugh in your face if you attempt to find a way out. Order is all very well, on condition that it's full of holes.'

But he was still in sincere mood.

'We must see Julius,' he said. 'You can explain your situation to him in person.'

'Is it absolutely necessary?'

'Absolutely.'

Madeleine had lately begun holding musical evenings followed by a buffet supper. They were more sought-after for the buffet than for Mozart. German uniforms mixed with scroungers, music lovers and those cheerful crooks Paris was chock-full of. Jean recognised the Pole, whom people were starting to talk about a great deal: an associate of the Bessarabian Joanovici, who was also Jewish, he was plundering France on behalf of the occupying authorities. His wife, a cold, distinguished-looking German, was said to be the mistress of General von Z, head of the requisitions commission. Inside a year, people said, this physically ill-matched couple with such well-matched morals had made a fortune. The Pole's name being unpronounceable, people called him Polo, a nickname he had quickly assumed to cover up his obscure origins and create an aura of familiarity around himself. Jean loathed him at first sight. In fact, he detested the whole tainted, dishonest, avid, self-satisfied world that had come to gorge on his country and sell it wholesale. The sozzled seriousness of the Germans listening to Sonata No. 40 in B flat major and No. 42 in A major for violin and piano was in stark contrast to the lack of attention of the French. A nation of music lovers? Then why had they started this war, and more importantly, how did they divide their lives between music and killing? It was said that Reinhard Heydrich, the Gauleiter of Bohemia and Moravia, who had died from the injuries sustained in an assassination attempt three weeks earlier, had played the violin to concert standard. The night before the attack, he and his wife had attended a concert. Yet the photograph of him that had appeared in *Signal* showed a man with the face of a dead salmon, already dead for twenty-four hours, a face so emblematic of cruelty one would never want to look such a person squarely in the eyes. Likewise the bevy of German officers sitting on Madeleine's Louis XV chairs, lost in the music as if in prayer, reminded Jean of the grotesque farce mounted by Obersturmführer Karl Schmidt in June 1940.

Palfy, it turned out, had not forgotten either. After the concert he came over to Jean.

'When I think of that idiot of an Obersturmführer ... Brahms! God, how boring. Now if he'd played us some Mozart, I'd have forgiven him for shooting us.'

'Are you bored, Constantin?' Madeleine asked, materialising behind them.

'Not here, not ever. Jean and I were remembering an incident from our army days that made Brahms repellent to us for ever. I hope there'll never be Brahms played here.'

She looked upset. She knew nothing about music, and until her worldly career had taken off had never ventured beyond popular ditties. Julius had observed that she became bored at the concerts he took her to and, passionate about music himself, had engaged a teacher who came twice a week to introduce Madeleine to the great German composers, choose the programme for her supper concerts at Avenue Foch, and teach his very malleable pupil the basic vocabulary that she could use without danger in the company of genuine music lovers. Within months she had become known in Paris as a great patron of music. Her education was naturally patchy, and the name of Brahms unsettled her. She had not heard the name before, or perhaps had forgotten it. She was also scared of Palfy's sarcasm and cutting wit.

'Don't worry, Madeleine, Brahms really existed. He looked like Karl Marx.'

'I know I don't know anything,' she admitted. 'Don't make fun of me! Jean … Julius is waiting for you in his study.'

The guests had left the drawing room and made a dash for the buffet. They had not noticed the absence of Julius, whom Jean found sitting at a Napoleon III desk, an annotated sheet of paper in front of him. It was not the same man. Where was his mask? Did the affable, benevolent, impassioned face of this great lover of the French way of life belong to the real Julius, while a false Julius, on duty, composed his features into a glacial, imperious frown? Jean, who had never liked him, was tempted to believe the opposite was true. At this moment he had the supposedly false Julius in front of him, with two lines suddenly appearing at the corners of his thin mouth and accentuating its true severity. Jean found him laughable, despite his cold, impenetrable stare. He sat down without being asked and crossed his legs.

'I'm listening,' he said.

Julius, insensitive to such nuances, told him that one did not withdraw without risk from an undertaking such as the one he had been entrusted with. Of course he understood the young man's motives, his scruples, his fear of arrest by the Portuguese police and handover to a foreign intelligence service, but that was part and parcel of the mission. He had not been chosen for an easy task. Since he had accepted the rewards, so he must one day accept the risks. Men of his age were dying in their thousands on the Eastern front to root out for ever the Marxist canker from Russia. Those who had the good luck not to be combatants owed it to the rest to possess strong nerves.

'I've carried out the mission I was given,' Jean said, 'but not in the name of anti-Marxism. In any case I hardly know what Marxism is, and even less what anti-Marxism might be.'

'Perhaps it's time you started being interested in ideas.'

'I occasionally have them. As luck would have it, they're not usually generalisations ...'

Julius smacked the table. The conversation had taken a wrong turn and he regretted having shown so little severity until now that Jean felt able to make fun of him openly.

'French irony has its charm, I don't deny it, and I congratulate you on possessing it. But we're dealing with something else here: you're withdrawing from a mission whose secrecy is its strength. I'm warning you now: it's impossible. If you withdraw I shan't cover you. Not even knowing the affection Madeleine has for you.'

Jean believed him. Julius's bald statement might have thrown him into a panic. As it happened, it came at exactly the right moment. He studied Julius closely, as if wanting to imprint on his memory the features, hardened by severity, that so ill suited this supposedly decent man mixed up in serious affairs who this evening was at home, having invited everyone who was anyone in the occupation to hear a performance of his two favourite Mozart sonatas. He understood that the time for games was over. The reality of the danger had not yet sunk in, but he sensed it nevertheless, and decided he needed a day's grace to ensure his freedom.

'I'm expressing myself badly,' he said. 'I need to think, that's all. I have an idea to put to you. I need twenty-four hours to see if it's workable.'

Julius was not easily deceived. There was too much at stake financially for him to allow Jean any leeway.

'What is it, this idea?'

'Give me till tomorrow and I'll give you not just an idea but a plan.'

'I can't run that risk.'

'In that case I'll leave you.'

Julius got to his feet, his face relaxed. The justice he had meted out satisfied him entirely. He stifled a surge of pride, came to Jean and put his hand on his shoulder.

'I'm sorry,' he said.

'So am I. Will you do me a favour?'

'Perhaps.'

'If your guests haven't cleaned out the buffet, I'd like to try your *foie gras*.'

'With the greatest of pleasure!'

They returned to the drawing room. Madeleine had been keeping an eye out for them. When she saw Julius smiling and holding Jean's arm, her anxieties vanished.

'Jean, I've kept you a cold plate and a bottle of champagne.'

'I'm leaving you in good hands,' Julius said as he walked away.

Jean tried to see who he was making for, who in this varied and chattering throng, released after the concert like a flock of birds, would detain him at the exit, but Madeleine was urging him towards the buffet, where several guests were still lingering. At a sign from her a butler bent down and extracted from beneath the table a plate attractively heaped with *foie gras* and cold veal.

'Madeleine,' Jean said after his first mouthful, 'your Julius has just warned me I'm in danger. I need to leave here without being seen. He assured me you'd help.'

She opened her eyes wide in astonishment. Her lover had never involved her in his affairs, and if a word out of place was ever uttered in her presence she pretended not to have heard.

'What? You want to leave without anyone seeing you?'

'Exactly.'

Madeleine's face tensed. She did not understand. Colour flooded her throat. Suddenly she was afraid, a defenceless woman in a world where, until now, her safety had always been guaranteed. Was it about to start all over again, the way it had been before, a life of obscure threats like those that had oppressed her during her hard life as a woman of the street? Moved by her disarray, Jean tried to calm her. 'It's nothing, absolutely nothing!' What good did it do to alarm her, to tell her the truth about the milieu in which she had blossomed so innocently, believing herself, in good faith, saved? The mirror over the buffet reflected a part of the drawing room in which the guests, glass in hand, spoke in small, languid groups, still slightly listless after the concert which, the Germans excepted, had rather bored them. In the centre of the mirror was Julius. He had taken Palfy by the arm and was speaking in his ear. When he looked up and caught sight of Jean and Madeleine together, acute annoyance appeared on his face. His expression hardened. Palfy seemed not to have noticed and had his head half turned, observing another part of the drawing room. Doubtless Julius had told Palfy what was going on. But what could he expect from Palfy? His friend's present course of action allowed no room for error. He was accumulating a fortune and would not sacrifice his ambitions for anything.

'What are you looking at?' Madeleine asked, curious at his sudden silence.

'Julius, in a mirror.'

She clasped her hands.

'I daren't do anything without him,' she said, sighing.

Her immaculately made-up face betrayed a moment's weariness. Her easy, sheltered life had relaxed her. The resurgence of problems hollowed her features, emphasising a dark shadow under her eyes.

'Sometimes when I wake up in the morning, I tell myself it's not real and that if I pinch myself the dream will evaporate,' she added.

With a gesture she took in her thirty or so guests, who in truth cared little for their hostess and spoke a language that was still largely foreign to her, though she tried valiantly to understand them. Yet she clung to them, for they symbolised her social rise. The dry pop of a champagne cork, eased out by the butler's fingers, attracted attention. Two couples rushed to the buffet, jostling Madeleine, as indifferent to the mistress of the house as if she had been the lavatory attendant.

'Nelly didn't come,' Madeleine said awkwardly.

Generously he lied.

'She's working tonight.'

'Well, of course, that's more important than anything ... What's she performing?'

'Musset.'

Madeleine was not very sure whether Musset was a play or an author. She made a note to ask Blanche next day and assumed a knowing and admiring expression.

'Are you and she still getting on?'

'Yes, very well.'

He pictured Nelly in a restaurant on Rue de Beaujolais, for that was where she was, opposite Jérôme Callot who had managed to get away to see her for an evening. It was good that she had found an opportunity to be alone with her ham of a co-star and to see him in real life, away from the theatre, in his tight-fitting suburban clothes. She needed to be disappointed. She would be. Afterwards everything would be better.

'I invited her,' Madeleine went on. 'Despite Blanche. Blanche thinks I mix anybody and everybody. It's true that Nelly's not always easy. She says quite impossible things. People get very annoyed. A month ago she took out General Köschel's monocle and pretended to try it out, you know ...'

'In front or behind?' Jean asked mechanically.

'In front. She claimed her "brown eye" was short-sighted.'

Jean laughed. General Köschel was considered an utter fool, and an unpleasant fool to boot. Nelly's aim was good. Nothing scared her.

'It's like Marceline,' Madeleine added, enjoying a chance to confide. 'I like her. She always amuses people, and Julius and Rudolf both say they never get bored when she's here. For me it's different: I don't laugh at the strange things she says. I'd still be saying those things myself if I hadn't been lucky enough to meet Julius. The truth is, I know all that too well … Oh, I don't mean I worked like that … far from it … Anyway, you know all that … you! It's impossible to imagine her as anything other than a madam. It's written all over her red face. But she's good-hearted and innocent, so innocent she's like putty in Constantin's hands.'

Julius released Palfy, who was left alone in the middle of the drawing room. He turned round, caught sight of Jean and Madeleine, and winked at Jean. Polo came up to him, frowning.

'That Polo person is vile,' Jean said.

'Yes, that's what I think, and I don't know why.'

'He'd sell his mother.'

'Julius says he's very intelligent.'

'Success can turn the lowest of the low into a superior being.'

'Do you think so?'

Jean sensed that these people intimidated Madeleine and that she would have given anything to send her guests away and stay on her own with Julius that evening, by their radio, listening to music. Julius genuinely loved music. As a young man he had played the organ. What had life made of this enthusiastic player of Bach? A conqueror, a businessman, and the beloved lover of a woman who had led the hard life of the street. Madeleine made Jean's heart ache when he glimpsed her fear that she was not what Julius dreamt of. She had by no means forgotten the past and quaked at the thought of her salvation being taken away from her. It was a terror and it paralysed her. Her second destiny was imperfect, for it was always overshadowed by her first. She could not get used to it. Yet no one had had the nerve to remind her of it. Besides, who, apart from Jean and Palfy, knew? No one here, not this evening.

Fortunately Blanche is there to watch over her. She corrects her blunders, points out the way forward. She may have spoilt her own life, but she will make sure Madeleine succeeds, and beyond her expectations. It is her cherished ambition. At this sort of evening she is like a chair attendant in the park: invisible and swooping down on the prey that fortune offers her. She has just noticed that Madeleine and Jean are having a private conversation. She whispers in Madeleine's ear, 'The lady of the house belongs to *all* her guests.'

Madeleine follows her meekly, ready to obey. She has not offered to help Jean, and he has not insisted. Let us watch her once more as she joins the prefect of police, who is getting bored talking to a German official with mediocre French. Her dressmakers and new young hairdresser (sought-after throughout Paris) have fashioned a new woman with such skill she cannot be taken for anything other than a lady. And as only appearances matter, she is actually in the process of becoming one, of erasing her past. We have mentioned that she was accomplishing her second destiny. She has a third she is not expecting, of which she remains unaware. As we shall not see her again, better to speak of it at once and salute this modest woman to whom Palfy gave her start in life, who has no other ambition than to feel secure, and whom Blanche will push to become what she herself can never be. In fact, Madeleine is to carry on living happy and carefree with Julius until that dawn of 21 July 1944, when the SS raided their apartment in Avenue Foch. The previous day, von Stauffenberg's attempt on Hitler's life had failed. The repression had begun. Julius, who had played the Wehrmacht card, was in the first wave. He was shot the same afternoon. Madeleine shut up the apartment, leaving it in the butler's care, and fled to Montfort-l'Amaury and the house Julius had bought for her. Let us remember the dates, which are important: the Allies are still in Normandy but Paris's liberation is not far off. The

German army is packing up. Polo has already left for Spain with his treasures; Palfy is married and living in Switzerland, free from want; Rudolf von Rocroy, posted to the front, has managed to get himself rapidly taken prisoner by the British. One society is scattering, and a new one has yet to take its place. Madeleine, who in her innocence has committed to neither side, awaits in starry-eyed trepidation the arrival of the officers in crepe soles. One of these, a major commanding a parachutists' unit, purposely seeks her out to inform her that he is the owner of the Avenue Foch apartment. He is deeply sorry to hear of the death of Julius, his friend of pre-war days, and reassured to know that nothing has been stolen. The only damage that occurred was when the SS raided the apartment and stupidly broke a Chinese vase.

'It's the price of war,' he says. 'I should like you always to consider that apartment your own. Julius was my business partner. If it hadn't been for him, I'd have nothing left. Whenever you come to Paris, you must make yourself at home.'

Madeleine does not hesitate. Major Bernstein is a gallant officer. So gallant that she marries him, partly to be back among the same servants, rather more in order to survive, because Julius had no time to leave her anything. She can return to Paris, head held high, under her new name. Her third act has begun, leaving her former life, her depressing Montmartre existence, far behind in the past. Now, when she talks about her memories, she feels no need to delve into her Pigalle period. She has another past to replace it with, that of her Avenue Foch years with Julius, her musical evenings among friends. At the same time she is able to negotiate the ordeal of the purges unscathed. Who would think of making trouble for Madame Bernstein, whose husband is fighting at Bastogne with his regiment of parachutists? Major Bernstein is, in short, an ideal husband, so undemanding in every way that he dies discreetly from a bullet in his abdomen in February 1945, leaving Madeleine a widow, Madame Bernstein, and in possession of a fortune large enough for her to live without cares from that day forward. In truth she would happily have retired to the countryside, the dream of city dwellers who have pounded the streets in their younger years, but Blanche is there, pushing her to become the muse of a small artistic clique. And so Blanche fulfils herself through another woman whom fortune has smiled on more broadly than her. Madeleine will enjoy an affair more intellectual than physical with a poet who makes frequent retreats to Solesmes. From it she will gain a discreet and fashionable glory. Ten years later, her Tuesdays will be the most sought-after in Paris. Every August she will sponsor an annual music festival in an ancient abbey. Age will suit her very well, and in her sixties she will take to wearing a velvet choker that hides the wrinkles on her neck. Need we add that Blanche will not leave her, hating her a little more each year and concealing it very well, wounded in her self-esteem to the point of feeling poisoned, to see Madeleine succeed where she herself has failed ...? Madeleine will only become aware of Blanche's hatred in the last moments of her life, laid low by a fatal bout of influenza in 1970, when Blanche tears from her ring finger a large emerald given to her by Major Bernstein on the last night of his final leave. She sees Blanche's mad stare in a face disfigured by greed and a haste to see her benefactress dead and buried. La Garenne had been right to mistreat his mistress and demand lewd favours from her. He would have made her a saint. Freed from his clutches, she stole from Madeleine, blighted her final moments with hatred, and discovered that when she in turn wanted to invite artists and writers to her own Tuesdays, not one of them was at all interested in her.

We have finished with Madeleine and Blanche. They have just spoken to Jean for the last time, and now he is aware of exactly how alone and ignored he is in this gathering. The author would like to add a footnote here. It may be, in truth, that we have shown a Jean too composed and too sure of himself. Let us not forget that he is only twenty-two and that he has already had his fair share of struggles, been aided by fortune, harmed by misfortune. He is beginning to form a more accurate idea of the world confronting him, and in which he must, at this moment, survive. He has responded to Julius's judgement on him with impudence, but impudence cannot hide an intelligent anxiety about his fate. His throat is tight. He has never found himself in such a tight spot, and is thinking about everything that will soon change around him, about Claude whom he will be forced to abandon, about Nelly whom he will not be able to see again, at the same time as scanning the room for the man who is responsible here for carrying out Julius's orders. We shall add that he has no regrets. It was a fine adventure, and he has savoured the trips to Portugal, even Urbano's unexpected friendship. But everything is crumbling: the way to Claude is barred to him, Nelly at this precise moment is perhaps already in bed with her fool, and he will never see the money he carefully deposited in a secret account in Lisbon.

He drank several glasses of champagne and thought of Antoine du Courseau and their last night before abandoning La Sauveté to the Longuets. Palfy touched his elbow.

'Are you dreaming?'

'I'm afraid my goose is cooked.'

'Marceline will be here in a minute. I've just telephoned her.'

'Then what?'

'We've confected a little stratagem. Be patient. Talk to someone. Julius is watching you.'

Palfy left him. The only person Jean felt like talking to was the butler, the one person worthy of the occasion, but the butler would not compromise himself by mixing with the guests. Polo walked over and collected two glasses.

'So, Monsieur Arnaud, you look rather out of sorts.'

He rolled his 'r's. It was an accent he claimed to have acquired as a boy, in his primary school in the Auvergne. He even occasionally came out with a '*Fouchtra!*' which he felt sounded very local, but which left any listener who really came from the Auvergne baffled.

'No, I feel excellent, thank you. I just know hardly anybody here.'

'Ah, the who's who of Paris! So difficult to break into!'

'Even more so if you can't really be bothered.'

Polo looked surprised. Since his ascent he felt at ease everywhere. This young man looked unconcerned.

'I'm delighted to have bumped into you – I wanted to give my wife a little painting. A very little one. On canvas. That you can roll up. I'll drop into your gallery tomorrow. I'm sure you can find something suitable for me. And don't fleece me on the price; I'm a friend of Julius's and Constantin's …'

He moved away, smiling, happy to have revived the young man's gloomy spirits with the thought of a painting. A very small painting that could be rolled up and slipped in a handbag for a journey to Switzerland or Spain. There was a stir: Marceline was entering the drawing room, a head taller than the women and almost all the men. In recent weeks she had filled out and looked practically voluptuous in a blue satin dress, in her hand a very large bag that she left on an armchair before walking over to Madeleine and saying in a voice both earnest and joyful the phrase Palfy had taught her and that people now expected from her, while restraining themselves from giggling: 'My own two in your dear ones,' and shaking both hands as she did so, surprising those who did not know her and were astonished by this impulsive irruption of a she-bull in a china shop. Jean did not smile. He had a soft spot for the ridiculous Marceline, so at ease with herself. After gushing greetings to Madeleine and others she moved in his direction, picking up a glass of champagne from the butler on the way. She smelt strongly of a cheap perfume that Palfy had identified as patchouli. Crossing the drawing room, she ignored Blanche, who was looking daggers at her. From her private convictions Madame Michette derived a poise that nothing could alter. Her activity, hilarious to start with, then by chance branching into genuine clandestine undertakings, had developed and magnified her authority. In all innocence she had believed she was working for Palfy from the moment she had informed him of her desire to serve, and it had not occurred to her for a second that he might have launched her on an unsuspecting Paris as a joke. That evening she was about to play her most important role: to extricate Jean from this trap, to spirit him away from Julius's agents.

'I'm getting you out of here, young man,' she said, speaking out of the side of her mouth, as if the slightest word might be read on her lips and give them away.

'How?'

'Go into the hall, discreetly. I'll be in Madeleine's bedroom. But quickly. There's no time to lose.'

He would have believed anyone at that moment. He slipped out without being seen and found Marceline in the bedroom. She was already undressing. She was wearing two dresses, one on top of the other, two pairs of stockings, two necklaces.

'Put these on!' she ordered.

In her bag she had a pair of high heels and a floppy hat.

'I'll never be able to walk in these.'

'I'll tell them you're drunk.'

He did as he was told, hid his suit in Madeleine's wardrobe, and let Marceline apply lipstick and eye shadow.

'For once it's useful to be a pretty boy,' she said.

Looking at himself in Madeleine's mirror, he felt he looked grotesque, no better than a clown.

'I shan't fool anyone.'

She placed a wig on his head and the floppy hat. She stood back.

'Perfect!' she announced. 'Time to slip away.'

She took his arm, supporting him as if he were a tipsy girl, and they reached the street door. There were cars lined up along the pavement.

In one of them sat four men in black. The driver turned to look at them, but Avenue Foch was deep in shadow and he saw only two women built like prizefighters.

'Female wrestlers,' he said to his companions, whose laughter wounded Marceline enough for her to hesitate, on the point of turning round and slapping the man. Her sense of duty won out. She shrugged, pulling Jean along with her. His ankles were buckling. They crossed the Étoile and turned into Rue Troyon. Two prostitutes stationed outside a dingy hotel sniggered.

'Look at the queens!'

Marceline retorted with an obscenity so vulgar that the girls, awe-struck, were silenced.

They walked for five minutes more, until they arrived at a barred gate opening onto a private path that led to small ivy-covered houses like the one where Claude's mother lived. Marceline knew the way. In the darkness she located a well-concealed entrance. She knocked three times and the door was opened by a man in braces, his feet in worn slippers. A dim light lit a table at which a woman put down her crochet work to observe them.

'He's a friend,' Marceline said. 'He needs a quiet place for the night to sort out his next move.'

'Has she got coupons?' asked the woman.

The man dismissed the ill-mannered question with a gesture.

'I said a man friend,' Madeleine corrected her, lifting off Jean's hat and wig.

Their host burst out laughing.

'Well, well, well!'

Marceline modestly acknowledged her success. Jean stood, embarrassed and conscious of how ridiculous he looked.

'He can sleep in the storeroom back there,' the woman said, getting to her feet with difficulty, her legs swollen by poor circulation.

'We'll make a bed up for him. Has he eaten?'

She could not bring herself to address him directly.

'Yes,' Jean said, 'thank you. *Foie gras* and cold veal. But I've been drinking champagne so I'm a bit thirsty.'

'We only have water.'

'There's nothing better.'

They looked at him, puzzled and anxious. The words '*foie gras*' and 'champagne' aroused a strange reaction in the woman.

'Perhaps the storeroom isn't very comfortable. We could put him in the boy's room. He'll have to leave the shutters closed in the morning.'

'I'll be here to collect him tomorrow before eight,' Marceline said. 'He won't be any trouble. I'll bring him a change of clothes. Where are your things? At Nelly's?'

'Yes.'

'Give me the key.'

'Knock before you go in.'

She raised her eyebrows, concerned, and he added, 'Nelly may not be alone.'

'I'll know what to do. Go to bed and sleep well. Tomorrow will be tiring.'

She seemed about to salute as she disappeared with decisive steps down the path. Jean thought that if she came across the two tarts in Rue Troyon again they would be in for another mouthful.

'My name's Jeanne,' the woman said.

'My mother was called Jeanne too.'

'I have a son your age. He's a prisoner in Silesia.'

'He was studying at the Arts et Métiers,'[30] the man said. 'My name's Paul. We'll show you your bed. You must be tired.'

The bedroom smelt of mothballs. Photographs of actresses plastered the walls.

'We'll have to open a window,' the man said. 'You'll get a headache if you don't. We have a lot of moths.'

Jean drank a glass of water, got undressed and lay down. For a few minutes he listened to them tidy the main room without speaking, before they went into the neighbouring bedroom, where he heard whispering. Their bed creaked, and Paul started snoring almost immediately. Jean lay with his eyes open in the darkness. Everything was unravelling. He thought of Julius, who must be mad with rage and anxiety, of Nelly packing a suitcase for him on Marceline's orders, of Claude assailed by anguish in her drugged dreams. He was distancing himself from her. Another current was carrying him away. His easy life was coming to an end. He felt a satisfaction so keen he sighed with pleasure: it was curious to be joining the Resistance, dressed as a woman, on the day of St Jean himself, to be borrowing the bed of a prisoner of war who, before being called up, had collected the photographs of three German actresses: Marlene Dietrich, Leni Riefenstahl and Brigitte Helm. The smell of mothballs persisted, despite the open window. A pair of cats fought furiously on the path outside until someone threw a saucepan of water at them. Silence fell again. Paul's snoring subsided. Jean wondered what the couple lived on, old before their time, withdrawn from the world in the heart of Paris in a tasteless neoclassical house, whose imitation Henri II furniture made it nearly impossible to move around. Without a thought for their own safety they sheltered the strangers Marceline brought them at night. In the wake of Madeleine's soirée they represented another, very different France that one was tempted to forget when one lived in the artificial, glittering milieu he had inhabited up till then. Paul made him think of the man whom he still, out of gratitude, thought of as his father. Albert and Jeanne, Paul and Jeanne. The same preoccupations, the same narrow horizon, but within the limits of its narrowness a generosity and courage that were there when they were needed. Jean hoped their son was aware of their qualities and did not reject them or reproach them for not belonging to the world of lovely film actresses in which he lived in his dreams, far from the braces and slippers of Papa, and the waxed tablecloth and crochet work of Maman.

*

He was awoken by the dawn and it took him a while to orientate himself in the unfamiliar bedroom. His first gesture had been to stretch out his hand for Nelly and encounter only the rough, tightly tucked-in sheet, and he immediately realised that from now on he would miss her more than he had expected. He tried to remember their embraces but could only call one to mind, of infinite force and happiness, when they had made love together on the rug in front of the open fire before Marceline had brought Claude back, soaked and bruised and already unhinged. How could he erase the last six months, rekindle the pure flame that had consumed him since the meeting in the café at Clermont-Ferrand? There would never be anything more beautiful than what he had lived through with Claude in the dismal Paris of those years of 1940 and 1941. He had not forgotten any of it and at the same time he felt her, the woman who would always be for him the very image of dignity, slipping away from him. He regretted having made love with her on the spur of the moment, at a stroke putting an end to the rapture which had united them and borne them on, leaving them more wounded than satisfied, overcome by the awful sadness of quenched desires. It had been much more beautiful when they slept chastely in each other's arms, like children, transported by a desire that only enhanced their tenderness. Blaise Pascal now waited like a spider in his web to pounce on Claude. The thought horrified Jean. The harm had not yet been done, but seemed unavoidable now that Jean had to flee, because, curiously, escaping from the arrest orchestrated by Julius, saving life and liberty, meant equally risking his life and losing his liberty.

At eight o'clock Marceline marched into the bedroom, carrying a suitcase. She burst out laughing.

'Just look at you!'

In the mirror he saw his face smeared with lipstick and eye shadow from the night before.

413

'I forgot that good girls take off their make-up before they go to sleep.'

'It's a question of self-discipline! I've always insisted my girls take care of their skin after work. With all the rubbish they plaster on their faces, by the time they're thirty they've got skin like a sieve. Cleanliness is the key to health.'

'Did you see Nelly?'

'Yes, of course, and I didn't need to knock either. She was on her own. She's packed you a suit and some clean underwear herself. She was crying. She wants to see you. Though now's not the time.'

'I expect you find it all a bit like something out of Corneille.'

'That's what I said to her. We'll arrange something later. For now we have to get you out of Paris.'

'I need to go to the gallery and get some money.'

'Constantin's dealing with it. He's going to let me have it later today.'

Jeanne made coffee for him and buttered some bread. In her dressing gown with her bare feet in slippers with holes in them, she looked more depressing than the night before. She avoided looking at him and he realised that she found it hard to cope with the presence of a man of her son's age. Paul was more friendly. Opportunities to talk were few and far between.

'Did you see Laval's speech?' he asked.

'Vaguely.'

'You should reread it. There's someone who thinks Germany ought to win.'

'Apparently he's negotiated a return of prisoners in exchange.'

Jeanne turned towards him, her eyes sparkling with anger.

'What prisoners? And who's going to choose them? I don't believe it.'

414

Paul looked down. His choice of subject was unfortunate. But what could he talk about? Everything was getting worse. Rommel had taken Tobruk, the Afrika Korps had crossed the Egyptian border and the Wehrmacht had reached Kharkov. The spring offensive was developing from the north down to the Caucasus. Nowhere was there a glimmer of hope. Paul was silent. He rolled a cigarette and immersed himself in *Le Matin*.

'Don't pay any attention,' Marceline said when they were in the street. 'They argue endlessly. Every time he opens his mouth she contradicts him. It's worrying her sick that her son's a prisoner. I've known her a long time. When Monsieur Michette and I took over the Sirène, it was her last year there. She was in a bad state, her legs were giving her trouble from climbing the stairs, and she was going to confession all the time. The priest married her off to Paul. He was working for the post office. They came to live in Paris because people were gossiping and they'd had a son, a handsome boy who's been scaring them this last year. He's too clever and he despises them. I've got a hunch that they decided to be brave so he'll despise them less. Did you see? Not one question.'

Jean learnt a great deal that day. He decided he would never laugh at Marceline again, who carried out her clandestine duties with the effective authority and discretion that she had acquired when managing the Sirène. She took control of everything, going to see Palfy who gave her the money Jean was owed, collecting his false papers. From now on his name was Jules Armand. He chose 'Jules' in homage to the nickname Nelly had invented. 'Armand' made the task of the producers of false papers easier. He kept the same initials and date of birth. The following day he was at Moulins, and that night a guide led him through fields and forests to a French army post south of the line of demarcation. Stationed in a barn which no longer smelt pleasantly of hay but of boots, uniforms and rifle oil, the section was keeping the man on guard duty supplied with wine. Another was cutting bread and distributing a piece to each man with a sardine. On the whitewashed wall the section's artist had drawn a red devil and written in black letters '152nd RI, France's finest regiment'. A staff sergeant entered. A soldier shouted, ''Shun!', triggering a lazy line-up, the men embarrassed by the wine and bread. The staff sergeant stood in the doorway, hands on hips, looking annoyed.

'What's that?' he roared, pointing at Jean.

'He's just crossed the line,' the corporal said.

'Have you got papers?'

Jean handed over his new identity card. The staff sergeant read out his details.

'Well, well, class of '39 ... You're eligible for service. You'll stay with us, in the armistice forces. Your lot hasn't been demobbed yet. Go and get yourself some kit.'

'Thank you,' Jean said. 'I wouldn't mind a bit of a rest. I'll get the kit later.'

'I'm not interested in what you wouldn't mind. An orderly will escort you to the command post.'

He summoned a bewildered-looking private, squeezed into his tunic, his jaw pinched by his chinstrap.

'Take this man to the command post.'

'Yes, staff.'

'Yes, sir!' the staff sergeant yelled. 'Sir, you ignoramus. It's a gold stripe, can't you see that? I'm in the cavalry, not the infantry. Nothing to do with you horrible lot. About turn ... right wheel.'

Jean followed, dismayed. Behind him the section was laughing, restoring the staff sergeant's good humour.

'And when you go through the woods, be careful of the wolf!'

Was he falling out of the frying pan into the fire? The memory of his army experiences made bile rise in his throat. He would not be part of that company of clowns.

'He's a nasty bastard!' the soldier said as they plunged into the undergrowth, whose delicious smell, heightened by the dew, enveloped them.

'And he doesn't care who knows it!'

'Find a way not to be in his section. He's always like that. I call him "staff" on purpose. Just to hear him scream that he's in the cavalry.'

'What's the captain like?'

'The cap'n? No better. There's no escape here. What's it like in the occupied zone?'

'So so.'

'The Fritzes all right?'

'More or less.'

'Given the choice, I still prefer it here. I'm from the Ardennes.'

Jean got out his cigarettes.

'Do you smoke?'

'Do I? They don't call me the locomotive for nothing.'

He pulled on his cigarette with relish and attempted a smoke ring in the still air. A squirrel crossed the path and bolted up a tree, disappearing immediately in the foliage. A little further on, in a clearing, some young people in battledress khaki were chopping wood and piling it up in a stove.

'They've got a cushy number, those Chantiers de Jeunesse,'[31] the private said. 'Reselling charcoal on the black market. Their mess tins're always full. And ciggies, you want 'em, they got 'em!'

Jean saw his chance.

'Do you want the packet?'

'Do I want it? You bet.'

His hand was already greedily outstretched.

'Not so fast! Maybe we can come to an agreement.'

'What do you want?'

417

'To get away.'

'Oh yeah! And I'll be on a charge. Two weeks, one in solitary. Thanks a lot.'

'You're right, that would be shitty of me. Let's keep going. Is the CP far?'

'Another two kilometres, on the edge of the forest. Just outside Varennes-sur-Allier.'

Coming towards them rapidly, with a supple stride, was a young man in blue shorts and a short light-coloured jacket and white socks, his beret pulled down over one ear.

'He's one of the chiefs,' the private said. 'They're all chiefs there.'

The young man stopped.

'You've just crossed the line! I can tell without asking. Good: we can always use another pair of hands to rebuild France. Are you Chantiers age?'

'I suspect I may be a bit too old.'

'In that case it's the Armée de l'Afrique for you. You're in luck!'

He shook Jean's hand and strode away to rejoin his group, who could be heard singing in their clearing.

'They're funny, that lot. Roll up their sleeves. Salute the colours. Sing songs: "Avec mes sabots …", "Maréchal, nous voilà". Roll on demobilisation! So what about those fags?'

Jean turned round. The young Chantiers leader was disappearing through the trees. The soldier held out his hand. Reluctantly, Jean drew back and punched him on the chin as hard as he could, muttering, 'Sorry, mate,' as the private crumpled to his knees, his eyes staring, a trickle of blood flowing from his split lip.

At Varennes-sur-Allier he caught a bus that took him to Clermont-Ferrand, where memories of Claude came flooding back. He felt ill: there was Rue Gounot where she had stood with the sunlight shining through her dress, Place de Jaude where they had met again, thanks to the net cast by the girls at the Sirène. He wanted to cry. He could not stay. At the Sirène Monsieur Michette did not recognise him, but Zizi threw her arms around his neck.

'Where's your friend?'

Palfy had left a lasting impression. Zizi no longer 'went upstairs'. She deputised for the *patron* and shared his bed. Business was not what it had been, but they could not grumble. Other trades had been worse hit by the restrictions. No, Jean did not need to stay. He was leaving for the Midi, where he planned to spend a few days before returning to the occupied zone. He had brought a letter from the *patronne*. That afternoon they found him a suitcase and a change of clothes that made him look like an ordinary traveller. A train took him to Lyon and another stopped the next morning at Saint-Raphaël, from where he telephoned Théo.

'Jean! We hoped you'd find a way to get down here, but we didn't expect you so soon. Where are you? Saint-Raph? Raining there, is it?'

'No. Lovely and warm. I feel like diving in the sea.'

'It's not the time or the place. Stay where you are. I'll come and get you.'

Half an hour later Théo was at the station, at the wheel of his wood-gas truck. They thumped each other on the back.

'It must have caused you a lot of pain,' Théo said.

And so Jean learnt that Antoine had died the previous day.

'The doctor was too late. Antoine, he was red, all tensified. It looks like it was a stroke … We sent you a telegram straight away, but you never know nowadays if telegrams get there. It's a real mess … Poor Antoine, he loved life, his Bugatti, Toinette … Ah my, Toinette, he adored her …'

Jean reflected that he had loved Marie-Dévote too and Théo had refrained from saying so.

'Just yesterday, before it happened, he was fishing his long line in front of the hotel and brought back two rockfish. We're having them for lunch. Can't let ourselves go without, these days. The funeral's at five o'clock. Have you got a black suit?'

'No.'

It really was a day for wearing black. Antoine, now stiff and cold, had deserted Jean, and he could not stop the tears welling up in his eyes. He had come to talk to the man who had been his childhood accomplice, and for the first time Antoine had failed to be there. How could you believe in death on the shore of this lovely blue bay bordered by maritime pines under a bright and carefree sky? Antoine must have thought he would never die.

'It happened so quick Marie-Dévote didn't understand what was going on. She was sewing in her bedroom. He went up to see her for a chinwag and he suddenly said, "I don't feel well." She told him, "Lie down." She went to get him a glass of water when he went all tense. Then he went red too. And that's it, he was dead. Completely dead, just like that. He didn't even say "huh". All over.'

They buried Antoine that afternoon in the cemetery at Saint-Tropez. Théo had ordered a 'mausoleum' that would be ready in a week's time. Until then a wooden cross, earth and armfuls of wild flowers picked by Toinette in the hills covered the body of this man who had chosen to live as he liked, scorning inherited wealth and the milieu he had been born into. Death had taken possession of him with a swift, neat discretion that was not its habit. Théo's explanations notwithstanding, Antoine had probably succumbed while making love for the last time to the beautiful, voluptuous Marie-Dévote. A happy ending that mingled the heat of desire and the coldness of death.

Toinette had cried so much before the service that she remained dry-eyed and dignified at the cemetery as the coffin disappeared under the gravediggers' spadefuls of earth. In her lovely, melancholy profile Jean looked for signs of the du Courseau line, but Marie-Dévote's Saracen blood and Antoine's Celtic blood had mingled so well that there were no individual traces left of either. Her grace was cooler than her mother's, and at the same time it was possible to detect a more highly strung will than her real father's. Several times during the ceremony Jean gave in to distraction, drawn by her faultless figure in black dress and stockings. He remembered by heart the note he had received in 1939 just after he had enlisted.

Dear godson, I send you my best warm wishes and a muffler. I hope it isn't dangerous there, where you are. Don't catch cold. Uncle Antoine sends you a thousand affectionate thoughts. He says you are his only friend. He kisses you, and I shake your hand …

He had been charmed. It would have been a pleasure to answer her if Antoinette du Courseau had not revealed the secret of his birth to him. And some invisible thread had, without question, connected them in the last summer before the war. Words had turned out to be futile. They echoed mournfully, no match for a secret understanding. When Claude had stayed at the hotel Toinette had remained in the background. Nearly indifferent. Spending almost too much time with Cyrille, as if Claude and Jean did not interest her. Now he could contemplate her only as a beautiful image, not without a hint of jealousy, for one day a man would come and carry off this happy creation of chance and pleasure. Selfishly he wished her a mediocre fate, one that would not fill him with envy.

That evening, after the funeral, a procession of neighbours dropped in at the hotel. Marie-Dévote had prepared for their visits. She set out glasses, wine and pastis on the table on the terrace. They talked in low voices, as though the dead man still lay in his open coffin in the middle of the living room and could hear them. The Midi accent lightened the tone of their condolences, and with the help of the pastis a note of cheerfulness permeated the conversations. Toinette disappeared and Jean led Théo out to the garage. He wanted to see the Bugatti again, still sleeping there, its headlights turned towards the sea. Antoine had left this place only the morning before: his large pipe lay on the workbench, a net was waiting to be repaired, and the car had just been wiped with a chamois leather, its chromework rubbed with oil.

'He really loved it,' Théo said. 'Like a woman! One day I came here barefoot; he didn't hear me: he was talking to it, he was saying to it, "My beauty. I'll keep you turning over as long as there's a drop of petrol left." Hey … wait a moment. I'll do it today. He'll enjoy the music in paradise.'

Jean wanted to stop him. Théo had decided too quickly that he was master of all at last. But the Bugatti, which for three years had started at a tug of its ignition switch, refused his orders. The starter spun unresponsively. The motor shuddered and stopped.

'It's flooded!' Théo said and moved around to open the bonnet.

'Leave her. Perhaps she's sad today.'

'I tell you: you're a sentimental one.'

Toinette appeared at the doors of the garage. Her face was tense, her eyes sharp and bright.

'What are you doing here?' she said to Théo.

'We were looking at the Bugatti.'

'You don't touch it, ever, do you hear me? Ever!'

She turned on her heel, certain that she would be obeyed. Jean went after her. She had taken off her black stockings and was walking barefoot over the sand, still warm from the day. The singsong voices of visitors reached them from the terrace.

'What do you want?' she said to Jean.

He felt guilty.

'I didn't want to start the Bugatti.'

'I know. Théo's such a baby.'

She called him Théo, never Papa, and treated him harshly. They were walking towards the far end of the beach, where Antoine had gone so often to sit and smoke his pipe, watching the sea from the grey rock where he sat. Jean stopped to take his shoes and socks off and walked like her, feeling an inexpressible pleasure in treading over the warm sand.

'How's Claude?' Toinette asked.

He told her what had happened, the arrest, the interrogation, her return in a terrible state, the madness that had taken hold of her. Toinette listened without comment, staring ahead as if she could see at the end of the beach the bulky figure of Antoine on his rock, lapped by the wavelets of the gulf. She was not interested in Claude.

'Cyrille must be awfully sad. I hope you take him out for walks.'

'His grandmother has custody of him. She doesn't let me near him.'

'What awful stories!' she said suddenly, as though the little boy's loneliness was the only aspect of the story that seemed sad to her.

Jean wondered if she knew everything.

'It's our second day without Antoine. I feel so unhappy.'

Her musical Midi accent gave the banal phrase a lightness that took away its sense.

'Did he talk to you about me?' he asked.

'Yes. Often. He loved you … Oh, come on. I mean, I know … You're his grandson and I'm his daughter.'

'At this precise moment, that seems really stupid to me.'

She turned to him with tears in her eyes.

'Stupid?' she said. 'You think it's stupid? I think it's … unfair.'

They had come to Antoine's rock, and she stopped, putting her hand on the rough stone.

'I can see him. As if he was here! Yes, it's unfair. It's all unfair.'

'I regret it. And he regretted it too. He would happily have put your hand in mine.'

She smiled. Two tears trickled down her golden cheeks. Jean was silent in the face of her strikingly natural beauty. At her side, he told himself, he would have forgotten everything.

'I'll never meet anyone like you,' he said.

'No. Never. And don't try. I'll never forgive you.'

He put his arms around her and kissed her. He tasted orange blossom on her lips. She pushed him gently away.

'No more than that. It's lovely like that. When are you leaving?'

He recounted his flight from Paris, where he would soon be called back. Saint-Tropez was a refuge. Caution dictated that he should not move from there until he received word.

'Say nothing to Théo,' she advised him. 'He's on the Germans' side, because they're winning. When they lose, he'll be on the British side.'

She smiled, sure of herself, and added more quietly, 'So it'll be me who leaves. I'll go to the mountains and stay with my cousins.'

'Why?'

'It's better. Let's not tempt fate.'

She thought everything through, with a disconcerting thoroughness. In this family the women were the thinkers, while the men spent their time in pursuit of pleasure.

'We'll go back,' she said. 'I need to stay with Maman. She's so sad. You know, Antoine was her real partner. Théo's her baby. She lets him have everything.'

They walked back to the hotel. Marie-Dévote, a black and watchful silhouette, observed them as they came. Jean wondered if she had seen them kiss, though it was unlikely. But Marie-Dévote did not need proof. She guessed and, like Toinette, thought it was better to separate two beings who were so strongly attracted to each other and could not come together without offending against the natural order of things.

Next morning it was left to Théo to explain.

'Toinette, she was choking with sorrow. I've taken her to the mountains, to her cousins'. The air's thinner up there. She'll breathe better. You wouldn't think so, but she's delicate, that one, delicate like the orange blossom.'

Jean remembered the taste of her lips. He spent the rest of the day so sadly quiet that Marie-Dévote took him aside.

'Antoine, he didn't want to hurt anyone, ever. If we're too unhappy, he'll start worrying himself sick up there. Don't stay here. Go with Théo. He gets around with his truck, sees some countryside. When you're passing, you can drop by our cousins and kiss Toinette. She'll be glad you haven't forgotten her.'

He and Théo crisscrossed the back country, as they had done the previous year. Théo was building up his business. Everywhere he was greeted, bottles were uncorked, goat's and sheep's cheese, home-made bread, black olives in vinegar, dried figs in salt water, tomatoes and cucumbers were brought out from cool larders for him. He lingered, argued endlessly, passed on the evening news from the wireless: Rommel was at El Alamein, the Wehrmacht was besieging Sebastopol, the Japanese had landed at Guadalcanal. Never before had Théo pored over the atlas so closely. Toinette was exaggerating: he was not 'on the Germans' side', but gleefully, and at a safe distance, followed the victories on both sides. The deployment, on Independence Day, of the first American bombers, B-17s, over Germany gave rise to intense excitement. To hear him, the war was like a world championship: he sought not the victory of good over evil or evil over good, but only wished the match to carry on until all the adversaries were exhausted.

'You'll see,' he said in a sudden flight of prophecy, 'they'll finish up on level pegging, a draw. No one will have deserved to win and no one deserves to lose. Remember, it was Théo told you so.'

They called on Toinette. She was not at home. She was picking lavender on the mountainside with her young cousins. While Théo was chatting Jean asked to be shown which way they had gone. He found them in the scrub on the side of a hill of wild lavender, each girl carrying a cotton bag, wide-brimmed straw hats on their heads. From the path he would have found it impossible to say which one was Toinette. They wore the same grey smocks and the same aprons, and were singing in Provençal, their piping girlish voices mingling with the sharp call of the cicadas. A face looked up and called to Toinette.

'*Té*, Toinette, he's here.'

So she had talked about him. He felt intensely proud to have been the subject of a confidence. The girls straightened up, charming figures on the blue-washed hillside dotted with the green of small oaks. He recognised Toinette when she put down her bag and smiled at him under her straw hat. Her lovely tanned face and light eyes were calm. She had pushed up her sleeves, baring her arms, the same golden brown as her legs.

'I came to say goodbye.'

'I thought so. You're leaving then? It's a shame.'

She smelt naturally of lavender, a fresh smell that would for ever, from that day on, remind Jean of her. Her three cousins kept their distance, consumed with curiosity. Toinette held out her hand.

'No,' he said. 'No shaking hands. We kiss our loved ones.'

He kissed her lightly on both cheeks and added, 'I'll write to you.'

'Yes, that'll be nice … Send me a postcard, to say which countries you've been to.'

He knew as well as she did that he would not, that it had been delightful and now it was over, that their feelings would vanish in the infinity of their parting. Whether it was the heat or emotion, fine pearls of sweat were forming on Toinette's face. Her soft olive skin glistened. She wiped her brow with the back of her wrist.

'It's hot,' she said. 'I don't know how you can wear a jacket. It's easy to see you're from the town.'

She picked up her bag. In a moment she would bend over and carry on picking. Jean would have given anything to stop her.

'Goodbye then,' she said. 'And safe journey!'

'I won't forget our walk to Antoine's rock,' he murmured very quietly.

She shrugged her shoulders modestly, then murmured in turn, 'You'll have long forgotten it when I still remember it.'

From the farm came the hoarse bellow of the truck's horn.

'Théo's getting impatient,' Toinette said. 'Don't make him wait. He doesn't deserve it. He loves driving so much. You know ... it makes him different from everyone else.'

She bent down to pick a stalk of lavender and held it out to Jean.

'Keep it ... for a little while.'

She smiled. After he had gone, her cousins would comfort her. He turned to the three girls, three young cooked plums whose eyes shone under the brims of their hats. One of them, at least, looked almost as pretty as Toinette.

Marceline's message summoned him to Lyon. He spent three weeks there in the company of a short man in glasses, whom he met each day at a different point in town: Place Bellecour, at the Tête-d'Or park, at Perrache station, in obscure bistros – Le Pot, La Baleine – where at the bottom of a few steps you entered a low, dark room. The short man was a wonderful connoisseur of the few places that served the best Beaujolais. It was his only weakness. Actually, to be fair, he had another: he had no sense of humour. When Jean grew tired of his Boy Scout precautions and allowed himself a mildly sarcastic remark, the man looked so hurt that he was filled with remorse. He learnt in dribs and drabs what was expected of him, entering, by small steps, into an unreal, hushed world whose organisational charts reflected an unknown hierachy. He quickly realised that Marceline's recommendation had been of the highest. He was not considered a run-of-the-mill operative; important things were expected of him. Leaning on a terrace bar at Fourvière with his companion one day, he confessed to him, 'You must be mistaken. I only joined your organisation because I had nothing better to do.'

It wasn't the sort of reflection to be made to the man. He did not understand such remarks and was offended by them. He came close to retorting that the devil made work for idle hands, but his pupil interested him; he was a quick learner, almost too quick, as if he might forget the codes and security measures as soon as he had committed them to memory. In mid-August Jean was directed to go to Rouen. He was to spend several hours in Paris between trains. Arriving at Gare de Lyon, he was about to take the Métro for Gare Saint-Lazare when he was suddenly tempted to go to Palais-Royal. He got off there and ran to the Français. The concierge did not want to let him in. There was a rehearsal. Jean asked for Nelly to be given a note. She came running down to see him.

'I've got a break,' she said. 'Let's go to the Régence.'

She was in a sweater and slacks. They ran across the square and found a small table near the window.

'I didn't know I loved you,' she said. 'I think about you all the time.'

'What about Jérôme Callot?'

'Oh darling, you make me so happy! You're jealous. You stupid idiotic scrumptious darling, your rival didn't make it past dinner for two. I'm free. Stay.'

It occurred to him that she thought he had left because of the other man.

'No, Marceline will tell you why I left. Do you see her?'

'All the time. She has permission from Vaudoyer to watch the rehearsals for *Suréna*. In the afternoons at home she goes through my lines with me.'

Some German officers sat down at a neighbouring table. They regarded Nelly wolfishly, wondering what she was doing there, in slacks and sweater on an August afternoon. The waiter told them. Nodding, they knowingly pointed out to each other the Théâtre Français, its great grey outline visible through the window.

'We've just got to make love,' Nelly said. 'I can't tell you how much I want it.'

He had an hour till his train. Hè went back to her dressing room with her and they barricaded the door. The stage manager called her several times, drummed on the door, and went away again, grumbling. Nelly laughed with pleasure.

'"Love, over my virtue", ' she said, '"hold a little less dominion."'

He had to admit it: her love was joyful and generous.

'I don't know what I'll do without you,' he said.

'Yes, it's madness ... darling Jules-who. You see how good it is to be together. The truth is that there's nothing better, and I'm going to cry when you leave me. I adore you, you know ... You were so obvious, and now you're becoming mysterious. It's magic. Women will love it. I'm going to be cheated on left, right and centre.'

She kissed him on the cheek and vanished down a corridor. He had to ask his way several times before he found the exit. He reached Gare Saint-Lazare on foot. Paris was not a city he could walk around with impunity any longer. In Rouen the following day, having delivered his message, he enquired about the times of trains for Dieppe. As the first one left in the morning, he booked into a hotel and spent the evening reading *Lost Illusions*.[32] Later, when he was asked what he had done during the last two years of the occupation, he always answered with the same sincerity, 'Nothing. I travelled and I read. Every evening, every night, in trains and cafés during the day. I read and I didn't think about anything else.'

On 19 August the Dieppe train did not leave Rouen station. The Canadians had landed. We already know how Albert met his end in that bloody adventure and its uncertain lessons. Antoinette told Jean the news by telephone. His last link had been cut. He would have liked to see the abbé Le Couec again, but that saintly man was under house arrest. He could not even go from the rectory to the public telephone at the post office. Jean found that his sadness was leavened by a kind of elation: he was on his own. He weighed no more than his own weight, and he was learning how to be a man by walking on the edge of the chasm, a difficult task that precluded self-questioning. He did not recognise his own reflection: another Jean was being formed in him, a stranger, timid to begin with, then more and more self-confident. The game itself did not bore him, though he brought to it a somewhat limited conviction. He spoke little, kept his doubts to himself, learnt to mistrust everyone and everything. All in all, the short, bespectacled instructor, with his immovable faith and his flow charts, had fashioned a fairly realistic Jules Armand. Jean regretted seeing him only rarely. The rules that governed the network's security did not allow it, although he stretched them now and then. He likewise met Nelly at the theatre, but their meetings grew more infrequent and Nelly drew away from him, though she was always as tender as before. She explained it to him gently.

'When I'm not working I need a man beside me. You're perfect, but you're never there …'

'It's because I'm never there that I'm perfect.'

'Stop being silly … and understand that I don't like sleeping on my own. It's physical.'

'Get a dog.'

'I thought of that … and I'd already have done it if it wasn't for the pee in the morning. Can you see me, eyes swollen, cream all over my face, naked under my coat, bare feet in my pumps, walking my pooch round Place Saint-Sulpice at eight in the morning?'

'You wouldn't be the only one. There are plenty of grannies out at that time of morning.'

'Jules-who, you're mocking me.'

They skirmished gently and rolled onto the couch. He saw her in *Suréna* as a Eurydice so passionate he felt she was talking to him, the only spectator in a full house. In the dress circle, between acts, he glimpsed Marceline Michette craning forward, an ecstatic smile on her lips. Having given Nelly her cues for so long, she was starting to think she was part of the company.

In March 1943 Jean passed through Lyon and met his instructor.

'You've been very useful,' that precise man told him. 'We can use you a little more effectively now that your probationary period is over. Do you speak German?'

'No.'

'But you know a number of Germans.'

'They all spoke French.'

'I suppose you haven't seen any of them for some time.'

'Since you ask, no. I'm rather keen on staying alive.'

'Do they all feel the same about you?'

'All of them.'

'You couldn't regain the trust of any of them?'

'Definitely not, but … wait … I do know a German woman, the girlfriend of a friend of mine.'

'What does she do?'

'She works in an important organisation in Paris. I don't know what exactly, but I should think she's more than a secretary. She has a good deal of freedom and she even has a car …'

A week later he was at Gif with Jesús, who was repairing the roof after a tree had fallen on it.

'Jean, you is Providence itself. 'Old my ladder.'

They talked for an hour, Jesús on the roof, Jean holding the ladder. Laura no longer returned every night. Petrol was running short. She stayed only from Saturday morning to Sunday evening. Jesús invited Jean to stay until she came. She would be very happy to see him; well, 'happy' was a figure of speech, for she showed her feelings as little as ever. Jesús felt that she lived with the constant memory of her brother's death in Russia.

'She's comin' tomorrow. 'Ave a walk. Go and see your Claude.'

Claude was no longer at the clinic. He saw Dr Bertrand.

'Madame Chaminadze was getting much better recently. She was well enough to leave with her mother and her uncle. I think they went to the country. You wouldn't have recognised her. Her expression had relaxed – she was still prone to having that distant look in her eyes, but that's understandable; she has some way to go. The affection of her mother and uncle had boosted her confidence.'

'You can't tell me where they are?'

'No. I'm sorry. You understand that because of her husband ...'

'Yes, I know. And what do you make of the uncle?'

'A character ... Anyway, I see enough of them to say that this one looked benign to me. He has a great fondness for his niece.'

'So I see.'

Jean was not unhappy. Claude belonged to the past. He was resolved to forget her, to forget Cyrille's small hand in his. The following day Laura enlightened him.

'She left three months ago. You wouldn't have recognised the bearded man from the forest. Love transformed him. Washed, shaved, very presentable. Not afraid any more. He's still careful though: they've moved into a house he bought for her.'

'Where?'

'I know where. But don't you think it's preferable for you not to know?'

She was right. Even so, he was so close to the truth, it hurt him not to know it in its entirety. Common sense dictated that he should avoid causing himself pain. Otherwise one day he would be overwhelmed by sadness, gripped by a desire to see Claude, and he would be unable to resist.

He had another conversation with Laura in which he took the risk of admitting to her what he was looking for.

'I've been waiting for this opportunity for a long time,' she said, looking him in the eye.

'You can have me arrested.'

'No.'

'Is it because of your brother that you're willing to help me?'

'Yes. You can count on me.'

'Betrayal doesn't scare you? You're betraying Germany.'

'No. Not the real Germany.'

'The risks—'

'I'll take them. Like you. My only condition is that Jesús mustn't know anything.'

The short man in glasses was so pleased that he left his Lyon refuge to meet Jean at Fontainebleau. They walked along a bridle path in the forest that the instructor knew every inch of. Occasionally he bent down to move a stone aside or pick up a bramble or a piece of paper that could frighten a horse. Jean concluded that his companion had been a cavalry officer, but found it difficult to imagine him riding at a hard gallop or jumping obstacles: he seemed too cautious, not athletic enough. Then he remembered someone once saying in his hearing, 'The officers of the Cadre Noir,[33] when not in uniform, all look like worried notaries, and the NCOs look like their clerks.'

So the short man in glasses had been a cavalry officer. He retained the ramrod-straight posture.

'Jules, I don't know when we shall see each other again. Perhaps never. A possibility we must never lose sight of. But with God's help …'

He crossed himself.

'… with God's help I shall watch over your future when the victory is won. We shall have to change our rhythm and make a difficult adaptation to peace, normal existence, and our real names. I've almost forgotten mine, which was too complicated in any case, and which I shall simplify if I get the chance …'

He must have had a double-barrelled name, a source of family pride and the butt of jokes he could no longer bear.

'… I don't know yours either. Jules … it's unusual. One hardly ever hears it these days. Who gave you the idea?'

'An actress who liked to make fun of me.'

'Yes, Jules makes people smile because of "pinching Jules's ear"[34] and a popular song that turned "Jules" into a synonym for "bloke" ...'

'Bloke' was a word he did not use very often, pronouncing it with an affectedly proletarian accent.

'We only notice those superficial details – name, rank, decorations, address, social standing. They all belie real friendships. I'm beginning to feel a genuine fondness for you, Jules, almost as if you were my son, which you could be, as I'm now fifty years old. After the war we shall lead very different lives from those we knew before the hostilities. I believe – I hope – that men will be more brotherly. Many of us feel that clandestine activity will lead to a political, moral and spiritual revolution. The word "revolution" frightens me a little. The truth is, I'm a traditionalist and a monarchist. I say "monarchist" because it's a bit more general than "royalist". My mentor, Charles Maurras, instilled anti-Germanism in me from my adolescence onwards. I've followed his teaching to the letter, although today I tend to think that Maurrassian anti-Germanism could have been more understanding and less virulent after the armistice in 1918, and by contrast ought to be more hardline now, during this occupation. I occasionally glimpse my old mentor in Lyon. He doesn't know me, so I stop to watch him hesitantly, deafly crossing Rue de la République in that big cream-coloured coat of his, its pockets stuffed with books and newspapers. He's still indomitable. I don't think he'd criticise what I'm doing now, whatever he writes about it. Perhaps he doesn't quite grasp the devastation of the men of my generation. But even if we can't follow him in everything, he's still, with Bainville, the only political thinker who saw the resurgence of Germany and the Nazis' alliance with the Communists. His warnings were useless. Now we must triumph or die ...'

Jean was struck by the simple tone of this unpretentious man, who ran his network with professorial seriousness and left nothing to chance. He was filled with admiration for his discretion and his leadership, and his willingness to open his soul to a near stranger. In the months that followed, they saw each other regularly at different locations, walking together in woods and parks, like two philosophers keeping each other informed about the evolution of their thoughts after they had exchanged the information Jean had received from Laura and Jean's own next orders.

In early August 1944 they met in Paris. The network had suffered two heavy blows, but the strict separation imposed by its chief had avoided a catastrophe. The final days of the occupation had been less uncomfortable than might have been expected. Marceline told Jean of Julius's execution. Madeleine had vanished with Blanche. Palfy, now married to Geneviève, was already in Switzerland, his new fortune safe. The Théâtre Français had closed. Nelly was idle at home. Jean joined her. In the evenings they lingered on her balcony. Shadows hugged the walls. The Germans, barricaded in the Palais du Luxembourg, fired salutes that shook the area like a firework display. The telephone kept working, by some aberration, and people called each other all the time to pass on news. Nelly opened her mother's last preserves: confit d'oie, duck pâté à l'armagnac, truffle salads, smoked eels. She started riding a bicycle, bare-legged and wearing a big beribboned hat, and came home with strange snippets of information: there was not a gram of caviar left in the expensive districts; there were only milk calves to be had at La Villette; all the children had pimples; the Café Weber was the secret command post of the Resistance; the Eiffel Tower was closed to visitors; at the Cherche-Midi prison the warders had asked the prisoners to protect them from possible reprisals; General de Gaulle, leading a commando unit, had liberated Champigny-sur-Marne himself and had a lunch of fried roach in an open-air café with General Eisenhower. Lovely, happy and free, Nelly invented stories with abandon. It was fine and hot. The days were long. People lived very well with an hour of gas and six hours of electricity a day. Jean raided Nelly's library and discovered a German poet called Rilke whom she recited to him, standing up, wrapped only in a sheet.

> *'I live, and at that instant the century turns.*
> *One feels the wind from an enormous leaf,*
> *one of God's and your and my written sheaf*
> *that on high in foreign hands revolves.*
> *One feels the radiance of a brand-new page*
> *on which everything can still become.*

'How appropriate that is, and from a German too.'

One morning Laura telephoned from her office. Her department was moving out. Trucks were being loaded with the archives, under the protection of an armoured car. Jean dashed to the Étoile to find her. Alone in the square, she watched the procession of green vehicles moving out of the 16th arrondissement, heading east.

'It's a rout, Jean. I'm going to try not to follow and reach Gif on foot. They're saying the Chevreuse valley has been liberated. I'm afraid for Jesús. Recently people have been turning their back on him, because of me.'

Jean was a better judge of the situation than she was.

'You'll make things worse. Don't go. I'll talk to the chief and you come straight over to Nelly's, but for heaven's sake not in uniform.'

'I haven't got anything else.'

'Go to a shop now and buy something.'

She reached Place Saint-Sulpice at the end of the day, wearing a raincoat over her uniform. Nelly gave her something to wear. The short man in glasses came to fetch her and took her to stay at his command post.

'Don't move,' he said. 'I owe you an enormous debt of gratitude, but my powers are becoming limited. I thought I was the only one in the Resistance but I'm discovering that there are thousands, millions of us.'

Marceline, who was now constantly at his side, added,

'At setting out we were five hundred, but being speedily reinforced
We saw ourselves three thousand on arriving at the port.'

'Yes, Madame Michette, your quotation could not be more apt. Three thousand just seems to me to be something of an underestimate. We are living literature. Your passion for Corneille reminds me of my youth. The theatre of moral nobility! It's certainly the moment for it. We shall badly need it ...'

With Laura safe, Jean began to worry about Jesús. Borrowing a bicycle, he cycled to Gif with a safe-conduct in his pocket for his friend, whom he found, as anticipated, a prisoner of the FTP,[35] locked in a barn with twenty other 'traitors'. The safe-conduct was no magic wand. Three colonels wearing new braid discussed interning Jean. Fortunately the telephone worked. They called Paris. The messenger's credentials were confirmed, and he was able to go to a devastated Jesús.

'To me! To me, a Spanish man! Jean, you saved my life. Where is Laura?'

'Safe. She was very worried about you.'

The local maquis controlled communications and vanished when a German convoy passed through. Jesús was given a hunting rifle. He was guarding the *mairie* by the time Jean reached Paris again, exhausted. At the beginning of September in *Les Lettres Françaises* he stumbled on an article devoted to two great painters of the Communist resistance: Pablo Picasso and Jesús Infante. There was talk of an exhibition. A photo in *L'Humanité* showed Laura kissing Picasso and described Jesús as a former Republican fighter living in exile.

Jean appreciated the honour. From the cell in which they had been ten men scratching, moping, exchanging their life stories, passing on rumours and hearsay, imagining Paris ablaze and the armies of Field Marshal von Rundstedt regaining the offensive and driving the Allies back into the Atlantic, he had been moved to solitary confinement. Through the cell bars he could see the prison yard and the circle of prisoners from whom he had been separated. The overcrowding, the chatter, the complaints of the weakest, the lofty contempt of the strongest and even the dignity of the best had robbed him of his energy. Ironically solitary confinement returned it to him. He resumed the exercise regime he had begun at Dieppe Rowing Club years before. Press-ups, sit-ups, warm-up exercises, shadow-boxing; his fitness began to return. It would have returned faster if he had been properly fed. He would have liked more reading material too. A book a week did not satisfy his craving. He paced round and round inside his four walls, attempting to recall every detail of the battle of Waterloo as Fabrice del Dongo had experienced it, or the scene of Julien Sorel reaching for the hand of Madame de Rênal. In between he recited to himself lines Nelly had taught him.

> 'Your brown hair and shining black mantle,
> Your hard bright eyes that are too gentle,
> Your beauty which is not one,
> Your breasts a cruel Devil corseted, perfumed
> with musk as he did your pallor
> Stolen from the moon at dusk ...'

He regretted not being able to remember how it went. Another couple of lines,

'Time for a greeting, all bedazzled
Time to kneel and kiss your slipper ...'

But they had left him a notebook and pencil and he resumed his previous discipline, his daily habit of noting down his thoughts.

A lawyer had been appointed by the court, an intelligent and over-quick young man named Deschauzé. It was not his fault: Maître Deschauzé had thirty defendants like Jean to defend and mixed up their cases, histories and sometimes their names. His heavy briefcase was full of hot air.

The first visitor Jean was allowed was the little man in glasses, whose real name he learnt at last: Jehan de la Ferté-Mondragon. He arrived in the uniform of a cavalry major. The warder, impressed by his decorations, left them alone.

'You see me as an officer for the first time. I'm leaving for Alsace tomorrow to rejoin my regiment. I thought I might be of some use in Paris, but life here is impossible. They don't want me. They're right. Officers are made to command soldiers, not to play at being a policeman during a purge. I had a lot of difficulty getting to see you, but I had a good excuse: to bring you the medal of the Resistance and tell you I've also proposed you for the Military Medal. Here's your Resistance medal. Don't chuck it down the toilet until I've gone. It would hurt me. Obviously I shall look after your interests as best I can. I may as well tell you it's very difficult. You have, it seems, engaged in proscribed activities. I'm not asking you to tell me all your secrets. All I require is for you to assure me you have not worked against your country's interests …'

'Absolutely not.'

Jehan de la Ferté-Mondragon misunderstood him.

'What? You can't assure me?'

'Yes. I can assure that I have not worked against my country's interests.'

The major looked relieved. He turned his blue képi in his short, chubby fingers. Sweat beaded on his forehead and he wiped it away with the back of his hand.

'It's hot in your prison.'

'Only in the visiting room. Lawyers catch cold easily. In the cells you have to break the ice to wash yourself in the morning.'

'We didn't fight for this. Full prisons, people condemned to death … torture … extra-judicial executions … I feel ashamed. I'm going back to the army.'

'I hope you won't feel ashamed of the army too.'

Jehan de la Ferté-Mondragon raised his arms.

'I hope so too … If I do, I shall resign and take holy orders. I've been tempted to for years. You know, the thing that pains me the most is that by doing this they'll turn you into a rebel.'

'Oh no … To rebel you have to have an idea. I don't have one, and I shan't do them the honour of acquiring one.'

'I should very much like you not to be bitter.'

'Don't ask for too much. But all men should go through the test of prison. When I get out I'll truly be free.'

'Perhaps you're right. I regret not having gone through that particular test.'

'A man like you doesn't need it.'

The warder entered, his back straighter in an officer's presence.

'Major, the prisoner's lawyer is here.'

'Then I shall go.'

'In any case I shan't see him,' Jean said.

'What?' The warder was astonished a prisoner should refuse even

440

the minimal distraction of a lawyer's visit.

'I said I refuse to see him.'

The major got to his feet, his képi in his hand.

'Jules, you're digging yourself in deeper. You have to fight.'

'Lawyers are part of a system I disdain.'

'Defend yourself! That's an order.'

Jean was touched by his severity and not brave enough to explain to him why he felt there was no point in playing the game.

'In that case, stay, please, Major.'

The lawyer came in. We have said that he was a busy young man, intelligent, brilliant even, but overworked. The officer's presence threw him into confusion and prevented him adopting the patronising tone he had prepared.

'My respects, Major …'

Jehan de la Ferté-Mondragon nodded without replying.

'My friend, I have good news for you. The examining magistrate has advised me that you are to be transferred to London to be interviewed there. Of course I shall go with you. It's a simple matter, there and back.'

'I thought you were very busy.'

Jean was not stupid. Maître Deschauzé had gauged from the unusual turn of events the level of interest his client was arousing. It was no longer a case of yet another small-time thug working for the Gestapo, the kind of case he had coming out of his ears, but a defendant whose alleged actions had had repercussions as far away as London.

'It's an international matter,' the lawyer said to the major. 'A tangled web indeed. If Jean Arnaud were willing to help me, I could do something for him.'

He saw, on the table, the medal the major had brought with him.

'What's that?'

'The Resistance medal.'

'And you didn't think fit to tell me?'

'Let's not get things confused,' Jean said. 'I'm accused of distributing counterfeit notes, which has nothing to do with my activities for Major de la Ferté-Mondragon.'

'Major, are you prepared to be a witness for my client?'

'Certainly.'

Jean felt distinctly bad-tempered.

'Maître, I didn't choose you. You were appointed by the court. I did not want a lawyer, and I warn you that if you make another such crude error, I will dismiss you in open court.'

Maître Deschauzé should have left. We know, however, that despite his self-satisfied exterior and certain mannerisms with his cuffs and his mop of hair, he was no fool. He had underestimated Jean, keen to be done with a complicated case and a difficult character. Quite suddenly, he had discovered his client. Instead of storming out and slamming the door, he stayed.

'I beg your pardon,' he said in a more measured tone.

'Jules,' the major said, 'you're doing the opposite of what you should. Let me embrace you before I go. If I'd married, I should have liked to have had a son like you.'

He hugged Jean and left unhurriedly, saluted by the warder.

'When do we leave?' Jean asked.

'Tomorrow morning. An inspector will accompany us.'

The lawyer began to walk up and down the visiting room, furnished with two chairs and a pine table.

'I'm sorry,' he said. 'Very sorry ... Don't judge a book by its cover. I'm also a human being. You're not angry with me?'

'Not in the least!'

'I'd like to get you out of here.'

'It'll be complicated.'

'Help me.'

'If you put it like that, all right.'

They shook hands. The warder took Jean back to his cell. Jean put the medal on the table, opened his notebook and wrote:

15 November 1944: I must write before my fingers freeze again. It's getting dark. Three lights have just come on in the 'recreation' yard. I long to hear the sound of children playing down there: it's so sinister. I'm lucky if I can make out the sound of police vans and the slamming of doors as they're locked. I've never been forced *to reflect so much. Not self-reflection, reflection on others. And so, just as I decide definitively and for ever that the human race is rotten, the major comes on the scene with a little cross in his hand. Balzac's young lions will do anything to win their cross, and I'm no young lion. There's no relation between that cross and what I did. Yet the major's attitude, his embarrassed words, his shy but genuine warmth give meaning to these two years. And then to cap it all, and show me how simplistic my generalisations are, the lawyer takes off his mask and I discover a young man like me, who makes a mistake and recognises it. So every day I have something to understand, something to learn. In the opposite sense, there was the day I went to see Cyrille (oh yes, that boy I loved so much and who two years later didn't recognise me and as I held out my arms to him asked, 'Who's he?', a little voice showing how much was lost, already forgotten) and Anna Petrovna kept me there with her honeyed phrases while her son went to fetch the police, far outstripping the lowness of which I thought that woman capable. In short, because I might have solicited the intervention of CP and R von R in Claude's ordeal, I was myself a traitor in the pay of Germany. Since her mother informed on me, my love for Claude has become horrible, impossible. But in any case, what could I do to save her from Anna Petrovna's machinations and Blaise Pascal's lust? The real answer, yet again, lies in that far too general idea that women slip through our fingers and that the great art is not to try to stop them and not to suffer from that fact. Talking of fingers, mine are freezing now and I'm going to stop.*

We shall not recount the journey to London because all that matters is the result. Jean became certain there that the British knew practically nothing about the currency trafficking that Berlin had launched on the foreign exchange markets in the middle of a war. A rumour was circulating, which they were doing their best to verify. Rudolf von Rocroy, tracked down in a POW camp, had been interrogated at length by the secret service. Jean was brought face to face with him and hardly recognised him in his grubby uniform. Emaciated and feverish, Rudolf no longer resembled the worldly colonel who had stuffed his pockets in occupied Paris. His detainee status and the interrogations he had been subjected to for two months had restored some character to the craven profiteer. He denied the whole affair, and in particular having used Jean to sell counterfeit notes in Lisbon manufactured by his superiors. The second surprise was produced by Urbano de Mello. The young inspector, having been promoted as expected, was now working at an international level. Summoned to London – which had at last clarified his connection with MI6 – he identified Jean and lied brazenly: the accused had not come to Lisbon to deal in counterfeit currency but to establish contact with a foreign intelligence network. Urbano expressed himself succinctly in bad English. Not a word betrayed what had passed between them. Jean was cleared.

Back at Fresnes prison Jean wrote in his notebook:

25 November 1944: Delightful trip to London, glimpsed through the windows of the car sent to meet us. I emerged from it in one piece, thanks to Urbano who, though he had no reason to, lied outrageously to save me. In short, I now stand accused only of having helped Claude escape from the clutches of the Gestapo. What wickedness! My brief is gloomy. He was dreaming of a big trial and now all he'll get is a piffling little one. Having said that, just as I start scoffing most loudly, convinced that I've found the key to the world – constant ignominy, basically – I'm confounded by examples of virtue. Virtus! *In* virtus *we find* vir, man. *Among my women friends, I still have: 1. Marceline, the transvestite dragon, and 2. Nelly, who leads her life like a man. The balance sheet of what I owe to women goes something like this: 1. sorrow (necessary!), 2. tenderness (pleasant but not indispensable), 3. pleasure (divine!), 4. the art of slipping away (essential!), and 5. an apprenticeship in lying by omission (useful!). In short, I owe them everything, and I haven't been any better than they have. So nothing is as simple as I'd have liked it to be, with myself and a clear conscience at the end of it. There are nuances to everything. It's all so difficult! However gloomy he is about my 'innocence', Maître Deschauzé is very free with advice. There may be no big trial at which he can play the great criminal lawyer (though there would always have been the risk of me wringing his neck in open court and he knows it), but I interest him. He thinks there's something going on and would very much like to be in on the secret. He won't be, and will have to make do with a swift little trial in a lower court. Yesterday he said to me, in a low voice so he wasn't overheard, 'I never really thought you were guilty ...'*

Liar! He didn't think so, he hoped so! But I've also learnt to dissemble (see above). In London he spent all his time swanning about. Was worried though when I asked him to put his liberty to good use and find Salah. The idea of meeting a black person – a former chauffeur, the former secretary to a prince, and living in my mother's house at Chelsea – rather startled him. Of course Salah made such a strong impression on him that he forgot he was dealing with a black man. The collection of paintings and sculptures played its part. It seems that even though she left the house five years ago, you can still smell Geneviève's perfume there. Maître D fell in love with her portrait. Obviously he had no idea what Salah was talking about when he asked him if I had thought about using the prince's letter. I don't even know where the letter is any more, and, since Palfy had the cheek to open it, I wouldn't think of sending it to its intended recipient, now living next door. I saw him yesterday in the corridor, Monsieur Low-down Longuet. He's been arrested for commercial collaboration. His son, who changed sides just in time and got in with the FFI, will get him out. Nothing hangable in Papa's case; he just topped up his bank account by building bunkers for D-Day. His cellmates benefit from his generosity, which doesn't seem to stop him being a sitting duck for the warders: 'If Monsieur le marquis de La Sauveté would do us the great honour of slopping out for everybody …', or the other prisoners: 'Hey, Longuet, when are you going to slip us a free ticket to one of your whorehouses?' Even if I had the magic letter, it would be addressed to thin air. The only person I can count on is me.

A few days after his return from London Jean was moved back to a cell with six other prisoners.

'Excellent, excellent,' Maître Deschauzé told him. 'You're no longer a special prisoner. It's the first sign of your acquittal. You're being brought back into society.'

Jean did not care for his return to society. He began to despair. Perhaps he was even afraid. Prison weighed on him. He clung to a letter from Nelly.

Darling Jules-who, I won't write to you to tell you I miss you and I love you. You know all that. No. This is better. I'm looking after you. Your major came in last night after the performance. He looked as if he'd gone down into hell. Backstage, all those bare shoulders, all those painted ladies terrified him. He wouldn't look at them. So why me? *To find out who I am and if* I'm worthy of you. *I don't think I passed the exam very well, even though I didn't say 'shit' or 'prick' once. That man loves you like a son. He's tortured by the thought that you're mouldering away in prison. I reassured him, told him 200 press-ups every morning isn't a man who's mouldering. We were trying to work out who could help you when Marceline turned up. She's here all the time. I adore her, she's my nurse. I think if I cheated on you, she'd kill me. The major has the greatest respect for her. Did you know she's going to stand for the Assembly when the war's over? As a Christian democrat. At Clermont-Ferrand she knows her clergy and notables inside out, so to speak. While she's waiting she's cooking up something at the Justice Ministry. She's talking about getting the brothels closed. Anyway, she swears she'll have you out of there for New Year's Eve. I've written to Maman to send us our liberation supper. To cut a long story short, the major was reassured as he left to go back to war. Your lawyer tried to put his hand on my bum. I said no. I'm fed up with the Théâtre Français; I may go back to the cinema when it gets going again. One producer's no big deal, after all. I saw Jesús at his exhibition. He talks about you very fondly, but I don't think he'd raise his little finger for you. Laura takes care of him. We didn't know she was a member of the Communist Party, did we? She'd stand up for you, but party discipline forbids it. She and I have had some bittersweet exchanges. As for your dear friend Palfy, it's better for him if he doesn't set foot on French soil for some time. He's a clever man; he'll find other places to go. Marceline swears to everyone that he was France's first 'resistant'. Some people rather doubt it. That's all the friends' news. Darling Jules-who, don't despair. I'm waiting for you.*

The same day Jean wrote in his notebook:

12 December 1944: a heaven-sent bout of flu has seen me off to the infirmary. I'm getting away from the atmosphere of the cell, of the past they keep harping on about endlessly around me, though with a good dollop of mistrust where I'm concerned. We're all in the same boat, but the guard went and told them about the medal the major brought, so they probably think I'm a grass. Which doesn't bother me. Yet every favour separates me from them. So: the day before yesterday the guard came to fetch me to meet a prison visitor. 'Politicals' aren't entitled to this treat. I had no desire whatever to go, but to get the others' backs up I accepted. Surprise, surprise: there was Michel in the visiting room, very soberly dressed, very serious look on his face. The conversation went something like this:

Me (aggressive): What are you doing here?
Him: I belong to a charitable organisation whose members visit prisoners. In reality I shouldn't have the right to see you. Our charity's interests lie with common criminals.
Me: Sadly I haven't killed anyone.
Him: Of course I'm not criticising you for that. Anyway, I was able to play on our possible relationship.
Me: What do you mean, possible? It's definite.
Him: Not legally. It's a question of blood.
Me: You don't say!
Him (disconcerted): You don't need anything?
Me: Nothing. Nelly sends me parcels and my lawyer brings me my post.
Him: I've been to see all the friends who could be useful to you.
Me: That can't have taken long.
Him: The major's the most likely one. An admirable man, a saint ... Jesús is very busy with his next exhibition ... La

Garenne …
Me: Not that madman.
Him: Don't be cross with him, he's having a difficult time. As for Blanche de Rocroy, I didn't know she was a resistant …
Me: No one did. Not even her.
Him: She speaks quite harshly about you.
Me: That hanger-on? Bugger her.
Him: Jean, you mustn't become embittered.
Me: I'm not embittered, I just want to get out of here.
Him: That's understandable, and I came to offer you moral support. It's impossible to forget our childhood.
Me: You hated me.
Him: I still reproach myself for that.
Me: Tell me about the abbé Le Couec, Antoinette …
Him: The abbé's in prison with a lot of other Breton separatists. Antoinette's married. Someone very decent. A widower to whom she has brought a dowry of her very fine qualities …
Me: Are you working on an exhibition?
*Him (*embarrassed*): The opening's tomorrow.*
Me: That's a shame for me.
Him: It's a very Christian exhibition. Quite painful, in other words.
Me: Well, thanks for the news. I won't hold you up any longer.
Him: I've brought you a book, something to think about in prison: the Confessions *of Saint Augustine.*
Me: Keep it for a pickpocket. I've read it and reread it these last two years.
Him: You're discouraging.
Me: Then I have good news for you: I have absolutely no wish to see you again.
Him: I'm not offended. I'm just doing my duty.
Me: A great satisfaction, I'm sure. Goodbye, Michel. We have nothing in common and, to be frank, I've only put up with you

449

because of Antoine. Since he died I've no reason to go on.

Him: That's it: get it off your chest, insult the people who wish you well, trample the past ... Afterwards you'll feel better and we'll talk more freely.

Me: We won't talk. I don't want to see you. *There are lots of people I don't want to see again. My life is elsewhere. I made it myself and I'm proud of it. Don't make me say something unpleasant – I'll regret it later.*

Him: I'll pray for you.

Me: Then ask for my flu to last a bit longer. I'm more comfortable in the infirmary than in a cell for six.

Him: I shan't say any more. You'll always find me ready to help you when you need me.

Me: Thank you, dear Michel. Now goodbye.

He left, wrapped in the arrogance of his deep humility. He's the sort of person who's permanently sheltered from reality. He deflects it. What's the point of telling him what I think of his relations with Senzacatso when he feels secure in going up to the altar every day for a perfect communion? It's obvious that he can only despise someone as decent as the abbé Le Couec. There's nothing Jansenist about him, in his cassock and wide-brimmed hat, with his huge boots on his feet and the ribbons of his Military Medal and Croix de Guerre on his chest. And now here he is, compromised again, yesterday's thorn in the side of Vichy, today's enemy of Gaullism. He'll never be acceptable. Nor me. So we've won, he and I.

On the morning of 31 December, as a result of sensitive judgment by a magistrature eager to have its changes of allegiance forgotten, Jean found himself a free man. His case had been dismissed: a most rare favour. Maître Deschauzé informed him that his release was the fruit of combined efforts by Marceline and the British Embassy, alerted by Salah. From the front line the major found a way to send a congratulatory telegram to Nelly's apartment. What is there to say about that first morning of freedom? There was no one waiting for him at the prison gates. It was a lovely winter morning, with a pale sun shining over the bare branches of the trees. The deserted streets, the vacant looks of passers-by and women with shopping baskets on their arms, the queues outside the cheese shops, their windows daubed with offers, the pavements strewn with dead leaves, and, pervading everything, a weariness and sad drabness, contrasted with the warm, sunny days of the Liberation. A tramp stepped in front of him, his hand outstretched.

'I've just got out of prison …'

'So have I,' Jean said.

The man looked at him, intrigued, then scornful.

'But you were a filthy collabo.'

And turned his back on him. The Métro had regained its rhythm. It was warm in the tunnels. Under their shabby overcoats men were wearing worn-out suits like his. The cheap rayon fabric creased as soon as you sat down. At Saint-Germain-des-Prés he finally began to feel he was back at the heart of a familiar world.

Nelly was waiting for him.

'I didn't dare believe it. Your lawyer called me last night. You don't look well.'

He looked in the mirror. He had lost weight, his skin was dull, and he had dark rings around his eyes. He had to smile to recognise himself. Behind his shoulder he saw Nelly's childish features, lit up with pleasure.

'I've made you a breakfast you'll remember for ever, but don't imagine it's like this everywhere. People are dying. There's still a war on. I've got a personal supply. An American colonel came to see me at the Français. His father was my grandfather's brother. He's called James Tristan and his pockets are stuffed with chocolate and cigarettes.'

'Good-looking?'

'There I really don't have any luck at all. He's the only American in Paris who isn't good-looking.'

Good-looking or not (Jean allowed himself a mild scepticism), he had provided porridge, powdered milk, bacon, coffee and tea.

'I had no idea I liked good things so much,' he said.

They spent the morning together. In the afternoon Nelly left for a rehearsal, from which she phoned him three times.

'Are you all right? Wait for me, I'm coming soon. It's so annoying here. I want to hear your voice.'

He did not leave the studio, did not even look out into the street. From Nelly's bedside table he picked up the book she was reading and saw the verses she had underlined in red pencil.

> *So having watered History with my tears,*
> *I wanted to live a bit more happily;*
> *Far too much to ask, it now appears;*
> *I looked to be talking unintelligibly.*
> *Well then, my heart, I beg you, let it go!*
> *When I think of it, in truthfulness,*
> *A feverish sweating lays me low*
> *That I might slip into uncleanliness.*

Jules Laforgue, whom she recited with such sweet sauciness. He would take it with him, to hear Nelly's voice behind the lines.

*

At four o'clock he could not hold out any longer. He walked down Quai Voltaire and along the Seine. The booksellers were already closing. He hesitated at Place Saint-Michel, then continued as far as Claude's building. Leaning against the parapet, he was standing motionless, incapable of a decision, when a hand touched his arm.

'I walked past you three times without being certain, but I see it is you.'

A clean-shaven man, his eyes glittering feverishly, wearing an Eden hat and carrying a cane with an ivory knob, stood in front him. His lips trembled.

'Do you recognise me?'

'Yes, you're Blaise Pascal.'

'Do you know who just turned the light on?'

'No.'

'Her husband. She went back to her husband,' he said. His words were choked by a sob.

In different circumstances Jean would have happily beaten him to death. But what was the point? He said instead, 'You're the lowest of the low. Try to show a bit of dignity at your age.'

'You can't teach me a lesson!'

'I bloody well can. I'm letting you off lightly. Where are your wonderful theories now?'

'Gone! I've been punished. I should never have left my solitude …'

'You're disturbing me. I came to say goodbye to an apartment window.'

'I come here every day.'

'Go away. Leave me alone.'

Blaise Pascal seized his arm with unexpected force.

'Listen to me … I know everything you can reproach me for, but listen to me … I have a right to be heard …'

Jean extricated himself without difficulty and started walking towards Place Saint-Michel. The man followed him.

'I didn't touch her. I loved her, that's all. Like an infinitely fragile thing … And I hated you because you came between her and me all the time. Now it's over: he's come back. He's erasing both of us for ever.'

Jean walked more quickly.

'That's an end to your little affair.' Blaise Pascal raised his voice. 'You don't want to listen to me … But it's over, I tell you, over … For both of us …'

Passers-by were turning to stare at them.

'We're equal in human misery now!' Blaise Pascal shouted. 'You'll never sleep with her! Never!'

Jean turned round threateningly.

'Shut up!'

'There's only her husband now. Only him: you don't exist any more. Like me!' His voice broke. 'So listen to me, Jean Arnaud. I only want one thing from you: the truth. It's true isn't it, that you never touched her?'

Jean felt a sudden, wrenching dizziness that weakened his determination.

'I was never her lover.'

'I knew it!' Blaise Pascal was triumphant. 'Why don't we talk about her, the two of us?'

Pushed violently backwards, he almost fell. Jean, running, was already on the opposite pavement as the other man, lifting his cane, shouted again, 'Let's talk about her, let's talk about her!'

Passers-by gathered around him, and slowly a policeman made his way towards the commotion.

On the stairs up to Nelly's studio Jean met Marceline wearing a sheepskin coat that made her look twice her normal size. She kissed Jean.

'I nearly missed you,' she said. 'Justice exists after all. France recognises her good children. And she needs them now, how she needs them! Obviously anyone can make a mistake. I was telling the minister yesterday morning. He completely agreed, but he can't be everywhere, poor man.'

'No, of course not.'

'One must try to understand.'

'Oh, I do understand.'

She looked reassured.

'I'm very *partisauntie* for reconciliation between all the French. That's my programme.'

'People are saying you're going to stand in the elections?'

Marceline put on a knowing air.

'"People" *have* asked me. I have to think about it. There are some good men in the MRP, but their hearts are rather over to the Left, and I'm more to the Right. Well, there's room for all sorts in the good Lord's house.'

Her life was taking on a new meaning. She believed in it. A wind of purity was blowing through the corridors of power. Monsieur Michette had had to retire.

'In my position,' she said, 'there would have been too much talk. He's retired to Carjac. Zizi's keeping house for him. I'm very understanding. Morals have changed too.'

She had something else to say, and was finding it difficult to say it.

'I've just come back from *Switzerland*.'

The look that accompanied her words was so knowing that Jean found himself nodding encouragement to her.

'Yes, I saw "our" friend. He looks very happy with his wife. A very attractive woman. Distinguished too …'

'Did he say anything to you about me?'

'Yes. Your transfer to London worried him a lot.'

'Reassure him. There's no danger. Tell him Rudolf played the fool, and he's very good at it.'

'People are nasty here at the moment. He was seen with the

Germans very often. When people question me, I tell them I was seen with them too and that I was worming intelligence out of them. Constantin thinks you shouldn't stay in France ...'

'That's exactly what I think.'

'But he's wrong! France needs men like you.'

'I doubt it.'

Marceline was sincerely disappointed.

'Come, come, you mustn't get disillusioned so quickly!'

'I've made my decision. Not on Palfy's advice; he'd like to see me a million miles away. Nothing he says is ever disinterested. But I haven't forgotten that he saved my bacon. Wish him good luck from me.'

Marceline remained convinced of Palfy's innocence. He had set her off on her current adventure. Jean did not want to disabuse her.

'Think about it!' she said.

'I've thought about it.'

'What about Nelly?'

'She'll find someone to comfort her.'

'It'll be like Corneille in real life!'

'I don't think so.'

She kissed him again and pulled a bottle of champagne from her coat pocket.

'I'm losing my marbles! I almost forgot. Wish me well at midnight.'

Jean was sorry to have disappointed a woman of such strong convictions, whose innocence was still intact, and he kept her a few minutes longer, in time for Nelly to appear.

'Mmm, lovely, Marceline, champagne. You're an angel! Stay with us, we're having a party.'

'In that case I'll take you to dinner at La Coupole.'

Jean would have preferred not to go out, to savour his newly won freedom in the intimacy of Nelly's company, but Marceline insisted.

'I won't stay late. I know what love is. I've seen plenty of men in a hurry.'

Boulevard du Montparnasse was plunged in darkness, but behind

La Coupole's blue-tinted windows the big, brightly lit dining room dazzled them. Jean felt almost dizzy. After a universe measured in square centimetres, the restaurant's space, the height of its ceilings, the smoke, the heavy smell of sauces from the dishes that the waiters in their aprons passed under their noses no longer seemed real. An absurd reflex held him back, as if he had no right to what, after life in prison, seemed like an insane luxury. A head waiter recognised Nelly and led her to a table in the corner.

'Here you can see without being seen!' he said conspiratorially.

He was exaggerating. Jean discovered that in two years Nelly had gone from being a gossiped-about, faintly notorious actress to a full-blown celebrity. Journalists came to talk to her, then some actors who were about to perform in a nearby theatre. There was a flash as a photographer took her picture. He asked for Marceline's and Jean's names for the caption.

'She's my confidante,' Nelly said. 'And he, oh, well, yes, darling, ta-da! This is my lover, Jules-who.'

When the photo duly appeared the next day, Jean Arnaud found out that from now on his name, as far as gossip columnists were concerned, was Joolzoo. Marceline, beside herself with happiness, radiant with wine and a glass of chartreuse, beckoned a short man in a cape who was going from table to table offering to draw caricatures. Looking up, Jean recognised La Garenne at the same time as he recognised Jean. He paled and, spinning round, turned his back on them and dashed for the exit, as if pursued by some terrible danger. Stripped of the treasures he had collected in his garret in Rue de la Gaîté, he had returned to his old trade as Léonard Twenty-Sous. The head waiter, who had seen what had happened, leant towards them.

'You must tell me what you said to get rid of him so fast, our Léonard Twenty-Sous. He usually sticks like glue, that one. We put up with him out of sheer weakness.'

*

Finally alone in the studio at Saint-Sulpice, Jean and Nelly fell into each other's arms.

'It can't be true!' she said, stroking his hair.

'But it is true!'

They opened Marceline's bottle and lit a fire. At a minute past midnight Maître Deschauzé telephoned.

'I wanted to be the first to wish you a happy New Year. It's all over. All that's left is for you to start again on the right foot. I have a message for you. Monsieur Urbano de Mello hopes very much you'll visit him in Lisbon. He'll support your request for a visa at the Portuguese consulate, if you so wish … I'd like to talk to you about it. I'm not far from you. I can pop over.'

Nelly, listening on the second receiver, signalled no.

'I'd prefer tomorrow or the day after,' Jean said.

'The problem is I have to go to the country tomorrow.'

'Well, I'll wait for you to come back. There's no hurry.'

'I promise it wouldn't inconvenience me at all to drop in on you and your charming lady friend now.'

'No, no, you mustn't put yourself to any trouble. We'll talk about it later. Good night and thanks.'

Nelly giggled.

'Talk about obvious! I'll admit he's not bad physically.'

Jean looked at her. He was very fond of her. They had had fun together and would never forget each other. But you didn't keep a girl like Nelly, and besides he had no desire to keep anyone. No one could know just how much he had been freed earlier that day. A few days more and it would all have faded, down to the last traces of prison smell.

'What are you thinking about?' Nelly demanded.

'That you're going to make a wonderful career in the theatre and cinema, and I'm going to feel a little pang in my heart every time I see your name in lights.'

They were sitting in front of the fire, the champagne bottle between them.

'Do you remember?' she asked.

'Yes. I've thought about it often. And then Claude's arrival.'

'Have you forgotten her?'

'I don't forget anything.'

'Jules-who, you've learnt a lot of things. Now you have to make the most of them.'

'That's certainly my intention.'

She smiled sadly and started to undress.

'When are you leaving?'

'As soon as I can.'

'Are you going far?'

'As far as possible.'

'Tierra del Fuego?'

'Perhaps.'

She took his face in her hands and came closer to kiss him on the lips.

'I just can't believe I love you as much as I do,' she said. 'Do you want me to leave the theatre for you?'

'In six months you'd be bitterly criticising me for it.'

'Ohh! You're right, you're so right, my scrumptious boy! I'll never have another lover like you.'

Her eyes glistened with tears. Jean knew he would never have another woman like her either, and that to have known her was an infinite stroke of luck. He was suddenly overwhelmed with cheerfulness.

'We're not going to get soppy, are we?'

'Oh no!'

'We're winners.'

'Yes, both winners.'

'And we'll show them we're better than everyone, and less idiotic.'

'And less idiotic.'

They stretched out next to each other on the rug, their feet warmed by the fire, holding hands.

He turned his head to look at Nelly's fine profile, her pretty nose, her red mouth in her pale face. She lay completely still and her bare breasts hardly rose and fell. She looked like a young boy.

'I don't know if I dare ask you to promise me something, darling Jules-who.'

'Say it.'

'You'll think I'm ridiculous.'

'I bet I won't.'

'All right. I'm the daughter of terribly bourgeois parents and I still have their values … well, it would just make me awfully sad if I heard you'd turned into a reprobate like your friend Palfy.'

'I don't have his skill. Look: he's sitting tight in Switzerland, having married my mother, who, when they first met, pretended she could never remember his name, while I've been spending my time in prison. Logically I should be taking him as my role model, but some tiny thing has always stopped me.'

'Yes, I know.'

She looked reassured and squeezed his hand.

'I believe in you,' she said.

'That's the only thing you could say to me that matters, and I shan't forget it. There's you and the major, which is extremely strange, because the two of you couldn't be more different … How serious we're being!'

'Once in a while it's all right.'

'Not too often.'

'Oh no, not too often,' Nelly said. 'Life would be unbearable.'

'I've learnt that too.'

'You're not unhappy?'

'Not in the slightest, now I know that you believe in me. I don't think anyone has ever actually said it to me, and it makes me feel …

how can I explain? … elated, yes, as though it's made me forget these four wasted years. I feel as if I'm finally not a little boy any more.'

'And you don't feel glum about getting older?'

'No, at my age it's marvellous. Later on, well, we'll see …'

Notes:

1. The Garde Nationale Mobile was the forerunner of the French territorial infantry, also known as *les Territoriaux* or *les Pépères*, a sort of Dad's Army for those between the ages of 34 and 49, although it also remained a separate auxiliary force for domestic defence, and after the French armistice in 1940 regained some importance.

2. A *mich* (slang) is a man who pays a prostitute.

3. *De l'amour* by Stendhal (1822).

4. The line separating French territory into an occupied zone and a free zone in the armistice of 22 June 1940 was referred to as the *Demarkationslinie* or 'demarcation line'.

5. Eugène de Rastignac's words addressed to the city of Paris at the end of Honoré de Balzac's novel *Le Père Goriot*.

6. Baron Frédéric de Nucingen is another character in Balzac's *La Comédie humaine*, a fabulously wealthy Parisian banker, who first appears in *Le Père Goriot* and later in other novels in the series, notably *La Maison Nucingen*.

7. The common name for France's colonial army, from 1900–60.

8. The FFI (Forces Françaises de l'Intérieur or French Forces of the Interior) were the result of the combination in early 1944 of the main military groups of the Resistance in occupied France.

9. An institution created in the First World War and revived in the Second to bring financial and social aid to French soldiers, their families, and civilian casualties.

10. *The Police Headquarters' Literary Review*.

11. The Society for the Keepers of the Peace.

12. *Intrigue and Love*, Friedrich von Schiller's bourgeois tragedy, whose plot owes much to *Romeo and Juliet* and contains an anti-British message.

13. A French company manufacturing aircraft engines, motorcycles and bicycles until the 1950s.

14. Cartoon characters created by the illustrator and scientist Marie-Louis-Georges Colomb, known as Christophe. Cosinus invents a series of wildly outlandish means of transport, but himself never leaves Paris.

15. The church of Saint-Gervais in Paris's Marais district, hit by a German shell from the long-range gun 'Big Bertha' on Good Friday, 29 March 1918. The shell killed 88 people and wounded 68, the worst single loss of civilian life in Paris in the First World War.

16. The tax collectors of France who, under the *ancien régime*, collected duties on behalf of the king.

17. Year II of the Republican calendar, which approximates to 1790 in the Gregorian (western) calendar.

18. *Crème chantilly* with chocolate inside.

19. Dépôt = part of the Paris Conciergerie on Quai de l'Horloge, used for prisoners awaiting judgment.

20. *Les Thibaut*, a multi-volume *roman fleuve* by Roger Martin du Gard.

21. Originally known as Jeanne Laisné, Jeanne Hachette ('Jean the Hatchet') was a French heroine who in 1472 helped prevent the capture of the town of Beauvais by the army of Charles the Bold, Duke of Burgundy.

22. Raoul Ponchon (1848–1937), a friend of Arthur Rimbaud's.

23. A Paris street kid.

24. 4 August, the night when the nobility traditionally renounce their privileges.

25. Angélique Arnauld (1591–1661), an abbess and important figure in Jansenism, the branch of Catholicism to which Blaise Pascal adhered.

26. Jean Duvergier de Hauranne (1581–1643), abbot of Saint-Cyran, who introduced Jansenism into France.

27. Théâtre Français, by which the Comédie Française is also known.

28. Édouard Bourdet (1887–1945), playwright of dramas of manners and artistic director of the Comédie Française from 1936 to 1940.

29. The Jerónimos monastery (Mosteiro dos Jerónimos) at Belém.

30. The leading French engineering training institution.

31. Literally 'youth sites', the Chantiers de la Jeunesse Française were a paramilitary organisation set up in 1940 after conscription was abolished in the wake of France's defeat.

32. One of the novels in Honoré de Balzac's series, *La Comédie humaine* (*The Human Comedy*).

33. The elite French equestrian corps.

34. '*Pincer l'oreille à Jules*' = a military euphemism for emptying the latrine buckets.

35. Francs-tireurs et Partisans, the French resistance group created in 1941 by the French Communist Party.